MIFFLIN DRIFT

LARRY T. ELEY
AND M. T. ELEY

CHAPTER ILLUSTRATIONS BY BRENDAN PATRICK LAUTH

Library of Congress Control Number: 2021952869

ISBN: 9781681063737

Printed in the United States of America
22 23 24 25 26   5 4 3 2 1

CHAPTER
ONE

N ow, I never knew all the particulars, but here's what led to me holding a tomahawk behind my back while E.A. Darnell banged on the other side of the front door, yelling, "Get the hell out of my house, *now!*"

It all started four years earlier in July, 1959. I was an only child who loved baseball and the outdoors, spending most weekends on my grandparents' farm if I wasn't playing ball. It was obvious to me at an early age that my parents were not in love: Dad worked constantly at his business, and Mom got a job at J.C. Penney's as a saleswoman. The writing was on the wall. Dad was a workaholic, and Mom wanted the nightlife to spend her commission dollars.

So one morning at two o'clock, after the biggest fight they ever had, Mom bundled me and our meager belongings up in the Campbell's-tomato-soup-colored '56 Bel Air and we left for her parents' farm outside of town. After we knocked on the door for a minute, my grandfather answered with his .25 caliber pistol in his hand. Mom explained we had nowhere to go, so they let us in. I slept on the old, worn couch under some musty, heavy blankets and tried to just think about the crickets chirping outside beneath the living room windows.

The next morning, my grandfather looked me up and down: nothing but a scrawny 11-year-old.

"We're baling the north field today, son—it's the biggest hay day of the season. I'll need your help."

"Yes, sir," I said. "I'll try."

Mom and Dad eventually got divorced. I felt like they flipped a coin and Mom lost so she got me. It wasn't that they didn't love me; they just both wanted their freedom from everything. Dad stayed around town for a while, but after his construction company had a lull in the fall he went to work for Trans World Airlines as a flight engineer. That was his original passion and what he'd done in the war. Even then I knew the divorce had taken what little he had, and while building homes wasn't awfully profitable, being an engineer on prop planes paid very well. He was a good carpenter but a better mechanic, making friends with every engine he met.

I saw him only a little less once TWA started flying him around the world. He'd come home about every six months, which was about as frequently as I was going to see him after the divorce, anyway. But when he was home, we spent time together, unlike when he was working 16-hour days. Around the farm, Gramps and I didn't talk about him except when my grandfather would mention the in-town mechanic was taking a week and 50 dollars solving a problem that "Tommy" could have fixed in an evening and for a ham dinner.

After the divorce, it seemed like Mom was gone every night and had little time for me at her parents' house. But Grammie insisted she pay attention to me, and we did start spending some time playing baseball. During the war, Mom had played on a girls' baseball team, and she was good. She would pitch to me using the barn as the backstop, then hit balls to me while yelling stuff like, "Man on second, one down, where's your throw go?" She taught me to play the outfield because that's what she had played, and I got good enough to where I always was a starter for the local school or summer teams.

Three and a half years passed with a whole lot of baseball, farming, and not much else. I never really felt the need to blend in too much at school; the farm was enough and seemed like the whole world. Then Mom's supervisor at Penney's invited her to a summer party he was having for his 15th wedding anniversary. He had wanted to take his wife to Hawaii but had lost the thousand dollars he had saved for several years on a longshot horse at that year's Little Brown Jug in nearby Delaware, so a simple cookout had to do the trick. One other thing: he had a bachelor friend who'd never been married and sold industrial-grade cleaning products—J.C. Penney's was one of his biggest accounts. His name was Edward Allen Darnell.

Edward, or "E.A." as he preferred, reminded me of a less-likeable Jackie Gleason. He had just broken up with a gal he'd been dating for a couple of years, apparently. When his friend told him the attractive young divorcée at Penney's might be coming, E.A. cancelled his fishing trip with his brother. On Mom's side of things, she was desperately looking for a reason not to be home that night: my grandmother's spinster sister Edith was visiting the farm for the weekend and was bringing her ukulele, supposedly. That was to be avoided at all costs.

So Mom went to the party, and I was told to compliment Great Aunt Edith on her strumming and yodeling skills. When Gramps came into the parlor and saw what was about to happen, he looked out the window toward the pasture and said, "You know, I believe one of the cows is going to have a calf . . . I'd better go check that out." He took his pipe and tobacco with him.

"I'll go Gramps, wait up!"

"Uh, no, son, she'll be nervous enough. It's her first calf. You stay and enjoy the concert." The first-calf bit was more for grandma than me; I knew we didn't have any out in the field.

Mom and E.A. hit it off, of course. After a whirlwind courtship, they got married seven months later, right after Valentine's Day. Following their honeymoon in Indianapolis, where E.A. conveniently had a few prospects for a new floor wax he was selling, we went off to live with him in Northglenn, a suburb of Columbus. Mom said it was "veteran's housing," built quick and cheap for all the guys coming home from World War II. In the sixties, they mostly got rented out to people like us. It sounded like the opposite of Gramps's 100-year-old farmhouse.

In the time I'd lived on the farm, I'd changed from the scrawny kid who had arrived there. I was about five-ten, 150 pounds, which was about as big as I ever got. Hardened by the farm work and sports, I guess I thought I was something. But when it came to love and romance, I knew nothing. A kid at school in Sunbury said that Northglenn was the big city and I would have to get a girlfriend at Mifflin High School or get beat up every day. I didn't plan on getting beaten up, but I didn't expect much in the romance department . . . much less the two girls who would come into my life that next year. Life has a funny way of setting things up.

But I dreaded my first day of school at Mifflin, when everyone in their already-cemented friend groups would realize I was the new guy. When I walked to the bus stop, all the kids looked at me like I had a third leg. Back on the farm, I lived in the country and went to school in the city. Here, I lived in town and went to a county school out in the country. There was a cow pasture right up against the baseball field, and athletes had to chase loose cattle so often that our school mascot was actually the "Cowpunchers." It felt like the world was having a laugh at my expense. As I got onboard, the driver was gruff, as if he'd had to move some cows himself that morning before starting the bus route. He jerked the thumb he'd been picking his teeth with towards the back.

"Yes, sir," I said quietly. As I walked quickly towards the rear of the packed bus, I noticed the seats had numbers on them on the back of the ones in front of them. There was a hood sprawled out across all of seat 16.

"Move over, man." I said. Behind him were two guys in seat 18. One of them looked like James Dean; the other had a burr haircut and looked like a future linebacker, real stout. They were watching like something was going to happen.

"Make me, punk," the hood replied. "You can sit on the floor."

We sized each other up like young guys do.

"Just move it, will ya?"

"No, punk!"

Teenage guys are like young bulls in a herd. They test each other to see who gives in first. I wasn't looking for trouble, but I wasn't looking to sit on the floor, either. So I slammed into him and he slid across the seat. I heard his teeth clack as he hit the window and the bus rumbled down the road.

"You're dead, idiot, dead," he mumbled, rubbing his mouth with the back of his sleeve. "After school: you and me go—"

At that point, the James Dean guy grabbed the hood by the collar and pulled his head back over the seat. "You had it coming, Ernie. You mess with him, you mess with me, understand?"

"Yeah, Butch."

"What? I can't hear you."

"Yes, Butch!"

At lunch, the burr-headed guy came over to where I was sitting off by myself at an end table. He put out a beefy hand.

"Mack Hall's my name. The guy that saved your butt is Butch Fuller."

"Well, I appreciate it. I don't need to get into a fight on the first day here."

"That might get you a good reputation at Mifflin," he chuckled.

"So that's what this school's like, then?"

"Well, that depends. You play sports?"

"Baseball."

"Well, you'd be fine here. Our team could use the help. Man, they're awful."

"How 'bout you? Play any sports?"

"Football. I played freshman football this year."

We sat and seemed to have run out of stuff to talk about. Then he asked, "Would you have fought Ernie?"

"Yeah, I've met punks like that before at Sunbury, where I was before. We called them 'townies.'"

"That up north?"

"Yeah. Would Butch have fought Ernie?"

"He wouldn't have to. Erine's already scared to death of Butch. Most people are."

"Are you scared of him?

"Me? I'm a lover, not a fighter."

"So why did Butch help me if he's got nothing to prove?"

"Well, you were in the woods down by the creek last Saturday, right?"

That had been our first day in town. Mom had gestured out towards the back yard like it was the Ponderosa and said I wouldn't miss the farm. I went to prove her wrong. I missed the cattle, the big barn, taking care of something. But what I found was a massive forest that nobody seemed to own, complete with several streams running through it. *Maybe this will be ok,* I thought at the time.

"Yeah, I was. So?"

"Well, we were watching you throw that tomahawk of yours at the dead tree."

"Oh . . . I guess I didn't see you." I was too busy pretending the tree was E.A., I admit.

"Exactly! We didn't want you to. Butch and me hang out in the woods a lot along with two other guys, so we know it better than the hallways here. But hey . . . you're welcome to join us. Butch wants you to show him how to throw a tomahawk. We figured anyone who could get 10 out of 10 throws at 30 feet could join the gang."

"Sure, I can show you guys," I said, a little surprised. Sure enough, the next several nights, I went with Mack and Butch to the woods, where I showed them how to throw an ax like the Indians did on *Gunsmoke.*

We were joined by another guy named Henry, who went to the local Catholic school, Desales, and was about as odd as the rest of us. He tended to yell into the woods like Tarzan, and beat his thin chest while doing it. They were all pretty interesting, I guess.

Everyone got good at throwing an ax after I explained that it was all in the way you pointed the blade and how you placed your feet. In return, they showed me more of the forest, which kind of surrounded the homes where we all lived. It really was several hundred acres, maybe more. Larger than my grandpa's farm, anyway, and a little more wild. They had trails and hiding places everywhere.

Mack and I quickly became good friends, so I asked him to spend the night a few weeks later so we could watch *Rawhide* and learn more frontier stuff to do in the woods. Mom okayed it and even said she'd bring pizza home after she got off work. When he arrived, we turned on the old, tiny, black-and-white that had come with the house and dragged the living room chairs about a foot away from the tube. E.A. always said he was going to get a new set but somehow the funds tended to get "invested" elsewhere. When the show opened, we both sat as close we could and sang along with the theme. "Move 'em out!" Mack yelled, moving his chair even closer to the set.

During the first commercial, Mack moved back and stretched. "So tomorrow, I'm meeting the guys at the Alum at eight. Butch found an old rowboat and we're gonna go all the way to where the Alum meets Big Walnut Creek 20 miles from here. Wanna meet up on the south side of the woods and walk Sewer Creek with me to meet them?"

"'Sewer Creek'? Sounds awful."

"Nah, it's just the creek that has Shanty Town's sewage in it. Sometimes you can see toilet paper in it!"

"What's Shanty Town?"

"Cripe! You have so many questions, Larry. Come tomorrow and maybe I'll tell you."

Sewer Creek seemed worth seeing. As far as Shanty Town, I'd never heard about it but it must have been pretty big to make a whole creek of sewage. Mack was already glued back onto the television, so

I figured I'd save my main question—how we planned on getting home once the rowboat reached its destination—for tomorrow. Mack was looking thoughtful as he chewed on a nail.

"Larry, do you think that Rowdy Yates will kill anybody on this show?"

"He always does. I'm sure he will."

"How come they never get where they're going, anyway?"

"I guess if they did, that'd be the end of the show, Mack. Now who's asking all the questions?" Mack laughed and punched my arm.

The drovers on the show this episode ended up lost at a saloon, dancing with some girls while the piano played. Mack eyed one of the girls who regular viewers knew showed up in every episode.

"Did you have a girlfriend at Sunbury High School, Larry?"

I hadn't. But although lying was wrong, it was an unwritten rule that guys could stretch the truth about their romantic life. So I said, "Oh sure, Mack, several. Uh, at the county fair last year one even kissed me."

"Wow! What was that like?"

"It was great. Of course, you get used to that sort of stuff." Mack looked impressed. Rawhide wound up and I switched over to the Flintstones.

"Ever wonder why don't they hook the dinosaurs up to the cars instead of running with their feet?"

"No."

"I mean, they could go faster. Plus, no blisters."

"You're a deep thinker, Mack."

At that point I heard the rear door open and Mom yell, "Pizza!" She brought it in along with two root beers. We both thanked her. It was always weird to hear other kids call her "Mrs. Darnell," but Mack was a charmer.

"You're welcome, boys." Then the phone rang, and Mom answered. We tried to pay attention to the Flintstone family, but got an earful listening to her side of the conversation.

"Hello? . . . Where are you, E.A.? . . . You're at Tubby's Tavern? . . .

Are you drunk? . . . E.A., don't say that . . . Why did you lose your job? . . . No . . . I don't want to hear you imitate a crow. . . . Come on, honey, stop this. . . . Get sober and come home. Fine, I'll come and get you. No, we are not leaving. This is not my fault!"

It was obvious E.A. was drunk again, but this time it seemed bad when Mom came in with a worried look on her face.

"Uh, Larry, you go to Mack's for the night. I need to go get E.A. Just a little accident."

"No Mom, I'm staying here with you." My face was beet red; I had hoped to keep E.A. a secret for a little longer, but the cat was out of the bag. To my surprise though, Mack played it cool.

"Larry's right—you shouldn't be alone here, Mrs. Darnell." He got his coat. "I'll go, but Larry, you know my number right?

"Yes, Mack." He pulled me aside.

"Hey, my old man hits the bottle, too, usually all of 'em. I know all about this stuff. So does Butch. You call us if you need anything, yeah?"

"Thanks, Mack."

"Listen, just make coffee and don't argue with him. Agree with anything. And get out of here if he threatens you. If not, call me in the morning, we'll meet up outside the woods. And don't worry, this'll blow over."

"Thanks, Mack. Take some pizza—sorry we didn't get to watch *77 Sunset Strip*." He waved me off, smiled, and made the Flintstones pedal sound as he started walking home. Without Mack, though, the situation felt a world more serious. I went upstairs to get my tomahawk, just in case, and watched Mack walk down the street toward his house.

From the opposite window, I could see headlights snaking their way up the road like they were avoiding bomb craters, sometimes going in reverse. Finally, the car lurched into the driveway and E.A. got out through the window, somehow.

And that's how I came face-to-face with E.A. Darnell, tomahawk behind my back, separated only by a locked kitchen door.

"Jane, take the kid and get the hell out of my house now! I'll . . .
break the window to get in if I have to!" he yelled.

At that point, Mom called a friend of E.A.'s named Pug, who lived
one street down, and asked him to come quickly. He got there in a
hurry, and I could hear him outside listening to E.A. say we were
to blame for him losing his job with the cleaning agent company.
Pug was a former alcoholic himself and now counseled people with
drinking problems, I guess, so he seemed pretty calm as I listened
through the door.

"E.A., face up to your problems. You probably lost your job because
of your fault, right?"

After three denials, E.A. admitted that was true.

Pug rapped on the door. "Jane, fix a pot of coffee, please. And put
the kid to bed." I stepped out from behind the dining room wall.

"No, Mom, we're leaving, we're not living here with him anymore."

"Larry, we can't go back to Sunbury. We can't. Your Aunt Connie
and Uncle Bobby are living with Grammie and Gramps, now. They
can't take us all in."

Outside, E.A. was now cawing like a crow, telling Pug that he
had drunk something called Old Crow and felt like he could fly, then
running down the driveway with his arms out, flapping them. Even
though it was going on 11 and it was late winter, quite a few neighbors
had gathered in their driveways to watch him try to join one of the
Trans World Airline flights taking off from the nearby Columbus
airport.

"Mom, we can't stay here. Look out the window—he's making a
fool out of himself and us! The neighbors are egging him on. And
laughing! Please, let's pack our stuff and go."

"Larry, put the tomahawk away."

"No!"

"Pug is going to bring him in. If he sees that, it could cause more
problems."

"Mom, as much as you and Dad fought, he never got crazy. Let's go!" I heard the door unlocking; Pug was using E.A.'s key, which he had had the entire time, to get in.

"Put the tomahawk away, son, it's okay. Go on, put it away before I let him in." Pug seemed amused but sad.

Mom nodded at me, so I went upstairs. I heard Pug say, "All right, Jane, he's sorry for all this. I guess he used company funds for tires on his car after they reneged on a bonus promise."

"I wondered where those tires came from," Mom sighed.

"But he's a good salesman, Jane. He'll have another job in no time."

Upstairs, I laid on the floor above the heat register where you could hear everything in the kitchen pretty clearly. E.A. started to apologize to Mom for everything he'd ever done in life, and then he started throwing up in the downstairs commode.

"Yeah, he said he's been at Tubby's Tavern since late afternoon," I heard Pug say as he sat the coffee percolator back onto the stove. After a few cups of coffee, E.A. started to make sense, kind of. He started off promising he'd never drink again but seemed to reverse course on that pretty fast.

"Hey, Jane, look! I won a hundred dollars playing pool down at Tubby's. The more I drink, the better I shoot!"

Mom seemed to be done for the evening and guided him to the stairs. "Tomorrow is Saturday, E.A. Let's go over to Northern Lights shopping center. You can use your winnings to get the fish tank you've been wanting."

"Can I get one of those little catfish, too? I'll name it Zerkloin Zeke, I'll get a big snail too and call it Jolly Roger. Say, wanna hear my crow imitation?" Mom didn't answer, but I heard "Caw, caw, caw!"

In a moment I heard the sound of heavy footsteps coming upstairs—it sounded too stable to be E.A., so I figured it was Pug. I got up off the floor and sat on the bed, sliding my tomahawk under the pillow. He leaned in at the door.

"Son, you're pretty brave for protecting your mother. No need for it now, though. I'm going to stay till E.A.'s asleep, okay?"

"Yes, sir."

"It'll be fine. I've known him for 10 years. Used to be his drinking partner 'till I landed in the county jail." I felt maybe more sorry for him than he did for me; having to explain your friend to the kid of the girl he met a year ago must be tough. He meant well, though, and advised me to give E.A. and the area a try. I did brighten up when he mentioned like Mack did that Mifflin badly needed ballplayers—I'd signed up to try out for the varsity team that last week and was worried I had set my sights too high for a freshman.

I got up the next morning at about eight. Saturdays I shaved and showered; shaving was new to me and I didn't have much even in the way of stubble, but it made me feel grown up. When I came out of the bathroom, E.A. was in the dining room, measuring for the aquarium stand. If he was hungover, he didn't show it.

"Chuh, bub! There's bacon and eggs in the oven staying warm. Have some." "Chuh" was one of his favorite lead-ins, kind of an annoyed sigh you spat through the teeth. "We're going over to the pet store to get a fish tank. Wanna come?"

I wasn't sure what to say to a man who had told me to get the hell out of his house 10 hours ago, but I decided to go with his mood.

"Uh, no, E.A., I'm hanging out with the guys down in the woods today." I helped myself to a big plate of bacon and eggs. Whatever E.A. was or wasn't, you never left a meal hungry if he had anything to do with it. I gulped it down and put on my boots. "Thanks for the grub, E.A. Uh, see you later?"

"Chuh! Some morning I'll make sausage and gravy for us. I learned how to make it when I was on KP in the army." He did not apologize for the prior evening, and I was glad, because it was all kind of awkward.

I called Mack, gave the all-clear, and we agreed to meet on the footbridge over Sewer Creek.

CHAPTER
TWO

Like a perfect gentleman, E.A. offered to go out and warm up Mom's car before she went to her half-day at Penney's. He also moved his clunker, a 1954 Buick with over 200,000 miles, mostly from his sales travels. It had more than its share of dents and scrapes, some of which were probably fresh from last night. As I pulled on my flannel-lined jeans and one of grandpa's old coats, it pained me to see him gunning the engine in Mom's Bel Air; my father had bought it new for Mom during one of their few good times, long ago. When E.A. came back in, he started to read the help-wanted ads from the previous day's paper as I put on my boots to go.

"Chuh, bub! Come with us, it'll be fun. I'll buy lunch at that new restaurant, McDonald's. Ya like burgers?"

"Eh . . . I'm late to meet the guys, but thanks anyway."

E.A. chuh'd and went back to reading the job listings and deciding they were all too easy. I doubled back around the house and snuck into the back utility room, where I'd moved my canvas belt, tomahawk, and hunting knife earlier that morning before E.A. got up. I didn't know if he had seen them last night, but it wasn't worth risking ruining his good mood by letting him see them now. To me, going into the woods armed was pretty natural; you always at least had a knife, and you never knew when you'd need a good tomahawk. I did once, and that was the only time I had come face to face with a coyote, although I was lucky he had better things to do than pay attention to me.

They did raise eyebrows in town, though: one of the neighbors who was taking out his trash laughed as I walked by.

"Hey there, chief, what's with the arsenal?"

"Going to the woods. Might need 'em."

"Ain't no Indians down there," he laughed. "Hey, did your dad ever get off the ground last night?"

"He's not my dad!" I responded hotly.

Mack was already at one of the hidden entrances to the woods, near what I guessed was Sewer Creek. It was supposed to be up in the 50s, but there were skiffs of snow in the air, which meant the sun wasn't planning on showing up anytime soon. Sewer Creek had ice at the edges and, as Mack had predicted, there was frozen toilet paper stuck in parts of it. Mack was picking off a piece with a stick when I arrived.

"Aw, man! Was afraid you weren't coming," Mack said. It was obvious he meant it. "Did E.A. wake up after you called?"

"Oh, I just waited until Mom went to work before I left."

"Good idea. He sleeping it off, then?"

"Oh, no, he got up and made us a big breakfast. He's getting ready for his new fish tank."

Mack laughed and said E.A. probably felt stupid from last night, which I figured was a polite way of saying E.A. was stupid. We trotted off about a hundred yards in dry brush before getting on the trail. Mack knew the path pretty well and was in the lead, about ten feet ahead; it wasn't much more than a worn deer path, about five feet wide through the thick tall grass and scrubby trees. Half the time you'd see deer in the streets in Northglenn, and it was pure luck for them they hadn't crossed paths with E.A. last night. I shook my head; I needed to get E.A. out of my mind for a bit.

"Thought we're going to follow Sewer Creek, Mack?"

"We are! But it curves back and forth for a bit before straightening out,, we need to make good time if we're not going to keep Butch and Henry waiting at the boat."

I nodded. "By the way, Mack . . . any reason why Henry has been talking in Old English the last few days?" Henry seemed to really work hard lately to say things in a way that made no sense, and I had started to wonder if he was always like that. Mack nearly got run over by a big freight truck the Sunday before when Henry had warned him to "Lookabouts for yon motor-chaise!" and Mack had turned to ask "what?" instead of dodging.

"Oh yeah, I meant to tell you last night. I guess he's in some Shakespeare play at school at Desales. He said it was *King Lear.* He's practicing his character. Still can't believe he almost let me get pancaked."

"It's annoying. Is this instead of Tarzan?"

We stopped to look at a smashed beer bottle someone had left behind—Weideman's, E.A.'s favorite. I put a narrow stick in through the neck and carried it along. There was an old shelter house on the trail with a rusty old trash can that was probably emptied every decade, but it was better than leaving it to sit in the brush and cut some poor deer in the hoof.

"Tarzan? Oh, that's his woods act. He has different characters, you know. You should see the way he treats his brother."

Mack went on to say Henry had several sisters and a brother and made them treat him like a king even when the family was at mass, which confirmed something E.A. had said a few weeks ago. Henry's family lived down the street from us and were always up to something in their yard, all of six of them, and finally E.A. had decided that the family was Catholic based on the fact that they had more than two kids "just like the Kennedy gang," which I guess went to show E.A. was kind of right every now and then. I didn't care about all that, but when Mack said that sometimes Henry would make his siblings smell his armpits as a punishment, it seemed like he was the least likely person to be part of Butch's gang.

"Why's Butch even let Henry in the gang?"

"Well, in Northglenn and in Mifflin especially, you gotta either be tough or act like it to survive. We're tough, and Henry . . . is good at acting like it. He's scared to fight, though, even though he gets picked on for going to Desales. He thinks he looks like John Kennedy, and he's afraid he'll get his nose messed up."

Saying you went Desales was asking for trouble around Mifflin. It was a private Catholic school that attracted rich kids even though quite a few Catholic families from our neighborhood went there, too. Last year, Mack had said, some seniors from Mifflin nearly got expelled for tossing a Desales freshman on top of the concession stand after their offensive line steamrolled our team. There were no repercussions after the Mifflin coach spoke on the seniors behalf and said it was an innocent prank.

We reached the shelter house, which was more of a forgotten concrete pad with half a roof, and I slung the glass bottle into the rusty trash can in one shot. It shattered some more and startled a few birds. Mack took a handy limestone pebble and bent down to draw a big "M" on the weathered floor, then started marking around it.

"Here's your geography lesson for the day, Larry. Mifflin's got lots of hoods, mostly from the East Linden area who don't get to go to Linden High. And we also got people who live in the Veterans housing, like you and me. Then there's another big subdivision called Amvets, about three miles from here to the south. I don't know why, but all the good-looking girls live in that one. Northglenn has all the good-looking tough guys like Butch, and me, and you!"

The snow was thickening up and starting to stick to the already-cold trees and icy-damp path, making the going pretty slick on the worn deer trail. Soon, we had to jump over to the other side of the creek; you did it by hopping on some small grassy islands and then up the bank to another trail. The islands were hard to spot since they were surrounded by ice and covered in it, too, but you could tell them by where the white suddenly got cleaner than the brown-gray ice of Sewer Creek. Even in the cold weather, it reeked; in the summer time it must have smelled like an outhouse. Mack said that Butch called the new path Troll's Trail, but it was nothing except a narrow path along the creek as its banks got higher and was probably flooded half the time.

Mack knew the woods like the back of his hand, but there was no question that Butch was the real leader of the gang. The real mystery for me, at first, was why Butch hung out with us when he could have been hanging out with kids his own age who probably already had cars. Mack said that he used to shoot pool in German Village in downtown Columbus until he got in trouble a few years back; the judge went light on the punishment but told him to get a better crowd to run in, and I guess he took it to heart at the wise age of 16, two years earlier. We all liked the outdoors almost fanatically, but after last night with E.A., I realized the obvious connection was that, except for Henry, we all had boozy dads who we spent most of our time trying to escape from.

Mack stopped suddenly and interrupted my thoughts. We had reached an area where Sewer Creek narrowed and ran between high banks on either side and you had to walk sideways with your back to the dirt embankment. Up ahead was the entrance of what seemed like a cave, just enough to walk in.

"Uh, have you met Possum Carlson yet?"

"Who?"

"Possum Carlson. Or as he prefers to be called, just 'Possum.'"

"'Opossum?'"

"'Possum.' Has to do with his father hunting possums, I guess. It's his favorite food. Like how the seniors a few years back called me Bacon until Butch and I slugged the teeth out of one of 'em.' I guess Possum likes his nickname, though." He was camping out in

Troll's Cave for the heck of it and had asked Mack to pick him up on the way.

"This Possum guy doesn't seem like Butch's type, either." I guess I was too proud of my new membership to admit anyone else.

"Eh, he's not, but somehow he always manages to come along." We got to the cave, a five-foot wide opening into the side of the hill. Mack said it went back in about 20 feet or so. There was campfire smoke curling out of the opening.

"Let's give Possum's call sign." Mack cleared his throat, then let out an "EEEEEE AWWWWWKKKK EEEEEEE!!!!" I held my ears.

"Mack, that's the call Porky uses on Lassie."

There was no response.

"Maybe the trolls got him."

"I'm sure they did, Mack."

At that moment something covered in brush and leaves came to the mouth of the cave, about five feet away.

"EEEEEEEE AWKKKK EEEE!!!"

I unsheathed my tomahawk faster than Tobeel on *Gunsmoke* before realizing it was Possum. Mack laughed and introduced us. The mass of brush went back inside and I heard some water being poured over a fire, and then he emerged with a big rucksack.

"So Larry, you're already in the gang?"

"I guess, Possey."

"Call me 'Possum!' Everyone does because I love possum stew. Do you? And Mack, Larry's in the gang? Aw, man!" Now that he had shed the heavy camouflage, I saw he was wearing some old surplus army fatigues about two sizes too big, except for the shoes, which were too large by even more. "Hey guys, wanna march along in the woods and sing marching songs? Hup, two, three, four, hup, two, three, four. . . . Come on, new guy, get in step!"

"No, I'm not marching . . . Possum."

Possum appealed to Mack.

"He's not a full member. He has to do what I say."

"No, Possum, he's a full member. Butch said so."

"But I'm not one yet. How come he gets to be one so soon?"

"Butch said so," Mack repeated.

We talked a lot less with Possum in tow. Despite the snow, the brisk walk and the big breakfast were working together to keep me warm, and Gramps's old flannel-lined jean jacket was as snug as it used to be on the farm; I was starting to fill out the shoulders. I wouldn't let Mom wash it because it still smelled like corn silage.

We soon found Henry and Butch at the mouth of Sewer Creek, hard at work on an old dilapidated rowboat that was turned over by an old mattress and two tires. Sewer Creek also served as the local dumping ground for Shanty Town, which meant you never knew what would wash down to the marshy point where it joined the Alum . . . if you could brave the smell.

Henry was smearing roof tar from a dirty old can on the hull, and Butch was trying to nail the tiller back on to the rudder with a rock. I handed him the tomahawk and he just nodded thanks. Butch was never one to speak much, but he did lift his eye at Possum.

"Why's he here?" he asked, pointing with the tomahawk's handle.

"He was at Troll's Cave," Mack answered.

"Should have left him there."

Henry turned around with a paintbrush that had half its bristles missing. "Welcome, Sir Lawrence and Sir Macintosh. We sail soon for yonder land," he said, pointing downstream with the bristles.

"So you're in a play, Henry?" I asked flatly.

"Yes, I'm the Duke of Burgundy in *King Lear.*"

"When is the play?"

"In April."

"You're not going to talk like this 'til April, are you?"

"I have to. I'm going to be a great actor someday, as great as Marlon Brando."

Butch handed me back the tomahawk. He and Henry then looked at the boat one final time, and we all dragged it to the creek, where it bobbed pretty lightly.

"Squire Possum, put thy chattel in the vessel," Henry ordered.

Butch then gave the actual seagoing order. "Larry, you and Mack in the middle. Marlon Brando, you stand in the bow—you're lighter. Watch for ice and sunken logs. I'll take the rudder. Uh, Possum, you push us off and observe from the shore."

I knew construction products because I had always helped Gramps do the carpentry repairs on the farm buildings. This roof tar wasn't going to waterproof anything for at least a day, much less while immersed in cold creek water.

But Butch bristled at being told his plan wasn't watertight and jerked his index finger into the boat, so I got in.

From off to the side, Possum started to climb into the already noticeably lower gunwale. "What about me? Don't I get to go? My dad was a vice admiral in World War II. Make the new guy stay behind. I know all about boats."

"Tell you what, Possum, I'll flip you for the tiller. Heads, I win, tails, you lose," Butch said, digging out a nickel. "Call it!"

"Tails."

"Aw, nuts! Tails. You lose. Hey, give us a push out into the Alum, will ya?

"Butch, I'm serious. This won't seal the boat," I said, looking at the old can.

"Do I sense fear in thy voice, sir Lawrence?" Henry goaded.

"No, your highness, but the Alum's up today, and I see ice chunks."

"It's always like this in late February," Butch growled. "I'm in charge, and I say we go. Anyone wants out, go now."

No one got out, to Possum's obvious disappointment.

"Good," Butch said. "That's settled. We're off. Push, Possum!"

The creek was higher than usual, and like I'd told Henry, there were ice chunks and debris in the water like something had happened upstream. We bobbed in the wrong direction for a few yards before Butch got us turned around with the rudder. We soon caught a current and were quickly zooming downstream.

Almost immediately, the boat began to leak. I said nothing but started to use the pitch can to bail the water out, glad I had worn my deerskin gloves or my hands would have frozen fast. Along the bank on the west side Possum was running along with us yelling and waving his arms.

"Hey, give me my pack back—bring it back!" I lugged it out of the pool at the bottom of the boat but continued to bail. Henry started rooting around in Possum's pack instead of looking for icebergs.

"Hey, guys, submarine sandwiches . . . thanks for the food, Possum!" he yelled as we quickly got out of distance.

"We're rolling now, guys," Mack exclaimed. "We'll make the end of the Alum in no time. And then—"

"Butch, we're taking a lotta water," I said.

Butch didn't answer as he had his own problem: the rotten old tiller had broken off, leaving him no way to steer. We started to spin around and were now headed downstream stern first, which made every eddy in the river feel like a ramp. Henry let out a Tarzan call facing upstream where Possum was a distant dot: "AHHH EEE AHH!" I thought I heard Possum return his call.

As we headed toward the big granite bridge that carried traffic on Agler Road over the water, we passed the golf course that was appropriately called Alum View Greens. There was a maintenance worker trying desperately to get an old tractor started. He turned to see us and started shouting.

"Hey! Hey! You crazy kids! Get out of the creek! The ice jam up near Westerville broke up this morning. It's coming downstream fast!"

Butch waved but cussed under his breath. The worker continued to shout.

"Hey! You guys listen to the radio? They say this valley is going to flood!" He waved us off and continued trying to gun the tractor. I felt bad for him, but there was nothing to be done. I knew from the farm that those old tractors hated running out of gas and would punish you afterwards by not starting up. We left him behind pretty quickly in the rushing stream, but he managed to yell at the top of his voice before we turned a bend, "I'm telling you, get out of the creek NOW!"

I think it hit us then that the situation was pretty serious: Henry told me that in the fall some trees had jammed up against a bridge up north and they had backed up ice and debris over the winter, making one of the largest ice dams on record for the area. There'd be pictures of it every now and then in the paper on slow news days. Now it was breaking after the previous week of warm sun. Our boat was starting to break up, too.

There were about two inches of water in the bottom with more coming fast, and the bucket didn't seem enough to make a difference anymore with the four of us weighing down the boat. The current had picked up noticeably, too, and upstream the water seemed to be turning a muddy, angry hue.

"Butch, what're we gonna do about this?"

Butch had had a few minutes to think, plus a cigarette, and had calmed down to typical Butch levels. "All right, throw everything over that we can so we can get past the bridge."

I dumped the pitch can, Mack cut the anchor rope with my knife, then threw the anchor in. Henry saw his chance to do his character.

"Sir Lawrence, cast Possum's chattel into the raging torrent!"

"No, Henry, it's his stuff."

"Thou quakebutt! Do as thy lord commandeth."

"Shut up, Duke Bumblebee!"

Butch was watching, and a grin came over his face. "All right, Larry, when I tell you, you punch a hole in the bottom of the boat. There's a stone shoal about 20 feet past the bridge. We're going to ground there."

As we passed under the big granite arches, I looked over the side of the boat at the pitch-black pools the pillars disappeared into. The water quickly turned gray again where they ended and Butch yelled, "Now, Larry, now!"

I hammered at the bottom with everything I had using my tomahawk's axe head and easily busted out a section about a square foot in size, which the current immediately tore off. We quickly took on gallons of frigid ice water and grounded on the shoal. The waves had gone over the top of my high boots and soaked my feet and socks instantly before we could scramble to get out and up the bank.

"Get the pack!" Butch yelled at Henry, who was coming out last and climbing up the bank while the boat started to scrape along the shoal. Henry shook his head as he pulled himself up.

"Let it sink with the boat! Serves Possum right for, uh . . . for being Possum."

I jumped back down on the stone shoal, knees-deep in water, got the pack out, and shouldered it. It was soaked but seemed extremely heavy even considering that. Free of all the weight, the boat was swept off and sunk stern-first in the pool beyond where we'd grounded.

We climbed farther up, but Butch advised us to run until we could clear the highest bank we found. "Let's get across the fairway at least. I've seen these ice jams bring a lot of water before. That guy was right about the valley maybe getting swamped."

Happily, the maintenance worker was long gone with the tractor as we sprinted across the number eight hole. Normally I could outrun almost anyone, but the heavy pack was holding me back, so Mack dropped back with me, huffing a bit. "I think we need one of the Flintstones cars now, Mack," I said.

"With or without dinosaur assist?" he laughed.

Possum was waiting for us at the club house, where we ended up after a nice sprint, and I plopped his sack down with a rattle. In the distance, the Alum was now a dull roar.

"Thanks, Larry!"

"What on earth is in there, Possum?"

"Oh, a blanket, food, my bowling ball, a first aid kit, uh..."

"Bowling ball, Possum? Really?"

"Yeah, it was for protection against trolls."

I nodded blankly. I guess a bowling ball coming out of a dark cave would be pretty good troll deterrent. Possum clapped me on the back and back into reality.

"You're my new best friend, Larry!"

"No, I am not, Possum."

Off to the side, Butch got his cigarettes out and offered them to everyone. Henry and Possum took one, Mack and I said nah. Butch looked pretty proud of himself for an adventure well done.

"Well, that was great. Everyone have fun?"

"I loved it, Butch! When can I join the gang?" asked Possum.

"A more fitting vessel is required, sir Butchwald, but—"

"Henry, if you keep talking like that, you're out of the gang and Possum can . . . uh, apply for your spot. Until then, Possum . . . once you find a general's combat helmet to add to those fatigues, you're in."

Mack and I agreed it had been a good time, and Butch was content enough to start us walking back home. After a few minutes, Possum decided to bring up the fact that we owed him for the sub sandwiches. Mack just burped and said to get meatball subs next time.

"Butch, make 'em pay," Possum wailed.

"No, Possum. Ask your admiral father. The law of the sea says whatever you salvage is yours. Although I think Larry paid you enough." Butch winked at me. "You did good today."

Butch, Mack and Possum all lived on Woodland Avenue, but Henry and I actually lived near each other on the main road, which was called Northglenn, so we walked back together. We made small talk, and to his credit he spared me his method acting, which I guess was what he called his Old English speak.

As I walked in the back door, Mom, and E.A. were setting up a new aquarium. After slogging home in cold boots, the house seemed like the tropics, and I carefully took off my soaked socks on the porch so Mom wouldn't see wet footprints.

E.A. was like a kid at Christmas.

"Chuh, come look, Bub. I got two big snails, a catfish, some angelfish . . . " he rattled on the names of all the new inmates. The tank was a 30-gallon one, and he'd already set up the air filter, the bubbling frogman, the water plants, and even the little castles for the fish to swim through. No fish, though. I quickly glanced at the trash to see how many beers E.A. had killed but was surprised not to see any.

"Uh, where are the fish, E.A.?"

"Chuh! They're in bags in the hall bath tub, I gotta get the water to a certain temperature before they go in." There went my hopes of putting my numb toes in cold water to warm them up before a hot shower, like you're supposed to. Mom came out of the kitchen and thankfully didn't notice my sockless feet.

"Oh, Larry, we got a letter for you from the school athletic director. Baseball tryouts start on Monday, apparently. Did you sign up to try out for the varsity?"

"Yeah, I did!" I had specifically signed up to try out for the varsity, not freshman or reserve. Mom had read the letter.

"Are you sure about trying for the varsity? I mean at a new school and all."

I gave her a quick hug. "Well, I had a good coach when I was growing up, Mom."

I went toward the back bathroom to take a hot shower and put up with my feet feeling like they were on fire. I realized, as my toes came back to life, that it never occurred to me to tell Mom or E.A. that I'd almost drowned today. I thought I might offhandedly mention it to see E.A.'s response, but when I went upstairs, I noticed three empty beer bottles in the trash can. So much for never drinking again. Mom came around the corner again. "Oh, one more thing. Do you know a girl named Aubrey at school?"

"Yeah . . . we're in home room together."

"She came into Penney's today. I saw her cheerleader jacket and told her you went to Mifflin, too. She said, 'Oh, your son is so cute. One of my best friends has a crush on him!'"

You might as well have said JFK had picked me for his running mate. Aubrey was easily the most popular girl in our class, if not the whole school. She was a reserve squad cheerleader and also the head of a group of girls that called themselves "the Rat Pack," just like Sinatra and his Hollywood gang. They were the envy of the school, with money, looks, and a full-nelson on the school's social scene.

If they flagged you as a favorite, you were in for good.

CHAPTER
THREE

Monday morning found me walking to the bus stop with a spring in my step. I did miss the farm terribly, but after that weekend's adventure it felt like the town belonged a little more to me, even though there was nothing here in Northglenn to take the place of the animals and farm work. The woods and the nearby streams were like what the old West must have been to Lewis and Clark, uncharted and unoccupied. Nobody really knew who owned all the land. We just assumed somehow they'd been forgotten by the developer who built the veterans' housing. Whoever owned the property probably didn't mind us traipsing over the fallen trees and helping clean it out, one old rowboat at a time.

Baseball tryouts started that evening, and that helped too. I had been looking forward to them for the past week, but I'd almost forgotten about them when Mom told me about the mystery Rat Packer who had a crush on me. I was still thinking about who she could be as I walked to the middle of the bus where Mack had saved a seat for me.

"Well, Mr. Baseball, today's the day."

"That's old news, Mack. What do you know about Aubrey and the Rat Pack?" Mack's eyebrows nearly lifted into his flat top.

"Wow-y, you've been here what? Maybe two months? And already got the Rat Pack chasing you?"

"One of her friends has a thing for me, I guess. I don't know which one, though."

Mack laughed. "Well, from what you told me about your love life in Sunbury, you probably won't have any trouble, pal. Still, I'd watch it. The Rat Pack always has an angle, from what I hear."

Mack was being sarcastic, but would have been even more sarcastic if he knew the truth about the Sunbury girls. Truth be told, I had only been kissed twice. The first brief kiss was with a girl on a hayride back when we lived on the farm, and she had told me I tasted like mustard. Maybe it was the hot dog I'd just eaten. The other time was at the fair when the high school senior fair queen had given me the ribbon I won in the cattle showmanship show. When she went to give me the ribbon, the local newspaper photographer popped out of nowhere and told her to give me a kiss for the paper. Under her breath, as she smiled, she muttered "Get over here, you stupid dork, and smile," then handed me the ribbon and kissed me while looking at the camera. Not really a strong background.

Aubrey was her usual coy self in home room. I'd first met her when I walked her home during a snowstorm the first week I'd gotten here. I hadn't known anyone then, but when she loudly complained in home room that her parents' car was in the repair shop and she had to walk a few miles back home in a blizzard, I volunteered, wanting to just know someone at school. All the way, I talked about the only things I knew about—farming, then baseball. Finally, she turned to me at the beginning of the old granite bridge and said that I was nice but surely knew about something other than cows and catchers' mitts.

Strangely, that broke the ice, and from then on we seemed to have an unspoken understanding. I always felt like there might have been a spark between us, even though she made it clear she only dated upperclassmen with cars. She was the social queen extraordinaire at Mifflin, and getting in her good graces was probably the smartest thing I'd done yet besides hanging out with Mack and Butch. Aubrey held power over all sorts of circles at the school.

I waited as long as I could to ask her about her meeting my mom at J.C. Penney's, but she didn't bring it up at all and just wished me good luck on making the varsity team. I made an attempt to pry it out of her with seconds to spare before class, but all she responded with was "Oh yes! Your mom is so nice, she really knows clothing styles." But the way she smiled, I could tell Aubrey knew what information I really wanted. For the next few days I tried everything I could think of to get it out of her, but Aubrey kept her lips sealed.

Baseball tryouts demanded more of my time, anyway; for the next week we were in conditioning, and that drained me pretty bad. I had already been running and doing endurance drills on my own, not to mention hauling Possum's pack across the golf course, but I wasn't as prepared for 15 30-yard sprints to help us clear bases faster. Thirty-eight boys tried out, but after the conditioning week 10 had quit. Fifteen would get asked to join varsity, and the rest would be the reserve team. Since there were not enough for a freshman team, that was canceled. I figured that best case scenario, I'd make the reserve team, which wasn't so bad for a new guy.

The second week was skill evaluation and left me zero time to talk to Aubrey. That was all right; I was hitting pretty well and making the right plays in the outfield drills. I knew I was doing well when the upperclassmen started talking to me in "son talk."

"Son, I'll be for saying you're gonna be for making the varsity!"

"Well okay, son! Way to be for hitting the ball, way to be for going . . . "

Son talk mostly consisted of exaggerated expressions like that. When in doubt, you could just start a sentence with "Well, okay!," then put "be for" in front of any action, then end with a drawn-out son. There were also mandatory phrases, like "saying okay" and "seeing it" that you had to be for saying. When I asked one of the upperclassmen to tell me what it was all about, he just shrugged and said, "Son, it's the newest way to be for talking."

This seemed dumb, but it meant you were in, and as it turned out, the son talkers were right: when spring training was over, I made the varsity team as a freshman. After seeing my name posted as an outfielder on the announcements board, I told myself, "Well, okay, son!"

I wasn't the only one checking out the roster. The next morning, Aubrey was waiting for me in home room. One thing I learned about Aubrey: she found you.

"Larry, you did it. You made the varsity as a freshman—I'll be for hugging you, son!" Aubrey said, mimicking the upperclassmen. Then she playfully put her arm under my elbow so all the junior and senior guys could see. Once they were good and jealous she walked me to a corner. "Anyway, I have a friend who, actually, she's my best friend, and she thinks you're so cute. But she's shy. When the time comes, I'd like to get you two together. I think you'd be such a cute couple."

"Well, who is it?" I asked excitedly.

"Kathy Martin." She got in front of me and analyzed my reaction. My jaw dropped to my knees.

"K-Kathy Martin?" I almost squeaked.

Even though I had only been here a short time, Aubrey might have just as well said Natalie Wood. Kathy was beyond pretty. From what little I had gleaned from locker room talk, her family lived in River View Manors, a swanky new development overlooking the Alum, in a beautiful new three-story home. Her mother had supposedly been an actress in the mid-forties in a few forgettable films, but she was still Hollywood royalty when she moved back home to Columbus and met her husband, who was now one of the area's biggest patent attorneys. He worked for a big firm downtown that owned a city block and seemed to sponsor half the local charities.

"You're serious?" was all I could say.

"Yes! Kathy. I mean, if you'd rather date Sharon or Rita, say the word. But I think you two would be perfect."

I nodded dumbly.

"Now, let's not rush things. In three weeks we're having the big sports benefit dance. Just leave it up to me and keep on doing everything you're doing. You're cute the way you act so hard to get!"

Well, I wasn't playing hard to get. Shy, maybe. Inexperienced, yes. Stupid about girls, probably. But if Kathy had made a pass I'd have looked about as pale as I did after the mustard-kiss incident. True to her word, though Aubrey wouldn't bring the topic up anymore, and I didn't dare go around her and talk to Kathy on my own. Not like I would—I was too nervous—or even could, because Kathy was exclusively with the Rat Pack. They formed an impenetrable defense around their members, like circled covered wagons, and only Aubrey could get you in. Besides, whenever I looked at Kathy, she seemed to be just turning her head the other way.

Baseball season started that next week with a bang. In the first eight games, I only got to play in three, once as a pinch runner and twice as a defensive replacement in the outfield, only batting twice and walking both times. I figured it was better than being on the reserve team, though.

Mifflin's baseball grounds were just a dirt infield and an outfield that was actually the parking lot for football games. What little grass that could fight past the gravel also had to compete with the cinders from the school's coal furnace that were spread there to stabilize the parking area. It was pretty rough to say the least, but it led to my big break.

The ninth game—the last before the big sports dance—we were playing Grove City and losing the second game 11-0 when our star center fielder came running in for a line drive, tripped in a tire rut and slid on some sharp cinders. His elbow looked like raw meat, and the coach used the whole bottle of hydrogen peroxide from our ancient medical kit on it. After they got the centerfielder on his way to the hospital, coach nodded at me and said, "Go to center, thirteen," referencing my number. That put me in our last inning at-bat. In the bottom of the seventh, the scorekeeper yelled out the next three batters, including me.

Hoyal hit a double, and Lehman walked. The pitcher was a real devil and didn't cut anybody any slack. When the coach called time-out and motioned me over to him, I figured he was taking me out because he wanted someone more reliable out there. Instead, he advised me to take the first pitch, then open my stance and swing away on the second.

As I stepped into the box, I endured the normal freshman razzing, lots of "Look out! Jim-Bob's gonna take your head off!" sort of stuff. The pitcher was Jim-Bob Manley, and we all knew he was being scouted by the Pittsburgh Pirates. He could throw the ball at you 90 miles an hour from about a foot above some of our heads—he was six-foot-seven and it looked like someone was throwing the ball at you from the top of Mount Everest when he pitched. As the coach predicted, the first pitch came in high and tight.

Behind me, the catcher laughed. "Go sit down, kid, you're not even going to see this next one."

Instead, I opened my stance like the coach said, meaning I moved my left foot a little towards third. This time, the pitch was belt high on the inside, and I was able to meet it out in front of the plate, lining it on a rope to the alley in left center. Hoyal and Lehman scored, and I ended up on second base.

As I stood there, Jim-Bob turned to me and dragged his finger across his throat. I imagined he meant to hit me next time I was up. Instead, when I scored on a double, the son talkers on our team exploded and were for dumping ice water on my head, son.

In home room-the next morning, Aubrey was all bubbles. "This is going perfectly, Larry. I heard all about it last night and this just makes it like something you'd read in *Confidential*. You're a star and Kathy's going to . . . Wait—you are going to the sports dance Friday night for sure, right?"

"Well yeah, that was the plan. Um, can I meet Kathy now?"

"No. She's too shy and won't come if she knows you want to come just for her. I've got it all set up. You just come and act cool—then, you'll dance in the snowball dance with Kathy and then she'll pick you as her lady's choice dance when they have that. The rest is up to you."

"Snowball dance?"

"You know, where the most popular guy and girl start dancing first, then you others start dancing."

"So that's you and the quarterback?"

"Someday, but you get brownie points for saying so. It's always the head cheerleader. Have you been to one of these before? You can dance right?"

"Uh . . . no."

Aubrey sighed but seemed to have planned for this, too. "Oh, well, never mind. I'll meet you in the lobby before the dance. It's easy. Anyone can dance." She looked down. "You do have better shoes than that?"

"Uh . . . yes."

She went through a grooming and manners speech that lost me 30 seconds in, then decided I was ready to go. I wasn't so sure. But I had no choice. I was committed.

Friday night came, Butch and Mack swung by the house to pick me up, and I was off to meet my very own Rat Pack girl.

Butch was going just to hang out and smoke and check out the hot cars that would be there; Mack was going to go because of the concession stand food and to hopefully to ask someone to dance, though I knew this didn't rank too highly on his list of priorities. Of course, before we even got to the bridge, Possum and Henry caught up with us. Henry usually went to our school's events to take his choice of the peasant girls, but I think it was because our girls were prettier. Possum was going for reasons known only to him.

Once the gang was there, Mack spilled the beans. "So Larry's got a hot date with a Rat Packer, guys . . . "

"Put a lid on it, Mack." I didn't want everyone to know, anything could happen.

But that set Possum off. "Tell us who, tell us who!"

"It's Kathy Martin," Mack said before I could yell over him.

"Mack!"

Henry butted in before I could change the subject. "Oh, I know her! She went to Catholic grade school with me. Red hair, braces, freckles . . ." in spite of Butch's previous warning about speaking in character, he couldn't help it. "Sir Lawrence, I am taken aback you would stoop so low."

"When was the last time you saw her, Duke Bumblebee?" The Duke thought it over while a black '57 Ford with a couple guys from the team pulled up alongside us. One of the seniors stuck his head out with his letter jacket visible in the streetlights.

"Sons, we'll be for guessing your feet are for doing some walking!" Inside you could hear the guys tearing up.

"Be for getting in, sons," the driver yelled.

Butch scoffed and flipped his cigarette over the side of the bridge. "Don't do it, guys."

I always felt like a part of Butch wanted to be in the in crowd, but then another part of him had beaten that part up. Anyway, Possum didn't listen and ran for the car and fumbled through his typically imperfect son talk.

"Sons, your son is getting in the car, sons, well okay!" Of course, as soon as he got close to the car, they pulled fifteen feet ahead.

"Sorry, Possum son, the car was for slipping its gears!" They were guffawing. This went on maybe a half a dozen times across the bridge while we hung back. Finally they got to the end of the bridge and sped off, with Possum running after them.

Butch sighed. "What a moron. Mack, I'm serious, he's not a gang member!"

When we got to the school, Possum was still out of breath and asked me to loan him fifty cents to get in. I said he should ask Henry, but I guess he was staying the night there and Henry was buying the pizza. Possum probably didn't want to take money away from him since then he wouldn't have any money to buy dinner. I gave him a 50-cent piece I'd found in the street the other day and went in looking for Aubrey. She was waiting for me and dragged me off to a side room.

"You ready to learn how to dance?"

"I'm ready to meet Kathy!"

"Cool it Larry. Some people would kill to be in your shoes right now."

Since the DJ wasn't there yet, the school had someone else playing records. A swanky, mostly-horns instrumental called "Wonderland by Night" came on, and Aubrey put her right hand on my shoulder.

"Okay, this is perfect practice music. Take my left hand, right? No, left hand. Correct."

"That's not so bad. Thanks, Aubrey."

"Idiot! And put your right hand on my back . . . lower than that. C'mon, were you a monk back in Sunbury? Not that low! Raise it, buster!" She reached behind and gave my hand a pretty good slap.

"You said to put my hand on your back!"

"You think I haven't heard that before, huh?" She led me around for a couple of minutes while people milled outside, and then the song finished. Finally, she sighed deeply and groaned. "Okay, obviously we should have done this in homeroom. You're lucky Kathy's head over heels for you. Just do the best you can and stay off her feet. And whatever you do—oh, shoot, she's here!"

I looked out the door and went back into the gym as Kathy arrived with another Rat Pack girl named Melanie.

"Now, like I said," Aubrey continued, "I have this all worked out. Once you see me go by in the snowball dance, that's your cue. So at the start, work your way over to Kathy. Wait until the lead couple goes by and I go by. Then, and only then, you will escort Kathy out onto the floor and dance. Later, she will ask you to dance for the ladies' choice."

"So the lead walks by, you walk by, then—"

"It will be so romantic and perfect! All right, gotta go. Bye!"

Aubrey had walked me to the gym door and went off to look over her brood. On stage, Jerry Shaver, the Channel Nine anchorman, was setting up alongside Miss Teen Beat herself, Donatella Montabella.

Oh, yeah, Miss Teen Beat. For the last several years, Channel Nine had sponsored high school dances to promote its Saturday afternoon dance show, usually teaming Jerry with an outgoing, peppy girl who they would crown Miss Teen Beat at the end of each school year. Her job was to kind of be a cheerleader-meets-girl-Friday at the dances and keep things lively. Donatella Montabella was all that and more.

She was from North Jefferson High and everything Miss Teen Beat should be: a cheerleader, an excellent dancer, a good singer, cute, and willing to talk like she was sucking helium every third breath. She could even act, which helped because she always had to appear like she was having the time of her life. I had seen her last fall at the Sunbury dance, and when she screamed "Hello, Sunbury!" I swear one of the gymnasium window panes broke.

Alongside her and Jerry Shaver's turntable, Mifflin's very own local garage band, the Piston Rings, were going to play. Mack and Butch were nowhere to be found, and I was on my own, trying to avoid Possum. The gym started to heat up and get humid as all us students putzed around and sized up the members of the opposite sex until finally, Jerry came out on stage with a spotlight on him.

"Hellllooooo, Mifflin! Are you ready for a great night?!?!" People started cheering.

"I SAID, 'ARE YOU READY?!?!'" More cheering.

"We've got music. We've got dancing. We've got surprises, annnnnd we have Mifflin's own band, the Piston Rings, here tonight. But, best of all, we have Miss Teen Beat, DONATELLA MONTABELLA."

She came bounding out from behind the curtain, down the stairs, did a cartwheel around the circle that opened up for her and then the splits, bouncing back up like a toy.

"HELLO COWPUNCHERS!!! What's first, JER?"

Jerry told her to start with a chain dance to the song "Loco-motion," which started blasting from the speakers before someone adjusted the volume. Kathy was sitting very properly on the auditorium bleachers, her legs crossed, watching me, and I decided to play it cool and sit this one out. The song went by in a second and Donatella announced: the snowball dance. Already?

Okay, it was time. I looked at Kathy: she was about forty feet away, smiling and still watching me. Aubrey had obviously prepped her, too. I knew she was thinking "Now he'll come over, it'll be perfect." Speaking of perfect, not a strand of her long, strawberry-blond hair was out of place. I looked down at my loafers; they had gotten muddy on the way over. I tried to wipe the mud off on the back of my pants before realizing I wasn't in the woods and mud looked bad on white khakis. "It's Up To You" by Ricky Nelson came on. I was looking at the beautiful girl waiting for me . . . and I started over to her.

At least, in my mind I did. My feet, on the other hand, didn't go anywhere. I was frozen like the Tin Man in *The Wizard of Oz*.

"Feet sons, be for walking," I said in my mind.

"No, son, we'll be for staying here." So I stood there the entire time.

When the song ended, Possum came running by and said that if I didn't have a girl to dance with, I should dance by myself, which is what he did. In the distance, Kathy looked at me, kind of held her hands out and tilted her head as if to ask "what happened?" With that, I regained my confidence and vowed I'd dance to the next song.

Aubrey walked up to me and burst my bubble. "Why didn't you dance, hot shot?"

"I froze. It won't happen again, promise."

"Thaw out fast. She's going out to dance with someone else 'cause I told her to!"

Kathy was now standing with one of the school's cool crowd, a bunch of guys who called themselves the Gents, and one of them wrapped an arm around her as the next song started. It killed me to see Kathy dance with some dumb senior when she had been waiting for it to be me. There was no way I was missing my next chance. Like Ricky Nelson, I'd make a cool joke about needing a second to get over how beautiful she was, and it'd be like I'd never goofed up. Perfect.

After a few more songs, Jerry took the mike. "Okay, gals, Ladies' Choice Dance. You know how it goes—if he's been too shy to ask, you go get him. Mr. Arwell, guard that door!"

Mr. Arwell, the school wrestling coach with banana-sized fingers, stood centurion-style next to the door.

"And Donatella, second surprise of the night—you're going to start with one lucky guy to dance with you!"

At that point, the song "Let the Little Girl Dance" started to play—of course, it was a song about a shy girl getting the nerve to ask a guy for a dance. Even Aubrey couldn't have planned it like this. Come on, Kathy! Get over here!

Donatella started to go out to find her partner. I stepped away, thinking it'd stink if she picked me, but bumped into Henry who was trying to intercept her. She dodged him like a fighter plane only to run smack into Possum.

Not missing a beat, he grabbed her hands and began dancing like he had lost his mind, pumping her arms up and down like a rail handcar and moving his feet like he was walking on hot coals.

"Stop it," hissed Donatella, loud enough for everyone to hear. "You're not even with the beat!"

Across the floor, Aubrey was playfully pulling Kathy with Melanie pushing her from behind. I stood my ground, confident, confident like a rock; I was Steve McQueen and Paul Newman rolled into one, awaiting my Rat Pack girl. Marlon Brando would have taken one look at me and quit. John Wayne would have nodded proudly. I was going to do it. I was going to dance with Kathy Martin. I wasn't going to run or freeze...

She was coming closer and closer. Without Aubrey or Melanie's help, she came right up to me and said in an almost hushed voice, "Dance with me, Larry?"

I gulped, nodded and stepped forward.

At that point, Possum let go of Donatella and grabbed her microphone off the stage. He began to sing in an awful voice and was butchering the lyrics. Donatella dusted herself off inches away, which caused the floor manager to put the spotlight on her, me and . . . Kathy. For Possum, this was the go-ahead to personalize the chorus in his best high-pitched imitation of Billy Bland, the singer on the record:

Let Larry and Kathy dance
Let Larry and Kathy dance
They've never danced before
So turn the spotlight up a little more
So they can get out on the floor! Yeah! Let Lar-

At that point the song had a saxophone solo bridge and Possum switched to miming a trombone. "Wrong instrument!" someone shouted as Jerry stopped the record with an awful scratch and called for Mr. Arwell, who strode over, wrapped his entire hand around Possum's forearm like a handle and yanked him off the stage.

I turned to Kathy and started to apologize and more importantly ask, very loudly, who on earth this Possum guy was. But she was standing there, biting her lip and fighting back tears. When I saw the glint in her eye, I froze up again and finally she turned and ran out of the auditorium.

"I'm going to kill him," I muttered to no one in particular. Jerry called for the Piston Rings to come out. I left and went out into the hall to look for Kathy, but instead, like a hawk hunting a rat, Aubrey nabbed me. I started stuttering, "Where is she? I am so sorry, Aubrey, Possum is a moron. I don't even know him."

Aubrey pointed over near the door, where I saw Kathy surrounded by Rat Packers. I could hear sobbing as she sputtered.

"I am so . . . humiliated! It's worse than when I wore braces and kids called me lobster-trap mouth!"

Melanie held her arm around her. "Nonono, Kathy, you're beautiful and he's awful, I can't believe that idiot had his friend . . . " I saw red and almost punched the wall.

"Aubrey, this is a huge misunderstanding. I'll go apologize and then the next dance . . . "

"You leave her alone, you hear me?" she seethed, pointing her finger directly into my eyeball. She read me the riot act, saying it was obvious I had Possum do his thing expressly because I was jealous she danced with someone else after goofing up on the snowball dance. Basically, I was to not exist within ten miles of Kathy, ever. "You better consider transferring to Linden or somewhere." Aubrey said. "We're gonna make your life AWFUL."

I tried to say something but couldn't get a word in edgewise, so I went back into the gym, where I numbly watched the Piston Rings play their signature cover song, "Sleep Walk." I leaned against the wall and let the blood mount to my head while couples slow-danced around the floor. It seemed like a bad dream I was bound to wake up from, soon, soon . . .

Mack was dancing with some girl from the neighborhood named Trish; they saw me and stopped to come over.

"Larry, what was all that about with Possum? You gonna dance with Kathy or what?"

"I don't know, but my night is ruined and the Rat Pack is probably going to murder me."

"Oh, don't worry, Larry," replied Trish, who I didn't know but seemed kind. "I know tons of people who would have thought that was hilarious and danced right along with you. Who cares what a couple girls think?" I tried to explain, but Mack gave me the eye and took Trish back to the floor.

After the dance was over, Butch, Mack and I went out the back door and started home. Mack had managed to get a box of hot dogs that made it through the night unpurchased and was handing them out, but I was more in the mood to throw up. As we left, I saw a brand new Lincoln being driven by a woman who looked like a forty year-old Kathy picking the girls up. They ignored us as the car roared by. Once we got out of their dust, Henry caught up with us, Possum trailing along.

Henry could not resist. "Sir Lawrence, who was the young wench you tried to dance with? Such a beauty is worthy of your King! Why, thou ought to have stayed with the chambermaid you spoke of..."

I was mad enough to fight, maybe both of them at once. Possum deserved at least a slug.

"Henry, that WAS Kathy. And Possum, what the heck you were doing? You humiliated us! She was crying! I'm doomed! I'm gonna have to transfer!"

"Uhm, uh, I was only trying to repay you for saving my pack a few weeks ago. What girl doesn't like a little time in the spotlight?"

"Squire Possum was trying to help. You were outright much perplexed," Henry said.

Butch sensed I was at a boiling point. "Henry, shut up. Possum, go away. Larry, calm down."

I ignored him. "You are an idiot, an absolute idiot, Possum. And you, Henry . . . don't talk anymore crap to me. You know what? That's it, Possum, let's go! You too, Sir Bumblebee."

I put my hands up and was ready to clock someone. Butch intercepted me and pulled me away before I took a swing. "Easy, Larry, easy!"

Off to the side, Mack motioned to Henry and Possum in between bites of the hot dogs he had in either hand. "You two split, now! And this isn't over, guys, you betrayed a gang member!" Henry said he had nothing to do with anything but walked off slowly with Possum.

Once Henry and Possum shuffled off, Butch let me go. "You're a handful, friend, and I don't say that to many people. You all right?"

I was cooling down. I started to realize I had come close to hitting Butch too, which would have ended with a trip to the dentist's. I just waved him off and kicked the dew off a big tuft of grass. It was one of those crisp spring nights where all you could hear were crickets and a distant plane drone. After the three of us had walked across the bridge, Butch risked interrupting the quiet with a comment.

"Larry, I, uh, know Aubrey's older sister, Candy. I'll try and put in a good word for you on Monday, okay?"

"We know you didn't plan that, Larry," said Mack.

"I was so close, guys. I know it's stupid, but I really wanted tonight to go well. My first summer here, I could have spent it with a Rat, ya know?"

Butch smoked with a wise look in his eyes. "Maybe it's for the best, ya never know. Anyway . . . Mack, call Henry and tell him I want to talk to him tomorrow at the footbridge at noon."

"What about Possum, Butch?"

"Tell him he's still on probation, for, uh . . . ten more years."

CHAPTER
FOUR

J ust about the worst thing that can happen in baseball is to strike out with the bases loaded. It happened to me, and no one even had the heart to boo me. As the weekend dragged on, that's what it felt like happened with me and Kathy at the dance on Friday night. Everything had been perfect: Aubrey, queen of the entire class, pulled every last string. I was so close to Kathy Martin that I could smell her perfume. It was one of those nice ones you smelled at Lazarus, the six-story department store in downtown Columbus that we went to maybe once a year. And I blew it. I kicked myself all weekend and replayed the evening over and over in my head as I stood at the bus stop Monday morning. For a new guy at school, it had been a dream come true; now, she and her friends thought I had put Possum up to the whole thing.

I got jerked out of my thoughts by the sound of bus three coming to a stop: the rattling bad muffler, the squeaky brakes, and the horn that sounded like a duck getting run over by a streamroller. As I stepped on, the first thing I noticed was that Mack was in the detention seat.

"What's up, Mack? Everything okay?"

He kind of frowned. "I'll explain later . . . no big deal."

The bus driver yanked the door closed and yelled at me to head back, so I did as Mack re-crossed his arms.

Among the 40 kids that rode my bus, we had a few members from the "Gents," the same group that the guy Kathy ended up dancing with belonged to. On Mondays, they all wore yellow blazers hand-embroidered with a big script G and thought they were hot manure, although Butch put it more precisely. I hadn't been here long enough to know much about them other than I thought they were phony and Kathy was probably going to marry one of them because of my goof up.

Even before the dance, though, I never quite liked these guys. They made fun of the poor kids who rode in from Shanty Town, the collection of shacks and run-down homes about a hundred yards to the west of Northglenn and the headwaters of Sewer Creek. Most of the shacks had no electric, some didn't have running water, and the kids all looked and smelled like the last shower they had was whenever the last rainstorm was. They wore castoff clothing and stayed mostly to themselves. But the Gents were merciless towards them, especially one girl named Harriet who couldn't hide her buck teeth.

Today, it was me who was the prime target. As I walked back to seat 19, I heard them sing "Let The Little Girl Dance" in a bad barbershop quartet imitation, obviously a poke at me. I ignored them and sat next to Harriet, who turned from the window. She was actually pretty, teeth aside: a quiet, red-haired girl in a ragged dress who seemed to always look sad.

"Look, please don't sit here. Those guys up front will start yelling 'spray' and say I'm contaminated or something."

"Harriet, I have to sit here. Just move over a little, please."

"Please don't," she whispered.

The bus driver yelled back for me to sit down or get off the bus.

Harriet moved over against the window, and the Gents erupted.

"Spray, spray, spray, he's right by the cootie queen!"

The bus driver didn't even notice, or care to look like he did. I still felt a little hot from Friday night and thought about going up and busting a few chops, but as a member of the baseball team, getting in a fight on school property was an automatic suspension. Butch was not on the bus that morning, but he'd told me never to get involved in this stuff, anyway. The Shanty Town people looked after their own, he explained, and sure enough he was right.

Behind us, another girl named Kaitlyn stood up, got out of her seat and marched down the moving bus' aisle, then challenged the guys who were yelling to a fight. When they kept yelling "spray!" she went so far as to walk right up to the second row and smack one of them. The bus driver turned around, slammed the brakes and said to get back in her seat.

"You won't do nothin', so I did. I'll fight you all, come on," she said to the driver and the Gents. She stood there defiantly while they looked pretty sheepish until she returned to her seat, spitting on the closest Gent's leather shoes to rousing cheers.

She patted Harriet's shoulder as she walked by. "Those guys are wimps, huh?"

I just nodded off to the side. As usual, Butch was right.

Aubrey didn't even talk to me in home room and acted like I was dead. During the day, everytime I tried to catch Kathy's eye, she looked the other way. Life seemed pretty bleak.

At lunch, Mack said "I told ya, you'd have hell to pay if you messed with the Rat Pack. You don't see me chasing them."

"At least I'm not sitting in the detention seat on the bus. What'd you do?"

Mack explained that he had thrown a cherry bomb out the bus window that morning a few minutes before I got in, which meant he was in the detention seat for the rest of the year, although that wasn't too bad since there were only a few weeks left. That meant I would be riding with Harriet till school was over, but it seemed like Kaitlyn had things under control. Still, it was bad enough with the Gents gloating over their victory at the dance.

That Monday and Tuesday at lunch, Trish seemed to find more and more reasons to come over and chat. When she finally asked if I was dating anyone, I felt uncomfortable because Mack was pretty interested in her.

"Uh, no, I'm not, but I thought you and Mack were . . . "

"Oh, no I didn't mean me. No way—you're not my type."

"Sorry."

"Forget it. Anyway, I ask because . . . you know I transferred here from Linden at the start of the year? I have a girlfriend that comes over a lot to visit. I just thought . . . Maybe if Mack's over and she comes over, well, maybe you'd like a blind date. She's cute!"

Usually blind dates meant the guy or gal couldn't get a date any other way, so I hemmed and hawed and gave a firm maybe, hoping Trish'd forget or find someone else. Besides, if she and Mack split, it'd be awkward if I was dating her friend.

With my romantic life on ice, baseball season took over as my main focus. We were awful: with four games to go until the end of the year, our record was three wins, 20 losses. There were teams cursed by Babe Ruth that did better. It was no surprise when the coach called a team meeting and said he was retiring this year. He'd been the coach since 1939, and there was only so much you could do to improve a team called the Cowpunchers. Replacing him was the assistant coach, Mr. Barnhart, a younger guy with a pretty wife who'd just moved to town. But what happened next was a bombshell to me.

In order to get your letter jacket at Mifflin, you had to play in at least half of the games of that season—and you had to play in at least half the games the team won. This somehow showed you had contributed. I was sure I'd be a rare freshman letter jacket owner, having played in twelve games and in all of the victories. Plus I had started two games while the regular center fielder healed up from his collision with the lava bed field, as we called it. The letter jacket was as good as mine.

But then the coach announced that with only four games left, he was going to play all the seniors and juniors as much as he could, so they were all guaranteed to get a letter. Well, we had a couple of juniors and one senior who were just dead weight, but he kept them around because he was soft-hearted. So that meant me and the three sophomores who had been playing were going to warm the bench for the rest of the year. Goodbye, freshman letter, I thought.

I was right—when the season ended I came up short. But after our final loss, Coach Barnhart called a meeting for all sophomores and freshmen, including the reserve team, right there in the dugout. He was just a few years out of Otterbein College, a local college with a decent team, and had heaps more energy than the outgoing coach.

"Listen up, boys. I've gotten us a sponsor for a summer team, and I want you all to play in it. Sinclair Oil is putting up cash for our uniforms and travel expenses if we name ourselves the Sinclair Dinos. I'm okay with it, if you are—but be warned, these uniforms aren't just green, they're shamrock green. But what that does mean is . . . you get to play ball and be twice as good come next spring."

About 10 guys said they'd play—I'm not sure if the rest just wanted their summers free or were turned off by the uniforms, but either way we would have to ask Desales and Linden guys to fill the other four slots. We had a core of interested people, but baseball was the ugly duckling at Mifflin and recruiting was unlikely. Coach Barnhart said that that would change next year, though, and ended the meeting with a rousing speech. "Guys, from this minute on, we do everything to build Mifflin into a district power. Next year, people will want to move here just to play ball. All right?"

"All right!" We put our hands together and gave a hearty cheer of "TEAM!" so loud it woke up the old coach, who had gone to his Studebaker for a cigarette and fallen asleep with his head against the steering wheel.

With baseball over and school ending soon, it was spring party time, celebrating the end of the year for some and the end of school altogether for others. This was showtime for the Piston Rings, but apparently this year they had competition. One of the strangest things that came out of the disastrous spring sports dance was that Possum started a band. He got three other guys who also thought they were entertainers, and they formed a band with the oh-so-original name "The Northglenners." Possum, their lead, could play the bugle and harmonica; plus, he would sing along with records. All this for twenty dollars.

As a gag, the Gents hired him to be the opening act for the Piston Rings at a bash hosted at one of their houses. The school was talking about it for days, but surprisingly I heard the most about it afterwards from Aubrey on the last day of school. I was eating lunch alone after Mack left early to go woo Trish when Aubrey slid up stealthily.

"Uh, I owe you an apology, Larry."

"Really?" I said, defensively. Aubrey was ruthless when she wanted to be and I figured I was being set up for one final kick in the pants. "Why?"

"I went to the Gents' party a few nights ago and that Possum guy was the first performer before the Piston Rings. He and his band were singing the Bristol Stomp—all the Gents wanted him to show them the dance he did with Donatella. They call it the 'Possum Stomp' now."

"What's this got to do with me? I'm not his friend, for once and for all."

"Possum didn't even realize that the Gents were just making fun of them. Is he dense?"

"That's one way to describe him."

"It's a good way. Anyway, the guy Kathy danced with—they're not together by the way—asked him to tell the story of how you tried to embarrass Kathy with his song. But he didn't understand at all. He just tried to speak in son talk. 'Sons, your son was the son that thought that up, Larry son didn't know I was going to do that, sons, be for giving the Possum all the credit, sons!'"

Aubrey was laughing into her lunch tray, but I wasn't enjoying the reminder of Possum's existence.

"That's great, Aubrey. You should try and teach Possum how to son talk."

"Okay, okay, what I mean is . . . I realize you didn't mean to embarrass Kathy. It really was that Possum guy's fault."

"Oh. So . . . am I back in the picture then?" I asked hopefully.

"Oh, yes and no. Look, we all hang out at Morningside pool the entire summer. It's the social scene here in Mifflin in summers, and maybe I can help you out. Come on over when you can and feel like you won't freeze up." She poked me in the side.

"What about Kathy?"

"Well, she got over the Gent fast. But now she's interested in a guy from Desales named Cubby, mostly because he lives close to River View Manors and you were out of the picture at the moment."

"I am not going to be a second choice. Or third choice. Let him have her." I admit, I was lying through my teeth, but Kathy seemed as inaccessible as ever. Aubrey just shrugged and said wait and see. "This wouldn't have happened if you hadn't frozen upppp!" she added in a singsong.

My good mood, boosted by a fresh outlook of what the summer could hold, was slightly dimmed that afternoon with the sight of E.A. putting beer in an eyedropper and squirting it into the fish tank for his new drinking buddy, Zirkloin Zeke the catfish. I noticed that the two snails had become the parents of at least a hundred children again.

I say again because, weeks before the dance, it had gotten so bad that E.A. decided to kill all the snails in the fish tank by putting all the permanent residents back in the bathtub, before taking the tank, plants, castles and snails out to the yard and leaving them there overnight. After scraping those snails out and hosing down the accessories, he then put the fish tank in the oven and baked it for 20 minutes. I heard him say, "Choo, snails, that'll kill you!" . . . but it hadn't.

Now, with the heat of June and a few hours of sun each afternoon, the snails were back with a vengeance. I woke up that Saturday morning to the smell of bleach and toilet bowl cleaner and heard through the floor register that E.A. was mounting a full chemical assault on the entire fish tank assembly while the fish waited it out in the bathtub. Then I heard a beer bottle get opened on the counter, one of E.A.'s favorite bar tricks. I opened my window, gasped for fresh air from the beautiful summer day outside, and decided I was going to evacuate.

Summer baseball was going to be great, but my baseball bat from the school team had developed a nasty crack, so I figured the best use of a Saturday morning was going and getting a new one in the strip mall where Mom worked at Penney's—there were a half-dozen other stores, one of which was Joe's Sporting Goods. They had an agreement with all the local schools and offered good discounts for student athletes in return for poster placement in the hallways. Looking out at the deep blue sky, I got the bright idea I would run the table today, to use one of E.A.s' phrases: basically, to get a lot done in one go. First, I'd leave and get away from E.A. Two would be going over and getting a new bat at Joe's. Three was the crown jewel.

Today'd be the day I'd walk right through Shanty Town to get to the shopping center. No one in our gang except Butch had ever done that, at least that I knew. Walking through Shanty Town by yourself was the sort of thing you could brag about to Butch and he wouldn't roll his eyes. Maybe I'd even fudge it a bit and say it was at night. If I did and lived to tell the story, it would make up for my bad night at the dance. I figured I might even go up in the pecking order of the gang, maybe even go around Mack for the number two slot, or at least avoid getting replaced by Possum. I took a deep breath, had my morning shower and shaved, and made it outside in 10 minutes flat. My eyes were stinging from the fumes coming from E.A.'s latest snail D-Day campaign.

Shanty Town began right after you headed west on Mecca Street and was exactly what it had been since the Depression. People had lost their homes elsewhere and went there when there was no other place to go, staying for generations that now included Harriet and Kaitlyn. It was conveniently near the railroad spur that led to the main drag, so hobos and homeless people stopped over in the collection of buildings as well. As I entered the little village, I smelled coal and wood smoke from the chimneys right away, plus the unmistakable smell of pork roasting. Mack had told me that even in summer the people here had fires going for cooking and hot water.

There were chickens and a few goats roaming freely along the street, clucking and bleating. I almost felt like I was back on the farm, except Gramps kept the place clean. Here, the overgrown trees kept the sunlight from doing anything more than barely illuminating gray, musty old buildings and people, but you could still see it was filthy. There were real outhouses here and there, too, not that they got much use. About halfway through, I saw a man carefully carrying a slop bucket from one over to a small ditch or stream running nearly through the street. He dumped the contents down the bank and I instantly had a better idea of why Sewer Creek was the way it was.

An old wino on a porch asked if I could spare a dollar, but I kept moving and tried not to eye a rusty old shotgun leaning up against a bent porch column. I was going to make it . . . wait till Butch heard this. But just as I turned the corner of one house, I saw that most of the people in town were gathered around a fire where someone was roasting a hog and basting on barbecue sauce. In the dim light coming through the giant maples, you could barely read a sign outside the last house that read:

D. R. Haskins
Mayor, Constable-Justice of the Peace
Pork Producer

An old bearded man came out to the street from the house just as I walked by and I had a feeling he'd been watching me since I stepped foot in the town.

"Hey there, Northglenn boy! What'r ye doing in my town? We don't want yer type here, so skedaddle!"

"Just cutting through to the shopping center, Mayor."

"Yer gonna stop right there, turn 'round and go the long way 'round town, sonny, and if I see ye —"

At that point, I saw Kaitlyn from the bus by the bonfire turn. She turned around and laughed. "Eh, he's okay D.R., let 'em pass."

"Jest this once, Katie."

"You lost, Larry?" she hollered.

"Nope!" was all I cared to say. I picked up my pace after that, though. The town line was just after the bonfire, and after crossing a footbridge and sneaking through a tight hole in a long, scraggly hedge, I was on the entry drive of the Linden Air Drive-In. Tonight's feature: The Ten Commandments. Even though it was an old film, it always drew a big crowd, and I wondered how Mayor Haskins felt about that many out-of-towners nearby. Then again, you'd miss the foot-wide entrance in the hedges if you were too busy thinking about Anne Baxter.

Ten minutes later, I got to the Penney's where Mom worked, more of a tough guy than I was when I'd set out, I guess—although when I told the guys, I'd leave out the part about Kaitlyn helping me get by the mayor. I saw Mom showing someone some blouses and there were people backed up at her register, but she still took a quick break to tell me to get my bat and wait for her at the new hamburger joint, McDonald's, where she'd meet me at 2:30. She was supposed to get off at noon, but she was on commission so she decided to work a while longer. With that, I headed over to Joe's Sporting Goods at the other end of the shopping center and got my bat. Joe turned out to be Joey, an older woman who looked like she had played some ball in her time. She knew her stuff and was able to peg me as a line drive hitter versus a power hitter, meaning I'd want a thicker handled bat. She pulled out a new, dark ash Nellie Fox model, thirty-three inches, $8.95. I swung it a few times and liked it right away.

I was in McDonald's around one-thirty, stomach growling. I was about to order when I noticed Mack's new girl Trish on the payphone in the corner. It was easy to see she was upset and almost crying. Waiting for her in the booth across from the phone was another girl, and I admit I couldn't take my eyes off her. She was darker-complexioned, like girls who went to the pool to tan too much wanted to be, with long, coal-black hair and dark eyes over a mischievous smile. What really got my attention was a long feather hanging about level with her left ear. I was stunned!

Trish got off the phone and immediately saw me. "Oh, thank goodness! Larry, can you believe it? Mom and I got our times mixed up, and she can't pick us up until five! We can't afford to just stay here for four hours . . . walk us home?

"Us?"

"Oh yes, Larry, this is my best friend, Miss Lynn Bennet; Lynn, Larry, he's Mack's friend. He's Mifflin's superstar baseball player."

I wanted to impress Lynn so badly but I was afraid to speak, thinking I'd repeat the chicken sounds I'd heard in Shanty Town. I tried to pull out something suave.

"Uh, 'miss?' So you're not married?" It bounced like rubber; she smiled and flipped her hair back.

"No, are you?"

I was having a hard time not staring at Lynn's feather, it was so distinct. Since I couldn't think of anything else to say, so I looked until she laughed.

"Take a picture, will ya? It will last longer."

I could have just kicked myself but then her face broke out in a big smile.

"Got ya! I just love to see people's expressions when I say that."

That broke the ice. The guys behind the counter were looking bored and cranky, so I said of course that Mom could drive them home if they'd wait with me until two-thirty. I got us a bag of burgers with fries and fresh Cokes all around.

Lynn's smile seemed to change me instantly from dorky teenager to someone easily as cool as Ricky Nelson. I was confident: conversation was flowing out of me like I was the smoothest talker of all time. We sat and talked like we had known each other for years—well, Lynn and I did. Trish tried to interrupt a few times but obviously saw what was happening and finally stole fries from me while I talked with Lynn. All too soon, Mom pulled up and honked the horn. I went out first to explain the situation, and Mom said of course she'd drive them back.

When they came out, Trish called shotgun. As I opened the door for her, she leaned over and quietly hummed the first few notes of the Wedding March in my ear. I blushed a brighter red than the car's original paint color. Mom had a box of curtains in the back, so Lynn and I had to sit close to each other. At that moment, if someone had said the name "Kathy Martin" to me, I would have said, "WHO?"

When we got to Trish's, Mom quietly said under her breath that I should walk them to the door in that way moms do when what you do next is life or death.

"What a gentleman," was all Trish said as she laughed. "But I know when I'm not needed. . . . see ya, Larry! Thanks for the burgers."

I still had my voice even though I had been afraid I was going to melt down sitting that close to Lynn in the car on the way to Trish's house. "Uh, Lynn, I sure hope you come to Trish's often. I just live one street over and uh, uh, I'd really like to see you again, sometime, I hope, I mean . . ."

"Me, too." She seemed nervous. "I mean, I'd like to see you again, uh, I didn't mean I'd 'like to see me again.'" She turned but just as she was about to go inside, she unclipped the feather from her hair and handed it over.

"That'll last even longer than a picture." She gave a flirty smile and wave over her shoulder while I floated in reverse back into the car. I was in love, hook, line and sinker.

CHAPTER FIVE

I lay in bed that next morning staring at the feather clip Lynn had given me and smelling the fresh, dewy summer breeze as it mixed with the fragrance of Lynn's hair. I had been mesmerized by Kathy, but the way I felt about Lynn was different. Kathy was a badge of honor. Lynn . . . I knew almost nothing about her, but that brief time I spent with her the night before had me wanting to know everything.

I suppose I would have stayed there all morning if I hadn't heard someone knocking at the front door. Mom had gone to work, and E.A. had left for the new job he had found a month ago selling a different line of cleaning products, some samples of which had been used in yesterday's assault on the snails. He had just taken over an established route from a retired guy who spent most of his evenings at Tubby's Tavern. The money was better than E.A.'s old job, plus the hours were longer, so he had to be home less often. It was a win-win situation.

"Larry, are you in there? Are you asleep? Come on, the gang's got a mission!" I heard Mack yelling up from outside. I tucked Lynn's feather in my pillow and ran downstairs to find Mack and Butch at the doorstep—Butch looked impatient. Mack explained that earlier that morning, they'd already been to the creek and seen the nudist colony of city slickers that was rumored to swim in the Alum just above the big pool where we sank the boat. This was news.

"What? Don't they know that people can see them from the road?" I asked. Butch shook his head.

"Not with the leaves on the trees. Come on, we're going to go chase them out of our area. I don't want to become a destination for people from Columbus." I gobbled down a bagel as Butch explained the attack and Mack slid in and took about a dozen cookies from Mom's cookie jar, which was shaped like a monk and said "Thou Shalt Not Steal." I coughed.

"Oh, uh, these are for Butch," Mack said. He gave him one but kept the remaining eleven in a paper bag he'd also taken from underneath our sink. Somehow, after only a few months, Mack knew where everything in the kitchen was, maybe better than I did.

We made the park in record time but hadn't gone a hundred yards in when a big, black Newfoundland dog crept up behind us and pounced on Mack.

"It's a bear, guys, run for your life!" he yelled from the ground.

Butch and I were bent over laughing—everyone recognized Elvis, the father of half the neighborhood's dogs. He was overly friendly most of the time, unless he was on his way to a date.

"Just give him the cookies, Mack, and he'll go away," Butch suggested. Elvis agreed and tore the bag from Mack's hand before running off.

"Oh, man, I was starved . . . We have time—can we go back to Larry's?"

"No," Butch said firmly. "We hafta make a detour to the Blains' farm first."

This was unexpected, but since Mack had a tradition of stealing food from all the neighborhood, I figured we were going to visit the Blains' produce stand at the end of their road, usually run by their daughter.

"I guess I could steal some strawberries. Marcie expects it now—it's a tradition," said Mack.

"No. We're going to pick her up," Butch answered.

Mack and I looked at each other but said nothing. I knew Marcie from school, but she never ran with us before. Butch hadn't planned on telling us, it seemed.

The Blains' vegetable and fruit farm was a small setup right before the golf course with a roadside stand at the end of their long driveway. From it they sold produce to grocery stores and local restaurants whose chefs and owners would pick it up themselves. Even then, it seemed old-fashioned compared with some of the newer marts going in in Columbus, but Marcie said they owned the land and did pretty well for themselves. Anyone with taste buds knew it was fresher food than the stuff shipped under-ripe from California on the refrigerated railcars.

We stayed on the south side of Sewer Creek and soon got to the area near Troll's cave. Instead of going in, we climbed up over the hillside that covered Possum's favorite camping site and immediately found ourselves in their strawberry patch. There was a small trailer with fresh-picked strawberries on it, and Mack couldn't resist going over and taking a quart.

As he turned, Marcie lept from behind the nearby tractor tire and pounced on him, tackling him to the ground like a linebacker.

"Help, it's the bear!" he shouted, half seriously, I think.

"Ah-ha! Mack Hall, caught ya red-handed," Marcie said proudly, wiping her hands off on her shorts. "You all think you're stealthy as coyotes but I could hear you plomping up that hill with the tractor running." She looked at me. "What are YOU doing with these delinquents, Larry?"

Marcie was the prototype tomboy but cuter than Christmas, and if I hadn't met Lynn the night before I might have tried to awkwardly be smart. But then something happened that ruled that option out entirely—she went over and hugged Butch.

"Hey, it's my guy!" she smiled.

Butch gave a chuckle and stifled it trying to look fierce, but what do you know: he was a human being after all. I asked Mack about it later; he wasn't sure but thought it had it started towards the end of the school year; I missed out on seeing it happen because of baseball. Even Mack didn't know it had gotten to the point of Butch giving out free hugs.

Once he'd peeled Marcie off, Butch laid out the mission.

"All right, everyone: now and then, a group of inner-city slickers come down to the Alum to swim, naked. They think this is the wilderness, apparently, but this is our turf, so they have to go. They got plenty of spots in the Scioto River north of Columbus they can do that crap in."

"Are there naked girls?" I asked.

Mack chuckled as Butch replied. "Yes, several."

"Guys, too?" Marcie inquired.

"Yes, but you can't look."

"Aww, gee, Butch," she whined sarcastically. "I'll look anyway."

"Mack, you got grenades on you?"

Mack's endless supply of M-80s and cherry bombs came from a wooden crate that his dad had purchased from a going-out-of-business fireworks store. I always worried one day I'd read in the newspaper that a local boy had died in what appeared to be a hydrogen bomb test, but so far Mack was still around and usually had four or five on him. They were almost waterproof, too, and he and Butch had plenty of experience fishing with them.

"Don't worry, guys," he assured us when Marcie said she didn't want to hurt the swimmers, even if they were city folk invading our turf. "We'll throw around 'em, not at 'em."

From Marcie's, the swimming hole was only a short walk along the bank of the Alum. At this point in the summer, the water was warm and almost hot in the shallows, opposite of what it'd been during our boat ride. The creek was alive now, with bluegills, water weeds, turtles and—

"Snake!" Butch shouted. He jumped up higher than some nearby bushes.

I looked at his last footprint in the muck and saw the biggest, fattest snake I'd ever seen. It had mottled markings that made it look like a copperhead, and you never wanted to take the time to find out if it actually was one. I knew that people got amputated limbs from untreated bites. All the guys took several steps back.

"Aw, jeez, guys," Marcie said. She calmly walked up to the fat roll of scales, put a handy branch squarely on its head, then grabbed it by its belly and tossed it into the water. It slunk off into the shallows. "Just a water snake. Wouldn't bite a lamb."

"I knew that—I tripped," stuttered Butch.

No one said anything, but we all had to stifle a snicker. Butch was liable to punch you if he thought you were laughing at him, and it was obvious Marcie had a special immunity.

We advanced along and eventually got to the crest of a shrubby dune before the deep pool—sure enough, we could hear a lot of laughter. Peeking out over the top, we saw several people in the stream, and yes, they were naked. I had never seen a girl nude before and as I reached the top of the sand dune after everyone else, I was hoping for girls who had just got done starring in an Elvis flick.

They were not. There were several older women, maybe 60-plus years old. Thin, pale, and saggy, except one who was calling herself Moby Dick—and Herman Melville would have agreed. Moby would get on her inner tube wearing only frogman fins, then dive in head first, leaving her behind out of the water, standing apparently on her hands kicking her flippers. When she came up, she would yell "There she blows!" before spouting water out of her mouth. I hoped for her sake that she had all her shots, as they were downstream from the mouth of Sewer Creek. I briefly flashed back to the man with the outhouse slop bucket from yesterday.

The only man was maybe 70, also very pale and skinny. He had a life preserver on and a pith helmet, but nothing else. As he stood up, Marcie groaned and covered her eyes. Suddenly, Butch's mission seemed a little more justified.

Each of us took a cherry bomb from Mack, and Butch got out his lighter. Once all our fuses had been lit, Marcie yelled "Nuke 'em!" and we tossed about ten altogether in the water around them. I think we got some assistance from the snake, as it swam through the group at just the right moment.

After the explosions in the water, which looked like World War II footage, the nudists made it to shore as fast as they could. Naked people were running all over trying to dress as they ran, including Moby Dick in her fins. We took off running, too, till we got to Marcie's farm, whooping and hollering as we went. Butch made us all swear to tell anyone else we saw summer students from Ohio State University who looked like they were from Shaker Heights in Cleveland and drove Cadillacs. Then he nominated Marcie to join the gang as a full member; Mack and I seconded. All in all, a full day.

Butch said he was going to help Marcie finish her chores, so Mack and I took a hint and left together. On the way home, he asked if I ever had plans to go to Morningside Pool like Aubrey had mentioned at the end of school.

"Your beloved Rats go there all summer, Larry," he laughed. "Maybe Aubrey can work her magic again."

"They're not my Rats Mack, and anyway I think I may have found someone else."

"Who?"

I then told him about the previous night with Trish and Lynn.

"I know this girl . . . uh, kinda dark, long hair, high cheekbones?" He was trying to be tactful.

"Yes, Mack, she's an Indian."

"I didn't want to say that, Larry, in case, uh, you know." He shrugged.

"Makes no difference to me. She's the most beautiful girl I've ever seen. And she's Trish's best friend, too."

"Her name is Lynn Bennett, right? I would never tell Trish, but she is pretty. I don't know much about her, but I heard at the pool last year she's had a hard time with the, uh, the Indian thing and all. But also I guess her family's not too well off."

"Well, she seems even better because of it."

"What's got you so worked up about her?" Mack asked.

"She's beautiful. She's got this mischievous smile, and she can dish it out as well as she takes it. When she said goodbye and kind of goofed up, saying she didn't mean to say she wanted to see herself, she got so shy but I felt like I saw the real Lynn. She wasn't trying to be perfect . . . she's already special." I wasn't making sense, but Mack was a good friend and pretended like he'd been there.

"What happened then? Did you guys kiss?"

"NO. I just kind of melted inside, Mack." I got beet red as I remembered the warm feeling in my gut from the afternoon before. "She gave me the feather she was wearing Mack, just like that. What do you make of that?"

Mack raised his eyebrows. "Okay, Romeo, listen. I've been going to Morningside pool for four years. It's not just the Rat Packers. Girls from Linden-McKinley, Mifflin, and Desales go there. It's the place for summer romance. That's where I first saw Trish last year before she transferred to Mifflin. Lynn was there sometimes with her, too, with that famous feather clip."

"Thanks for the tip."

We walked along for a little bit and Mack lit up all of a sudden. "Hey, this is pretty neat that she and Trish are friends. We might end up being brother-in-laws!"

"That's not how it works, Mack."

We agreed to go to the pool the following Monday as I was busy with baseball that weekend and had to re-shingle the shelter house in the woods—one thing E.A. had done for me was win me some jobs that used the skills I had picked up from working with my grandfather around the farm. E.A. was becoming quite the big wheel in Northglenn and was a real man of the people, at least some of them. He had shown up so frequently at community council meetings to complain about this or that that they appointed him to fill a vacant street captain's slot, figuring it'd shut him up.

In fact, E.A. got right to work for the greater good. In the month he'd been on the council, E.A. had already potentially solved one of the biggest problems facing the neighborhood: the constant flooding of the municipal baseball field and park by Sewer Creek. Any time it rained longer than a day, Sewer Creek turned into a smelly, frothy river and covered the grounds, leaving behind wads of toilet paper and a distinct smell for days. The solution was a dike, but the council could never raise enough funds. E.A. had never been stopped by that problem before. When he learned that they were widening nearby State Route Three, he took me along to meet the general contractor to see if we could have the excess fill dumped at the park.

"Watch how I handle this guy, Larry, watch and learn," he said, getting out of the company car in one of the rare moments he didn't call me "bud" or "bub." I rolled down the window and heard him ask for the superintendent, who came out in dirty overalls with a worried look on his face.

"Hey bub!" E.A. began. "There's mud all over the streets. It's making my driveway look like a construction site. Who's gonna clean this up?"

The superintendent didn't need angry calls going into the state office. "Look guy, it's almost impossible to keep the streets clean as we're widening, but I'll have a brush team take care of it tonight."

Ed looked around with a wizened gaze. "Look, I spent a little time in the engineering corps in the Army. . . . you got too much dirt around here. Why don't you drop it off at the Northglenn municipal park? I'm the street captain, I'll calm folks down about the dirt." The engineer smelled a deal and shook E.A.'s hand right then and there.

Sure enough, the next day there were 20 truckfuls of dirt piled up along the municipal drive in big mounds. All that was needed was an excavator to build the dike. E.A. got on the phone and found a local excavator to build it for free in return for naming the park after his deceased father, who originally owned the land Northglenn had been built on in the forties. The council was in awe. Everyone forgot about the flying-in-the-driveway incident back in March, and E.A. celebrated by repeating the trip to Tubby's Tavern. This time he did not drink Old Crow.

One thing E.A.'s political career had not benefited was his fish tank. A few days after the last extermination effort, the snails returned en masse. When I got home from baseball the day after E.A.'s victory lap at Tubby's, I noticed the fish tank was empty again and reeked of cleaner. E.A. was prepping an old rag with Drano and really going at it in the interior of the little castle.

"Chuh, bud, this'll be the last of the snails," he said. Unfortunately at that moment, we heard the bathtub draining and E.A. went in to find Zirkloin Zeke had escaped down the drain. I patted E.A.'s shoulder as he shed a single tear into his Drano-soaked sock. They got a new Zeke that evening at the store, but it was lazy and didn't seem to want to eat scum, so E.A. flushed him that weekend and replaced him with yet another catfish, who ate not only scum but some of the smaller fish. Meanwhile, the snails returned. It was a bad week for E.A. but a good one for the salesman at the aquarium store.

Despite the fish tank, it felt like I was living on cloud nine. It seemed like the summer would go on forever, and it was a good feeling, the first I'd had like it since before we moved from the farm. Summer baseball, adventures in the woods with my gang, and Lynn—Lynn was all I had thought about for a week. She was on my mind when a Monday breakfast came and found me home with E.A., with Tommy Dorsey and Frank Sinatra's "I'll Never Smile Again" playing on WBNS 1460. E.A. and Mom loved the pre-war oldies; they were the soundtrack of my mornings.

"Bub, I'm staying home today to clean this fish tank and kill the snails for good. Want some grub?"

"Sure, E.A. What's the plan this time?"

"Take all the fish out, scour the tank with gasoline in the drive, spray it out, and broil it in the oven on high for 45 minutes, not just a little for twenty. It'll be a proper home for Zirkloin Zeke the third."

"Won't the glass crack?"

"Not if I heat it up slowly."

"Sure those snails aren't just hiding out in the filter when you do your cleaning?"

Ed looked at me like I had suggested the pebbles were actually snail eggs. "Chuh, bud, no snail's going to get inside that filter. I know this stuff." He plopped himself down another pancake and cracked a morning beer.

About 11:00, Mack came to the front door.

"Larry, I'm gonna buy your lunch today," he announced. "In honor of it being our first day going to the pool and all."

"Thanks Mack, I appreciate that."

"I just need you to pay my way into Morningside."

"Ah-ha." But I did some quick calculations, figured I could eat more than fifty cents' worth of food, and the joke was on Mack.

We shook on the deal. Mack declined some cookies to go, so I figured we really were going to chow down if he was willing to bet his empty stomach on it, maybe at Doris's, the local corner deli. That was easily a dollar if I played my cards right. But when we got there, Mack went straight for the back, where they had placed a small tray of slightly over-ripe tomatoes out on a cart. It read "Free—help yourself."

"First course, dig in, pal."

Somewhat miffed, I picked them over and found a good one.

"Gee thanks, big spender, you're so generous."

Mack laughed and chomped his tomato. When we got down to East Linden Grade School there was a mulberry tree with overhanging branches full of berries that needed a week or two before they were ready.

"Course two, monsieur, only the finest food for you," Mack said as he bowed like a French waiter. I nibbled on one and puckered up bad.

"I want to see the manager. These are sour as heck, Mack."

He only kept heading down the road, but I figured I had a strong case to renege on our agreement. Once we got to Hudson Street, there was a little old-time druggist with a temporary lunch stand outside. I smelled the heavenly aroma of barbecued chicken wafting from a grill manned by an attractive young woman. A sign advertised a one-dollar lunch and I wished I'd brought enough money to splurge, because Mack had welshed on our agreement.

"Here boys, try a sample of our new chicken recipe. One dollar gets you a whole lunch and an ice cold Coke."

I started forward but was blocked by Mack's beefy arm. He got close to the girl as if he was going to say yes, then began to sniffle.

"Ma'am, that smells just like the chicken my mom used to make before."

"Before?"

"Before . . . well, ma'am, before she died." He then blew his nose loudly on a napkin he took off the stand's counter.

"Oh my, young man . . . that's just awful." I looked at her and then at Mack and realized she was really buying this.

"Not as awful as the fact that . . . well, she never told us the recipe, ma'am. Me and my father can't manage it. That's the first time I've smelled that in months. Everything we try just tastes like cardboard."

The girl broke down. "No, no, no! Here, you and your friend are going to have a full plate, and not a drumstick either, you two take a large piece."

I started forward again. Even if Mack had outright lied, I was starved. But Mack whacked me back with his arm again.

"Oh, ma'am, I just couldn't. We're all right, we can manage. But what if a needy person came along and you didn't have any chicken to give them? No, we must go. . . . We must leave and continue our journey," Mack quietly said.

By now she had tears in her eyes, which was good because I was rolling mine.

"Oh, if only more young men were polite like you instead of being beatniks and bums. Please sit here at the table, I'll be right back."

Mack stayed in character while she was inside, quickly dabbing a napkin from an open pitcher of lemonade onto his face for fake tears. The young woman came back with a tray and two styrofoam plates and loaded them with chicken, coleslaw, and baked beans.

"Please," she said, "be our guests. We've got so much more chicken in the freezer, so no one will go hungry."

When she went back in for brownies and Cokes, Mack looked over and gruffly said, "Dig in and look grateful, will ya?" then laughed.

When we got to the pool, I paid for both of us.

After waiting a half an hour to let Mack's feast digest, I got changed into my trunks. While we were waiting, I'd watched a long line of boys at the high diving board as an older guy with a clipboard looking on—one of them was Cubby, the great Desales athlete and the very same guy who Kathy was apparently interested in. I looked over and saw Kathy watching him dive, he was actually pretty good. "YAY, Cubby!" she yelled every time he dove. I didn't forget about Lynn, I guess, but I hadn't forgotten about Kathy, either, and it annoyed me.

The only swimming I had ever really done was to take some basic classes at the county pool up in Sunbury, when we lived on the farm. Plus, our farm neighbors, the Loars, had dammed up a spring on their farm and had let all the local kids use it as the swimming hole. I never had dived off a board before, but us guys would do somersaults and stuff off the bank into the spring. I'm not sure what came over me, but I chose that moment to get in line and jump off a high board for the first time.

"Can't say I've seen you around before, son. What's your dive going to be?" As I looked up, I realized the shirt of the man with the clipboard also read "DIVING COACH."

"Oh, I'm just going to jump in," I said.

"If you're trying out for the pool's diving team, you have to state your dive so I can grade you." He was getting impatient and Cubby and his friends were behind me, asking what the holdup was. I looked over at Kathy—she seemed to be enjoying my situation. Not wanting to be outdone, I boldly said I'd be doing a somersault, finishing in a swan dive.

"Okay, go ahead and dive, then, let's see what you got." I didn't want to be on any old diving team, but with Kathy watching and the memory of the dance still lingering in my mind, I had no choice. Up the ladder I went.

I tested the board's spring, it seemed okay. More responsive than a creek bank. The whole pool seemed to be looking up. I stepped forward, sprung off the board, tucked and began my somersault.

I got halfway through and froze with my legs straight out and my stomach facing skyward. I seemed to lose all inertia except down, where I was headed for the world's biggest back smacker.

"Ohhhh shii—" I yelled for what seemed like an eternity.

"Look out, he's doing a smacker!" Someone yelled over me. I thought for sure I heard a woman scream. Then with a crack you could hear all the way back home, I hit the water. Going down, I wanted to just swim out the drain, through the filtration equipment and eventually into the Alum. Instead, as I surfaced, I heard a lot of mock applause by Cubby and his cronies.

The diving coach yelled, "Are you okay, son?" When I nodded, he shook his head. "Don't know what that was supposed to be, but I don't think you're ready for competitive diving."

I went over to where our towels were and Mack was lying in the sun. "Did anyone see that, Mack?"

"Yeah, everyone! That was cool, do it again! The lifeguard got out of her chair and grabbed the life doughnut. The water splashed all over the picnic area, too!"

I wrapped my towel around my head and laid on the deck chair, wishing I had never taken Mack up on his offer.

Then, I heard a soft voice, obviously a girl, say, "Are you okay?"

I didn't answer, I figured it was the lifeguard. I stuck my thumb up.

"Larry, are you okay?" I unwrapped my towel, only to see that it was Lynn Bennett.

"Oh, hi, Lynn! Yeah, I'm okay, just a little —"

"—embarrassed, maybe? Were you showing off for the Rat Pack?" Mack snorted off to the side.

"Wha—how do you know them, Lynn?"

"Everyone knows who they are. They run this place—we just swim here. Hi, Mack. Trish has told me alllll about you!"

Mack blushed and turned away, so I continued. "Not really, Lynn, I just wanted to jump off the board and I got caught up in the . . . the diving competition, it looks like, uh, I don't think I'll win this one."

She motioned for me to come join her on a nearby bench away from Mack, who was still bright red. "I was hoping you would come to the pool sometime, Larry, but that was the dumbest thing I have ever seen," she laughed. "You have a thing for one of the Rats?" She was about the most straightforward person I had ever met. I just kind of sat there staring at the pool, not knowing what to say. "Well?"

Did I really owe this bossy little girl an explanation? On the other hand, the rush of feelings had returned, like we'd known each other for years. I decided to level with her, kind of.

"No, I don't, but Aubrey tried to fix me up with one of her friends and it didn't work. I wasn't here to see them. Actually, I was here to see you—" I summoned up all the courage I had "—Lynn."

She smiled and brushed her hair away. "That's the safe answer, Larry. I like that."

We sat and talked, and soon we picked up right where we had left off that night at the hamburger joint. Too soon, she said she had to go, but told me that she came to the pool on Mondays and Tuesdays. The other days she waited tables over at Maddie's Diner on Hudson Street. Then she got up and smacked me on the back.

"Don't pull another stupid stunt like that again, Larry. See ya tomorrow?"

I gulped and said sure. As she walked away, I saw Kathy and Aubrey drilling holes in us with their eyes.

When I got home, the fish tank was on the curb with the rest of the trash. Mom said that when E.A. had filled it up with water after letting it cool following its 45-minute broil, a few snails appeared within minutes, and E.A. decided then and there to give the remaining fish a 21-flush salute and be done with it. Besides, now he had a new project.

E.A. loved holidays with the best of them, usually because they converted some weekday nights into Fridays. When he found out that there was no Fourth of July celebration in Northglenn, he'd gone to work. Since he'd only come into power in early June, he had less than four weeks to get it done. But in short order he got four food vendors plus several games whose owners were in between county fairs. He even got an octopus ride and a Ferris wheel from a small circus whose lead acrobat was recuperating after a fall at one of the hospitals he sold product to. Finally, to make sure he had a good time, he had Tubby's Tavern sponsor a pool tournament, bringing in their own billiards table underneath a big canvas tent. His ace in the hole was one of his biggest sales clients in Columbus, the Ugly Bull Brewery, which promised a beer truck and other entertainments. The council was split in half; half of them loved it, and half of them felt it was rapidly becoming a non-family event. E.A. was the deciding vote.

But he was a man on a mission and was determined to win over his opposition by making his 4th the most family-friendly event of the century. The next night he sat down at the kitchen table, put the telephone's base on his left, a notepad in the middle, and his Rolodex on his right. Then he cracked his knuckles and started dialing like a stock broker.

Pulling a few strings with his work contacts, he got the number of a local TV wrestler named the Thunderchief and convinced him to agree to be the grand marshal. He sealed the deal by noting that several big car dealerships that typically sponsored the TV matches would be advertising in the parade, and it'd be a great tie-in since the car dealerships usually sponsored the local wrestling hours.

"E.A., are there really going to be cars at this parade?" I asked. He held up a finger and started dialing. The next call was to the local Chevy dealer, one of his clients for cleaning products. They agreed to lend four new convertibles for the parade, under the promise that he'd get the highschool cheerleading team to fill them, as well as TV's Thunderchief, who was a "close friend." He winked at me while saying it was a done deal.

E.A.'s coup de grace was calling Coach Barnhart and convincing him to do the work of rescheduling our Fourth of July game with the powerful Hilliard Hawks to take place at the park. In return, E.A. would introduce the coach to the local dealers for sponsorship potential. But it wasn't just for me: E.A. knew from the school directory that Mrs. Barnhart was also a teacher and the new cheerleader advisor. "Now Barnhardt," I heard E.A. say as he popped a bottle cap, "these car dealer guys need to appeal to the younger audience, or at least their parents. You get Mrs. Barnhardt to bring the Mifflin cheerleading squad for a little school spirit in those convertibles, I see Chevy logos and sleek pinstripes on your boys' chests for summers to come." I remembered telling E.A. how much the coach hated the Sinclair green, and apparently that info had gotten filed away in his internal Rolodex after all.

I wondered how many businessmen went to bed that night not realizing they were just pawns in E.A.'s chess game against the city council. As I turned up my transistor radio and looked outside at the stars, I thought about the more important fact that with the cheerleaders filling the convertible seats, I'd be seeing plenty of the Rat Pack on the fourth. Oh, well. Feeling Lynn's feather as it hung on my bedpost and thinking about how my diving humiliation plunged me lower in Kathy's eyes but had gotten me my second conversation with Lynn, I figured that if things could work out for E.A., they could work out for me, too.

When 10:00 came the next morning, I headed right back to the pool again, avoiding the lady selling chicken. I decided that today I'd make the classiest impression on Lynn possible. If Morningside pool was known for summer flings and flirting, I had a real shot at something here if I didn't goof it up.

As it turned out, Lynn and I were about to become part of the pool's romantic history.

CHAPTER
SIX

E very Monday and Tuesday for almost the whole of June, I managed to be myself, who it turned out Lynn liked. It started out with classic low-risk moves that got bolder with the days: sharing food, sitting side by side, sharing a lunch, swimming together. Since she only came two times a week, I would go over and eat with her at Maddie's a couple times when I could. With baseball and my new job service and Lynn, I was about as busy as a person could be, and since Mack and Butch also had girls, none of us minded the temporary lapse in gang adventures. And if it bothered Aubrey and Kathy at all, they never let on. With no more offensive maneuvers by Aubrey, Kathy started to become history.

At the end of June, the first summer dance at the pool was announced. I felt bold enough to ask Lynn to go, but she said no. Her mom worked at night cleaning offices in addition to mornings at Maddie's, and Lynn had to stay with her sister, Kristy, who was only eleven. I tried to learn more about her family, but Lynn clammed up pretty fast on that topic. She wasn't ready to tell me, I guess. We never really admitted to each other that we were an item, and though we were always together at Morningside, there was really nothing to make us public, so her having an out the evening of the dance did seem a little disappointing. But as June came to an end, we agreed to meet at the pool on the last day of the month and the day after the dance.

When I got to Morningside, the Rat Pack was playing a game of keep-away with a beach ball. I knew most of the guys who were in the water with them, and I had become familiar with all the other Rat Pack members at school, if only as one of their thousands of admirers. I just stood and watched as Lynn wasn't there. Then Aubrey sidled up to me.

"Ready to play in the big leagues, Larry?"

"Hi Aubrey, long time, no chat. What do you mean?"

"Kathy and Cubby fell out last night at the dance. His fault, he's been Mr. Fickle and two-timing her with a girl from Desales . . . real bad news for Cubby. She's through with him if you're through with what's-her-name. Linda Lonnehan?"

"I'm not through with anyone, Aubrey. Her name is Lynn Bennett! I'm not interested in Kathy." Aubrey looked like a sorcerer who just found out her magic was mostly firecrackers, but she recovered fast.

"Nonsense, Larry. Look, I know what you're doing, but now's not the time to play hard to get. We're about to play war horse, and Kathy doesn't have anyone now that Cubby's too afraid to show his face around here. Now, you volunteer and you'll see."

She walked off; I think she was mad at me. Sure enough, a game of war horse broke out—where the girl gets on her guy's shoulders and everyone throws the ball, trying to knock other couples off their feet. Guys were circling like sharks around a horse-less Kathy, but Aubrey was fending them off while looking at me and winking like she had a bug in her eye.

Suddenly I was pushed into the pool from behind. In the clear blue water, I saw Lynn jump right in beside me with a big grin. We both emerged at the same time.

"Come on, Trigger, get down so I can get on my horse!"

I ducked down and she got up on my shoulders, and turned my head to the left. I saw a frowning Aubrey had let a guy through to Kathy, and Lynn was steering me right towards them . . . so I went. Lynn splashed so much water that Kathy shouted, "Stop! Stop! Enough, enough!" and got out.

Lynn was on a mission: she wanted to go after Aubrey, who had found the head lifeguard and made him into her horse. "Turn right, Trigger, right!" But before we could attack, the backup lifeguard blew the whistle for the rest period.

"Down, down boy," Lynn laughed as she got off into the water. When she tried to jump on me again, I dodged and tried to dunk her, but she was surprisingly strong. It was more fun to make her think I was going to do it than to actually dunk her, anyway.

We got out and lay in the sun and had a wonderful Sunday afternoon beneath the all-blue sky, talking and listening to her little transistor radio with all the hits on 1230 WCOL. After a few mornings of E.A. and Mom's favorites, it was refreshing to hear a girl sing some of the new songs, which were my favorites, too. At four, she announced she had to go home.

I offered to walk her, and she furrowed her eyebrows before nodding, wrapping her towel around her shoulders and shivering in the slight breeze. For some reason, she had come over in her swimsuit and a long shirt and did not bother to change. I tossed my towel on her and she wore it like a nun as we walked back on the hot pavement.

"Well, I showed those Rats who was boss today."

"Whaddya mean?"

"I just sent them a message that you're not available, that's what."

I was getting a little smarter about girls. Four months ago, I would not have picked up on opportunity knocking like this, but now I was streetwise like Butch. Lynn didn't want congratulations. I stopped and was going to say something, but I lost it in my mouth when I saw her smile. I think my eyes told her all she wanted to know. Now and then, the less said, the better. But I did have an invite to make.

"You know, Lynn, on July 4th we have a game at Northglenn Park, where the old semi-pro baseball team used to play as part of the Independence Day celebrations. You should come."

"I'll be there, Larry. Hope you're better at baseball than diving." At that point, I felt her hand take mine and my heart actually skipped a beat.

We had gotten into a residential area that was progressively getting more and more run-down—not quite Shanty Town, but more brown and rickety than Northglenn. I thought it was somewhere in the area of Tubby's and wondered if I'd see E.A. When we came to a two-story, four-family brick apartment that was in sorry shape, Lynn stopped.

"All right, this is as far as you go."

"Is this where you live Lynn?"

"No, I didn't say that. I said, 'This is as far as you go,' Larry."

"I can walk you all the way, I don't mind."

She shook her head and told me she would see me at my game. "Bye, Trigger," she said with a smirk and a wave over her shoulder. I just waved as she turned the alley around the house. Then I remembered something.

"Hey, Lynn! There is a parade to start the day in Northglenn," I yelled. She turned and laughed.

"I'll think about it!" But she winked, too.

July first saw a bit of change in E.A.'s plans for the glorious fourth. Ugly Bull Brewing had agreed not only to send a beer truck with fresh, cold brew, but their mascot, Ugly Billy Bull, as well. For a dollar, you could get your picture taken with Billy handing you a fresh frothy mug.

"Chuh, Jane," he said to Mom with a celebratory bottle of Weideman's in hand. "We'll make a fortune for the Community Council on Billy pictures alone. I told those bozos I could do it, I told 'em." And it was true. Half the community wanted him to run for township trustee in the fall. As I went upstairs to bed, it started to pitter-patter on the window panes.

That was the start of a two-day washout that I think some of the more conservative members of the community council hoped would cancel the holiday plans and give them a year to oust E.A. from the council before he could plan any more summer festivals. But his dike held fast. He went out three times in the storm to make sure it was staying put, and even invited me the third time. He seemed strangely heroic, standing in the downpour with a flashlight in his hand, its beam stretching out into the park. We were all in E.A.'s aquarium now.

The three-state-long band of rain clouds moved past Northglenn the morning after I watched E.A. face the storm, and a bright July sun quickly dried up what it had left behind. E.A. was no civil engineer, but he'd somehow managed to create the region's best-drained park, and after a day of sunshine the ground was damp but hardly soggy. E.A. triumphantly woke up at 6:00 a.m. on July fourth, earlier than I did, to take in his big day. It was my big day, too: the parade, the carnival, our game with the Hilliard Hawks, and most of all Lynn being there. I was beginning to think of her as my girl, I guess. We had only been together for a month, as Mack kept on reminding me, but what a month it had been! Sometimes it felt like we'd told each other everything already, and at other times it felt like I'd barely scratched the surface of her world. Both impressions felt good.

E.A. was already up on Woodland Avenue placing the parade participants by the time I got into the shower. I guess I was whistling extra loud, because Mom knocked on the door.

"My, aren't you the songbird this morning. Are you performing a solo in the parade?"

I came out wrapped in a towel and said. "Remember Lynn, Mom? The girl we took home a month ago?"

"I do. What about her?"

"She's coming today!"

Mom smiled and just went "ah!" I put on my baseball uniform and headed over to Trish's; she was already on an old lawn chair waiting for the parade.

She anticipated my question and raised her sunglasses to wink. "Lynn's on her way, Larry, but you had better get in formation. We'll be cheering for ya." With that, I headed into E.A.'s staging area.

At the head of the lineup was a big white convertible with Thunderchief, the famous TV wrestler, as our fearless grand marshal. He was dressed in war paint already. He had his scalping knife with him and was already practicing on the air, to the annoyance of his driver. Behind him were three more cars filled mostly with the cheerleaders. Of course, the Rat Pack, including Kathy, made up the bulk of the girls. Kathy wasn't a cheerleader, and neither were some of the others, but Aubrey had invited them to fill in slots. Aubrey leaned down from the back of the car and whispered.

"This is your day to make your move if there ever was one. I heard your old man is the organizer!"

I was in too good of a mood even to correct her about E.A., so I ignored her and kept walking down the parade lineup. After the cheerleaders and a few other local celebs came the Ugly Bull Brewery delivery truck, two fire engines, the township police, and a few others with hastily put together floats from local groups. Even the army sent a jeep with four MP's in chrome helmets and spit-shined shoes from Fort Hayes with brochures urging us to sign up for the draft or do the noble thing and enlist. The mascot for the Ugly Bull, a guy dressed in a bull costume, was currently asking them about Mr. Darnell to find out his place in the parade. The MPs looked like they'd rather be in Korea than here and kept ignoring Mr. Bull . . . until he pulled the bull's head off and we realized it was an attractive brunette. At that point they were all ears to Mrs. Billie's questions.

But E.A.—strictly professional today—walked right up, pointed to a clipboard, and said he'd registered the bull to run up and down through the parade. The lady sighed, replaced her head, and trotted off as E.A. saluted the MPs. Off in the distance, you could see Mrs. Bull trying to cool herself off by blowing "steam" out of her nose and running into the mist.

The final addition to the dealership's convertible lineup arrived at exactly 9:55, when Possum and his band rolled up in a red Chevrolet covered in American flags. The band was dressed as the Revolutionary War fife and drum corps, the "Spirit of '76" one. Possum was the old guy with the drum, with flour or something making his hair seem white and powdery. They quickly got to the front, with Possum adjusting a bloody bandage that looked like a ketchup rag around his drummer's head; I could see the driver of the convertible nervously dabbing the suede seats with a cloth. I pulled E.A. aside.

"Are they supposed to be up there?" I asked.

E.A. consulted his chart and nodded.

"How'd you convince them to do that?"

"Convince them?" E.A. looked offended. "'Chuh bud, I got those boys to do it for free in return for 15 measly minutes on the main stage tonight after the main band plays."

As I hustled off to join the Dinos as they took their spot behind the cheerleaders in the cars, emergency vehicles began warming up their sirens. After a nudge from Aubrey, Kathy turned and waved, then smiled what I had to admit was a gorgeous, flawless grin before turning back really quick.

"What was that?" one of my teammates said.

"Darned if I know—" but then the fire department really got going with their sirens and the parade was off.

Up ahead, all I could hear besides the wee-oh wee-oh of the sirens was Possum calling us to attention, then hup-two-three-four, hup-two-three-four. I laughed and remembered that day in the woods back in early spring . . . Possum had gotten me to march after all. This time, though, he was playing Yankee Doodle on a recorder while his band beat on some old snare drums. Halfway down Northglenn Drive, Thunderchief stood up and let out a screech and slashed the air with his knife, and that really got the parade-watchers in their yards going. From where I was, it looked like he needed a longer loin cloth, though. Aubrey let out a squeal, and Kathy turned around toward me with a red face.

As we went by our house Mom waved at me like I was coming back from a war, and I sheepishly tried to wave back without embarrassing myself in front of the guys or Aubrey. The parade continued on toward Lindale drive, with Possum limping like a wounded Continental Army soldier. At one point he stumbled like he'd been shot, and that gave me a chance to turn around and see that everyone had left their yards and followed us, with the parade having become a mob. The fire chief got Possum up and he led us, like a modern day Moses, to Sewer Creek and E.A.'s brand new park at the end of Mecca Drive.

Mecca was, of course, where Trish lived, and as we approached their yard I could see her, Mack, Butch, and Marcie all sitting in lawn chairs and enjoying some icy Cokes while they heckled me.

"Get in step, 13!" "Where'd you get those uniforms, the museum?" "Fill 'er up!" I admit, I was more irked by the fact that I didn't see Lynn. But just when I was starting to worry, I felt a hand take my elbow. There was Lynn, with a new feather clip, turquoise earrings peeking out from underneath her long black hair, blue shorts, a red pullover, and a white scarf. She was dressed for the fourth for sure.

"Where'd you come from?" I said, tripping a bit.

"Snuck up on ya, didn't I? I'm walking the rest of the way with you, if you don't mind," she said, grinning. I'd known Lynn long enough to know that her wardrobe was limited, but she always looked sharp and you could tell she put thought into what she wore. This combination was new, though, and boy, did she look like a dream. Of course, you can think elegant thoughts like that, but all I managed to get out was "You are so pretty!" Lynn blushed but stayed Lynn.

"I know that, 'cause you say it so much," But she winked. Kathy and Aubrey turned around to check us out, but Lynn stared them down. "Mind your own business!" she yelled. And they did, the rest of the parade.

The open field was filled with concession stands and carnival games, and crowning it all was an old, wooden Ferris wheel, whitewashed and all jeweled with colored glass bulbs. The parade quickly broke up and the Dinos naturally filed into the ball field, even though we didn't have any of our equipment. Once we all had stopped, assistants of E.A's came over with small bullhorns and announced the MP's from Fort Hayes were going to raise the flag for the first time on the shiny stainless steel pole at the top of the rise that rimmed the park (donated courtesy of E.A.'s cleaning company, of course). Everyone stood at attention and sang the Star Spangled Banner, maybe all two hundred of us against the backdrop of the birds and summer wind.

After that, one of the assistants got on top of the back of a convenient convertible and started to read a list of the day's activities, but Thunderchief grabbed the bullhorn and bellowed savagely. "Thunderchief give five silver dollars to any man brave enough to wrestle him on grass!"

The silence was thick. No one came forward, and after waiting ten seconds for effect the Chief laughed. "Turkeys! Gobble, gobble!" I looked at Lynn and she seemed entertained, although confused.

Then a big hillbilly guy in bib overalls stepped forward and yelled, "I'll fight ye, red man!" The chief took off his war bonnet, put his knife down, crouched into a pose, and motioned him forward. The challenger ran at him arms swinging, but the Chief sidestepped him and let him run out into the grass. He tried it again with a whoop and the Chief effortlessly put him in his signature deadly totem pole hold. Once he cried uncle, Thunderchief let him up and gave him the silver dollars, anyway. The Chief whooped some more and asked if anyone else wanted to try. Billy the Bull came snorting and charging and Thunderchief gave a good show running around the field before disappearing while the crowd applauded.

Lynn snorted once the Chief disappeared. "Who is that guy?"

"What, you don't know Thunderchief? Don't you watch the Chevy wrestling hour on Saturday nights?"

"No, we don't have a TV. And I wouldn't, even if we did. TV's stupid." All right, I thought to myself, maybe Lynn wasn't completely perfect.

By then it was 12:30, with two hours until our game. I wanted to go home to get my equipment and eat, but of course I wanted to hang out with Lynn, too. I figured Mom wouldn't mind an extra mouth and invited Lynn to come home with me. The concession stands had long lines, anyway, as Northglenn enjoyed the summer's first feast of burgers, brats, chicken, grilled onions, and funnel cakes.

I went into the house first, just in case Mom was busy. "I'm home, Mom, and I got someone special with me!" But Mom seemed to be expecting a guest, in the form of either Lynn or Mack, and had already set out three places. "Mom, you remember Lynn from uh, that one time," I said, trying to act like I'd not thought about it every night for a month. "Lynn, this is my mom, Jane Darnell." Of course they did that thing where girls hug someone they just met and we dug into chilled chicken salad sandwiches and coleslaw.

When Lynn excused herself to the bathroom, Mom leaned over the table. "Larry, she's just gorgeous, and so sweet!" I nodded. "Aren't you glad I made you walk her to the door?"

"Yes, Mom." We headed back soon afterwards, my duffle bag in hand while Lynn carried the same bat I'd gotten the day I'd met her. The Hilliard Hawks had already arrived and were stretching in front of their two matching red and white Volkswagen buses, complete with painted banners that read "Look Out! Here Come the Hilliard Hawks!" I looked over at the humble station wagon that Coach

Barnhardt used to pick up all of the out-of-town guys and knew we were today's underdogs even if it was our home turf.

There were only small bleachers at the park, so most of the crowd, including Butch and Marcie, had already sat down on the bank of the hill along the third base side. I got ready to introduce Lynn to Marcie, but to my surprise she ran over and hugged Marcie. It turned out that Lynn often came over to the Blains' farm with the owner of Maddie's to buy produce for the café. I admit, I was a little jealous seeing Lynn giving out hugs left and right when I'd only held her hand a few times.

Marcie sent Butch off on an errand at one of the concession stands, and he looked at me and drew his fingers across his throat, meaning I wasn't to tell Mack he was taking orders. Laughing to myself, I headed off to the diamond while the girls found a nice shady spot to sit down. The Dinos warmed up on the field, and soon enough the ump called out "Play ball!"

The game was tough right from the start. My first time up, I struck out on three pitches and came back to the dugout redder than a tomato. My first game in front of my girlfriend! And Aubrey didn't let her little dig slide, either. As I walked to the dugout I heard her say from the bleachers, "Ha, guess your little dream catcher isn't working!" to giggles from Kathy and the Rats.

Lynn couldn't have heard them, but from their spot on the grass she let out an ear-piercing whistle. "Get 'em next time, thirteen!"

That felt good, and next time up, I hit the ball hard to the opposite field. I thought it was enough to be a home run but the right fielder went to the fence and pulled it down. Coach shrugged and reminded me to focus.

I decided that it was time to step it up and impress everyone. This time, unlike the diving board, I actually knew what I was doing. In my last at-bat in the bottom of the seventh, I led off with a line drive double into left field. We were down two to one and things weren't looking good for the team. We'd only had three hits off the Hilliard pitcher all day. As I stood on second base, the Hawks' coach called timeout and went to the mound to talk to his pitcher and plot how to keep the Dinos down where they belonged. You could feel the game's tension in the air, and their catcher was trying to pick up on any signs from Coach Barnhardt as to what we were going to do next.

But he got nothing from us and the pitch was a chest-high fastball. The Linden slugger creamed it and it cleared the fence by five feet—I was nearly to third by then and all the Hawks could do was watch me and our catcher circle the bases. Game over, three-two. Coach Barnhardt was elated and looked like a college student again. He told us all to go have fun at the carnival and take it easy the rest of the week. We had beaten powerful Hilliard in a real show of skill. A lot of these guys were the same guys we would be playing against that next spring, and they knew it.

As I walked out of the dugout, Lynn met me and took my hat, tried it on then put it back on my head backwards. "What's with the cartoon dinosaur on your jersey, Larry? You look like Fred Flintstone."

"Sinclair Oil's our sponsor," I said flatly.

"Sure you don't need a big stone bat instead of that wood slugger? We could go down to the quarry south of downtown to size something up."

"Not sure if you could carry it then," I winked. "Good ol' ash wood will have to do. I'm going to change my jersey and shoes in the restroom. Give me a minute?"

"Why not change out here, Mr. Modest? You wear a lot less at the pool." She raised her eyebrows a couple times like Groucho Marx.

I knew that but it didn't seem quite right. "Gives you time to think about what you want to do," I justified. When I got back, Lynn was on the grass making dandelion necklaces.

"All right, first, feed me . . . then win a bear for my sister. I know you can throw. Kristy was going to come but changed her mind, but that's okay. I want to talk to you on the way home later, anyway."

I gulped and wondered what that meant.

For a girl who probably didn't weigh a hundred and five, Lynn had a huge appetite and scarfed down two big burgers like it was nothing. I was glad I had been working a lot lately, because together we ran up quite a tab at the burger stand and my pockets were growing light. Then we tried several games to get Kristy her teddy bear, with me finally knocking out a milk jug triangle with the old trick everyone in the country knows—aim for the middle. When I knocked the third tower of weighted bottles down in a row, Lynn clapped me on the back and did that whistle again as the carny unhooked a gigantic teddy from the tent poles. It felt like half the carnival looked at us, but I didn't care.

Somehow four hours flew by like they were nothing, and then it was dusk. The operators turned the Ferris wheel's colorful lights on against the darkening blue sky, and it all looked just like the poster. I wanted to go on it with Lynn because the only other ride was the Octopus, a rattling, whirring contraption that looked like it could fly off the trailer at any point like a giant helicopter, but of course that's what Lynn wanted to ride. Those things made me throw up faster than the smell of a dead cow, and we had just eaten greasy burgers.

"No, please Lynn, I don't really do circular motion." I saw my chance. "I'm a Ferris wheel man, you know. So much more peaceful and uh, romantic," I pleaded.

"Okay, sissy, I'll go on the kiddies ride with you. But I might tell your friends."

But it was a beautiful old wheel with those wispy steel lattices and creaky wooden benches that looked like they couldn't hold anything heavier than a toddler, with happy carnival tunes playing from a portable organ down below. I told her it reminded me of the county fairs I used to go to as a kid as the old man put the bar down in front of us and engaged the old electric motor with one of those old-timey bracket switches.

"You miss the country, don't you, Larry?"

"Terribly." I looked off into the distance at the fields up against the Mifflin area. "If you were up in Sunbury, I think life would have been complete." I figured the romance of the ride had gotten to me, so I backpedaled. "But from where I'm sitting, Northglenn looks all right." The seats were wide enough for three, but Lynn scooted over right up against me.

"Gotta admit, I'm scared of heights." I found it hard to believe she was scared of anything, but went along with it, even when she peered over the edge suddenly and caused the bucket to sway a bit.

"Whooooaa . . . wow! I can see everywhere from up here. I actually just live over there beyond that tower." She was looking about two miles away past one of the older, rusty barrel-shaped water towers that serviced the area. I turned to scan the houses in the dying red light.

"That's a ways away from where I usually drop you off, isn't it?"

She blushed in the electric glow of the light bulbs and caught herself. "Well, it's over there somewhere."

You always have to come back down to earth in life, but that's especially true on Ferris wheels. When the ride was over, we walked to where a clean-cut band in flashy suits was setting up. At that point, someone tapped me on the back. To my dismay, it was Possum.

"Larry, great, you're here! You can watch us play after these amateurs. My band is the entertainment tonight!"

"Are you the leader of the Doo Wop Bops?" Lynn asked innocently from the side, gesturing towards the small pavilion. The band setting up looked far too professional to be affiliated with Possum.

"Who? No, we're the Northglenners! We're playing after they warm up the audience."

I tried to usher Lynn away. I just knew he was going to ask about her feather clip or something. "Good luck with your gig, Possum— see ya, sorry we can't talk, gotta go, uh, you'd better go, too. Is that Donatella Montabella over there?"

But he had to say it.

"Hey, Larry, this isn't the girl from our spring dance. Who's this?"

Fortunately, Lynn had run into a friend and was girl-talking at a hundred miles an hour. It didn't seem like she heard him or saw me lean close to Possum and look him dead in the eyes.

"Possum, if you don't leave, I will attach you by your pants to one of those Ferris wheel buckets." I said through my teeth. "Don't ruin this for me." To Possum's credit, he nodded and left. Lynn came back and we watched a half-dozen songs from the Doo Wop Bops, and then she got up to go, saying she had to work a double the next day. I had figured it was time I headed home, anyway, and I was certainly not going to let her walk home by herself. But as we got up to go, we noticed a ruckus off to the side of the pavilion and a literal cymbal crash, followed by some riffs: it was Possum and his band. He had run several extension cords out from underneath one of the food trailers to his one amplifier, and he and his band were starting to set up where the extension cord ended, about 20 yards or so from the actual pavilion. They were going to have a battle of the bands rather than wait their turn. Several folks from the carnival committee came and asked to see his permit. He reminded them he was owed fifteen minutes for leading the parade.

I couldn't believe what I did next, but I went and got E.A., who came over like John Wayne and said Possum was owed fifteen minutes, or four songs, whichever comes first. I worried E.A.'s political enemies were going to use the guaranteed disaster against him next election cycle, but he had obviously been enjoying the free Ugly Bull Beer and didn't care. He staggered off without even noticing Lynn, back over with a couple of his cronies in the Tubby's Tavern pool hall tent.

By then, a crowd of about 20 people had gathered to hear Possum's music, and Lynn asked to stay. I sensed defeat and agreed. Besides his signature bugle and harmonica, Possum's Northglenners consisted of another guy on a six-string guitar missing two strings, a third guy on an ancient squeeze box that kind of coughed notes, and a fourth guy on bongos and a single small cymbal on an old stand . Off to the side was the record player to play the records they sang along with. As they practiced, it sounded like a polka band trying to fight Frankie Lymon and the Teenagers inside a cave.

"I want to see what they do. I play drums in the concert band at school. This could be cool," Lynn said, sitting down with her legs crossed.

"Ughhhhh," I moaned. At that point the guitar player stepped up and took their only microphone from Possum to begin the introductions.

"Hi, we're the Northglenners, I'm Paul, I play guitar." He then tried to do a quick riff on the four available strings. "Behind me is my brother Ralph on the squeeze box." Ralph then quickly played the first line of "We Three Kings." "Over on congos is Ca-raaaaaazy Mike." Mike beat the daylights out of them for about five seconds. "And up front, our lead man 'POSSUM' CARLSON."

At that point, Possum started the "Bristol Stomp" on the record player and began to play along with his harmonica. The audience erupted. Apparently word about the stomp had made its way to the streets and everyone knew the steps, though not as well as Possum. Halfway through, he started out to look for a girl to dance with . . . and he was headed straight for us. I put Lynn behind me.

I shook my head but Possum was nearly in my face. "You touch her, you'll eat your harmonica," I said.

Possum didn't miss a beat. He grabbed an older lady by the hands and they did the Possum Stomp all the way around the stage. When the song was over, the crowd was actually cheering and demanded an encore. Had I entered the Twilight Zone?

Possum started to put on the next song, but before it began, he held the needle up and grabbed the microphone from Paul.

"Now, fans, I'm dedicating this to my best friend, who is here in the audience. I always play this for him and whatever girl he's with at every dance we do. It's . . . 'Let the Little Girl Dance!'"

With that people started turning around to see who he was talking about; I did too, and looked at the people behind us.

"Who is he talking about, Larry?" Lynn inquired.

"Beats me, it's probably just part of the show. Man, they're actually good!" I said, acting innocent.

Possum did two more songs and then yelled "Goodnight Northglenn, see you next time!" as E.A. unplugged his extension cord and made a big "X" with his arms.

"Who is he?" Lynn asked. "You seem to know him pretty well. Is he one of Butch's gang?"

"No. Well, that's hard to describe, Lynn. Sometimes he runs with the gang. He's on probation right now, I think," I said as we started out into the cool summer night.

"I see." We walked about two blocks in silence, since I didn't want to talk about Possum. It was getting cold, even though the asphalt was giving off some warmth, so I gave Lynn my jersey to wrap around her shoulders.

She looked at me beneath one street lamp and stopped suddenly. "You really like me, don't you?"

Gosh, Lynn was blunt. I responded kind of exasperatedly. "A whole lot!"

"I've never had a real boyfriend before you, Larry. I just want to be sure this is real." She paused. "But I think it is."

I went with a gut feeling and asked a tough question. "You've experienced some hard things from people in your life, haven't you?"

"You mean, 'cause I'm an Indian?"

"Well, yes. I know you're not Thunderchief," I laughed. "But there's more to you than that."

"There is. It's a little of that, though. My mom isn't married, and she never married my dad, and she's divorced from Kristy's father. So yeah, I've heard it all, along with all the nasty things that go with it. Maybe more than you can imagine." She looked at me. "I like the way you're so respectful of me. You even opened doors for me and held the chair for me at lunch. I like that." Then she laughed. "Even though you're kind of awkward when you do it."

"Thanks."

"You are the kindest person I have ever known, outside my family. Trusting is hard for me, but I trust you, Larry." I went all in.

"Lynn, you make me feel so special when I'm with you. Of course I'm going to treat you right. Yes, you're . . . gosh, beautiful, but you're also smart, witty. You believe in yourself. You're fearless. I don't think anyone could stare you down."

She blushed a bit. "Thanks," she said quietly. Then normal Lynn returned. "Or at least, so you think. I know how to bluff. Try and play poker with me, and I'll fleece you." We walked a little more until the next bright spot underneath a street lamp.

"I guess I'm concerned about us, Larry. We don't go to the same school, and I know you're on the Rat Pack's wish list. Was that who Possum meant? Kathy? Were you guys a thing?" Lynn had asked around.

"No! I'm on Aubrey's list but none of them are on mine. I decide who I like." I felt guilty about not telling the whole truth about Possum and the spring dance, but there were tears in Lynn's eyes.

"So you can honestly say it doesn't bother you that I'm an Indian, with no dad, and a mom who works two jobs to barely make ends meet? When Miss Perfect is right there waiting for you in the convertible?"

I realized that the scene had made more of an impact on Lynn than I realized, so I cautiously took both her hands and looked her right in the eyes.

"Lynn, when I look at you, I just see my girlfriend, the most wonderful person in my life." That sounded stupid, like I was 15, which I was. But I had always been so mature everywhere else that now felt like trying to swing a bat for the first time. We were one street lamp away from where we always parted. "Please, Lynn, let me walk you home. I don't care where you live."

I saw a glint in her eye. "I know, Larry. But I do." We arrived in front of the run-down apartment building and I stared at my shoes before I finally spoke.

"I'll see you tomorrow at Maddie's, okay?" I started to go.

"Hey, doofus," I heard behind me. "You can hug me if you want."

I never held anyone so long or so close like I did Lynn that night. Finally, I thought of the only thing I could to leave her with.

"I won't hurt you, Lynn. Not for anything," I said, as softly as I could above her hair.

When I got home, Mom and E.A. were already in bed. Typically, I took a shower after games, but I could still smell Lynn on my shirt and shoulder, so I decided I'd wait. I felt like I was sleepwalking as I looked at the moonlight on the linoleum floor and thought about the Ferris wheel bright against the night sky. Finally, I put the feather clip on the pillow and fell asleep reviewing the entire day in my head like a movie.

CHAPTER
SEVEN

rue to my word, I went over to see Lynn at Maddie's. After she clocked out, she took my hand and led me to an old wrought-iron pedestrian bridge a few blocks away that went over railroad tracks that led to Union Station in Columbus. She had made sandwiches for us from the leftover meatloaf at the diner and spread them out on her apron on one of the benches, then poured lemonade from an old thermos into two Styrofoam cups. After the night before, it strangely seemed like there wasn't much to say about us, so we wanted to watch the passenger trains leave town.

"I like imagining where they're going," she said, waving at passengers onboard in the glass-top dining car. A few waved back at us, two kids on a bridge. "Sometimes I imagine I'm going there, too. Pittsburgh, Washington, Philadelphia, maybe even New York. I've never been on a train, though. Or a plane."

"I've flown with my dad a few times, back when he lived here and he had his old Piper Cub," I said. "But he's in southeast Asia somewhere, working for TWA."

"Which one's that?"

"Trans World Airlines. They fly overhead all the time in Northglenn."

"Does he ever come home?"

"He probably will, this summer. But it seems less and less since they got divorced."

"What's he like?"

"He's nice! But he and Mom just couldn't get along at all," I shrugged. Lynn nodded but was obviously sleepy after her long day at work. She adjusted her head on my shoulder and fell asleep right then and there. Carefully I put my arm around her and held her. Somehow we sat there for 30 minutes, without me or the trains waking her up, even as a big diesel chugged towards the east underneath us, its big bulldog nose lamp lit up in the overcast afternoon.

When she woke up she chuckled kind of embarrassedly. "Well, I've never done that before. Did I talk in my sleep?"

"Yes, you were talking about all your boyfriends. Who's 'stranger on the shore'?" I teased, referencing the song Mom and E.A. always slow danced to when it came on.

She slapped my shoulder and said adamantly, "I only have one, and I've never been on a shore, unless you count that Sewer Creek you all like hanging out around."

The walk home was filled with lighthearted talk and hand holding all the way, me making sure she was always on the inside of the sidewalk away from the traffic. We agreed to meet at the pool on Sunday afternoon, and I slyly acted like I was just going to go at our usual cutoff point.

"Forgetting something mister? Like a hug?" Lynn said, pulling me back. I held her close.

"Nope, just seeing if you remembered."

I floated home but was brought down to earth pretty fast by the sight of Possum sitting in our yard in a lawn chair E.A. had left out the night before.

"Larry, I forgot to give you these last night as thanks for getting us in the show." He then handed me two scraps of notebook paper that each read: "Free pass to any Possum and the Northglenners show." I flipped them over. "Value if redeemed: $1,500."

"Cool, Possum, can I just redeem them now?"

"No, Larry, you obviously can't keep a girlfriend. I'm trying to help you with things to take her to."

"Thanks then, I guess. But listen to me, Possum, that girl last night's name is Lynn Bennett. She is my only girl okay? I want you to remember that."

Possum got out a piece of paper from his pocket and wrote it down.

"Now, please go. We'll try and make the next Northglenners appearance, but no promises."

He laughed. "You are truly my best friend, Larry," and ran off humming and whistling the "Secret Agent Man" theme. I went inside to find Mom getting off the phone. She called E.A. in.

"Dear, my father called. He wants us to come up next weekend to help bale hay, it's a bit much for him. My sisters and their families will be there the next day for a cookout, too, so we'll make it a family event!"

I heard E.A. groan before I could say yes. "Oh, honey, you know Joe and I may go to Michigan to fish next weekend. Sorry to miss the cookout." E.A.'s brother Joe seemed to exist to get him out of stuff, but he was good at it. "Uh, Larry, you can help your grandpa, though. You know me. City boy all the way."

No question there. Mom knew I was as good as already in the car, waiting to go. Even if it meant missing out on a potential afternoon with Lynn, the prospect of heading back to the farm was like getting invited for a preview of heaven. I admit I thought about finally returning to the farm as much as I did about Lynn. When I told her about it two days later at Maddie's, she surprised me and said if it was okay with me, she wanted to ask her mom if she could come up with us, if there was a guest bedroom. I was all aboard for that, but I saw her mom shake her head "no" almost immediately.

So Saturday found me and Mom alone in the Bel Air on State Route 3, going up through the little town of Westerville and the endless fields and forests. It'd been six months since I'd been home, and truthfully I was kind of glad E.A. wasn't here to muddy it up with his antics. True to his word, E.A. had headed out that morning with an old dusty fishing pole and a heavy tackle box that gurgled and glugged as he picked it up.

Finally, we were surrounded by the familiar landscape of the Sunbury area, little groves in well-kept fields along the Big Walnut—the creek that wound along Columbus just miles from the Alum. We turned onto Route 36, and I could see Gramps's farm coming into view.

I felt like the prodigal son coming home, stepping back onto the familiar barnyard. There had been some changes since we'd left that winter, but the farm dog, a border collie named Gypsy, hadn't changed at all. She hadn't forgotten who I was, either, and was all over me in a second. Mom got out, hugged her dad as he walked over to me, and went into the house where Grammie was. As I peered into the barn, I saw the front end of a large, green tractor.

"Gramps—down, Gypsy!—ya got a bigger tractor!" I said. It seemed better than hello. Gramps hated hellos and goodbyes equally.

"I did, son! Thirty-five horsepower."

"What'd you do with the old one? You didn't sell it?" I asked with some worry.

"We still have it, son. But I've always wanted another tractor since the old Ferguson gave up the ghost. Trying some new crops now that we don't need all that silage. That big fellow will pull a three bottom-plow, believe it or not." That was more power than anyone needed this side of the Mississippi. Gramps had sold the old dairy herd to a neighbor and bought ten more Hereford breeding cows, almost doubling the beef population. It wasn't like some of the mega-ranches you read about out west, with a thousand head of cattle, but for a family of modest expenses that owned the farm, it had kept them in comfort with full bellies even during the Depression.

"Things are better since you were here last," Gramps continued as we walked into the barn. "I don't have to milk twice a day or grow quite as much corn just for silage, although I bought a few more hogs, too. So we're still making about 20 acres of corn. Mostly pasture and hay, some oats and soybeans. I'll turn the beef cattle onto the corn and crop stubble in the winter to graze. It's free fertilizer."

Gramps was grateful for the audience, you could tell. Grammie was great, but she didn't care for this sort of field talk; he'd been saving all these observations since February.

"What about the new 'A,' Gramps? That's a big tractor. Sure you're going to use all that horsepower?"

"Oh, yes. Besides, a neighbor down the road gave up on it so I got it for a bargain. The electrical components are about as complex as a radio, drove him nuts and he couldn't get it right. Well, Tommy came up a little while after you all left, before he headed out for TWA. You know how he can fix anything."

I'd not heard my dad's name said aloud since the last time I was here. I don't think E.A. gave him much thought besides his being the guy who bought Mom the '56 Bel Air, and Mom never mentioned him at all. When we lived at the farm he'd send airmail letters postmarked from around the world—TWA gave him free postage— and I think Mom had been jealous of his travels, so talking about him wasn't at all common. When we moved to Mifflin, the letters had stopped, although I wasn't sure if it was because he'd not been given the new address or just didn't want to write to the "Darnell" residence.

"Your dad is actually coming home next week," Gramps said, interrupting my thoughts. "He writes that his days as a flight engineer are over. Everyone wants jets, now. Said that if he wanted to stay in those prop planes he loves so much, he'd have to stay in a little country called Vietnam and some company called Air America. Sounded disreputable to me."

"Who's he going to work for, now?"

"Thinks he might get back into construction, like before . . . well, before you all moved here. I'm glad, because no one else can fix anything quite as well as he can."

Dad had stayed close with "Mr. Mallernee," as he called Gramps, even after things went south with Mom. There seemed to be a polite understanding that things were not entirely his fault and that was that.

"Come on, son, Grammie wants to see you too," Gramps said, interrupting my thoughts. Grammie had two cold A&W root beers waiting for us out of the icebox and gave me a big hug like I'd returned from the dead.

Sipping my root beer, I felt surrounded by all the old familiar farmhouse smells: the breeze always seemed to blow through the house from the west, and I could smell the sweet aroma of ripe hay drying in the field where it was wind-rowed and ready to bale. The kitchen always seemed like something was just baked in it minutes earlier, which mixed pleasantly with the warm scents of the outside.

After a good dinner—they called it dinner, not lunch—of mush and sausage, Gramps took me to see the new beef cattle.

"Hup, hup!" he called out to Gypsy, who was lying under the grape arbor watching a toad. "Darn dog. With all the stock to watch on this farm, she is downright fascinated with that toad that lives under the grapes. I believe she thinks it's her pet."

The folks had bought this farm during the Depression in the thirties, a result of having kept their savings in cash and not in the banks. It was 120 acres of rolling ground with two streams and a back field that Gramps got entered into the local wildlife conservation program, meaning it wouldn't get bought anytime soon by developers. I had learned to hunt and fish on this farm, alongside just about everything else I considered useful. When we first moved here, Gramps had given me his breech-loading J.C. Stevens rifle and a box of cartridges, and that rifle and Gypsy were my constant companions in my exploration of the fields and streams during all seasons while we lived there.

"Never aim at anything you don't want to shoot, and never kill something you won't eat, other than a rat, coyote, or a groundhog," he used to say. "And watch out for quicksand by the sycamore tree." Other than that, Gramps felt I was all right enough to leave to my own devices on their farm, and I never shot anything I wasn't supposed to.

As we entered the pasture, the cows raised their heads in curiosity and then went back to grazing once they realized they recognized the tallest figure. He showed me his new bull, who was now walking proudly over to check us out.

"Bought him this spring. He cost almost 400 dollars, if you can believe that. I'm going to raise and sell breeding stock from here on out, not feeder cattle. If this works, I'll make a good living, better than milking cows. If it doesn't, I've got the crops to back things up."

The bull snorted at us and rolled his upper lip back; if it had been later in the fall, we would have seen steam for sure. But at that point, Gypsy went into action, growling and showing her teeth. The bull backed off and went back to his harem.

"Well, son, are you ready to bale?" I'd been waiting for that question for six months. "While you were with Grammie, I got the wagons in tandem behind the B. She can take them out easily, but we'll need a little more power to pull one along behind the baler while it's walloping away. You go get the A now. She's hard to start because of how big those cylinders are, but you'll get it."

"Is driving it different than the B?" I was nervous about all that power, not to mention a far bigger frame to work around the tight gateways of the field.

"Just bigger, son, just bigger. Go slower and you're fine. Now come on, time's wasting."

To my surprise, the A started right up, and I wheeled her out with the baler already attached. Gypsy was slowly walking along behind, wagging her tail. Compared to the B, its engine was like a muffled M-80 of Mack's going off every quarter-second.

"Now, you're going to drive," Gramps shouted from the ground as he adjusted the drive shaft connecting the baler.

I throttled back so he could hear me. "You sure? I can load them while you drive!"

He shook his head firmly while moving the wagon by hand to the tail of the baler. "Don't look at me like that! I'm only 72. I'll work the wagon!" Living in Northglenn, I'd forgotten that guys his age were even capable of that sort of thing. The baler had just shot out its first bale of the day when Mom came out with a jug of lemonade. We throttled back and got down to talk to her.

"Heading out to meet some old friends in town," she yelled. "And Larry! You get off that tractor right now and load that hay for your grandpa."

"Jane," Gramps growled, "I'll tell you what I told your son: I'm only 72." He motioned for us to start.

We made two wagons of good timothy-clover hay and had it in the mow before dark. Baling hay worked up an appetite, and when Gramps announced supper was on him at a diner downtown, I had no problem agreeing. Grammie was at work in the kitchen prepping for the cookout with the family tomorrow and said to just go by ourselves.

"I admit, I was kinda counting on Jane's help, but she is just like she was in school, always wanting to be a-running off somewhere," she said a bit sadly.

We took Gramps' old Desoto pickup to the Hub, our usual old-fashioned haunt that was still somewhere in the thirties compared to the polished chrome of the new McDonald's in Northern Lights. You ordered at the counter-window yourself and a waitress brought it out to you at the old leather booths with their well-worn wooden tables. When Gramps went up to order three hamburgers with fries—

two for me, one for him—I settled into memories of the place. Then I heard a familiar voice.

"My guess is you'll need both of these."

I turned around and saw a gorgeous young waitress with two containers of mustard. I looked over at Gramps, who'd met a neighbor and was talking business, then back at her.

"Uh, no, just one will be fine." I looked at her again, and then it hit me—it was Elaine, the girl who told me I'd tasted like mustard when we kissed a few years ago on the hayride. When you leave a place, you always figure all the people that were a small part of it vanish, but here I was after months of adventure and Morningside, still good old' mustard mouth.

Elaine laughed. "Don't ya recognize me?"

"I didn't!" Two years ago on the hayride she had sported a short pixie hairstyle and was about as scrawny as I was. Now she had a beautiful long, blonde ponytail, had tanned about as much as I had and was gorgeous.

"You've filled out some, Larry," she said, feeling my shoulder. "Love the Beach Boy-style hair, better than that awful flat top."

Happily Gramps was still distracted.

"Well, I play baseball down in Northglenn, now and I have my own construction company."

"Where?"

"Just outside Columbus."

"Oh, nice! My folks bought this place . . . I work here on weekends and as a lifeguard at the pool during the week."

"That explains the tan," I said awkwardly.

"Whaddya up here for, Mr. Construction-Company-In-Columbus?"

"Just visiting the folks."

Gramps came back and she brought out our order. I had loaded my burger up with extras, so she playfully took both mustards. "I'll keep these for now. You never know what could happen tonight, Larry."

"Know her?" said Gramps with a glint in his eye.

"Eh . . ."

We chowed down and were about to pay at the cash register when another man came up to us.

"Ralph, got a question for you . . . looking for some feeder calves for fall. Do you know where I could get them?"

I'd forgotten what a wheel Gramps was in Sunbury; people looked up to him and respected his opinion. I could see it was a long conversation so I went out to the truck and rolled down the windows, smelling the cool, midsummer night while listening to the radio. In a few minutes, Elaine came out with an ornery grin.

"Hey, I'm off in a half-hour. You might remember, they show free movies down on the lawn at city hall on the side of that big canvas screen. Tonight's The High & the Mighty. I recall you talking a lot about John Wayne before you kissed me."

I blushed, but thankfully it was too dark to notice. "Aw, well, unfortunately, I didn't drive up here," I said, trying to imply with my confident tone that I had a 63 Stingray back in Columbus.

"Oh, that's no problem. I can take you home after the movie. I'm sixteen now, and I can drive. Or we can just go driving and uh, I'll bring the mustard."

I once saw a Three Stooges short on television with Mack where Curly had a tough decision to make over something. A little angel Curly had appeared on one shoulder and a devil Curly on the other. It was actually impressive how they got it to look so real. I imagined I had a similar gang on my shoulders.

"Go for it, man, she's hot and what do you have to lose?" devil Curley said. "Think what Mack will say!"

"You'll never see this girl again," said the angel Curley. "Think of Lynn. You got a chance for a real romance there."

"Or Kathy," said the devil.

"That's true," said the angel. "But I'm rooting for Lynn —"

Then the angel ran across my shoulder and knocked the devil off with one of those coconut-conking sounds that Larry's nose made. My eyes returned to Elaine's.

"Uh, I have a girlfriend, Elaine," I said weakly. It was water off a duck's back.

Elaine threw her head back a bit. "What happens in Sunbury stays in Sunbury. How serious can it be?"

"Thanks, Elaine, but she is nice and well, I did have the spicy mustard tonight. Might be worse."

She laughed, and mercifully Gramps came outside.

Back home on the farm, we watched his favorite program broadcast from Cincinnati, a bluegrass musical show called Midwestern Hayride, featuring mostly local banjo pickers and stand-ups from full-time feed mill workers, though every now and then they had someone good. Evenings with the grandparents weren't exciting, but they were peaceful.

We ended the night on the front porch, enjoying Gramps's other summer pastime of watching the traffic go by, though I had started to realize this was more something to do while talking.

"Well, do you hate the city?"

"I'm trying to make the best of it, Gramps. I don't mean to live there when I'm out of school."

"You know you have to serve your country right? Like I did in World War I. Everyone does."

"Yes, sir."

"You have a girlfriend yet, son?"

I told him I did.

"Figured there was a reason you'd rather be watching cars with me than whatever that waitress invited you to," he smiled. "What's she like?"

One thing I had with my grandfather that I tried to replicate in my Mifflin friendships was total honesty. I started with the fact I worried he might be most concerned about.

"Well, she's Cherokee, and she probably is the most beautiful girl I've ever seen. Even more beautiful than the waitress."

"Twenty-eight! That makes 28 cars. Must be something going on in Delaware," Gramps observed. At that point, the grape arbor toad must have gone to bed, because Gypsy trotted up on the porch and hopped between us on the glider.

"Good girl," I said, quietly.

Gramps sighed. "Well, maybe you were worried I'd look down on the Cherokee in your life, but I knew a Choctaw gal afore I met Lorena. Down in West Virginia when I was paymaster for the coal company. Thought quite a bit of her." He counted another car, but seemed to be thinking past a few memories. "If I had married her," he looked over his shoulder, "instead of Lorena, you'd have dark hair, because you get your blonde hair from her." He took his pipe out, thought about it and put it back, stepping off the glider and patting Gypsy.

"Good night, son. Come to church with us in the morning, will you? I know Jane won't."

"Yes, sir."

When I went to bed on the old familiar couch, I laid awake for the longest time, reviewing the summer so far with Lynn and wondering what Elaine was doing. But oddly, I ended up dreaming about Kathy. I never thought girls could cause so much trouble for a guy.

The next day after church, I took the breech loader rifle Gramps kept in the closet and Gypsy for a long hike, wrapping up some of the biscuits and cold bacon from breakfast in a canvas bag tied to my belt. We headed for the backfield where the stream ran through and still made quicksand by the sycamore. Since the field was in the state's conservation program, Gramps was paid to let it go as wild as it could be, keeping the cattle away from its marshes. As we entered the thicket, a big twelve-point buck leaped in from the right, his horns still in the velvet stage.

"Heel, Gypsy, heel!" I called. She came back after snorting along his trail for a few yards. The stream seemed flooded and out of its banks; further downstream, a small colony of beavers had dammed the creek and set up a settlement. Even though the water was over the top of the grass and brush, it was clear as could be; you could see the intricate loggerheads the beavers had set up with white-barked sycamore branches. Bumping up against the smaller twigs were smallmouth bass, just waiting for a shiny lure to fool them. I marveled at how different it was from Sewer Creek.

"Shoulda brought a fishing pole, huh, girl?" I said.

When we lived there, I said things to Gypsy all the time like she understood, and I figured she hadn't forgotten too much English. We sauntered over to where a spring came out of some rocks. Gypsy looked up for permission and dove in when I nodded. After she had her fill, carefully, drinking upstream from her muddy legs. I did the same, and then I divided the food between us.

The farm was like heaven on earth to me, and I wished we had never left it. But then I wouldn't have met Mack, Butch, Lynn, or anybody. And well, at almost sixteen, I wasn't about to give up and return to being a loner like I had been. Butch and Mack were the best friends I had ever had. Mifflin had a much better baseball program now that Coach Barnhart had taken over. And heck, if I had stayed here, I wouldn't have even been able to get out the compliment about Elaine's tan last night. I was no ladies' man but I was learning, I figured. I vowed to continue making the best of it in Mifflin, because I had Lynn and the gang, and suddenly going back that night didn't seem so daunting.

There wasn't much time to waste: Mom's sisters arrived with their families at about 2:30, bringing loads of cousins so young I didn't really know them. Most of Mom's sisters had moved to town like she had; there was no son to stay and help work the farm, and the daughters sure weren't interested. I wondered what would become of this paradise one day.

In the afternoon, we played croquet and horseshoes around the old pits in the backyard. No one could beat Gramps at horseshoes. Losing to him was sort of a tradition—no one let him win, we just couldn't beat him. After that, the day wound up pretty quickly and we were soon in the car. Gramps came over to the car while Mom was talking to her sisters.

"Thanks for the help, son. If you and your mom had stayed, I had had plans to enlarge things around here, double the dairy herd. But I can handle beef all right by myself." He looked over at Mom, then back at me and lowered his voice. "Listen, I've always thought of you more as a son than a grandson. You know that. Maybe because you're quiet, like me. Well, you bring that pretty Indian gal up here. We'll show her the place together."

"Sounds like a plan, Gramps."

"What's her name?"

"Lynn Bennett."

"What kind of Indian name is that?"

"She's only half-Cherokee!"

He laughed. "Well, you take care of her."

By now Mom was in the car, and he reverted a bit to his solemn self.

"Bye Gramps, see ya."

"Bye, son. Bye, Jane."

We drove along in silence for a bit while Mom collected her thoughts for when E.A. was set to roll in tonight. I chewed things over in my own mind. A new year of school loomed on the horizon, and Lynn, of course. I fell asleep against the window as the car rolled along. Something about being back on the farm assured me life was good.

CHAPTER
EIGHT

fter I caught Lynn up on my Sunbury adventures—minus the part about Elaine—she welcomed me back by showing me a countdown calendar she had in her book bag until the day we would both be sixteen and could "officially" car date. That of course meant we wouldn't need a chaperone whenever we went somewhere out of the ordinary. The wheels I was sure I was going to get after I turned sixteen and Mom and E.A. upgraded to a newer car opened up a whole realm of possibilities in and around Columbus. But we were months from her birthday in April, which seemed an eternity. Still, we had already started to plot for the coming months and years.

Lynn and I were both planners, you could say; one of our favorite topics on our walks was always about what we wanted to do with our lives when we were adults. She knew I wanted to be a builder, and maybe go back to farm life as a sideline. She wanted to go to nearby Ohio State University and eventually get her doctorate in physics, maybe working for one of the big research firms that were cropping up around the aviation industry in town. Most of it was over my head, so to speak, but we were two kids with dreams.

"Larry, will it bother you that I'll probably make more money than you?" Lynn asked suddenly with that ornery little smile on her face as we neared the corner where we always stopped. The question was so loaded that I froze up and the old speechlessness returned. "At least that way we can afford a farm . . . "

"Uh . . . "

"Got ya again!" She burst out laughing. "I just love watching your face when you don't know what to say."

I was recovering, but I knew she meant it when I saw her smile. "I guess that way I can spend most of my time on the ranch up in Montana." I retorted. "But you're serious, aren't you?" As I looked up at the old, rundown apartments, she squared off in front of me and did an awkward little boxer's dance acting like she was going to cuff me.

"Hate to tell you but I'm no housewife. Pow! Pow!"

I dodged her right hook and chuckled. "Well, here we are at the drop off point where I have to leave Dr. Bennett in no man's land, since she won't tell me where she lives."

"Oh, I think a little mystery in our lives keeps you interested in me," she replied mischievously. "If I tell you everything, you'll get bored." I gave her a hug, which was the only good part about saying goodbye.

"See ya at Maddie's tomorrow. Save one of the blue plates for me."

It took about 25 minutes to get home. Just inside the gate, E.A. was sitting in a lawn chair in Bermuda shorts and a Hawaiian shirt with four dead beer bottles on the ground. More interesting was seeing Marcie there, without Butch, listening to him discuss biodegradable sewage. The look on her face was a cry for help.

"So you see, Marleenee," E.A. continued, "without oxygen, it all turns into methane gas. You burn that, you got free heat and free hot water. If I could find a cheaper way to collect it, I'd be a Rockefeller.

Breweries could burn it for heat AND one of their main ingredients, for instance. That Sewer Creek would make a great site for a brewery. No one would care if ya discharged the waste right back into the stream. You'd be doing the work of a treatment plan and a half!"

Marcie saw her escape path and said, "Larry! Hi! Wow, it's good to see you. Thanks Mr. Darnell for telling me all about that, I hope you get it figured out someday."

"You're welcome, Mary, uh, Mary Lou."

I called an option play to get her out of there. "Marcie, you must be here to collect on that bet I owe you. Lunch at Doris's?"

"Sure, sure, I am, thanks. Well, goodbye and thanks again, Mr. Darnell."

I escorted her away from E.A.'s methane research lab and up Northglenn Drive.

Her face turned serious. "I'm not hungry, but thanks, Larry. I expected you to be home. I only hung around because I gotta talk to you about Butch. He's in trouble."

"What's wrong?"

"His probation's up at the end of summer, but he hasn't done all his required community service yet. I've been ragging on him to get it over with, but he hates everything they suggested. If the idiot would swallow his pride and pick up trash on Route 3 for three weekends, he'd be done!"

Butch had been on probation the last two years. We all knew that—it added to his tough guy rep around school—but he never told me why. As usual, Mack filled in the backstory one afternoon at Morningside when Lynn wasn't there: public intoxication and fighting down in German Village, a rough side of Columbus. He admitted to drinking as a 16-year-old but pleaded innocent to the brawling charge. Three kids had pulled up in a new Cadillac convertible in front of Butch and his friends at the time and started catcalling a woman and her young child. When they tried to coax the woman into the car, Butch went into action and pulled them out of the car faster than they could gun away. Two of the three had front teeth knocked out and the third was last seen running down East Whittier Street, fast.

Mack said it all would have been okay except the guy who'd gone running rang his old man at Columbus City Council before Butch could get back to Northglenn. Calls were made, and the public record said the guys were saving the woman from Butch, who got two years' probation and community service time for disturbing the peace. He did some of it, but still owed some hours before he could shake the probation. But all of the suggested services— nursing home visits, cleaning up public roads, attending local youth groups—were things Butch would rather die than do.

"Whaddya got for Butch to do, then?" I asked Marcie.

"Well, Henry is in a play with the Linden Players, some local theater troupe, all washed-up types. He said he can get Butch a part in the play if Butch lets him back in the gang."

"I bet Butch hated that."

"Oh, yeah. And he also says he wouldn't get on any stage and act like a dingdong with Henry. But the other option is for him to help build sets and be a stagehand. But he's not great with tools."

"Say no more. I'll help with the backdrops and build whatever he needs to do. Can't be too complicated."

"You're a lifesaver, Larry. The play's in 10 days, and it's all volunteers so I know you'll have to take time off from your paid jobs. If it makes it easier, I'm asking Mack and Trish to help, too. Maybe Lynn can come along," she said, nudging me in the ribs. "Anyway, show up at 8:00 a.m. sharp this Wednesday at East Linden Grade School."

Despite the name, East Linden was actually Mifflin's grade school and was where all the kid brothers and sisters of us Mifflin students went. It was on the way to Morningside, so it was fairly central to everyone. I figured this was a cheap way to get Butch out of the grips of the juvenile system and easy way to spend some "chaperoned" time with Lynn.

On the way home, I stopped at Henry's to find out more about this play. He was sitting in the backyard with a beer bottle in his hand. He appeared to be drunkenly staring off into the distance.

"SHooo, yas thinks I can't hold me liquor?" He frowned. "Sho! Yas thinks I can't hold me liquor?" He nodded stupidly this time and roared, "Well, Séamus, I'm twice ta man yous will ever . . . Well, Séamus! I'm twice ta man yull ever be, ya louse!"

"Hey, Henry, you okay?" I asked cautiously, just in case. After taking a moment to get out of character, he said he was just practicing for the play and that he had heard Marcie was lassoing me into helping Butch build sets.

I nodded. "I guess you're back in the gang, huh, Henry?"

"Yeah! Butch had to come crawling back to me. I knew he'd let me back in."

I snorted. "Henry, I wouldn't say that to him. You might be calling in your lines over the phone from the hospital. That is, if you could talk."

"Haha, I know. Still, it's good to be back."

"Well, tell your director or producer or whatever I'll be there on Wednesday, so have all the materials because I don't have a car to go picking stuff up in. I can build backdrops, and the girls will paint. I think Trish is artsy. How many acts are there, anyway, that we have to make stuff for?"

Henry informed me the correct term was set and there was only one, a rundown Irish bar. With that, he started rehearsing again, and I left him and Séamus to it.

When we arrived the first morning, the director came over and looked us all over through a pair of wire-rim glasses. He was a sweater-wearing sort of guy who looked like he had stepped off the TWA flight from New York City, but it turned out he was just from up north in one of the college towns.

"I . . . am Jack A. Lowe. If you are at all current in theater affairs, you will recognize me. If not," he sighed, seeing the name didn't impress us, "then . . . you must be my stage crew."

"Yes, sir," I said, indicating me, Lynn, Butch, and the rest of the gang. I didn't like his tone, so I decided to push his buttons and show off a bit in front of Lynn. "Do you usually work with kids to build your stages?"

"Young man! Have you ever performed in the theater, let alone . . . the charity theater? It is difficult work. Few are up to snuff. Do you think you can do it?"

"Sir, I just understand construction. Although usually I get paid."

Butch snickered and Jack A. Lowe deflated a bit. He took his glasses off and rubbed his temples.

"Our usual help wanted to be paid, but there is no budget. I am doing this for charity, and my own take is hardly enough to pay my expenses. Do you expect to be paid?"

"No, sir."

"Excellent. Because you cannot be." With that, we got to work.

The play was called *The Old Lads:* two wrinkly Irish men who had been longtime pals but were now bitter over their joint ownership of a bar and business dealings. Henry, with the aid of makeup and gray hair dye, was playing one of the men. The Linden Players consisted of people in their teens but also folks up to about 50 years old or more, so the guy playing Séamus needed no additional makeup besides some light eye shadow. Butch and I were the stagehands, shuffling things on and off in black pants and long-sleeve t-shirts that smelled like old tobacco and mothballs; Mr. Lowe had brought them down from whatever college he'd convinced to hire him as an acting coach during the school year. Marcie and Trish took tickets and were in charge of refreshments, donated in part by Maddie's and Doris's deli. Lynn got the unenviable job of standing off stage left with cue cards in the event that they were needed.

Even though it was an amateur production, a big crowd was expected because proceeds were going to Children's Hospital down in Columbus, and Mr. Lowe expected perfection because he got 5% of those proceeds. He got very little of it from Henry, who had been having trouble with some of his lines up until opening night. Since the last play Henry had been in was King Lear, he kept slipping into his Shakespeare character and injecting old-timey English into his Irish brogue. This, of course, would cause the director to stop and have it all done from the top. Some of the more experienced troupe members were grumbling to let someone else have his part, but it was too late now.

For days, we built backdrops, painted, and generally made a mess while the actors rehearsed. At the end, we had built a passable set that looked like an old-time bar. Really, Trish and her mom were the production's true heroes; without them, it would have been a bunch of beige-looking walls with my sturdy framing behind them. They even painted individual bottles on a shelf, labeling them stuff like "Booze" and "XXX" and "White Lightning." Butch was overwhelmed at the effort on his behalf, but of course he didn't know how to show it, so he just acted gruff and kept saying, "You all didn't have to do this," like he was mad, so we all knew he was happy with us.

Well, most of us. Henry was pretty high and mighty throughout the week about getting back into the gang, but he was pushing his luck. I thought I saw a new vein in Butch's forehead when Henry actually asked him to go and get him a Coke because he deserved it after a good run-through. I saw Marcie squeeze Butch's hand and lean over and whisper something before the two of them got up to get a bottle from the vending machine.

"Henry, are you insane?" I said.

"Yeah, buddy, Butch has friends who could hide your body real easy," Mack cautioned. "What the heck do you think you're doing giving him orders? We're all here giving you our summer vacation, you know."

"Nah, Butch knows I'm just having fun," said Henry with confidence. "Besides, he knows I'm his ticket out of the Franklin County juvy system. He can suffer a little bit longer for kicking me out of the gang." Mack and I shook our heads but didn't feel like saying anything else as Butch returned and tossed a Coke at Henry. Henry was right; if Butch messed this up or Henry did for him, we would probably see less of him while he fulfilled some other requirement.

But two nights before the play, Butch's probation officer stopped in. She was a short, dark-haired lady with her hair shellacked onto her head, all business. I think if she had smiled, her face would have broken. She headed straight for Mr. Lowe, who had been bothered to keep track of Butch's hours and effort, and I heard him say "satisfactory" many times before telling the officer he used to do live theater as an artist in New England and would return once he found "triumph" here. Finally, she came over to us and told Butch she was pleased to see him complete his probation.

"I will file the paperwork with the court, Norman. As far as the Franklin County Court system is concerned, you have completed your probation." With that, she slid icily out the doors. Marcie ran over, hugged Butch then kissed him.

"Marcie!" he growled. "Not in front of everyone."

"Oh, shut up, Norman," she said. Mack and I expected Butch to pound Henry as soon as the probation officer left, but he was as cool and collected as could be, probably because he was taking smoke breaks out back. But before he left for the next one, he turned and squared off with all of us.

"I'll say it exactly once. Thanks for all this, but if any of you ever call me 'Norman' to my face or behind my back, I'll kill you."

Friday night came and was an opening night full of jitters and mild disaster. Twice, Henry quoted lines as his character from King Lear. Lynn had to almost step on the stage with the cue cards. Teddy, Henry's younger brother, had the job of director's assistant and sent the wrong actress out twice. Butch and I tried out best to imitate thunder with old rubber tarps, but it sound like slowed-down hiccups. The director could be seen in the rear of the auditorium beating his head against the wall when he wasn't talking to the cute representative from Children's Hospital. But the audience loved it and cheered all the same. Henry helped himself to four curtain calls and blew kisses to the nurses who had come from the hospital in support of our efforts.

Nonetheless, after the audience had left Mr. Lowe called us all together. He stood on the stage while we sat in the remaining folding chairs. He had been drinking a glass of Alka-Seltzer just before.

"Never, in my 23 years in the theater, have I seen such a bumbling show. Between now and tomorrow night I suggest you all renew yourself toward a better effort. I can only hope the press doesn't get hold of this, or it's curtains for all our careers." He stormed out, and then Mack got up and did an imitation of his lecture, which helped ease the tension. I think Henry was mad that Mack was about as good an actor as he was, but Mack told him that he could never get over his stage fright, so his career was safe.

When Saturday night came, the director again called a meeting for the cast and crew beforehand, mounting the stage as we all sat down once more in the folding chairs. Amazingly, he was calm, if not a bit tipsy.

"Let me say that we will do better tonight. I want you all to know that the director for Columbus Finer Arts is in the audience this evening, and she controls nearly all of the grant monies given to Central Ohio theater. We expect a full crowd, too, so break a leg. This could be my big break." He caught himself. "Or yours!"

After everyone left, he pulled me and Butch aside. "Stage hands, I managed to borrow a better thunder sound simulator. It's those two square pieces of tin on stage left, so please go out back and practice a bit before the audience arrives." He hiccuped, a bit like the rubber tarps, and we left.

The great Jack A. Lowe was right: we had a full house and the cast was performing flawlessly. As the play started, Henry was spot-on perfect. In the scene I'd first seen him practicing in his yard, people actually applauded after the heated discussion that culminated in Henry's storming off stage. The play progressed through the first two thirds without a hitch. Applause was long and loud at the end of each scene.

As the curtain closed before the final act, I went over to Lynn to see how she was doing.

"Your friend Henry is actually good tonight," she said. "I've only had to prompt him once."

"Yeah, I hope he gets through the death scene okay. Last night he was laughing." My mind really wasn't too much on Henry's acting career, I admit: these last ten days had been great. I managed to get two home runs in my last baseball game and Lynn was here with me if she wasn't working. As the lights dimmed for the final scene, I just put my arm around her shoulder and whispered "my girl!" and she snuggled into the hug.

The play's big conclusion was that Henry's partner at the bar pretended to have a heart attack, but in reality had a revolver in his waistband and was going to kill his old friend for ownership of the pub once he was close enough to give the medicine. As Henry's character came rushing around the bar with the bottle marked "Rx", he was supposed to yell, "Grab him and lift his legs, for all that's holy!" which would cause the bar's bystanders to lift his friend and accidentally cause the revolver to go off, killing the would-be killer. It was a bit far-fetched for anyone who knew real quality drama, like Rawhide, but the director dabbed his eyes every time in rehearsal.

Anyway, because Henry had fumbled that all the night before as "Lift him and grab his legs!" the director instructed one of us to put the line in large black letters on the final cue card in Lynn's stack. But unbeknownst to all of us—including Lynn, who hadn't actually read the cue notes—Butch and Marcie had plans of their own.

"Oh! Oh! My heart!" cried the old guy playing Henry's friend as he started to collapse. I could see between the curtains the director sitting in his old folding leather chair, biting nails on both his hands. On cue, Henry grabbed the medicine bottle then made his way around to give it to him, ad-libbing all the way.

"Séamus! Séamus, don't die, I'm coming, my boy!" Henry's character, who was supposed to have had a few drinks himself, tripped at the end of the bar as required by the script, looking helplessly at his dying friend a few yards away and the spilled medicine. He looked to the stage left where Lynn stood with the cue card and seemed bewildered. Lynn gestured furiously at the words, pointing and mouthing what she thought was written there. Only then did I look and see something very different written in Marcie's usual roadside-sign font:

"THE THEATER IS ON FIRE."

"FIRE, FIRE! Get out of here, everyone, there's a fire!" Henry shouted hoarsely to the audience. His dead friend sprang up, looked crazily about, and galloped stage left, dropping the percussion cap revolver. Henry jumped up and followed. The audience applauded. I heard "He wasn't dying after all!" from the front row as the audience pieced together what they imagined was the cleverness of Henry's character in seeing through his enemy's plan. I saw Jack A. Lowe rise up and run behind the curtains that led to stage left, probably to strangle Henry. Instead, there was the deafening sound of thunder. I looked over at Butch, who looked at me; we'd completely forgotten the thunder scene! We had left the tin sheets right in the path of the director. Not knowing what else to do, we dropped the curtain to a standing ovation.

After the play, the director left without a word, but it seemed like the audience and nurses from Children's Hospital had enjoyed themselves. A few stayed over and helped put away the chairs, but between Lynn, Trish, and Marcie none of them got anywhere near us guys. Lynn was staying overnight at Trish's, so Mack and I rode home with them when Trish's mom came to pick them up. Butch triumphantly left the grade school with Marcie as a free man. Henry, on the other hand, had been told he would never be allowed to perform with the Linden Players again, even though his brother Teddy convinced everyone the director had miswritten the cues. But at least he was back in the gang, and humbled enough to stay in line for a few months. I don't think Butch ever told him who had swapped out the cues.

On Sunday morning, I let myself sleep in after an eternity of heading over to the grade school relatively early, knowing that the day would be spent with Lynn at the pool. Just after I arrived downstairs, the phone rang and Mom handed it to me with a teasing look in her eyes. "It's a young lady."

On the other end, a familiar voice said, "This is your wake-up call, sir. Breakfast is being served at Trish and Lynn's Diner in one hour . . . that's Trish's house."

I had never spoken to Lynn on the phone, but I knew right away it was her. After I said bye, I set the world record for the quickest shower and shave. Today was a bonus: Morningside Pool and breakfast!

Even though we'd been together all during the play preparation, this felt like the first time in a while that I was going to hang out with Mack on "our" turf, too. We'd all been in our separate zones the last ten days, especially since Lynn and I were working together alongside Butch. Marcie, Mack, and Trish had been zipping back and forth, with Mack helping Trish with the paintings on the wall, although mostly he seemed committed to staying as far away from Marcie as possible. I think part of him resented us three guys not goofing off too much during the play as the girls kept us occupied and in line, and he held Marcie responsible because of her hold on Butch. I had told him there'd be plenty of time for that in the fall since neither of us were going to play football.

But there would be less goofing off than I'd hoped: during the week at East Linden, Mack announced he had gotten a job at a local gas station and mechanic's shop, where he could pursue his newfound love of cars and get paid while he was doing it. Mack was actually a year older than me and had his license; he had just failed ninth grade the year before we moved in and was repeating it.

"I'm going to be a stock car racer when I get out of school, Larry," he had said stubbornly. "And you don't need a diploma to do that."

He had somehow purchased a '57 Bel Air with no engine and was now saving for the motor. As I walked into the kitchen at Trish's, he was already there beside Trish and Lynn.

"Finally, you're here. We can eat," he moaned. He started serving himself scrambled eggs. Trish playfully slapped his hand and gave him a large cloth napkin. The girls had gone all out: eggs, bacon, hash browns, orange juice, biscuits, and coffee, even though Lynn was the only one who drank it, and she added about half a glass of milk and two tablespoons of sugar. Against the wall was a handwritten sign that read "Lynn and Trish's Diner, Estd. 1963." I thought it was great, but I could see it was irritating to Mack. He tucked the napkin into his t-shirt and then raised a forkful of eggs to his mouth, but then Trish interrupted again.

"Let's say grace before we eat."

"GRACE!" Mack yelled. "And her sister Margie, too!" He then gulped down the forkful while stabbing the bacon with the tip of the knife. The look he got from the girls would have melted steel.

"Mack, we say grace here in our home, you know that!" Trish said with a forced smile.

"Hey, I said 'Grace!'" Another forkful of hash browns and eggs disappeared. Then I saw something I'd never seen before: Trish started crying.

"Just leave, Mack you're rude and you've been rude since this morning and I'm sick of you talking about how me and Marcie and Lynn are turning you guys into wimps!"

Lynn scooted closer and put her hand on my knee underneath the table while Mack grabbed his plate and stormed out, slamming the door and causing Trish's mother to come in from the living room.

"I'll go get him," I said, to ease the tension. As I went out the door, he was already at the end of the driveway, setting down an empty plate.

"Hey, Mack, get back in here. Come on, what's wrong?"

He turned. "See this?" as he put his fingers in a circle and held it up to his face. "There ain't no ring in my nose. You and Butch can't say the same. Did we say grace and have napkins for our lunch? No, sir. Before long those girls will have us dancing like Pinnochio on strings. Not me, buddy!" With that he did a 180 and headed for the woods. "I am going to where there ain't no girls. You can stay here for all I care."

I went back in, and we finished in a pretty awkward silence. After we were done, Lynn said we would help clean up.

"No, you two go on," Trish said. "I want to be by myself." Lynn got her things and we left. After we walked a block she stopped and looked dead at me.

"Look me in the eyes and tell me if you think I'm changing you into a wimp!" Before I answered, she continued. "I don't want to go to the pool. I want to go to the park near the grade school. I had something I wanted to tell you all week, but Mack kind of spoiled it, the butthead."

We got to the park and sat on the swings near the side of the little pond that ducks sometimes went on duck dates in.

"Well go on, look me in the eyes and answer me."

"No, Lynn, the only changes I've made since I met you have all been good," I said. Here I was again with a perfect opportunity to sound mature and romantic like "I"m the best man I can be around you, li'l lady" in a Cary Grant voice, but that was all I could come up with. She knew I was telling the truth, though; she put her head down and a tear trickled down her cheek, just one.

"Thanks, Larry. I know people joke about how . . . how girlfriends grind their guys down into perfection, but I actually liked you from the start." At that point the ice cream truck was jingling down Perdue Avenue and Lynn perked up. "Now go on and get me an ice cream bar, go on." She dug in her short pockets for a nickel. "And I'll pay for it, so if you see Mack, he can't say you're a wimp."

I jogged over and came back to the same old Lynn, no sign of a tear. "What were you going to tell me, Lynn?"

"Oh, oh yeah! So . . . I've decided I'm going to go out for the marching band this year!" she said with a smile. I had known from previous discussions she was considering this.

I thought about all the baseball games she had sat through for me and figured it was the least I could do to attend a few of her games, and I knew she'd been thinking about this since July. "Sure, you bet, Lynn."

She finished her ice cream bar and I gave her a few good pushes on the swing; once she got going she leaned back and let her long hair just flow behind. Watching her, I felt like my heart was just swelling up. I felt a bit bad for Mack that he couldn't see that a girl really wasn't all that bad.

We started walking back and forgot that morning completely, making plans for the rest of August and into the fall. I wanted her to meet my dad once I'd actually seen him a few times. And she wanted me to meet her mom and sister before school started. I assured Lynn that I had a friend on the baseball team who dated a girl from Hartley High School, a few miles distant, and they were great together, and we would be too.

I was looking forward to the remainder of summer now that baseball was over, and I was certain the coming school year would be the best one yet. Mack would come around, too, I said, once he got to spend some time tinkering with his car, and that made her feel better about where I stood in relation to her best friend.

After I left Lynn at our usual corner, I ran the entire three miles home without stopping, I was so on top of the world. I'd worry about Mack later.

CHAPTER
NINE

hen I got back, I noticed a white 1956 Buick Roadmaster sitting in our driveway. There were three people sitting on the porch, too. I could see Mom and E.A., but the third person had his back to me and was wearing an Australian bush hat over what looked like Elvis's thick, black hair. All I could see were the sideburns and the slicked back of his head.

Whoever he was, E.A. obviously had a captive audience—his favorite kind. From 30 feet off, I could hear that he was talking about one of his favorite topics of late, a sleazy local businessman named J.D. Wellington. E.A. had the cleaning product contract for J.D.'s convenience marts, and he idolized him because he seemed to be able to con his way into anything. He was so excited and was trying to talk so fast that I could see spittle flying from the corners of his mouth in the summer afternoon sun.

"Chuh! So ya see, what he did was draw up the false quarterly reports and had his dimwit brother sign them. He never read the things! The court practically gave him the business after that."

As I got closer I heard Mom say, "Oh here he is now, Tommy!" The man turned and I realized—it was Dad! The look on his and Mom's faces was like they had just been saved from a burning house.

I was surprised, too, at how civil they appeared to be acting to each other compared to the last time I'd seen them together. Either that or they were both so numb from E.A. that they had formed an alliance out of desperation.

My dad started to wave, but E.A. interrupted. "Tommy, do you want another beer?"

Dad had hardly touched the first one. "No, thanks . . . hello, son! Look at you, you look like one of the Beach Boys!"

I was double surprised. First, he knew about the Beach Boys; second, he was cutting loose with a beer, something Mom used to complain about him not doing enough of back in Sunbury. But I wasn't surprised that E.A. was serving him Billy Bull Beer. He still had a couple of free cases from the fourth of July and was keeping his private Weidemann's stock for himself, which he was drinking out of a frosted mug.

Like a male lion E.A. made an attempt to lay claim to his territory. "Chuh, Jane, go get me another frosted mug of beer. Pick Tommy up another bottle too."

Mom got up, then goofed. "Do you want Billy Bull or Wiedemann's E.A.?"

He burped adamantly. "You know what I like!" If this were a competition, it was E.A., one, Tommy, zilch. Dad held his bottle up and was looking at the sediment in the bottom while I stood there, neither of us sure what to say.

When Mom came back she set E.A.'s mug down with a clunk. "How was your day with Lynn, Larry?"

"Great, Mom. She's going to be in the marching band this year. Think I'll go watch her when they're playing at home. It's not too bad a walk."

Dad interjected. "That's a good sign for a girl, son. Remember Jane, when you were in the band in high school? Those were fun days."

"Yep, head majorette," Mom proudly said. E.A. snorted into his mug, kicking up a wave of foam on his nose. Point to Tommy, one to one now. But Mom got wise and told Dad to take me up to the A&W drive-in for dinner. "E.A., since you did so well on your sales route today, you can take me out to the Green Gable Inn in Gahanna." As Dad and I got in his car, I figured Mom won that match, 2-1-1.

At first, it was still awkward between Dad and me, even without E.A. It'd been over half a year, and unlike with Gramps, I couldn't really pick back up where we started. He remarked again about my longer hair. "Larry, you do look like one of those beach type people I saw in L.A. All they do is surf."

"Yeah, Dad, I got tired of the flat-top look. My girlfriend kinda designed this," I said with a grin. Dad smiled and raised his eyebrows.

"What about you, Dad, Mr. Elvis and drinking beer now?"

"Oh, in Australia the water was so bad it was either beer or nothing. Down there they brew this stuff. E.A. would hate it. They call it small beer. Just enough alcohol to keep it sterile, but you'd have to drink twenty to get tipsy. And for the hair, you saw my service pictures from China in '44. That's the way we all wore it. You kids think Elvis invented the swept-back?"

After that, it did feel like we were back to old times. We settled in at the A&W and ordered two frosted mugs of root beer and two burgers apiece from one of the booths.

"So you're not going back overseas, are you?"

"No, son, I'm home to stay. In fact, I'm in the middle of buying an established business from another contractor up in Sunbury. You remember Mr. Henry, don't you? I bought his company, which includes his trucks and tools and his clientele. He's retiring to Arizona." Mr. Henry had been Dad's biggest competitor back when Dad had been in business. Friendly competition aside, Mr. Henry thought well enough of Dad to sell him everything. I wondered if J.D. Wellington would have approved.

Dad asked to see the school, so we drove there after dinner, with me showing him the bridge over the Alum and catching him up on the rowboat adventure and everything else that had happened since we'd last seen each other. Telling it all at once, I felt like he'd been gone for years. I ended with the play and Dad sprung a question he'd obviously been saving.

"Well, Larry, sounds like you have a girl, but she seems to only be around the last few months. What's she like?"

"She is the most special person I have ever known," I said honestly and a little boldly. Dad playfully acted hurt but said to tell him all about her, so I filled him in on all the details, from her giving me her feather clip, to that morning at the playground. He nodded thoughtfully as he took the long way back to the house and seemed pretty pleased.

"Oh, by the way, son," he said as we pulled into the driveway. "This week on Wednesday, a couple of my old TWA buddies are bringing a Connie into Port Columbus Airport on their way to take it to a private buyer in Texas. I owe them a favor and they need me to look the engines over. I'd be driving right by Northglenn—how about I pick you up and you go with me? I'll see to it that you get to sit in the pilot's seat."

I knew from Dad's stories that a Connie was Lockheed's Super Constellation plane, a funny, three-finned transport with four big engines to get its massive body off the ground. Jets were taking over and the old prop planes were being sold off, so getting to see one up close and in the cockpit was no small offer. He'd sent me pictures and postcards of them, but I'd never seen one in person, at least on the ground.

"That would be great, Dad! Um . . . could my girlfriend go?"

"Hmm . . . Well, I guess why not? I'd love to meet her." With that, Dad drove off waving before E.A., feeling brave after dinner at the Green Gable, could attempt a rematch.

The next day, I told Lynn about the plane and asked if her mom would be okay with us going someplace new since Dad would be there and she could meet him first. Lynn screwed up her lips and chewed on her pencil's eraser.

"Mom won't be here, actually. Believe it or not, Mom's 31 and still can't drive! A friend is taking her to a big parking lot somewhere to practice parallel parking for the test." She said it like she wasn't paying attention to me.

"Oh? Was all I said. Then her eyes popped like she'd let out something I wasn't supposed to know. Lynn was 15; without asking, my brain did the math, but I didn't feel like it was worth mentioning.

"Well . . . she's not here 'till about three. But I think I can make it happen. I'll call you about this tonight or tomorrow, okay?" We said goodbye as her break was over, and I left.

She didn't call until the next day. All I had going on was a couple of lawn mowing jobs in the afternoon, but Lynn managed to call twice from the diner while I was out. She got me the third time and said her mom had OK'd the trip to the airport, provided the restaurant's owner could meet my dad and make sure we were on the level. I said we'd make it happen, and it was the first thing I told Dad when he picked me up that Wednesday morning.

"Sure, son," he said, happily. Dad was in his element today. His hair was trimmed neatly and he was wearing an Air America hat.

"Gramps said you didn't end up working for Air America," I said as I buckled in.

"Well, they brought me over on contract some of the time. I could have gone to work for them full time, and they were promising some pretty nice wages. But I would have had to commit to some small country named Vietnam. Lot of fighting there, some old French colony. But I can see the States getting tied up in it somehow. Last place I want to be is in another Korea."

Lynn was waiting for us outside the restaurant. The lunch crowd was already starting to mill in, but Dominic, the owner, came out and pointed to a prime parking spot beside his Lincoln. As I got Lynn, he stared us up and down like we were asking for jobs. Finally, after chatting with Dad he stuck out a big beefy thumbs-up and reminded us we were supposed to be back at three. Lynn was in her prime today, too: feather clip, bracelets, earrings, and more confidence than I thought I could ever have if I met her mom. We got in the back of Dad's car and were soon at the airport.

Dad showed his TWA credentials at the field gate, a guard waved us through, and we drove right up to the big, beautiful Constellation, its three tails gleaming in the sun. We got out and the pilots waved Dad over.

"Come on up, Tommy. She's a beaut. How do you like being grounded, friend? This sure ain't Asia," they said, along with some aviation ribbing I didn't get. He introduced me and Lynn, and the pilots motioned us up a steep set of rickety stairs.

"Come on kids, take a look at this bird. Some rich Texas oilman bought her and we're hopping her down to his private field at his ranch. Some friend of Lyndon Johnson, if you can believe it. He's going to turn it into his private plane. How'd ya like that?"

Lynn went in first, and I followed her. The inside was empty—no seats or anything, just a hot cavern of metal and windows. But the pilot pointed us forward, where we stepped into the tight cockpit full of levers, dials, and other things I didn't even recognize. I had been in a dozen small planes with Dad, but this was the major leagues.

"Tommy," the head pilot said from behind as Lynn squinted at the dials. "We're getting a low oil-read on number four, but oil levels on the dipstick are just what the book says they should be. What should we do? We got no flight engineer on this trip, and I don't feel like landing in some podunk field in Tennessee."

"Can you start her up without any hassle from the airport? I'll hafta hear before I can tell you." I realized Dad hadn't brought any tools, just his senses.

The captain reached forward and grabbed his headset. "Let's call the tower and let them know. . . . No, stay seated young lady, might need your help."

Lynn's eyes looked like she just won a game show. I left the pilot's chair, and he sat down and threw some switches. The number three engine woke up lively and then the rest got going. Dad and the copilot stood behind us and watched the dials as they spun up, looking out the window from time to time. I knew Dad was listening more than he was looking.

"All right, young lady . . . now you put your hand there with mine . . . let's throttle up. Not too much—these brakes can only fight so much." The engines really got going with just a push from Lynn's hand, and the look on her face was priceless.

Fifteen minutes went by in just seconds. Finally Dad motioned for the engines to be cut. While the props wound down, Dad concluded the plane would get them to Texas, no problem. "But note in your final report that the engine bearings are worn and it needs an overhaul, okay?"

We still had an hour and a half to kill before Lynn had to be back, so they showed us the entire plane. Lynn was over the moon.

"I have never gotten to do anything like this," she said as we walked around the massive lending gear. "I've never even been in a plane!"

"Well, Lynn, Larry should call you up next time I'm down here in my Piper Vagabond," Dad said. I realized my father must have really done well the last few years, I nearly had to put Lynn's jaw back in place. I winked at my dad; we were a hit.

Dad was super when we got back to the diner, too. "Well, Lynn. I look forward to seeing you again. I mean it about the Piper . . . it's no Connie, but the world sure looks beautiful from 3,000 feet."

Lynn for her part gave Dad a hug. I told Dad I wanted to meet Lynn's mom and it would be good to walk home, so he drove off. But as it turned out Mrs. Evers, or Kelly, wasn't back yet, so I ate with

Lynn. Then she got back into her restaurant uniform, minus the jewelry, and I left for home.

We tried to pack as much into the next ten days as we could before Lynn had band camp. I knew I'd come over to Linden High School and maybe watch them practice toward the end of camp once they knew the routines, but summer had been almost daily moments together, and I think we both dreaded school cutting that short. Once I got a car, I assured Lynn, things would be back to normal.

The Rat Pack was out in full force on our last day at the pool. After the airport, being back in their world felt like coming back to a playground, but they were in charge and it was obvious to Lynn the battle was back on. They were making no secret of parading Kathy front and center every time they walked by.

"Look at them. They watch everything we do. If we get in the water, so do they. If we get out, they get it out. I think if I went to the bathroom, half of them would swarm you while the others ran ahead so I had to wait in line."

"They're just playing around."

"No, I just know Aubrey is going to try to hook you up with Kathy once school starts." At that moment, as if to prove her right, one of the Rats put a quarter in the jukebox and played "See You In September," an oldie about having a flirtatious fling during summer before you went back to school and got serious about your regular guy or gal. Lots of groups had recorded it, and I wasn't even sure who was singing. I decided to seize control.

"Lynn, you're my girl, you're the only one who means anything to me! The Rats can go suck an egg."

"Larry, you're a lot of things, and most of them are good or at least tolerable. . . . " But she smiled when she said that. I think she got it from a book. "But you're not a girl, and I can smell trouble ahead with them."

I told her she was wrong, then scooped her up and dove in the pool holding her while she screamed, then laughed in the water.

The lifeguard gave me 30 minutes on the time-out bench while Lynn swam circles, but it was worth it.

The Sunday before Lynn's band camp started, Trish had an end-of-summer cookout for all of us . . . except Mack. Any hope I had of them making up was gone when Trish made an announcement while we were burning marshmallows.

"Guys, I'm moving on. I don't want to break our group up, but I probably will start dating again once school is here. I know that's probably hard for you guys, being Mack's friends and all." Marcie and Lynn told her not to be hasty, but Henry kneeled to the ground and offered to be the man in her life, saying they could keep the gang whole and fill the hole in each other's hearts.

"Henry, that's so romantic. What movie is that from?" Henry started to answer but Possum interrupted him with "Moon River" on his harmonica. Butch took it away from him and chucked it into a bush. While I watched Possum run after it, Lynn nudged me.

"You're closest to Mack. You talk to him, get him to apologize. Otherwise, this is going to stink."

I nodded and just watched the campfire burn for a moment as the first stars started to come out in the cool evening air. I put my arm around her and pulled her close. "Okay, I will."

For just a moment I thought she was going to kiss me but then Trish's mom came out, saying "Who wants hot chocolate?" and all the girls jumped up.

Lynn was staying overnight and I had a job helping to build a garage with a neighbor that started early the next morning. Soon after the hot chocolate, we made our way out to the driveway, where she'd given me the feather clip months ago.

"Bye, Lynn. Be ready to tell me all about camp next weekend, okay? If you're not a majorette by then and too important."

"I will, even when I am." Then she slugged me on the shoulder. "I'm just glad you're too busy to get to the pool. One less thing for me to have to worry about."

I looked at her and realized I was as mesmerized by her as I had been the first night, then hugged her for what seemed like forever until I heard a muffled voice inside Marcie's old Jeep, which was parked by the side of the road. It was Butch.

"Will you two just say goodbye instead of hugging for the entire night?"

"Quit it, Butch," I heard Marcie from deeper inside the jeep. "They're in love, can't you see that?"

Butch could, so he started the Jeep and we all said goodbye as Henry and Possum came out and left together. I heard Henry saying, "What did I do wrong, Possum?" Possum, faithful to Butch, said that gang members couldn't pursue other gang member's former girls, ever.

As I walked home by myself beneath the stars, I felt good about the coming school year, even if it would be mostly weekends and a few nights like this. We were going to be fine.

CHAPTER
TEN

The garage job went well and was a nice break from my regular fix-it jobs. I enjoyed the chance to actually build a whole structure and could see why my dad wanted to turn it into a career. What was also nice was that all those hours kept me away from home, where things had taken a swift turn for the worse for E.A.

His drinking had picked up again after the fourth of July, which I didn't initially understand because it had turned out so well. I learned from overheard conversations that despite that victory, he had been missing, rescheduling, then re-missing key morning appointments with heads of the Ohio State University physical plant, a whale of an account for his cleaning product company. Apparently he had tested the patience of his boss once too often the week prior and had finally been fired. Needless to say, things were tense at home. I came back to eat lunch quickly outside on the front steps the entire week and would often stay as late as the garage owner would let me. By Friday night, I'd worked so much that we already had the roof on, and the owner paid me a nice little bonus and told me to enjoy my weekend.

He didn't have to say that twice! The plan was to meet Lynn at the pool at 1:00 on Saturday and catch up on all that'd happened at band camp. I got there as soon as Morningside opened up, but the lady who ran the pool and prided herself in knowing the kids and all their dramas laughed and shook her head. "Nope, she's not here yet."

I went over to a place where I could watch for Lynn, but an hour passed with no sighting. I was getting concerned—Lynn was very prompt. At 3:00 I decided to swim some laps just to pass time and not look like a lost sheep. Out of nowhere, Aubrey joined me in the water.

"Where-oh-where is your other half, Larry?" she said, splashing water from six feet off.

"Probably had to work today at Maddie's," I replied. "She fills in for folks all the time." I decided to act on it and head over there right then and there. As I walked out to go change, Kathy was watching me more intently than ever.

To my surprise, Maddie's was deserted. No one there, and on a prime summer Saturday. A sign on the door simply read: "We are remodeling, closed 'til November 16th. See you then!" I went home with a worried stomach and pretended to watch TV, figuring all would be explained the next day.

The next day at the pool was a repeat of the day before: no sign of Lynn. I didn't wait for Aubrey to come over and rub it in. With no phone and no idea where she lived, I did the only thing I could do: I went to Trish's.

But after I explained my dilemma, she just shook her head at the door. "No, Larry, I haven't heard from her, either. I assume she's at band camp. You know how busy summer training is, Mr. Baseball."

"Maybe something's wrong, Trish. Let me at least know where she lives so I can check in on her. Please!"

She came out and shut the door behind her. "Larry, I know how much you care for her. But look, even I don't know where she lives.

She made me promise never to ask. I don't know why. But if I do see her, I will tell her she needs to talk to you. I know there's a good reason for this, though." I was getting frustrated and nearly said something smart-alecky but walked away in a huff.

Lynn was all I could think about that week, with a thousand worst-case scenarios going through my head. When my garage client said he had to take his wife to the dentist Tuesday afternoon and that I could take the afternoon off from finishing touches, I figured it was my shot to walk over to Linden-McKinley High School and meet Lynn at band camp.

It was a good half-hour walk down Cleveland Avenue, but with hardly anyone on the road on the hot afternoon I was able to make good time. Sure enough, the marching band was out on the field practicing the routine they famously called the Panther Attack, after their mascot. I scanned the field for Lynn, but everyone was wearing hats and marching band jackets, even in the sweltering heat. When the director called for a water and shade break, I beelined for a girl I recognized from the pool.

"Hey, Jennifer, you're good with that baton. How's practice going?"

"Larry! Long ways from Mifflin, aren't you? Thanks. What's up?" I got to the point.

"Is Lynn here today? Lynn Bennet?" I asked.

"You know, actually, no. It was funny—she came to the first two practices last week and I haven't seen her since. I was just about to ask you the same question. We need her for this darn maneuver. There needs to be a drummer on every corner of the attack, and we're down one."

At that point an assistant director walked by with a clipboard and pad of paper. Jennifer of course knew Lynn and I were a couple, so she took the initiative.

"Mrs. Snyder, is Lynn Bennet still in the band?" She turned to me. "Maybe she just called in sick. These summer routines are brutal."

The director flipped a couple of pages. "Mmm . . . no. Lynn told me last Tuesday she was not going to participate this year, which was a surprise. She worked so hard to apply."

"Did she give a reason?" I asked. The lady didn't know me from Adam, but I had to know. She just shook her head.

"Sorry, son, she just said it was personal. We don't make inquiries about stuff like that."

I left and went back home feeling bewildered and perplexed. The only thing missing for my mood was a can to kick all the way home. That evening at dinner, I pushed my half-finished plate of meatloaf aside and went to bed early. Mom knew something was wrong and I explained it to her hastily, not wanting to be stupid and cry.

"These things have a way of working out," she said, and I brightened up. Then she continued, "Just not always how we want. But sometimes that's better. You just wait. Life'll have some good news for you soon!" But I didn't just want good news. I wanted to be with Lynn.

The contractor paid me that Friday and said he'd refer me to some friends who were also looking to remodel and needed a pair of skilled hands. Nice as that was, rather than go home, I went to the woods; the only job E.A. had found to keep us going while he was looking for another sales position was at Tubby's as a bartender, and Tubby was going to let him hustle pool on the side. His hours were irregular, and I wasn't in the mood to be home in case he was there.

I wandered around the old familiar trails, wondering how and why life had so quickly fallen out of the sky. Finally, I came to a big old beech tree that had its own little knoll to itself. We all called it the guestbook tree, because it had many years' worth of names on it from generations of folks who'd lived in the area. I got out my Barlow pocket knife and carved out the following:

L. E.

+

L. B.

08/18/63

That was the last day I'd seen her, and it seemed like an eternity ago, almost farther back than when I had first seen her at the McDonald's at Northern Lights shopping center. Then I sat down and in my head the song "Theme from a Summer Place" was playing . . . it was our song, from the pool. We always stared into each other's eyes when it played and thought about things to come, or at least I did. After about a half hour I left, softly whistling the tune.

On my way back, I passed by one of the Gents' houses, where there was a party going on. You could hear the Beach Boys records from a block away. There was only a four-foot fence and I could easily see the Gents in their blazers, holding Cokes like beers and talking to, of course, the Rat Pack. I was about to shift into sixth gear and hightail it out of there . . . when, who should I see with one of the Gents but Trish.

That stopped me long enough to get noticed by Aubrey, who beelined over to the fence. A thousand questions were running through my head. Of course, Aubrey already knew about Lynn 's disappearance.

"Hey there, stranger, didn't see you at the pool this week. Listen, now that the Indian princess is gone . . . ready to come back to Earth?"

"Who the heck told you that?"

"Oh, I have my spies everywhere, even over at Linden." She nodded over at Trish who looked up at me, blushed and looked right down. "Now come on, you've just passed your summer fling course with flying colors. Even I had one—keeps you on your toes," she said. Looking back at Kathy, she sang the next comment in a high-pitched opera melody. "If you're ready for real romance, so is sheeeee!"

"Do you ever give anything a break, Aubrey?"

"NO!" she said, almost proudly. "Come on, hop this fence."

"I'm not invited."

"I'm inviting you. Come on, the Gents won't care. What's one more mouth to feed?"

I looked over at a card table where the Gents were picking at a platter of what E.A. called horse do-overs, which he said was French for tiny portions.

"No, I'm going home. This will never be my scene." And I left. I think it was the first time Aubrey had ever been told no. Looking back, I saw her go over to Kathy, who started nodding her head.

Still not in the mood to go home, I changed directions and walked back up Mecca Street to see Mack. It'd been a few weeks, with both of us hard at work at our new jobs, me moping, and him banned from anyplace Trish might possibly be. He lived two houses past the Woodland and Mecca intersection, just five houses from Trish's house. That had seemed perfect earlier in the summer.

When I walked into his yard, I could see him through the window of his front bedroom, which was just to the left of the main door; he seemed to be looking at a picture. Oddly enough, he also had some M-80s lying on his bed; it looked like he had taped four of them together with electrical tape. I didn't want to be a peeping Tom, so I threw a twig at the window panes.

"Mack, it's me. Can I come in?" I caught enough of the picture to see it was last year's school photo of Trish, but he quickly shoved it under his pillow.

"Sure, climb on in through the window." I pulled it up and jimmeyed up over the sill. I knew Mack had parents, or theoretically had to, but I never saw them. They were always gone or had just left or were on their way home or something.

"Mack, whatcha up to? That's some high powered stuff you got lying around," I said, pointing at the four M-80s.

"Yeah, I know. I wanna see if it will knock down that old tree stump near our hideout. I read somewhere that four of these are equal to a stick of dynamite."

"Well, hey, I'll go with ya," I said.

"Sure your leash is long enough?"

I wasn't sure if he knew about my situation with Lynn, but I didn't feel like bringing it up. I sat on an old chair and sunk about a foot, to the point I was looking up at him on his bed. There was a spring stabbing my back, so I leaned forward.

"Hey pal, do ya even miss Trish?"

"No!" he yelled and pointed to his face. "See this? No ring in my nose. That's what she wanted to do. You only see the nice Trish. 'Oh, Larry, you're so polite. Oh, Larry, you are so nice to Lynn. Oh, Larry, please pass the bacon to the left.' You should see her breathing fire."

"Can't be that bad."

"'Mack, wipe your shoes. Don't blow your nose out on the ground! Mack, we should go to church, Mack, you should get rid of your stupid firecrackers. On and on."

He leaned against the pillow and sighed. I heard the cellophane of the photo crinkle.

"So you don't miss her at all?"

He snorted "Yeah, but I want to be me and me isn't —"

"Mack, I get it. I'm still figuring it out myself, you know. I guess girls are a part of life we can't live without, even if they do seem more trouble than they're worth." At that point, I was talking more to myself than to him, so I got up. "Look Mack, give me a call when you're ready to blow that stump up. I'd hate to miss it." He nodded and with that, I climbed back out the window. "Don't crush the picture," I said as I left.

I went to bed early and slept in as much as I could, lying in bed and just watching Lynn's feather blow in the breeze against the bed post. I wasn't big on sleeping in, but the thought of going back to school the next Monday without Lynn to look forward to just seemed unbearable. Around the fifth time I'd turned over to snooze, I heard my mom coming upstairs.

"Someone here to see you, Larry."

"Boy or girl?" I asked, hopefully.

"He says his name is Arnold."

Well, that was a surprise. The only Arnold I knew was a member of the Gents, and I'd seen him the night before. I admit, as far as the Gents went, he was probably the best of the group and halfway decent to folks outside their clique. But what was he doing here?

I threw on some clothes and went downstairs, where Arnold was waiting outside the door. E.A. was still in bed, so I let him in.

"What's up, Arnold?"

"Wish you had stayed last night at the party, Larry!" He grinned. "From what I hear, there was a very pretty girl there who's got a thing for you."

"So?" Mom was in the kitchen, and I knew she could hear everything. As soon as I said it she came in with two glasses of pineapple juice and gave me a dirty look and Arnold a smile simultaneously. Arnold was smooth and knew my last name wasn't the same as E.A.'s.

"Why thank you, Mrs. Darnell, I love pineapple juice!" She smiled and retreated back to the kitchen.

"Look, Larry, Aubrey told me all about it. I know she's got her angle, but Kathy is the prettiest girl in our class, maybe the school. I know what it's like to lose a girl, but let me do you a favor and tell you that the best way to get over a girl is to get a better one. Plus, being friends with the Gents has its perks. The Rat Pack's now our sister sorority, so if you're in with us, you're in with them, and then you're in with everyone."

"What's your point, Arnold? I asked.

"Look, if you're too dumb to help yourself, help me out. I'll owe you a favor. How about you come to the state fair with us tomorrow. You're a farm boy, right?" He knew I was—he was one of the people who made mooing sounds when I first got here when I would get on the bus.

"Yeah, yeah, I moved here from the farm. But what do you need me for at the fair?"

"Well, I'm dating the newest member of the Rat Pack, a girl named Judy Donner. She just transferred in from Brookhaven High School." Everyone knew Judy. Supposedly, she was so pretty that Aubrey had made her a member immediately to keep her under control. She looked like the TV actress Tuesday Weld. "Well anyway, Judy loves horses and . . . ha, I'm a city boy. I don't know anything about them. Would you go with us as a sort of animal expert? It'd mean a lot to me. Do you know anything about horses?"

I started to tell him that Gramps hadn't had horses on the farm since about when I was born, although you'd still find their lost shoes turned up in the tilled fields from time to time.

But then Arnold added, "Oh, and Aubrey and Melanie and Kathy are going, too. And if that doesn't interest you, then Trish is going with Roger. They just started dating, and she said something about a friend of hers from Linden-McKinley might come, too. If that's your girl, you can play her and Kathy off and come out a winner anyway. Whaddya say?"

Well, I had no intention of playing anyone against anyone. But if Lynn was coming, sign me up to be an honorary Gent.

"Sure! I was going to go anyway. What time?"

"Be at my house tomorrow afternoon at 1:00 sharp. Thanks, Larry. You'll see, going with us has its advantages." He turned to go but stopped and kind of stammered for the first time. "Oh, and look, uh, please don't take any offense at this, but could you wear something other than cutoffs and a baseball shirt? The Gents have a dress code we observe in public: slacks and tight shirts. But no blazers, since it's at the fair and there's animals."

"I'm not a Gent, Arnold."

"Yeah, but maybe you could be, if all goes well tomorrow. The school year can go a lot easier if you're one of us."

Mom rushed in before I could say something sarcastic. "Okay, Arnold! He'll be there right on time, slacks and all!"

Arnold was satisfied and left. I groaned.

"Larry, this is just the sort of thing you want to happen to you, and I'm not going to let you ruin it. You can wear that new blue shirt and your light brown slacks . . . but polish those loafers. They've not seen the outside of the closet since we moved here."

Sunday was the next to last day of the fair. I'd thought about going there and looking at the livestock and tractor displays before Arnold came along, but not like I was dressed for church. I secretly hoped that I'd be able to break from the Gents and wander around by myself, but Mom anticipated this and told me under no circumstances was I to leave the group.

She starched and ironed my clothes so much that I felt like I was wearing more armor than Prince Valiant on one of his expeditions once I strapped on my belt. I was glad none of the gang saw me as I walked to Arnold's, although I had a close call with Henry as he went to afternoon mass.

Arnold and his mom were already in the front of her car. He nodded at her as though to acknowledge that Gents had moms, too, and turned the radio on. We rode about a block and stopped at Trish's house. I hadn't been there since the infamous breakfast date and eagerly waited to see Lynn bounding out of the front door, more beautiful than any Rat Packer. Instead, it was just Trish who came out the front and looked like she was on her way to a funeral once she saw me. When she joined me in the back, she muttered under her breath.

"Larry, what are you doing here?"

I pointed to Arnold. "Is Lynn meeting you at the fair?" was all I could think to ask.

Trish looked confused and hissed in reply. "What? No, the band is up at Cedar Point this weekend. They're marching in a parade and giving a concert in return for free passes on the rides. I haven't seen her at all since she started, like I told you last week."

"She's not in the band. . . . " I said quietly before we pulled up to her date Roger's house. I don't know if she heard me. She looked a little like one of the nervous actresses about to go on stage at Henry's play.

It was one of the hotter summer days, and the sun was bearing down hard on the metal roof of the car and making me sweat in my starched armor, so I had cracked a window. I could smell Roger's cologne the moment he left his house. He must have opened up a whole bottle and dunked his shirt in it. He got in on the opposite side of the car and slid right up to Trish, putting his arm around her.

"My girl for the night!" he said, loudly. She didn't look comfortable, but off we went.

Arnold had turned the radio off at this point and turned around in the big upfront bench while his mom drove like a chauffeur.

"All right, Larry, roll up that window so we can hear each other. Whaddya know about horses?"

It was time to put up or get out. I racked my TV cowboy shows knowledge and started spitting. "Well, uh, horses eat oats and hay; if they're brown, that's a bay. Did you know they wore iron shoes?" Trish was watching from deep within Roger's arm and I could feel the sweat on the back of my shirt. "John Wayne owns quarter horses, I rode a horse once bareback—that means no saddle. Ever watched the Kentucky Derby?"

I made a few more attempts to establish myself as a horseman but finally concluded that if Judy had any questions she could just ask me, as I didn't want to overload Arnold. It didn't seem quite what he was hoping for, but it was all I had.

The plan was that Arnold's mom was going to drop us off and we would meet the Rat Pack at a designated spot. Roger had other plans. Once Arnold's mom dropped us off, he took Trish's hand and announced, "We're off to the Tunnel of Love—see you guys at nine, alright?"

"NO, we are not," Trish protested as they walked off, but Roger seemed pretty determined. I was already ready to split; worst case scenario, I could walk home from the state fairgrounds in two hours and it only involved one bad neighborhood. I didn't need this night.

If I could just go see the livestock, get a few pamphlets on the new John Deere Tractors, and leave, I'd have made the most out of a lost long shot on Lynn being there.

But then, out of nowhere, the Pack descended on Arnold and me: Kathy, Aubrey, Melanie and the new girl, Tuesday—I mean Judy.

"Looook who's here, girls," announced Aubrey. "And he's wearing pants, not jeans! Larry, you look like a Gent!" She moved in closer while Arnold hugged Judy and Kathy and Melanie stood off to the side. "You made the right decision, Larry. And look who came!"

Kathy was obviously happy to see me but not happy enough to really say hello, it seemed. "Oh, great, silent Kathy," I said, low enough so only Aubrey would hear.

"Give her a chance. She had to watch you all summer with little Miss Linden-McKinley." Judy attached herself at the hip to Arnold and said she wanted to go to the horse barn right then and there. He nodded to me and I was on the clock, though Aubrey kept maneuvering me toward Kathy as we walked through the cavernous horse barn.

Judy looked at every horse, and we were there for an hour. Toward the end, even the girls were tired of it. Finally, I skipped ahead at the end of the final row of some big horse farm's line of Tennessee Walkers and memorized everything on the info card that had been posted by one big gelding. When Arnold and Judy arrived, I repeated everything on it verbatim. From behind Judy, Arnold nodded and gave two thumbs up.

"That's exactly the kind of horse my dad is going to buy me. That's what I want," Judy said at the end of my speech as we exited into the cooling evening air outside. Judy was eyeing an overflow building of draft studs when Melanie finally pointed at an old-timey circus tent.

"Freak show, guys! They're always fun."

If ever there was such a thing as a nice Rat Packer, it was Melanie. She was a little more down to earth than the rest of them and seemed kind enough at times. She fell behind with me as I regained my mental energy after an hour of horse talk.

"Why are you here, Larry? I thought you and that pretty girl at the pool were a couple."

"So did I, Melanie. I actually kind of came—" but then I thought better of it. That sort of thing would go straight to Aubrey. "—well, to help out Arnold."

"That's so nice! He's such a city slicker," she said as we filed into the ancient circus tent that was Freak Show Alley.

It was home of the four-eyed goat twins, midget men married to five-hundred pound women, ladies who ate fire . . . you name it, they had it. Then we hit the main attractions, starting with "Maja," the Snake Woman. The posters outside had shown a snake with a woman's head, strangling a man. "She will AMAZE you," it promised. But inside her section of the tent, it just smelled damp and musty. Maja was dressed in an outfit that looked like snake scales, but was obviously a human. She had a lethargic yellow python across her shoulders, and when she saw us enter she turned to her assistant and requested her black mamba. When the helper tried to remove the yellow python, it hissed and struck at him but he wrapped it around a mannequin arm and carried it off while the poor guy tried to squeeze the arm to death.

He then returned with a six-foot long black snake. He swore it would kill anyone it bit in just two minutes, but even in the dim light I could see it was a common enough black rat snake, the kind that hung around every farm in Ohio. Seeing our doubt, the snake woman cried out to come closer and kissed the snake, then acted like she was dying.

"Oh, children! Help me, help me!" she moaned sadly. The assistant ushered us out of the tent.

"Is she dead?" Judy asked.

"Yes," said the assistant, gravely.

"If she is, the people coming in after us are going to get rooked," I said. Melanie slugged my arm off to the side.

Next was a smaller tent beneath the big top that had a sign reading Borg Falstafingraf, the Viking Giant. One painting showed an eight-foot-tall warrior in a longboat with his sword pointing the way to England; another showed him fighting 30 men with a spear.

"We gotta see this!" Aubrey exclaimed.

Inside was an old man asleep on a massive throne on top of a platform. Around him was "REAL PHOTOGRAPHIC PROOF!" of him being a giant at different ages: at age six, he was already five feet tall. Another photo showed him riding a horse with his feet dragging the ground. Another showed him dunking a basketball without even jumping.

Aubrey went over and tapped his foot, since he seemed not to have heard us enter.

"Big Viking, wake up, wake up!" Judy was looking at the pictures off to the side.

"What kind of horse is this, Larry?"

I squinted and saw it was obviously a regularly-sized man on a smaller horse. "Foal, I think." Judy was still impressed, though.

When four other people came in, a man dressed in a cheap leather kilt and breast plate appeared and announced, "And now, ladies and gentlemen, Borg Falstafingraf the Viking Giant, awake!"

Borg looked down at us with bleary eyes, stood up, and drew his sword. His head was touching the underneath side of the tent thanks to the platform. He then blew into some kind of animal horn, and that was the show.

I had seen a lot of these shows at the Delaware County Fair before I moved here, so I was about done.

"Uh, Arnold, thanks for the ticket. Looks like we're all horsed out. I'll find my way home. I'm going to go look at the livestock and machinery," I said.

Aubrey put an iron grip on my forearm. "No, Larry, we want to eat and ride the rides!"

A prisoner of Aubrey's actually impressive pinch, I headed with them to the concessions area. They all had hoped to meet someone to take them out and had brought no money as a result, except for Kathy. Melanie asked me to loan her a dollar, and I thought, so much for a clean escape.

"Okay, girls, what do you want? I'll buy," I said, straining to be polite.

Aubrey went first. "Foot long with coney sauce!"

"Dumbo ear!"

"Curly fries!"

Kathy had her money out by this time, Possum wasn't there to trip me up. In my first ever words to her, I said, "Wait, Kathy . . . I will buy your food."

She did not respond but just pointed to the corn dog concession stand with a smile and nod. I got everyone their order, handing Kathy her corn dog first. Aubrey snatched it away, took a bite, and then gave her the rest. I rolled my eyes and scarfed down a sausage sandwich with steaming hot peppers.

Off to the side, Judy started to whine about going back to the horse barn, which immediately caused the other three girls to start chanting, "Rides, rides, rides!"

I looked around. We were near the Alpine Express, a ride that went up and around and around against a backdrop of the Alps. It had paintings of happy couples holding hands, hugging, and even kissing. I gulped and said, "Hey, how about the dodge-em cars? They're always fun."

Kathy was looking at the kissing couples on the paintings, then she glanced my way and said softly, "Let's ride this, please."

There was no way out of it. Why had I just eaten that sausage sandwich with peppers?

"Am I paying, Melanie?" I asked innocently.

"Oh, please would you, Larry?" she begged. "I'll pay you back first day of school." She climbed into a car with Judy and Ron. Aubrey and Kathy and I shared our own car, or in this case, "Alpine Lift Chair." As soon as we got in, Aubrey took the wheel and started to spin us around before the ride even started.

"AUUUUBRREEEYYYY!" I yelled but there was no effect on the two Aubreys now sitting across from me. Then the engine started, and up we went. I didn't care about heights, but when we started to go around and around and around, up and down and around, I could feel the sausage sandwich wanting to leave.

I looked at what appeared to be four Aubreys and heard her ask if I was okay, but I just shut my eyes and held on for dear life. To the left and right, sometimes, was Kathy.

Mercifully, the engine wound down. I got off and made a beeline for the restroom and gave the sausage sandwich back to the fairgrounds. After I splashed my face with cold water, I came out to find Judy was in Arnold's face about something.

"Okay buster, so Melanie is afraid of 'quick movement,' but you didn't have to make a quick move yourself and hold her hand the whole ride! I came to see horses. I should have come with him." She was pointing to me. With that she stormed off in the direction of the telephone banks. A bit flattened, Arnold suggested we find Trish and Roger and go home as the other girls came out from redoing their hair in the bathroom.

Just then, Trish found us first. She was by herself and immediately took my arm.

"Where's Roger?" asked Arnold.

"Uh, he found someone he knew from school. Think they're still by the Tunnel of Love—oh, here they are." Rodger sidled up with another girl in tow. We all walked the Rat Pack to where their ride was going to pick them up and shot the breeze by the main gate until Aubrey's older sister Candy pulled up in the family Edsel. She rolled down the window and flicked a cigarette out the window.

"Get in, you little creep, I've been circling for 20 minutes. If I miss The Great Escape with Jeremy tonight, you're dead."

Aubrey put her thumb behind her teeth and flipped it while the girls laughed.

Melanie came over and hugged me. "Listen, you're okay, guy! Remember: when school starts—" here she lowered her voice to a whisper—"she has a huge crush on you." She was pointing at Kathy, who quickly turned away.

Aubrey slid over while her sister yelled at the rest of the Rat Pack and stuck out a half thumbs-up. "I give you a five out of ten today, your best score yet," she said. Then she jerked her hand at Kathy, who was calming Candy down. "Coulda been a ten if you played your cards right. But thanks for the fair food—it's my favorite."

After they left, Arnold and Roger were talking about Roger's new date. I looked at Trish, who hadn't really left my side, and asked what was wrong.

"Oh, Larry . . . stay with me, please? I called Mom. She said Dad is leaving work from downtown and will pick me up in a half hour on his way home. I spent most of the time walking around by myself in the commercial buildings, just looking at stuff."

"Didn't you and Roger go into the Tunnel of Love?" I joked, but I regretted it immediately as she looked hurt.

"No! Look, I made a mistake, Larry. I admit it. I wanted to be in the popular crowd, I wanted to get back at Mack . . . and I miss my friends at Linden. I wish we had never moved to Mifflin, no offense. I used to be in the in crowd, but this doesn't hold a candle to that." I guess that after she'd refused to go into the Tunnel of Love, Roger had let her know that certain things were expected from girls lucky enough to get a date with a Gent, and she'd ditched him then and there only to see him boarding minutes later with his new romance. We looked up to find that the Gents and Co. had vanished.

"Figures. You won't leave me will you, please?"

"No, of course I won't, Trish," I sighed, resisting the urge to ask about Lynn even though I knew she'd told me all she could. "Where's your dad meeting you?"

"Seventeenth Avenue gate. We'll give you a ride home too, of course." She took my arm again and I could see she was pretty badly shaken. I gave her a few minutes before asking the question I second-most wanted answered.

"Look, Trish, What about Mack? Is it really over?"

"Well . . . it all started the day the four of us had breakfast a few weeks ago. He upset me when he yelled 'Grace, and her sister Margie.' Saying prayers is important to me, and he knows it. After you guys left, he came back but just kept yelling and we had it out. Mom eventually came and told him to never come back. I haven't seen him since. No, I don't want it to be over, but he was so rude. And how on earth do you come back from that?"

"So no word from Lynn, huh?" It just kind of slipped out.

"Honest, no, Larry." I explained how I knew she was not in the band and that Maddie's had been closed for a month. She bit her lip. "I can't call her, Larry. If she doesn't contact me, I have no way of getting hold of her. It's not just you she keeps secrets from. She just . . . I dunno what's wrong. I wish I did."

When her dad arrived, he was hopping mad. The call he got from his wife made him believe Trish's date had been rude to her and she was scared, so as soon as he got out of the car he lit into me and grabbed by the starched collar, which fortunately protected my neck.

"What's the big idea, buster? What's going on with my daughter, and on the night before the first day of school, huh? You ever fought a chef? I tenderize my steaks by hand—"

"Daddy, Daddy, this isn't him! This is Larry, Lynn's boyfriend. It's okay!" I could see he was more concerned about his daughter than mad, and he downshifted immediately.

"Oh, okay . . . sorry, boy. You okay, honey?"

"I am. Larry stayed with me the entire time, Daddy, Roger left with someone else. Larry's the one I told you can build things. He can even do the attic loft if you want."

"Well," Trish's dad said, wiping his hands on his apron—he'd not even taken the time to change from work downtown at one of the big hotels— "We'll see about that. But that's a pretty good commendation, son. Sorry again about the collar."

When we got to my house, Trish turned to me from the front seat. "Larry, I know how much you care for Lynn. Believe me, she feels the same way." She shrugged and waved bye. I took some comfort in that as I got out of the car.

The dining room light was on, and I saw that Mom had stayed up for me and was going through her backlog of gossip magazines. "Well, honey, how did it go? Are you a Gent now?"

"No, Mom. You could say they ended up being the opposite of gentlemen."

"Ah, I see. Funny how that happens. Did you at least see Lynn?"

"No." Mom frowned but saw I was in a better state than I'd been in previous nights.

"Aw, I'm sorry. I so hoped you would have a good time. You look so good, too, although your collar's a bit bent. Did you at least get to see the fair?"

I gave her a hug. "Let me tell you about Borg Falstafingraf, the Viking Giant . . . "

CHAPTER
ELEVEN

ummer was suddenly over, and the usual school morning routine returned in full. Mom had WBNS going with all the big bands and oldie crooners. Glen Miller serenaded us with "In the Mood" as bacon sizzled on the stovetop.

"First day, Larry," she said, shuffling some bacon on a plate beside toast and eggs. "This'll be an exciting year for you. You'll turn 16 halfway through. Enjoy these years—trust me, they go quickly."

"You seem in a good mood, Mom." Right then, E.A. came in dressed to the nines—for E.A.—in a delivery man's uniform.

Oh yes. Today was the first day of E.A.'s new job. On Friday night, an old pal had called him up to see if he still had his commercial truck license he'd gotten back in his army days. In a rare bit of foresight, E.A. had kept it current, although he had primarily been behind the wheels of sales cars, so he jumped on the opportunity. His friend had dropped off uniforms Sunday while I was at the state fair. He looked like a bus driver, minus the bowtie.

"Oh, don't you look good!" Mom said, and E.A. turned around for us, then headed off on a three-day run up to Michigan. As he picked up the brand-new day-trip bag Mom had gotten him as a congratulations for the job, I heard the familiar tinkle of bottles. After a dry sales trip out to Pittsburgh once, E.A. never went without his Weidemans.

Inwardly, I was really hoping the truck gig worked out. There had been no repeat of the infamous flying-crow affair like the last time he'd gotten fired, but I'd noticed that E.A.'s more violent moments came in spells, and though I was getting good at avoiding them, you just never knew. Most of the time he was okay. But there was no explanation of what might trigger another outburst like that one, so I always feared it was around the bend. With E.A. being gone half the time, I figured it was a good bet that it'd happen there and not here.

As I walked to the bus stop, I half-imagined that standing somewhere not too far away was Lynn, waiting for a bus to take her to Linden-McKinley. Maybe it was the early morning heat, which made it seem like summer was just beginning and not ending, that made me feel hopeful that somehow, in some way, things were going to work out. I was feeling only slightly less sad than I had been the weekend before, but it was something.

It was clear on the bus that a few things had changed. Gone were the Gents. I assumed that they were now driving, since a couple of them were upperclassmen, and that way they could keep their blazers clean. The gals from Shanty Town now sat throughout the bus and actually looked calm. A few were even asleep.

Mack and Butch had taken over the front seats now that the yellow-blazers weren't there and were holding one open for me. I looked back and saw Possum waving frantically.

"Back here, back here, Larry, I saved a seat for you!" I tried to look away quickly but instead saw Trish sitting a few feet back, by a head of black hair turned towards the window. My eyes must have lit up because Trish only shook her head.

"Haven't heard from her, Larry," she said quietly, but then Mack looked her way and she buried her face in her book. The other girl turned and it was just one of the Shanty Towners that were usually in the back.

In home room, I looked at my schedule for the year and saw that I had typing class in 6th period: it wasn't a mandatory class, but E.A. said I should take it, and that was his contribution to my education. The class was taught by a woman who was rumored to be at least five hundred years old. Mack said she had an autographed painting of George Washington that he had given her when they were dating.

"Seriously, Larry, Mrs. Minnery came over on the Mayflower," he said, looking over at my schedule. "But hey, looks like you get to join the road warriors this year." He was referring to the driving classes I had twice a week. E.A. had heard that the school was offering free classes and insisted I learn there rather than through one of the summer intensive schools.

"Choo, bud, when I was your age I was already taking the old man's Buick out on joy rides," he explained. "Don't need to spend $50 to find out how to do that." The school's driver's-ed cars were legendarily beaten-up junkers; little kids would follow them around yelling "Student driver, no survivors!'" But at the end of the course, you were one step closer to wheels. Maybe by then, I'd have a girl again to drive to and see.

My mind came back to Mrs. Minnery right as I ran into her. She was standing in the doorway like I was late. But as soon as she let me through, she resumed her position waiting for other students.

"Take a seat over near those girls," she said, pointing a bony white finger toward Aubrey, Melanie, and Kathy. Aubrey turned around in the middle of a conversation.

"Guess what? Melanie and I made the varsity cheerleading squad. That means we're getting our varsity letter before you do." She laughed and stuck out her tongue. Kathy glanced up and glanced down.

I needed a drink of water so I went outside to the fountain. For some reason, getting to sit beside the Rat Pack made Mrs. Minnery seem a lot nicer and less likely to have dated any Founding Fathers.

Even if my heart was still stuck on Lynn, it seemed all right to enjoy typing class a little if it meant some quality time with the Rats. When I came back, Kathy had traded places with Melanie and was sitting beside my seat. Kathy turned to speak to me, and then—

"Insert a sheet of paper into your typewriter, now. Let us begin," a croaky old voice began. I looked up at Mrs. Minnery, who had rediscovered her centuries-old glow. Darned old witch. Just a moment ago, she looked so young; it was obviously a spell. The classroom filled with the loud clatter of typewriters, and Kathy rushed off to another class as soon as it was over.

It was Melanie who took me aside after class. "Listen, Larry, just give Kathy a chance. I know you had a girl at the pool and I'm not saying forget her, but at least be kind to her, will ya?"

"I guess . . . "

"You didn't go to junior high with us and you just can't imagine how much she has changed, especially this last year. Have you ever read that fairy tale about the ugly duckling becoming the beautiful swan? Trust me, Larry, that's her! But she's so shy, and when Cubby two-timed her last summer she kinda went backwards. So, why not make your play? Oh, here's that dollar you loaned me yesterday."

I turned the two half-dollars over in my hand and wondered what old Benjamin Franklin would do. Something about a bird in hand being worth two in the bush. Right then and there, I thought: Why not?

It was interesting for the first week after that. Somehow, we found new ways every day to avoid talking to each other, but the glances were there. On Friday, when I forgot to bring my paper, she reached over and inserted a sheet in my rusty old Underwood typewriter, which was older than Mrs Minnery. I decided over the first weekend that I'd be the one to say hello on Monday and maybe even ask to eat lunch together. I didn't even feel guilty about it when I saw Lynn's feather in my bedroom, now almost faded from months' of summer afternoon sunshine. But I admit, I took it and carefully put it in my desk drawer.

But the next Monday morning, Kathy wasn't in class. Tuesday was the same. I knew she wasn't sick, because I had seen her at her locker. Finally, I screwed up the nerve to ask Aubrey.

"Where is she?" I asked, pointing to her chair.

"Where is who?" she asked stupidly.

"Her," I said, pointing to Kathy's empty chair.

At that point Aubrey raised her voice and said loud enough for everyone in the class to hear. "Say her name and I'll tell you!"

"Kathy," I hissed. "Where's Kathy?"

Melanie, who I figured was my ally, butted in. "No! Not 'til you say her whole name!"

I growled. "Kathy Martin."

In her cheerleader crowd-friendly voice, Aubrey jumped and yelled. "WELL, I'LL BE DARNED, HE KNOWS HER NAME!" The whole class was riveted, now, but Aubrey resumed her hushed tone. "It's simple. She transferred to distributive education. She works half days at her dad's law office. She leaves here at one o'clock three days a week and gets paid to type—unlike you, who still doesn't know where the letter "f" is. And you thought this was going to be easy? No way, José."

Well, I had no horse in the race at this point, so I just shrugged, inserted my sheet of paper, and started pecking out the vowels as Mrs Minnery entered the classroom, A E I O U, A E I O U. Aubrey seemed miffed that I wasn't more downcast.

I was alone at lunch time until a pretty girl I'd seen around the halls since last March stopped by. She had a look on her face like we'd known each other forever.

"Hiya, I'm Roxanne, I write the column 'Overheard in the Hall' for the school paper."

"I'm Larry, Roxanne," I said.

"Oh, I know that," she laughed.

In addition to being on top of the school grapevine, Roxanne also was the keeper of the WOW Book, a tattered notebook I had only heard about the year before. It was nothing more than an old notebook, bound in tape, with a page for each person's name—well, anyone who mattered in the eyes of the upper crust. If you wanted to, you could write a comment and give a rating of one to ten, with ten being the best and Wow being beyond ten, meaning you were crazy over that person. It was the best way to broadcast how you felt about a girl or guy, as well as get embarrassed if you weren't an item within the week.

"Listen, I know you just moved here last year, but here, take this—you're in it! Read your comments and give it back to me once you've read through everything and made your own wows." I nodded. "Listen, when a Rat Packer gives a Wow, it's hot, and I'm all over this. And right now, you're hot."

"Is any of this stuff even real?"

"Oh, sometimes the Gents will put something in there just to cause trouble. But I was there when the Rat Packer in question wrote it. It's bona fide . . . I'm not supposed to tell, though, so shh!" She winked and sidled away. I took the notebook and retreated to the school's front step where I could browse in peace. The notebook was in pieces, and I cautiously took it out of my beat-up E.A.-hand-me-down leather case.

It was a classic early autumn Ohio day with a hint of color in the massive old maple trees on the school grounds. For just a minute I regretted that I hadn't gone out for football. But as I looked at the trees, instead of leaves I saw money hanging on the limbs. I felt I could make 25 dollars on a good weekend raking and burning them, and the smell of a good leaf fire beat the smell of the locker room any day. I inhaled and could smell someone getting an early start a few blocks away. I admit, I was savoring the moment.

FInally, I cracked open the famous WOW book. The first pages were basically the Gents and Rat Pack saluting and complimenting each other, a real hot-air-blowing contest. I read a few of the comments and thought, yuck. Then I flipped to the jocks' page and found myself toward the back. I looked around and dived in.

"My name is Sheila, I wouldn't date him if we were on a desert island and he was the only man left on earth. He ignored me at the pool all summer. 1."

Sheila who?

"If he took me horseback riding, I would date him. But I hate baseball, so 7."

Thanks, Judy.

Melanie started helping me after that. "Well, '9.' He is so kind and I kinda went on a group date with him, he paid for everything. But I have a friend who is in love with him and I'm 6' 2" so . . . basketball players only for me."

A Rat Pack pledge we all called Lesser Brenda wrote, "Aubrey says I can have him if Kathy doesn't want him. 10."

Aubrey wrote "0." "If he listened to me I'd give him a six. Come on Larry, [this part was underlined] listen to Auntie Aubrey this year!!! And life will be a breeze."

Trish: "He is cute, I like him, but he belongs to my best friend. For her I say, 'Wow'!"

Aw. A few more back-and-forths from the peanut gallery, Then, down at the bottom, in the prettiest cursive I'd seen:

"Why can't we get together? I know I am shy, why can't you be the one to start a conversation? I waited all summer. Are you available now? I am! Just because you can't dive off a diving board, I don't care. WOW 10 WOW 10."

There was no name.

I leaned back and listened to the wind in the leaves, thinking about that one, then put the book back in my case, and walked back to where Roxanne usually hung around in between classes. Well, okay, first I flipped to the back and wrote in my best imitation of Aubrey's handwriting:

"Possum, take me on a romantic date in the woods and play your bugle and harmonica for me. WOW ever since you sang for Miss Teen Beat.—Aubrey M." For extra effect I drew a heart around a letter P.

I wasn't sure when Kathy had written her WOW, but I knew it'd been her, and it was nice to hear it from her, so to speak. With Aubrey there was always a sense that and Kathy and I were part of a grander plan that ended with her—Aubrey—being elected queen of Mifflin, but if Kathy was willing to go on public record . . . that had to mean something.

I soon found out why Kathy hadn't signed the book. The following week was the week before homecoming, and the school was buzzing with excitement. The voting for homecoming queen was slated for that Friday, and each class also voted for an attendant. True to Aubrey's promise, the Rat Pack started an all-out campaign to nominate Kathy as sophomore representative. The halls were full of posters and slogans, with Kathy plastered over her competitors—the Rat Pack was vicious, and I think Lesser Brenda's brother worked at a local print shop, so Kathy's posters were professionally designed. Obviously, Kathy wanted to appear to be available, not tied down, a political choice Aubrey probably inspired.

Friday, we all assembled in the auditorium to hear the speeches and decide who to vote for. Truthfully, I almost felt sorry for Kathy, because I remembered how badly she had been embarrassed last spring. She probably hated getting up in front of all of us. She was the last of the four speakers, and they'd all been pretty good. Mack gave me a nudge as she walked out onto the stage.

But calmly, Kathy took the podium with both hands—maybe her actress mom had given her some advice. She looked out at the audience and found me before she started. I gave her a quick wave and a smile. But then some goofball named Weasel Warren yelled out just as she leaned into the microphone, "Do the scene from 'Vampire Nurses!'"

We all knew the scene. It wasn't something most people admitted to seeing, but everyone knew it was when Mrs. Martin—Kathy's mom—died in the movie in a rather seductive manner. It'd been a little risqué, but chances were it was what got Kathy's mom in the big leagues in Columbus and eventually in a brand new Lincoln sedan with a lawyer husband.

Without missing a beat, Kathy grinned. "Mom will be thrilled to know folks are still watching that movie. We get a dollar every time it plays on TV."

The auditorium roared. Kathy continued, "Listen, Mifflin. I would love to be your sophomore attendant. If I don't win, I promise I won't sneak up behind you and bite your neck."

I actually voted for her, not that she needed my vote. She won in a landslide the following Monday during ballot day. In typewriting class, though, I made the mistake of wondering aloud to Melanie whether I should ask Kathy to go to the homecoming dance. Melanie looked at me like I had celery growing out of my nose.

"Larry, you're a sophomore."

"Yeah, so is she."

"You can't go to the dance unless you're asked by an upperclassman. Or in your case, upperclasswoman."

That was news to me. I blurted out, "Well she's in our class. How will she go?"

That's when Melanie gave me the full scoop: the star fullback of the Mifflin team had broken up with his flame of two years, he'd already asked Kathy, and she'd accepted. I regretted my vote immediately and even more the next morning when they arrived at school in Mr. Fullback's dad's classic Mercury woodie. Kathy got out of the car laughing and walking side by side with him.

All I could imagine after that was Kathy riding on the back of my Schwinn bike to the dance with Possum running alongside us. I went to the homecoming game that Friday night dejected and watched the homecoming court riding around the field in new convertibles, donated for the night by the same dealer E.A. had gotten to sponsor the parade—the Rats had been good advertisement. The fullback came out of the team meeting in uniform, face painted black like a warrior, and escorted Kathy to her place at midfield with the other girls. Once the queen—a senior named Patty Gallion and maybe the only girl more powerful than Aubrey—was announced, our fullback hugged Kathy while the Rat Pack lifted her off the field. My only comfort was the shellacking Mifflin received from Gahanna, 52-7. I smiled every time the fullback got crunched.

Saturday was spent raking the first crop of leaves and enjoying a handful of fires, plus 20 dollars more in my pocket. Mack swung by at 6:30 and asked if I was down for an adventure or if I was going to mope outside the homecoming dance at Mifflin.

"I'm a free man, Mack. What's the plan?"

"Wanna sneak in the back of the Linden Air drive-in? They're playing *The Alamo*."

"I can pay, ya know."

"Well, not really sneak in, Larry, they don't care as long as we buy food and be quiet. Never hurts to get a free entry. Plus, Butch and the gang are going!"

I swallowed and accepted that Kathy had come and gone like a whirlwind, and Lynn, well . . . it had almost been a month and a half. I was starting to think that maybe she was just a summer fling like everyone had said—but my friends had stuck around for good. I'd spent the whole day staring into the burning leaves thinking about the Linden-McKinley High School homecoming and which upperclassman was taking out a certain sophomore, and I wanted to forget it fast.

Once I'd gotten my shoes on, Mack coughed. "Oh, Possum's coming, too."

"Heck, I don't care."

E.A. was in from off the road for a few days, so of course they were out partying. I just locked the house and left a note on the counter.

We stopped at Henry's along the way and yelled his name from the sidewalk. After three minutes he came out in a cowboy hat about three sizes too large and was twirling a lariat and wearing chaps.

Mack beat me to it. "Henry, I'm gonna regret asking, but are you in another play at school? I'm not building another saloon or anything."

"Howdy, partners, I shore am. I'm a fixin' ta be in *Oklahoma*. I'm Dancing Cowboy Nummer Two in all the hootenannies."

"When is it, Henry?" I asked, knowing we would be seeing this till it was over and steeling myself for the answer.

"Well, partner, when the moon is full next month I'll be a-settin' tall in the saddle."

With that, we moseyed on to the corner of Woodland and Mecca, where Possum, Butch, and Marcie were waiting. Butch took one look at Henry and said, "Not a word, not a word 'in character' or whatever you call it, cowboy. If you so much as say 'ya'll' . . . "

With that, Henry lassoed the fire hydrant. Butch sighed loudly but got down to business. "Okay, we're going through Shanty Town, so just stay together. Larry, you've done this before, right? It's the fastest way to get to the rear of the Linden Air and we're late—"

Possum interrupted. "What? Are we sneaking in?"

Butch nodded.

"No, we should walk down Agler and Three-C highway to the entrance and pay. That's the only right way."

"Go ahead, Possum," Butch said as he started walking the opposite direction, towards Shanty town.

Possum turned to me. "Larry, you'll stick with me right? Can I bor—"

"I'd rather eat dirt, Possum," I said, a little mad that this was my evening while Kathy danced with a fullback and Lynn, well, who knew what Lynn was doing? He ran off and we were quickly in Shanty Town.

The streets, if the dusty clearings beneath the sick-looking locusts could be called that, seemed deserted tonight. The trees had dumped their leaves early but no one had asked me or anyone else to rake and burn them, so they just crunched underfoot. Near the edge of town was the big, bright glow of the same bonfire as before, and you could see the outlines of a lot of the residents. They all sat on logs from trees that had been cut down so they could watch the movies from the tall silver screen of the Linden Air, which hung in the distance. From where we were, we could already see the opening credits of the film.

"Evening Butch, how are ya?" The mayor was on his porch rocking with a puppy on his lap.

"Good, D.R. We're going to the movies. See ya got a new dog."

"Yeah, he just showed up. Y'all enjoy, and come back here for some moonshine if you're up ta it."

Butch looked at Marcie who shook her head. "Naw, but thanks D.R. We'll bring ya back some popcorn, though." The justice of the peace just chuckled and spat out a half-gallon of tobacco chew. Butch never stopped amazing me the way he always fit in anywhere outside of normal society. With outcasts, he was like a smooth politician running for senator.

After Shanty Town, it was an easy climb up a hill to the rear of the drive-in. Marcie and Butch went to get food, and I realized this was their homecoming date: Butch was a junior who should have been a senior and could have gone. When they came back, I motioned to Mack and Henry to come with me to the concessions and give them some alone time.

The Linden Air drive-in was famous for what they called their Hickory Dog. They cooked all the hot dogs outdoors over a hickory fire until they blistered and were perfectly smoked, then drowned them and their buns in baked beans that had been sitting off to the side and were just as smoky. No boiling in grimy old water for them or rotating for eternity on oily rollers. It was one of the reasons the Linden Air was successful despite newer, bigger screens on the outskirts of Columbus. Plus, they kept real good root beer on tap. No cheap, knockoff root beer poured into paper cups; these were real glass bottles with enough sarsaparilla in the beer to open a drug store.

Mack and I ordered, with Mack ordering so much the guy actually thanked him twice. Henry walked up to the counter, with his oversized Hoss Cartwright hat sitting down over his ears so he had to lean his head back and look at the concessions guy down his nose. He had his lariat over his shoulder.

"I'll just take a plate of grub!"

The man was too tired for Henry's antics. "Listen, we don't give any theme discounts. We got dogs, candy, and popcorn, Hopalong."

"Welllll, partner, give me a big sarsaparilla and the hind leg of a steer." The man got a hot dog and poured a half-empty bottle of root beer into a paper cup.

"This is on the house if you don't come back. So far, you're the weirdest guy I've seen this week."

John Wayne and Frankie Avalon had just arrived at the Alamo when a couple of hoods came over to us and stood in front of our view. We'd seen them making the rounds by the back row of cars. Two of them had leather jackets that dully reflected the light from the movie. The third one seemed to be the leader in a grimy tee shirt and a mechanic's coat that said "Toby" on the front.

"Okay, kiddoes, we're the drive-in movie police, and you're under arrest for not paying. Ya got two choices: one, pay a dollar fine, or two, give us your food and get out of here." With that, he flashed some kind of a badge.

"You ain't the police. I know what they look like. Get out of the way," said Butch, looking around him.

"Maybe we'll take your food, your money, and this ugly girl too. If she is a girl, that is," said one of the goons. That was a mistake. Butch came out of the folding chair like a cannonball. The punk tried to throw a punch but Butch was quicker and threw a right cross that knocked him on the ground. When he hit, I saw blood and teeth in the silver light of the screen.

"Toby, kill him!" the hood cried.

That's when everything started to happen at once.

The two others started for Butch. Mack and I stood in front of the second punk, then Henry lassoed him, sort of. It went over his head and dropped down around his waist before getting caught on his leather jacket's buckles. The guy on the ground was whimpering and looking for his tooth. Toby started for Butch, who by now was in his fighting stance, waiting. The hood who had been lassoed crawled out of the rope and started for Henry, who took off running like a giraffe with the top half chasing the bottom half, his 50-gallon hat flying along attached to his neck by a cord. Then he came back and faced Mack and me. I think he was trying to determine which one of us to try and go through.

Marcie yelled, "No, Butch! Don't fight! The police will come! No, no, NO!"

Toby laughed. "Even your girlfriend don't want you to fight. What's your last name, Butchy, so I can get the tombstone right?"

"His name is Butch Fuller, and you're the one gonna need a tombstone," Mack yelled. He had taken his eye off the third hood, leaving me alone with him. I wasn't too scared; I just hoped some of the stuff Butch had shown us wouldn't fail me now. But Toby took a step back.

"Crap, you're Butch F-f-fuller?" But Butch wasn't talking. He was in full go mode, calmly waiting for Toby to make his move.

"Yes, he is," Marcie said off to the side.

Toby was stammering now. "Uh, you're the bouncer at Blackjack's Pool Hall, aren't you? Sorry, it's just dark here, uh . . . " Butch was calming down a little. Maybe it was hearing Marcie's voice.

"Was. Now I'm a farmer. Still know a few things."

Toby turned to the other guys, including the one who had found his tooth. "I told you it looked like him. You guys are idiots. Sorry, Butch, just a little mistaken identity here. We're leaving."

"No. Not until he apologizes to her."

"Go on, Willie, you still got a tongue."

"Sorrphy."

Butch shook his head, and Toby kicked Willie in the leg. "Like you mean it!"

"I'm sorphy for sayphying that about you, I was wyphong."

Butch wasn't completely happy with that, but Marcie told them to get out of there. The people in the cars around us were looking at us, and it only took one complaint to the police to land Butch back in juvy with that witch of a corrections officer. Lucky for us, there were no more hoods after that, and we got to watch John Wayne die bravely after killing ten thousand Mexican soldiers.

We parted ways outside Shanty Town after the flick, with Mack and I hanging a right onto Mecca. I wasn't quite sure what had happened to Henry or Possum. Of course, Mack's house was completely pitch dark. Instead of going in the front door, we went in through his bedroom window like I had a few weeks earlier.

"Your parents ever home, Mack?"

"Nah, same as yours, always out partying." We raided the fridge for some cold cuts and cheese. "Listen, Larry, can I ask you something? I kind of need your help."

"Sure Mack, what is it?"

"Look, I miss Trish. Will ya help me win her back? Looking at Marcie and Butch, and . . . seeing how sad you've been without Lynn and missing out on Kathy, it makes me realize that maybe . . . I had a good thing. Maybe . . . I'm willing to do some different stuff to keep her around."

"Wow, Mack, that's a one-eighty."

"Nah," he said, cracking open a Coke. "Just not a three-sixty." He made a ring around his nose with his fingers. We laughed, and I agreed to do what I could with Trish.

CHAPTER
TWELVE

I was in my room studying that Saturday when Dad called the house and said he had a surprise if I was willing to stay over that evening at his house in Sunbury. Surprises weren't really Dad's thing, but I think I shocked him more when I agreed to come up and spend the night without even hesitating. My social life had kind of dried up due to how much me and Mack had been working as of late at our respective jobs, and Butch of all people was inseparable from Marcie. How different it all was from that summer, when the three of us had girls and typically the six of us were together. Now, it was just Butch and Marcie. I figured in two years, they'd get married, once they both were eighteen.

But a girl-less life made time feel like it had no meaning. I was doing a good job staying busy and distracted, to the point that some days I didn't even really think about Lynn or Kathy: cleaning yards, mowing, minor maintenance jobs here and there. Doris at the deli even convinced me to help her stock the store one evening when her usual help wasn't able to come. Suddenly, it was getting to be late October and I'd really not done anything besides make money.

Figuring Dad had gotten a new car and his old Buick was mine, I jumped at the chance to actually do something other than work that weekend.

There was a surprise alright when we got to his house. Sitting on the porch swing, reading *Little Women*, was a woman he had dated several years prior when I was about 12. I had nicknamed her "The Ice Queen," then, and four years hadn't changed much.

As we got out of the car, Dad said "Betsy, you remember Larry, my son."

"How do you do, ma'am?" I asked, figuring there was still time to talk Dad out of this. As it turns out, there wasn't.

"Larry, this . . . is my wife! We got married at the courthouse, just the two of us." I struggled to keep my jaw from dropping as she shook my hand formally.

I swear I tried to be nice, but nothing worked. It was the longest evening I had ever experienced in my life. Betsy was 44, five years older than Dad, but had never been around any kids other than her nieces and nephews. She took an instant dislike to me when I told her no, I did not not want to take a bubble bath that evening. I was fuming, thinking of the hoods Butch and Mack and me had almost beaten up several weeks before—and she wanted me to hop into pink bathtub of bubbles!

"That's what my nieces and nephews like to do," she said, a little tense. The bath smelled like bubble gum.

"They're six or seven years old!" I said.

It was downhill from there. No snacks, according to the list of rules posted in the kitchen. Breakfast was half an over-easy egg, a dry piece of rye toast, and a dixie cup of prune juice. I think the other half of the egg was supposed to be for the next morning. Dad and I had planned to go flying that morning but ended up staying in the living room as she was afraid that Dad would miss the weekly outing with her parents. So Dad took me home after Sunday's lunch—a small piece of liver with a side of dry, lima beans.

On the way home Dad said, "Give her time, Larry, I think she likes you."

"Dad, I want to see you, but . . ." I summoned up all the courage I had from feeling grown up. "I don't want to come back here again unless you or Mom make me."

I could tell Dad was hurt but he said he understood. "Betsy comes from a very old-fashioned, strict family, Larry. She tries to fit in but . . ." At that point his voice trailed off and we rode in silence. Then he spoke again. "After the divorce with your mom, a friend of mine introduced us. She was there when I needed someone, Larry, and that means a lot to you when you're smarting from a divorce. When I was overseas working on planes, she'd send me letters and things from back home that wouldn't go stale. We began a kind of long-distance romance, I flew her to Hawaii when I had a short leave—separate accommodations, of course—but we got engaged on the beach at sunset." He smiled at the memory.

I tried to see my dad as human, which meant I had to try to see his new wife as human. Mom had been a partier, so maybe having someone who went to bed at nine was a relief. I swallowed and said, "I'll give it time, Dad. But I think day visits for a while would be nice . . . until I get to know her a little better?"

That made him smile so I felt a little better, even though I was swearing in my mind to never see Betsy again. As I got out, Dad leaned over.

"Oh, say hello to Lynn, I really liked her. Maybe the four of us could go out to eat sometime, Betsy would like her, too."

"We're not together anymore."

"Oh, I see. Well, I'm sorry . . . anyway, I'll work something out with your mom about seeing you down here. Maybe Betsy can come down in a month for lunch?"

On the bus the next day, I told Mack that it was awful, just awful.

"Did you at least go flying? Or did you go back out to your folk's farm?"

"No. We were prisoners. It was the worst two days of my life."

"Tell us!" Butch turned around. "But be quick before the bus picks Marcie up. She always has to defend people." I noticed that two rows back, Trish was leaning forward in her seat to hear.

"Basically, my dad got married to a woman I used to call the Ice Queen when I was 12. He wanted it to be a surprise. Well, maybe she's nice to him, but she seemed to think I'm still 12. She actually had a tub filled with soap bubbles for me and wanted Dad to take a picture for their album like I was some kid. After I managed to get out of that, we spent the evening looking at her family's photo album and watching some dumb musical about a young girl in New York."

At that point Trish leaned forward and exclaimed, "Oh, yes, Love's Perfect Stranger! I watched it too. . . . " She looked at Mack. "But I had to watch it by myself." He and Butch rolled their eyes, but Mack was blushing a little bit. We were at Marcie's and she bounced onboard.

"Hey gang, what's new?"

"Larry took a bubble bath this weekend!" Mack shouted, trying to draw attention away from himself.

"I did not, you wastoid!" I yelled as I put him in a headlock. Trish leaned back in her row and looked pretty proud of herself.

Despite everything with Mack, Trish was sitting pretty tall in the saddle as of late. One of the non-royalty events that had happened during the school pageant elections was that Trish had been elected to student council; it was less showy, but technically had more power. She seemed far happier at Mifflin than she had been the year before, and certainly more busy. She had tactfully implemented some ideas I knew came from Linden, like having a student cheering section to work with the cheerleaders at basketball games. Thanks to her regular meetings, it just so happened that afternoon that we both stayed late for meetings and ended up walking home together. I'd made up my mind to bring up Mack's willingness to start things up again, but Trish beat me to another topic.

"Do you know it's been almost a month since you have asked me about Lynn?" she said coyly, looking over the Granite Bridge at the Alum Creek rolling by as its usual muddy brown self.

"Trish, look, she's been absolutely AWOL." I didn't mention that I'd kept one of the football programs that had pictures of all the homecoming court—Kathy included—on my desk for a week. "It hurts to hold on, so I won't. I don't expect anything from anyone." Trish didn't have a response for a few minutes. Finally, she stopped us in front of the Blain's farm and looked me in the eyes.

"Larry, if you really care for her . . . be patient. You think this is fun, having your best friend disappear? But I know her better than you and I know that whatever it is, it's serious!"

"Serious enough to not even call you?"

Her voice rose again, "Larry, next to Mack pre-break-up, you've become the best guy friend I have here . . . so drop it. I've known her ten times longer than I've known you. Look, maybe she has talked to me. Maybe I do know a little more than you. But it's awful and if you knew what'd happened you'd . . . try to fix everything, like you always do, you know? And that's not for Lynn. At least not now."

Well, this was news to me. "How can there even be a future if I can't do anything for her?"

"She may let you pay for her burgers, but she's not the sort of girl who is going to come whining to her guy. She has to work this out. And she's going to work it out on her own. If there's anyone more stubborn than you, it's Lynn, by a landslide."

I felt irritated but remembered I was here for Mack, not me, so I changed the subject. "All right, let's table it for now, Trish. Look, are you going to do anything about getting Mack back or are you just going to take potshots at him from two rows back the entire year?"

"Get him back? He's got to do the getting!" she said, but she was smiling.

"Romance takes two people," I shot back. "Look Trish, he wants another chance. He knows he was rude and says he's sorry."

"Maybe he's told you, but he hasn't told me."

"Well, I believe him."

"Do you? Because I won't put up with the way he acted again."

I wanted to say I felt the same about Lynn, but this was for Mack. "Yes, Trish, I do."

"Then you may tell him to call me, and we'll see."

Her comments left me feeling strangely angry as I saw Lynn's feather clip in my drawer when I went to grab a pencil that night. I admit, I felt a little betrayed. I fumed around by myself a little in my bedroom before going downstairs for one of the rare evening dinners when E.A. was at home. Mom had made a big pot roast, and even though it was Monday E.A. was celebrating the "mid weekend," as he called this three days back home every seven. I could hear him belting out Dave Dudley's "Six Days on the Road." He finished with a little shimmy in his chair as he stabbed the roast with a big fork and plopped a half-pound on my plate, then dumped carrots and peas and taters on with the ladle. Mom sure knew how to cook.

"Chuh, bud, if they don't draft ya in two years maybe I can get ya a job riding with me. Wanna see the world?"

"Thanks, E.A.," I sighed. I had a mental image of me and him riding along in a Peterbilt truck singing truck songs and eating greasy food three times a day. Chuh, Bub!

"We could be a tandem team and start driving long hauls out to the West Coast. That's where the real money is," he said. Then, under his breath, "Bub, some of them truck-stop waitresses out in the Rockies ain't bad, chuh!"

"Edward!" Mom said, whacking him with a spatula. It was probably the only time I'd ever heard his, uh, Christian name, I guess.

"Uh, yeah, E.A., I'm not sure that would be the life for me. Motion sickness and all, right?" E.A. considered the case closed and went back to Dave Dudley.

The next day at lunch, Possum sat down beside me just as I was watching Kathy three tables away and straining to pick up the conversation between her and Aubrey. I noticed she was no longer an item with Mr. Fullback and hadn't been for at least a week. There had to be a window of opportunity I was missing out on because Aubrey was too busy plotting. Of course, Possum sat right in my line of sight.

He got to his point pretty quick: he'd gotten suspended for two weeks from his paper route with the Columbus Dispatch because he had spent the money he owed the paper from his customers on a guitar for his band. He wasn't in trouble, legally; his dad covered his bill. But it was his parents who were punishing him. He had forgotten to tell the Dispatch they needed a new paperboy, and they naturally assumed the papers were going to be delivered.

"That's where you come in! Will you carry my route for two weeks, Larry? I'd pay you 20 American dollars. Please, friend of friends?"

"Ask Henry, since you're such good buddies."

"I don't want anyone else to know. I can only trust you. My parents are serious. They won't even let me out of the house."

All the leaves had fallen and I'd raked and burnt most of them, so I figured my work schedule was wide open until it started snowing again. I had the money for my varsity jacket next spring after I lettered, but another 20 dollars would let me buy my letter sweater too.

"Okay, Possum, 20 dollars for two weeks."

I went to his house the next day and took his books, paper bag and route chart. He invited me to dinner, but the smells coming from the kitchen made me want to retch and I began to believe that the stories I had heard about his family eating possum stew were true.

The next two weeks in the increasingly dim evenings, I carried his paper route with no accidents. The only hiccup was Sunday; I missed one house and the owner called Possum, who called me. I hustled out there and got him his paper by mid-afternoon, although he chewed me out about how I'd ruined his Sunday routine. Other than that, I didn't see anyone, except one day when Mack accompanied me on the route. He hadn't screwed up the courage to call Trish quite yet.

"Mack, act now, today, right now!" I said, like E.A. on one of his sales calls. "Before someone else moves in on her."

"All right, all right," he said as tossed a newspaper squarely into one customer's open car door.

I'd begun to notice life came in bursts and lulls; school was quiet, and Kathy was definitely free again. Aubrey said she was busy downtown at her dad's law office, and I should be so lucky as to have a job like that; they'd overheard that I was delivering papers. Aubrey made it seem like if I asked her out now, Kathy would deny my very existence, so I waited. The WOW Book, though, almost gave me enough confidence to go around her.

The night of the last football game was the same night I had to collect the money for the paper and be done with Possum's route, and I was glad for the distraction. I didn't feel like watching Kathy go onto the field one more time with Mr. Fullback, even if he had been nowhere near her side during school. As I made my rounds and imagined I could hear the crowd cheering for her miles away, I noticed that 2203 Northglenn was four weeks behind. That meant even Possum had forgotten to go there and collect. Or was too scared.

In the last months, Mack and I had started following Thunderchief from E.A.'s Fourth of July, and I quickly learned he lived in a lonely bungalow at the end of a cul-de-sac in west Northglenn. Mack had said he had threatened construction crews who'd arrived to construct his neighbors' homes with his famous tomahawk and that was why that cul-de-sac had remained wild and woody except for the Thunderchief residence.

If I'd known as much about Thunderchief back in July as I knew about him then, I probably would have warned E.A. against putting him anywhere near women and children. He wasn't just a star of the Chevrolet Wrestling Hour; he was its central figure, and his segment's body count was high. He had a horrible temper, and he occasionally scalped his opponents right on TV. Mack and I even saw him put a guy in the deadly totem pole hold and kill him one night. There was no return if he got you in that hold, but for some reason the television studios continued to film it for guys like Mack and me on our grainy 12×12-inch screens.

But the balance on the account threatened to put a big dent in my cut for doing Possum's route, so up the steps I went after a big breath of the cool evening air. Cautiously, I knocked on the door. Some people said TV wrestling was fake, but I wasn't sure about that. There was no denying it was funny, when you were safely separated from the Chief by a couple of rayon tubes and fifty miles. But even if people did live after meeting the Chief, you really couldn't deny some of the injuries they came out of the ring with. Butch said we were dumb to watch it, so around him we laughed and made fun of it, but privately we both knew the Thunderchief was probably a direct descendant of Sitting Bull.

A pleasant-looking woman answered the door.

"Yes?"

"Dispatch, ma'am."

"Oh, just leave it by the door."

"Can't. Uh, I want to, but you're about four weeks behind on your dues, ma'am. They won't let me deliver without collecting first."

"Well, you need to see George, dear. He's in the back watching TV. Come on in."

That was a relief. Maybe George was a mild-mannered relative, a brother or cousin who took care of the place while Chief was rampaging through the tri-state area.

As we walked through a warm and well-furnished home, the woman asked where the regular boy was. When I replied he was sick, she chuckled.

"Oh, dear. Well, he's so odd, maybe he needed a break. George, pay this young man."

I nearly leapt for the window. There, in the living room, was the Chief himself! Just jeans, no shirt. He was flexing his pecs like he did on television, just for fun, and I knew the tomahawk was close by. And he was laughing like a maniac. On his new color TV was a cigarette commercial about frogs on a lily pad singing the words "Johnny Smoker, Johnny Smoker, can you play your violin?" When they got to the second part, the middle frog would roll his eyes crazily and the Chief would bust out laughing.

"George, George, turn that stupid thing off. You owe this young man money for the paper."

The chief clicked the television off and stood up to his full height, which seemed somewhere north of six-foot-six. From experience, I knew the chief did not speak English, just catch phrases like "Chief not like white man or his talk;" I figured his wife would interpret for us. But to my surprise, he quietly reached under a magazine and pulled out his wallet.

"Oh, I was wondering why you'd not collected lately," he said calmly, though still wiping tears from his eyes from laughing. "How much do I owe you?"

"Four weeks, Mr. Chief," I gulped. "Two dollars and 60 cents." Here it came, the totem pole hold. I loosened up like I remembered Butch telling me to do if a tough guy put you in a hold. You broke less bones that way.

He pulled out three dollars and said to keep the change. "Just Mr. Agnew to you. So, you know who I am?"

"Oh, yes, sir, I watched you almost win the world championship a few weeks ago against Flying Fred. You would have won if you hadn't gone to get your tomahawk and let him hit you with the chair . . . but it made sense that you did, sir, I would have, too," I added.

He thought about that. "Oh, yeah. Taped that match last July. You know that's all on tape, don't you? The announcer just sets up in a sound booth and acts like he's announcing the match, we tape our interviews, and they splice them in. The boys in editing help it make sense. Some days I tape three or four matches. Sometimes there's an audience. They usually dub that in too, though." My eyes must have grown wide because he chuckled. "Have you ever noticed that it's always the same people in the crowd?"

I guessed the chief figured I was past the age of believing everything I saw on TV, so I didn't feel too sheepish.

"So, Chief, do you really hate Flying Fred, then?" I asked, risking one last well-known fact.

"Freddy? He's my best pal. He's got a boat up at Lake Erie. We fish around the islands whenever we get a chance. Great guy. Hey, don't be telling everybody my secrets, okay?"

I felt pretty special after getting the low-down from the chief as I walked down Northglenn Drive back home. He'd even said to come back when it started snowing and he'd contract his driveway out to me for the whole winter. That was a win and sure bragging rights.

Saturday morning, I went to give Possum back his gear and get my money. But after I handed him the bag and the customer's cash, he just said "thanks!" and closed the door.

I knocked again. "Uh, Possum, what about my twenty dollars?"

"Larry, I don't have that kind of cash laying around." He started to close the door again, but I put my boot toe in the way. They were gramps's old steel-toes, so Possum could squeeze all day long.

"Sure you do, I just gave it to you." He came out and closed the door so his parents wouldn't hear.

"Larry, I owed my folks for the guitar and I took it from the band's funds. But now I owe them and they'll quit and form their own group if I don't pay them something. Help me out, will ya? I promise that I'll play at your wedding for free someday."

I wanted to tell him hopefully that when that day came we would not know each other, but after 10 more minutes of senseless conversation I let it go. "Okay, Possum, you're obviously in some kind of trouble, so this one's on the house. But see if I ever run your papers again."

"Thank you, Larry. I promise, the band is on the verge of making it big!"

Maybe it was life paying me back for Possum's sake, but starting that next Monday, things suddenly got better. At lunch, Roxanne showed me her latest "Overheard in the Hallway" gossip column. The headline read:

MIFFLIN'S ROMEO SNUBS SOPHOMORE ATTENDANT

The article detailed how Mr. Fullback was now back with his old flame, with an actual quote (according to Roxanne) from him saying he was just giving "the kid" —Kathy—a break by taking her out to the homecoming dance. This was after the old girlfriend ran out onto the field during the football team's last game, when I was at the Chief's, and walked in with him in Kathy's place, hence the snub.

"How's Kathy feeling about all this?" I asked Roxanne. "Did you try and get a quote from her?"

"Oh, I only get quotes from people I don't like. She's fine. She's even ok with being jilted by him, I think she has her eye on someone else." Then Roxanne winked at me. I admit, the room felt like it spun a little. "Something good has happened to that girl's confidence, at least, since her homecoming speech with the vampires. But you know all about that."

"Wha-huh?"

"Rumor has it that you're the one who smiled at her when she started her speech, and that helped her get through it and make the gag about her mom's old movie. She's been talking about it ever since, even at play practice a few days ago. My sources told me all about that. So? Did you smile and give her a look?" I noticed Roxanne now had her notebook out.

"Yeah, I did. End of quote." Roxanne smirked and got up. "Wait, Roxanne. You said 'play practice.' She's going to be in the drama club play?"

"I told ya, something changed when she was elected to the court and you smiled at her. She signed up for all sorts of stuff. When's the last time you talked to her?"

"Uh, typing class at the beginning of the year?" I said. I realized everything I was saying was on the record so I zipped my lips shut.

Roxanne went off to collect dirt for her next piece, and I basked in the moment for a while. Then she reappeared.

"Look, here's a free tip in case you're being a typical dense guy." She slammed the table between each word for emphasis: "She! Likes! You!"

I got up that Saturday, the 16th of November, and headed for Maddie's Diner about 10:30, knowing they were re-opening that day and were sure to have a big crowd. With this news about Kathy, I was tired of playing games and waiting for Lynn to reappear, but there was still a part of me that felt like I owed her a final effort. If she or Trish wouldn't give me resolution, I'd get it myself. If she wasn't there, Dominic could fill me in. He'd remember me from the summer. Maybe they had moved away due to some family circumstances. I recalled her saying that her mom's parents lived in another state out in the big prairie. Either way, I knew I was happiest when there were no loose ends, and it wasn't fair to expect anyone else to tie them up for me.

"Larry, you have just been putting this off because you know it's over, man, move on," I said, giving myself a pep talk as my tennis shoes pounded the pavement. But I couldn't believe what I saw as I ran into the parking lot.

The old house beside Maddie's had been torn down. The parking lot had poured over into where it stood and the restaurant was easily doubled in size, with shiny new red stripes around the roof and flashy neon on the inside and out. It had been almost exactly three and a half months since I had been here, but it looked like years. There was a sign out front, too: "Closed until December 1, Remodel Taking Longer than Expected."

That took the wind out of my sails. I was ready to get my resolution with Lynn, but for nothing at all to happen was the worst thing. So I thought a lot for the rest of the weekend about the best way to put an end to the Lynn affair in a way that didn't make me feel like a chump. When Monday came, I got it.

With a smirk on her face, Aubrey sat down beside me in home room and started in immediately.

"Hooooww would you like to be Kathy's escort to the drama club after-play party on the 22nd of this month?"

That was this coming Friday night! I thought. Aubrey continued.

"She is in the play *Our Town* if you've not already gathered that from talking to Miss Dear Abby at the newspaper. Yes, I still watch you, even if I've been punishing you for not caring about what Auntie Aubrey thinks."

I bristled. "Well, I, uh . . . "

"Annnnnd she would love for you to ask her."

I decided to take the offensive. "Two things, Aubrey," I countered. "One, has she run out of upperclassmen to take her? And two, why doesn't she just ask me herself?"

"Because, ass-brains, I'm her best friend and I love being a matchmaker. At the rate you guys go, you'd be lucky if she kissed you this century."

"Why don't you just let us figure it out? Go help Lesser Brenda if you want to matchmake."

"Oooh, testy today, aren't we?"

"No, Aubrey, but life isn't a chessboard and I don't like being a pawn. Leave my Oreos alone," I added as she rifled through my lunch. Pushing her hand out of my lunch sack, I quickly weighed the facts a final time.

Lynn had disappeared and not even contacted me. I mean, she could have called me on a pay phone, she could have mailed me a letter. I disliked how Trish was holding out on me, too. That could go on for forever. Still, Lynn and I had been as much of a couple as any of the other innocent romantic twosomes that had popped up at Morningside last summer. We even had started making plans about when we could really date, maybe beyond that.

Kathy, on the other hand, was an unknown even after a thousand near-misses. A very beautiful, shy person who was still interested in me after all this. That meant there was something real there. Maybe my smile had sealed the deal. My memory of the speech was starting to grow more and more like Roxanne's version of things. I could feel Aubrey looking at me, so I sped up my thoughts.

For a girl who came from a wealthy family with everything she wanted, Kathy seemed well-grounded. I often wondered why she was in the Rat Pack. She didn't need them, and they seemed like a bunch of loudmouths in contrast to her usual reserved self. While they pushed the school's dress code, she always was dressed like a model in the high-end section of the Penney's catalogues Mom brought home, with great outfits and matching accessories. But for all that, once that fall I had seen a girl from Shanty Town going through the lunch line until she was turned away when she couldn't pay. Without saying a word to anyone, Kathy ditched the line and paid the attendant. I heard her lean over to the girl and say, "It's okay," then vanish. No waiting for compliments, just a little act of kindness.

Suddenly, it clicked. It was time.

"I'll do it, Aubrey. Only if you stop eating my lunch."

Aubrey looked shocked. I think she was enjoying me putting up a fight. But she recovered quickly.

"Great, Larry. Uh, wear a nice shirt and tie. Really talk to her about anything but baseball. Talk about the play and get her a rose. This is her first attempt at acting and, well, you know her mother was famous."

"Oh, I know about *Vampire Nurses*. And wasn't she the girl who hit Moe in the head with a brick in *Stooges Conquer New York*, too?"

"Okay, have your fun. Maybe you've learned some tricks from me, playing all hard to get. You are kind of a celebrity with the girls around school you know. I heard girls in gym class saying, 'Oh, I wish my boyfriend would smile at me like that!'"

Now the memory was cemented in my mind after hearing it retold by Roxanne and Aubrey. It was me beaming at Kathy in front of thousands of Mifflinites with the kind of applause Mickey Mantle got after a grand slam World Series home run.

"I'll eat lunch with her Friday, okay?" I asked, since Kathy was usually around on Fridays and not in Columbus.

Now Aubrey was back in form. "Nope. You can't, her civics class is down watching live trials at the Franklin County Courthouse this week. But maybe you could see her in the morning before they leave for court. . . . I'll be there, too."

On Friday, I made a point of being near her locker and looking cool. She was there talking to yet another Rat Pack pledge. I waited and when she saw me, she actually smiled and waved . . . and in her hushed voice, said, "See ya tonight!" before trotting off.

At lunch I was saving a seat for a friend from the baseball team who I hoped might be able to provide some tips, since he'd dated a decent amount. I was thinking about the questions I wanted to ask when I smelled very expensive perfume and turned as Kathy sat down by me.

She had on a beautiful brown plaid dress and jacket, with a black sweater underneath. Her strawberry blonde hair was perfectly combed in its shoulder-length style. It was like having lunch with a model. Ten months ago I would have mumbled something about as awkward as I did with Elaine on the famous mustard-kissing-bandit adventure. But not today!

"Thought you were on a field trip at the courthouse."

Contrary to her usual whisper in Aubrey's presence, she spoke right up. "No, I didn't go, actually. I figured you and I are going out tonight, and I am going to eat lunch with you. We are going to get to know each other before we have this long-overdue date. Does that sound fair to you?"

I gulped and nodded, then tried to crack that famous smile. She returned it with ease.

"Well, look, If Possum comes over to sing this time, at least I know you aren't responsible," she teased.

That put me at ease. Possum didn't come, although our shortstop sat down on the other side, but he quickly saw what was happening and high-tailed it out of there. For about 10 minutes we talked slowly and awkwardly, but then it caught on. We went outside and sat down after we ate.

"Listen, I do want to thank you for the grin you gave me during homecoming elections. It helped more than you know," she confided. "I was scared, Larry, I really didn't want to be up there. When your mother's an actress, everyone thinks you're comfortable up on stage, too, but . . . I looked out and wanted to run, but I saw you and it helped."

"Oh, that? That was nothing. Just wanted you to get up there and be yourself."

"I was hoping we would get to know each other last summer at the pool. You know, I was going to ask you to my family's Fourth of July barbecue, but you were always with the girl from Linden. Uh, are you two . . . "

"If you're going to ask me if we're a couple, I've not seen her for almost three and a half months." I was trying to be so polite: something about her made you feel like you were talking to the first lady, Jackie Kennedy. Kathy was so instantly likable. Just a small grin creased her face. Remembering her experience with Cubby, I continued, "I don't two-time girls."

The conversation flew by and after the bell rang, we seemed to teleport in front of the door of her English class. She turned to me before opening the door. "Well, after the play tonight, meet me in the cafeteria. That's where the party is. It's just cake and ice cream. By the way, I'm Mrs. Gibbs in the play. I'm wearing a lot of makeup to look older."

"I'm sure you'll look great even 40 years from now!"

She laughed, then actually reached over and touched my hand. "Listen, I'm allowed to date, but Mom likes to meet the guys I go out with." I must have furrowed my eyes at the "guys" part, because she continued. "I've only dated Joe, the fullback, and that didn't turn out so great. Mom is one of the host mothers tonight, so sometime I want to introduce you to her this evening, if that's okay."

"Sure thing, Kathy." Inwardly, I relished the fact that she didn't count Cubby last summer as a date. I felt like the biggest man in the school as I headed to my next class.

The day dragged on like a trip to the dentist office. By the time seventh period Spanish class started, I felt like years had gone by. I was doing the math on exactly how many minutes remained until I'd be able to see Kathy again after the play, when a little after 1:30 the PA system came on. It was the principal, Mr. Sullivan.

"Students . . . we are getting word that President Kennedy has been shot in Dallas." The classroom gasped. I thought for sure I could hear Mr. Sullivan's secretary sob off to the side of the mic. "At this time we really don't know much. But he appears to be alive and is in the hospital. Please remain calm and stay at your desks."

CHAPTER
THIRTEEN

en minutes went by with the entire school as silent as a winter's midnight. Then, the PA came back on. Mr Sullivan cleared his throat, started to speak, lost his voice and tried again.

"Students, I regret to tell you: our President is dead." He paused. "I have ordered the school closed, and all extra activities are canceled until further notice. You will be notified on the news stations about school resuming. That is all."

Of course, that meant no play, and it was just as well. I ended up walking home. I had missed the bus because I wanted to try and see Kathy, but she was in a meeting with the drama club. I assumed they were discussing when the play would go on now that this terrible thing had happened. And with each step the full weight of the world seemed to hit me.

Mom was home when I got there; Penney's had closed as soon as they heard the news.

"Ed will be home from his trip to Ann Arbor at about 7:00 tonight. . . . We got off about 2:00. We didn't even put away the carts for what we were stocking."

"Anything new on the radio?"

"They think they've got him. Apparently, he's killed a police officer too."

We watched the same news over and over on the television. Every once in a while some new little thing would pop in, but mostly it was newscasters reading the same report: John F. Kennedy was dead.

At about 3:30 we were told Lyndon Johnson was now our president. The pictures of Jackie standing by Johnson as they swore him in on Air Force One, the president's blood still on her clothes, were heartbreaking, and Mom was crying. I tried to comfort her but realized there wasn't much I could do, and I felt pretty low myself. Finally, I said I was going out and asked if she'd be okay.

"Yeah, I am going to start a big pot of chili for Ed. We'll eat when he gets in. If you're hungry, there's sandwich stuff and cheese in the fridge." I wasn't, so I walked off to the woods and came to the tree I had carved Lynn's initials on. I took out my pocket knife and carved the president's initials and the date.

Then I walked to the other side and put my hand over my and Lynn's initials. Part of me wanted Lynn to be here just to hold her. This seemed like the sort of thing that'd be easier if there was just someone there to bear it with you. We had talked many times about how much we loved our president, like every person under the age of 40 in America. Maybe, magically, it would be better if she were here. Maybe everything would be OK. Maybe it was selfish to think about romance at a time like this.

Nothing in my world would ever be the same, or so it seemed. My first love had come and gone. The nation's president was gone, and life was upside down. I sat in front of the tree for a few thoughtful minutes in the cold November breeze and then hit the trail.

Like school, the neighborhood seemed dead; lights were off when they should have been on. The only light seemed to be the flicker of TVs. People sitting in the dark with just the tube for light.

The few people who were out hardly made eye contact. Those that did looked like they were in shock. I wondered if I looked like that to them.

At about 7:30, E.A. rolled in.

"Chuh, bub, the Mafia sent their calling card to old Joe Kennedy and his clan," was the first thing he said. Then he laughed. "Payback for him daring to cross them back in Boston."

"No, Ed, they got the guy," I insisted. "He's an ex-marine and he shot the president with a mail-order rifle. His name's Oswald. He's not even Italian."

Ed just chuh'd.

In the morning, I didn't feel like getting up. It was a Saturday, but it felt like the first Monday of a year of Mondays. It seemed easier to stare at the ceiling and pretend the world ended somewhere outside the house on this cold, gray day. Around 8:00 I convinced myself to get out of bed only to find Mom and E.A. getting ready to go to the Albers grocery store. I got cleaned up, turned the TV on, and helped myself to some pancakes and bacon Mom had left warming in the oven. Then I heard a knock on the door.

It was Henry and Teddy. Being Irish Catholic, I imagined this was especially hard for all of them—I could see Teddy had been crying. For once, Henry spoke to me as himself, not as some character in a play.

"Larry, we're, uh, going to a special mass to pray for the country. I know you liked the president too, even though . . . What are you, Methodist?" I nodded. "Well, would you like to come with us?" His parents and little sisters were in the car in the driveway.

"Thanks, Henry, I appreciate it. I think I'm just going to stay here today. But thanks for asking."

Teddy blurted out, "He's dead. He's dead!" and started bawling again. To my surprise, Henry put his arm around him and walked him to the car.

Like every red-blooded American boy, of course, I had a crush on Jackie. It was awful to see the look on her face whenever they showed the swearing in of LBJ, which was every 10 minutes when the newscaster ran out of reports to read. I was watching it for the third time when there was a soft knock on the door.

I mumbled to myself, "I bet it's Possum telling me he is flying to Dallas to help with the investigation." I even thought about not answering the door. But I heard the same knock again. I took a deep breath and went up front, ready to duck down and pretend I wasn't there. But when I looked out the window, I couldn't believe my eyes.

It was Lynn.

Her hair was longer, almost to the middle of her back. She had a Linden windbreaker jacket on but she was shivering. I stood looking at her like she was a mirage and felt like I was dreaming.

"Remember me?" she asked when I opened the door. I stuttered. "Lynn!"

"Can I come in? It's cold out here."

After all the dreams I had had about her, I wasn't sure that this was real. Maybe these last two days were just a dream: JFK was still alive, and Kathy wasn't any more a part of my life than she'd been that spring.

"Where have you been, Lynn?"

She didn't answer but looked around the kitchen.

"Do you have any coffee? I started walking this morning, and I couldn't sleep last night. I just listened to the radio say the same thing over and over, and then I made up my mind to come over here. I wasn't sure if I should stop. But I saw you talking to Henry so . . . here I am."

I warmed up the coffee percolator and had her stand over the floor register in the kitchen. She put so much cream and sugar in her cup it was more like a milkshake, but it was the way she liked it. When she saw the bacon in the fridge when I got the cream, she asked me to wrap a couple of pieces in a leftover pancake. It felt like I was in a *Twilight Zone* episode called "The Return of Lynn."

"Are your parents home?"

"No, they're at the grocery store. They'll be back in an hour."

"Is there somewhere we can go to talk that would be private for a little bit? I, uh, we need to talk if you want to."

"Of course . . . why don't we just sit here while you thaw out, first?"

She just sat right on top of the furnace grate. I turned the furnace up, and then I got down on the floor with her and pulled her close. Just her presence seemed to melt my heart even after all this time, although I had a growing feeling that I was betraying Kathy. It was so strange to be hugging Lynn and thinking about someone else, but there it was.

"I was afraid to come here, Larry, I have to admit," she quietly said. I started to speak but had to admit to myself I agreed. I thought about the feather clip she had given me, now sentenced to live in a drawer. Part of me almost felt like I should give it back.

"Let's go to the park, down to the foot bridge over the creek, Lynn. No one will be there today. Here . . . you need to wear something more than that windbreaker." I got her one of my big flannel shirts to put on underneath.

Lynn put it on and looked down at it and laughed. "I have dresses shorter than this!"

I was waiting for her to bring up the elephant in the room the entire way to the creek, and it seemed like she was waiting for me to ask as well. Finally, when we got to the bridge, she went first.

"Before I start, I want to say that I'm sorry for not being in touch with you." Before I had a chance to reply, she launched into a speech that I felt like she'd rehearsed over and over. "Larry, my mom got appendicitis the day after I left you at Trish's. She spent the next two weeks laid up in the hospital and then got an infection. The clinic was one of the big Methodist charity ones, but we could hardly afford just her not working. Then she was in bed for two months and I had to go back to work at the diner weekdays, weeknights, and weekends till they closed for remodeling, which stopped that. Then the cleaning service Mom works for said they had to let her go because two months was too long an absence, so I asked if I could take her place. Larry, we had enough for two weeks, not including rent. So I had to. I would take the bus down to Union Train Station in the afternoon and clean restrooms until ten, and then try to study on the way back. The school let me skip the last two periods each day. I was the low girl on the crew, so I got the worst jobs. Have you ever cleaned a men's room in a train station?"

"But Lynn," I said in surprise, "Band camp, you were supposed to go up to Cedar Point, and . . . "

"There was never time or money for it, Larry. Don't you get it? I never went. Mom was in the hospital. I had to stay with Kristy. How could I go up to band camp and leave my sister and Mom alone waiting for charity from the neighbors?" I felt like I'd said something hurtful so I just zipped it. Lynn gulped and continued. "Mom's back to work now. Even with me working, we never would have made it without Dominic's wife's help. She brought food and made sure Mom and Kristy were OK when I worked. I think she paid the rent in September. . . . Someday, we'll pay her back. Someday."

There were a couple of young boys fishing at the bridge. I started to tell them not to eat fish out of Sewer Creek, but realized as we got closer that they were really just smoking. When they saw us they lit out of there, but I just motioned to Lynn to keep walking. My legs seemed drawn to the initial tree. Part of me was sad about her miserable situation, but the other part of me was hurt. Who cares what Trish thought? I would have helped as best I could if only she had just asked.

We were now in front of the beech tree, and I showed her where I'd carved the president's name and the date yesterday in the thick papery bark. It was still fresh and a little damp, surrounded by other couples' names from long ago. She nodded and softly said that her name had never been carved on a big old tree like this before. Without a word, I took her to the other side and showed her what I'd carved months ago, although it seemed like years.

L. E.

+

L. B.

08/18/63

"That's the last day I saw you. Before all of this started. When'd you carve that?" she asked hopefully.

"About a week after you stopped showing up." She wiped a tear from her eye and I cleared my throat. "Lynn, I'm so very sorry about all this. I can't imagine how hard this is. . . . I know you and your family have had a very bad time." I didn't really know what to say. My concern had been replaced by hurt. How could I be a part of Lynn's life if in one of her worst moments she wouldn't even turn to me for comfort? Didn't I even mean enough for her to even reach out, as embarrassing as the situation was? Maybe our relationship hadn't been all I'd hoped. But I knew the smartest thing to do was keep quiet, so I didn't continue and let her keep talking about how awful working had been.

She showed me her red, dry hands, with her fingernails cut short. "This is from all the cleaning chemicals," she laughed. "I smell like Chlorox more than anything else these days. And I cut my fingernails short so I wouldn't get the dirt from those awful bathrooms under them . . . can you believe that men throw cigars in the toilets? And other stuff too." With that thought fresh in my mind I wasn't sure I wanted to eat, but it was all I had left to really offer Lynn. My mind was just kind of numb.

"On a completely unrelated note, I guess . . . you hungry at all, Lynn? If you are, we can head home. Mom has chili, and I'm sure E.A will make his special four-cheese grilled sandwiches."

"Ooo, that sounds good!" Lynn said cutely. She took my hand but then let it go when I didn't quite go for it. But as we walked back through the woods, she got close to me and tried again.

"Larry, I am sorry for not contacting you. Please don't be angry at Trish. She pleaded with me to let her tell you what was happening, but I guess I was just . . . so embarrassed. I kind of withdrew from her, too. Being here with you now makes it seem all so silly. Did I really have to put us through all this?"

"It's a good question," I said honestly. "but Trish is a good friend. She never lets you down."

"I just didn't want you to see me or my family in that condition, I just couldn't."

Then I blurted out, "I was your boyfriend!" I was going to continue but then realized that I'd said *was*. Either she didn't notice, or she let it go.

When we got to the house, Lynn saw the Bel Air in the driveway. "So is this your car when you're sixteen?"

"Yep," was all I said as I opened the house door with Lynn behind me. I wanted to quickly make sure E.A.'s mood hadn't changed. Mom had her back to me at the table; E.A. was further away reheating the chili, singing the chorus to the Barber of Seville at the top of his lungs.

"Figaro, figaro, fiiiiiiii . . . "

"Mom, you remember Lynn Bennett," I said loudly. Lynn did a little wave and gave that cheerful smile of hers.

"Of course I do!" Mom got up and hugged Lynn. "Oh, dear, you're so cold. Larry, you should have given her a warmer coat . . . oh, your grandpa's old flannel. Well, I must have raised you half right."

"Fiiiiga—" E.A. turned and did a double-take. Lynn then asked Mom where the ladies room was and was directed to Mom's personal, off-limits-to-me-and-E.A. bathroom by the stairs. Then E.A. whistled and said real low, "Is she a Hawaiian? Or Venezuelan? Or what is she?"

"She's a girl, E.A."

"Yeah, I can see that. Anyone with half an eyeball can see that."

I wasn't in the mood for nonsense, nor did I care what he thought at the moment, so I went for it. "She's Cherokee, Ed."

As we ate, Lynn watched me put about 15 crackers in my bowl.

"I'm sorry, Mrs. Darnell. I tried to teach him manners over at the diner last summer." I could tell Lynn was trying to test the waters with little humorous things. I almost felt sorry for her. I wanted to reach out and say she was fine, we were fine, just not to do it again, but I couldn't. I just couldn't go back to feeling like I had that summer.

Mom laughed. "You've done well, Lynn, he just likes a little chili with his cracker soup."

Over at the gas stove, E.A. was making his fancy grilled cheese sandwiches as promised, though I wish we'd skipped it instead of making this lunch go on any longer. He let loose another Figaro.

The TV was on and we heard the announcement that plans were being made for the state funeral on Monday. That seemed to dampen the mood a bit, and Lynn said suddenly that she needed to get back. "Even today, the trains are still running and the restrooms need to be cleaned," she said quietly when Mom was in the other room with E.A. She said goodbye, E.A. bowing like a butler, and we left.

When we walked by the deli, Doris had the place open and was watching the same old television broadcasts, and Lynn wanted more coffee.

"I've been living on this stuff for months," she said. "Everyone says it's either cigarettes or coffee that keeps you going, but I've seen what cigarettes do to your teeth. My smile might be my only ticket out of here," she winked.

"Jeez, Lynn," I said, watching her pour the milk and sugar. "You sure that's any better?"

"Yes," she insisted. "I can brush this out at night."

"If we walk a few more blocks, I can get you an A&W milkshake. It's the same thing."

I strangely felt myself losing interest in Lynn's shenanigans, and we really didn't say much the rest of the way. She was shivering despite the flannel jacket and my coat, which I had given her, and I was at a loss for words, so we just listened to the sound of the neighborhood slowly coming back to life. I was the sort of person who needed a day or two to digest things, and Lynn seemed to expect me to come to terms with her excuse for a four months' disappearance just like that.

Maybe I had just misread Lynn all summer. Maybe she was so independent she didn't need me or anyone else when the chips were down. And that was fine, but I guess I thought I was a major part of her life, and what was more, I wanted to be.

As we approached the apartment building where we always parted, she turned and smiled, although it seemed a little cautious.

"So . . . where do we stand, you and I? Us?"

"What do you mean?"

"I mean, can we get back together? Now that this is all behind me, or soon will be. Mom's going back to work, and I can finally have my life back."

I waited a full 10 seconds before quietly replying, "Lynn . . . I guess you could say that I've started going with someone else." Lynn's eyes bugged out.

"Who?"

"Just a girl at school, Lynn." She seemed to step back and screwed up her fists.

"Larry, I have been through a living . . . a living hell, these last four months. I came to you today because of what happened yesterday and because I felt so awful that I finally couldn't bear to hide it all from you anymore. I knew I should have talked to you sooner. I've said I'm sorry. So sue me for wanting to see the one positive thing in my life besides my mom and Kristy. I thought you'd be ready to understand it all and now, now, you've moved on and just tossed me aside? Who even are you?"

"I am not tossing you aside, I never did, Lynn. But after not hearing from or seeing you for three and a half months, I guess I did move on. I had to. I thought we were through. I tried everything, I came to Maddie's, I went over to Linden band practice one afternoon. I begged Trish to tell me something. I was even going to stand outside Linden High School in the morning but I figured I'd be picked up for truancy from Mifflin. Are you mad because I didn't stay down in the dumps for four months?"

That stopped her. I thought I saw a little tear in the corner of her eye. "Okay, I admit I should have contacted you. I'll admit it again. I was wrong, okay? Come on, what do you want from me?"

"I wanted to hear from you, Lynn. So I could at least help."

But Lynn came unhinged right then and there. "Help? You mean be the White Knight, again? Like you were at McDonald's, rescuing two poor girls with no ride home, then rescuing Butch from probation, oh, and of course rescuing Trish from her awful date at the fair?" She yelled. "Yeah, you bet I know about that!"

"That's just . . . what I do, Lynn."

"Well, sorry to have denied you the chance to rescue my mom and her two orphan daughters! Sorry I beat you to it! Here!"

She took off my jacket and started tugging at her windbreaker so hard the zipper broke, and I heard her stifle a sob. Then she took off my big flannel shirt and threw it at me. I peeled it off my face.

"I'd rather freeze than wear this another minute." She turned without a word and was gone.

CHAPTER
FOURTEEN

School didn't resume until the day after the president's funeral. The mood in the hallways and in the cafeteria was solemn, with kids walking like zombies, looking straight ahead. I admit I felt a little like that myself after the scene with Lynn, but like everyone my mind was mostly reeling from the flow of news surrounding JFK. After the accused gunman was murdered by a nightclub owner with criminal connections, I felt that we would never know the truth. In five short days, we had gone from innocent high school kids who only cared about classes, sports, silly pranks, and teenage romances to a mood of complete despair. It seemed like we had all aged like in one of those awful time-machine fast-forwards where they put makeup on the actor over the course of hours but made it seem like seconds. Now, as you sat in the cafeteria you would hear things like, "You know, he lived in Russia," "No way a guy could get off three or four shots with an old rifle like that in a few seconds," "There had to be at least two gunmen." In a week we all became forensics experts and nightly television watchers. You always felt like there was some new detail just about to be released; but nothing could bring him back, or Jackie's innocent smile, either.

After that, though, normalcy seemed to return like the first flurry of winter. The class play was rescheduled for the second Saturday of December, the 14th. People started talking about Christmas gifts and visiting grandparents. A few days after the funeral, I waited at Kathy's locker to talk to her to see if things were still the same. It wasn't that the assassination might have changed how we felt, but we were all mourning. Even Mack seemed glum and hadn't gone on many joy rides in his newly re-engined car.

"You're here early," she remarked as she hung up her coat.

"My friend Mack got the engine in his car, so I rode with him today. Kind of its maiden voyage. Hey, I saw on the bulletin board that the play's back on. It's okay if you say no, but do we still have a date for afterwards?"

She looked at me and smiled, her perfect teeth showing. I got distracted by her hazel green eyes, reddish-blonde hair, and very light freckles, and forgot what I had asked. "Uh, are your ancestors Scottish by any chance?

"Gee, how did you guess, Larry?"

"Girls from Scotland are always pretty," I said using my newfound romantic confidence, though I'd never seen any Scottish girls outside the Bond films when Mack and I snuck in and watched them at the Linden Air. Kathy connected two and two with ease.

"Yes, Mr. Connery, it's still a date."

"How about going to the basketball game this Friday as kind of a warm-up date first?" I held my breath.

"Sure!"

Wow! I was on a roll. But as confident as I was, inside I couldn't help but congratulate myself like I'd just won the lottery. The out-of-place farm boy was going on not one but two dates with Kathy Martin. And I didn't have to join the Gents!

As Friday came, I realized that I had been so absorbed with the Kennedy assassination I had not noticed that our first opponent for basketball was Linden-McKinley. But Lynn was in the past. I had asked Kathy to go, and whatever happened would happen. I walked over to the school that night and waited at the dropoff area for Kathy.

Soon enough, the new black Lincoln Continental convertible pulled up and muscled its way to the curb around the seniors' old junkers. Kathy was sitting on the passenger side. She rolled down the window and motioned to me.

"Larry, get in the back, I want to introduce you to Mom." I opened the door; the car was immaculate and smelled like the entire J.C. Penney fragrance section combined.

"Mom, this is Larry, the boy I've told you about. Larry, this is my mom, Beverly Martin." She turned and smiled.

"Kathy has said so many nice things about you, Larry."

I had never been in the presence of a movie star, not even a washed up movie star, which for some reason doesn't matter in person. Even though she was probably 20 years older, I recognized her as the young woman who had clobbered Moe with the brick in one of my favorite Stooge shorts. I politely said hello and thought to myself that this is Kathy in 25 years; the resemblance was unbelievable.

"Anyway, young man, it's so cold. Kathy said you probably walked or something. After the game, we'll take you home. No buts!"

"Thank you, Mrs Martin," I said. As Kathy and I got out of the car, the Linden-McKinley student buses were rumbling in. I couldn't help but glance over at the kids piling out. After a second, I didn't want to stand out there gawking at both buses, so we went on inside the school.

Kathy and I found a seat, but not in the student section, which was packed. "Larry, it's so loud there and it's nice to be able to talk . . . and basketball is not really my game."

"Oh?"

"I hope you won't just think I am saying this, but I like baseball, and I know you play. I watched you a couple times last spring. I just come to these games cause it's a social thing and Aubrey and Melanie are cheerleaders."

Our previous lunch date had been all the polite get-to-know-yous that didn't really mean anything. Once Kathy started to talk this time, I realized that she was totally different than I thought she was. We talked a bit about our semesters up until recently, and I mentioned that I saw her pay for the girl from Shanty Town's lunch. She blushed a bit and brushed it off.

"Sometimes, Larry, those kids go without eating."

"I know, I live near there and come in on the bus with most of them."

"Oh, I know where you live."

"How?"

She wrinkled her nose and laughed. "I have my sources, Larry."

After the reserve boys game was over, there was a show before the varsity teams played. Mr. Sullivan walked to the center court and took the mic. "Ladies and gentlemen, please rise for the national anthem." We all rocketed to our feet as we remembered our fallen president. But that was quickly eclipsed by the next line, "Tonight we, uh, have Mifflin's own Paul and Ralph Ramone, accompanied by their band."

"Oh no," I grimaced. "It's the Northglenners." There they were, the Ramone brothers, plus Crazy Mike and Possum, who were shouting "NORTHGLENNERS, NORTHGLENNERS" over the applause of the student section. Possum pulled a pitch pipe out, hit the note for the brothers, and began to accompany them on harmonica softly into the mic as they got to the "dawn's early light" part.

Kathy reached over and squeezed my hand, "He is kind of responsible for us meeting, you know." She kept giggling about Possum during the anthem and the people in front of us kept turning around. Finally she buried her head against my shoulder.

The old man in front of us turned and eyeballed me. I noticed he had a navy tattoo on his arm so I said assertively, "Uh, her brother is in the service. This reminds her of him." He gave me a short, snappy salute and turned around.

I admit, Paul and his brother could harmonize very well. Possum just provided a soft background for their a cappella rendition. It would have actually been great if Crazy Mike had not been going "doot-doo-do-wah, doot-doot-da-doo" all through the song. When they finished, Possum waved and handed out cards to Mr. Sullivan, the referees, and the team captains as he walked off the court.

Mifflin was no match for Linden, whose front three averaged six-five and whose guards were as quick as leopards. Mr. Fullback (now Mr. Point Guard) tried to dribble his way through them, but Linden played like pros and stripped the ball out of his hands every time. I was waiting for Kathy to make a comment about him; she seemed to sense that and turned and said as he fouled out of the game, "Okay, I know you're thinking it. I wanted to go with you the entire time. Aubrey will back me up on that. But we couldn't, Mom insisted I accept his offer and besides, we're both sophomores. Next year for sure," she said, squeezing my hand.

"That's fair."

"So what did you do on homecoming night, Larry?"

"I snuck into the Linden Air drive-in with Mack, Butch and Marcie and got into a fight. Well, Butch did."

"I would have rather done that! I've never really had any crazy adventures, ever."

That response almost knocked me off my seat. As pretty and proper as she was, I wondered if she would have worn a sweater and skirt to the drive-in. At the start of the fourth quarter, Kathy and I were hardly even paying attention to the game as we talked. One of my baseball friends came up the steps and said they were going to Brendan's Big Slice Pizza after the game. He offered to drive us home if we came with him and his girl.

"I have to call home," said Kathy, "but I think that's okay." We then went out to the lobby, but it was six deep at the payphone. "Just wait here. I'll just go up to the drama club room. There's a phone in there no one knows about."

I retreated to the wall and watched some of the Linden crowd already leaving. This had hardly been more than a practice for their team, so the away-team audience was pretty thin. In the distance, I could see Kathy coming back.

Then, all of a sudden, I felt a tap on my shoulder.

"Hi," I heard in a hushed whisper. I turned to see the back of Lynn as she slid away and vanished into the last of the Linden crowd.

I looked to see if Kathy saw that, but thankfully she'd stopped at the drinking fountain. "Can ya get me home by 11:00? If you can, I can go," she announced. My friend owed me a favor from that summer when I got a double that scored our winning run. He had won his pitching debut that game, so he just nodded when I asked. I looked around for Lynn as we got into his car, but the Linden buses were gone.

Brendan's Big Slice Pizza was the hangout for Mifflin after football and basketball games, complete with a musty party room that smelled like breadsticks. For game nights, it was a pizza buffet—all the pies from that day they had left over on single-slice orders—and if you wanted to go, you just paid a dollar per person for all you could eat and drink. Soda, of course! There were pictures of old Mifflin teams on the wall and the latest rock-and-roll blaring from the jukebox.

"I've never actually been here," Kathy said as we walked in and I snagged us two available seats.

"Really?" In the back of my mind, I figured Mr. Fullback had taken her after every game this fall.

"No, really. I told you, I've not dated much." Then she lowered her voice. "Truthfully, no one ever paid attention to me until last year. Mom always encouraged me to get out and have fun anyway, so I did, and that's how I met Aubrey and the gang. Gave me something to do all those nights when Mom was out with her girlfriends and Dad was out on business."

Of course, I paid for us, as did all the guys for their gals. Even though I was a bona fide member of the baseball team, this was a whole different environment. I was hoping to fit in because I was a team member. But with Kathy as my date it seemed to seal the deal, so to speak.

The Northglenners arrived late and did a crazy version of the school's fight song until the manager came out and motioned for them to cut it. I hoped against hope Possum would not see me, but he did, and he raced over to our table.

"Well, I guess I got you two together after all! And you were so mad at me last spring, Larry, but see? It all worked out."

"Yes, Possum," I said through clenched teeth.

"Where's the other girl, Ly—"

Kathy kind of recoiled, but I made a quick recovery.

"Possum, this is the only girl there is. Do you actually know Kathy?"

"Well, I'm in her science class, but we have never spoken—"

As quickly as I could swing a bat, I interrupted. "Well, good. Let's keep it that way. Hey, nice performance tonight, Possum, way to go with the harmonica . . . and the brothers can really sing."

At that point people were yelling for him to do the Possum Stomp, and I stretched out my hand to the open floor. He winked at Kathy and puffed his chest out.

"Ah, fans. They never leave you alone," he sighed happily before gesturing wildly and stomping his way out to the floor where the baseball guys had cleared a space.

I knew we would be in the gossip page in next week's paper when on the other side of the clearing, I saw some kids that Roxanne called her watchdogs looking at us. Well, let her write a whole column. I didn't care, and she was my friend. "Baseball Star Finally Gets With Homecoming Court attendant!" I could see the headlines now.

At 10:30, just as the night wound down with Possum harmonica-izing with The Shadows' "Apache," I told my friend I needed to get Kathy home. He had to work at his father's poultry business the next morning, and mentioned that he and his girlfriend were hoping to go watch the submarine races down by Hoover Dam. I didn't tell Kathy about the last part, but she seemed happy after her first taste of Brendan's Big Slice.

In the backseat on the way home she cuddled up against me and I felt pretty good about it all. She even leaned in close and whispered: "We made it! We're finally dating!"

I felt pretty bold, so I responded, "Yes, and without Aubrey's help!" She giggled and I was glad the car was dark, because my ears were red.

Like a perfect gentleman, I walked Kathy to her door once we got to her house. I had never been to River View Manors, the only bit of Columbus wealth in our area, but it was clearly first-class. Kathy's folks' home was built on a bluff overlooking Alum Creek not too far past the shoals where we'd grounded our rowboat, and it wasn't hard to see they were rich.

"Kathy, I had a great time . . . looking forward to being your escort to the play," I said outside the car.

"Of course. Me, too." Before her mom turned on the porch light, she snuck in a quick hug. "Thank you, Larry. You're wonderful. And it's a date next Saturday. Our second one!"

My luck didn't continue that next week, though, as by Wednesday the play had been canceled again. Four of the cast members got the mumps. I had had the mumps long ago, but Kathy hadn't. It worked out, though, as that evening ended up being the obligatory visit with Dad, who'd brought Betsy. We went to a place she'd selected. She said she loved it because it was cheap and the portions were small. At least, she said the first part, I imagined the last bit.

As I got out of the car at home, she gave me a list on a sheet of scrap paper that had already been her grocery list on the other side.

"Here! This is a list of things you may not get me for Christmas under any circumstances." It read: "notebook paper, hankies, any type of perfume or fragrance, books of any type, gloves, cans of nuts."

"Was this your groceries?" I said, but then I turned it to the other side and it made even less sense. "How about I just take you and Dad to a nice Italian restaurant I know about down here?"

"Only if they don't serve too much bread. It's so wasteful when they do that." I backtracked when I thought of the prospect of running into Lynn.

"Well, maybe we'll take Grandma and Grandpa to the L&K restaurant in Delaware next Sunday after Christmas?" She said she hated burger joints, but Dad interrupted.

"That will be fine, son. What do you want for Christmas?"

"Just take me flying Dad, the next time you go." Betsy huffed but I managed to muster up the nerve to give her a big hug, which made Dad happy.

Even with no Kathy, the week went by surprisingly fast. Somehow, I got through that first stepmother Christmas. At least, it was nice to see my other grandparents. They didn't get out much, so even the L&K was a treat.

With everything that had happened the last month, I realized I had been a little scarce around the gang. We still talked and stuff, but we all maintained a bit of a facade, I think, while we digested JFK being gone and other stuff going on in our lives. Mack was back with Trish, Butch and Marcie were off in their own world, and I of course was distracted by Kathy. It was Mack who invited me to catch up over lunch at the deli, which I thought was a sign that Trish was already taming him. Even in the cold of last April, Butch and Mack's meet-ups were usually in the privacy of the shelter house where no one minded a few M-80s going off.

Mack got there first and came over to the booth where I was waiting for them. His cheeks were swollen and puffy.

"What . . . what's wrong, Mack?" He just muttered illegibly. Then Butch came in: he was all swollen up too. I wondered if I had missed a fight and hadn't been there for the guys, thanks to Kathy. Butch tried to explain but could hardly get any words out.

"Guys, you sound awful. Here, Mack, write it down." I slid him a napkin and a golf pencil that was on the table.

"GOT MUMPS," Mack wrote out, then waited. When my eyes got sufficiently big, he continued: "FROM DATING RAT PACKERS."

At that point both of them pulled cotton wads out of their mouths and busted out laughing.

"Okay, guys, joke's on me."

"Lunch, too?" Mack asked hopefully. I shook my head.

"He's gotta save, now," Butch laughed. As we ordered they razzed me about being in high society; word was out across the school since the basketball game and I didn't even get the pleasure of telling them. Evidently they'd decided that today was the day to drag me over the coals for it.

"Next thing we know, Mack, he'll be living in River View Manors and too good to talk to us."

"I wonder how much a three-piece suit costs."

"Is it too early to start looking into law school?"

This went on till Doris told Mack he had a call from someone named Trish, and then it was Mack's turn to blush. Butch got serious when he left.

"Larry, I hope you don't get burnt playing with those Rat Packers. I know they were your goal last spring, and you've made it, so have fun. But . . . uh, a word of advice?" He leaned in.

"Yeah?"

"Avoid Marcie. You're on her hit list and so am I 'cause I haven't punched you yet. She really likes Lynn and thinks you ruined a good thing, although I tried to stick up for ya."

"What about you, Butch, what do you think?"

"Hey, we all liked Lynn. But I understand it was a hard time for her and you. My pride woulda been hurt too if my girl didn't reach out to me for months. Marcie doesn't get it, but I do, I think you did what you thought was right. Just don't burn any bridges for Miss Columbus."

Mack and Trish phase two seemed to be going much better than the first time around; for one thing, Mack could take as good as he could give. For another, Trish seemed to like cars now. Mack proudly boasted that they went cruising in the cold evenings.

"But we keep pretty warm," he said, wagging his eyebrows.

"Only 'cause you just fixed your radiator," Butch snorted.

The following week, as New Year's approached, I was hoping to go to a party of some kind. The year before I'd watched Gramps and Grandma doze off about 10:30 to the radio broadcast out of New York City while Mom and E.A. were off at some shindig that they didn't come home from for two days. Besides, I was starting to fit in with some crowds outside of Mack and Butch, and I admit it felt good: I was the only one who played sports, so I suppose that was the reason. Being a ballplayer brought a certain clout that I didn't quite grasp during my first year at Mifflin. And it didn't hurt to have a Rat Packer chasing you.

And of course, the most sought-after invitation was the one at Kathy's house. Her parents were having a catered event for themselves, and Kathy's party would be in their recreation room in the basement. Roxanne had written it up in the last edition of the paper and had handed me last year's write-up, which read like a gala ball at the Governor's house down in Bexley. I didn't dare call Kathy and invite myself, though. But as I thought about how I could swing it a few days before New Year's, I got a call that evening. Happily, I beat E.A. to the phone.

"Hello, Larry!" It was Kathy. She had never called me before, but had managed to get my number somehow. I wasn't surprised. "I am sorry we haven't seen each other at all, but I had to do my school work from home while I was in quarantine. I'm fine, but it's been a drag."

"Well, everyone missed you."

"Did you miss me?"

"You bet I did!"

"Well, to make up for it, would you like to come to my house on New Year's Eve as . . . as my date?" I stretched the phone as long as the cord would go away from the living room.

"Of course, Kathy! What time? What are we wearing?"

"Be here at 8:00 sharp. The party goes till 1:00. It's all sophomores and their dates. Lots of food, and we're turning the basement into a rock-and-roll club. Just dress sharp. Can I count you in?"

"Well, I don't know, I may have to turn down some invitations," I pretended.

"Mom may play *Stooges Take New York* on the film projector if that helps," she laughed. "See ya then."

"Sounds good, Kathy."

As luck would have it, the next morning as I shoveled snow for Thunderchief, I saw Trish out walking to the corner store. We'd not intentionally stopped talking, but she had to know Lynn and I were through. I broke the ice by asking her if she and Mack had any New Year's Eve plans. She seemed pretty civil but a little reserved.

"Uh, no, Larry, I'm working at the Neil House downtown, busing and waitressing. Not sure what Mack's up to, probably eating a sandwich at midnight." She kicked a mound of plowed snow. "You probably don't care, but Lynn's going to be there too. As a guest. You at all interested in working down there? Twenty bucks and tips, plus you get to see Lynn!"

"I've got an invitation to the sophomore party," I said, truthfully but a big vaguely. She had to know where that party was happening.

On New Year's Eve, Mom dropped me off at Kathy's. I had to find my own ride home as they were headed to Tubby's Tavern for his New Year's bash. She peered out the window at the large, warm windows that lined the road that ended at the Martins'.

"Wow, Larry, who are these people?"

"Well, Kathy's dad is a big-time attorney. And her mom, back in the forties, did you ever hear of an actress named Beverly Anderson?"

Mom thought a bit and finally chuckled. "*Vampire Nurses*?"

"That's Mrs. Martin."

"Not too bad, Larry!"

Kids were arriving and getting dropped off in the half-circle drive. I went in and wondered if I'd just be a fly on the wall. The house was massive on the inside, and there seemed to be four or five tables with snacks, hors d'oeuvres, and drinks for the adults. But it seemed I'd not walked ten feet before Kathy found me and took my arm.

What a spread! Her dad had hired a catering firm to do the night, no expense spared. Cocktail hour was upstairs, and the high school party was downstairs, but the menu was the same: huge platters of meats, cheeses, finger foods (as Kathy said), and what seemed like hundreds of small sandwiches. Now and then, Mr. or Mrs. Martin would do a chaperone walkthrough, but if they were paying special attention to me, they hid it. The biggest surprise of the evening, though, was that Aubrey and most of the Rat Pack were not there. I asked my best baseball buddy who'd made the invite list why not.

"Larry, it's chaperoned." He winked. "And there's no booze here, either. At least, not for us."

Whatever the reason, Aubrey's absence gave Kathy a chance to be herself. She seemed more relaxed than ever and was a great hostess . . . and an even better New Year's Eve date.

Towards ten, the chant went up from Weasel Warren—the same doofus who interrupted Kathy's campaign speech for sophomore queen—for *Vampire Nurses*. But Kathy played it cool. The film projector was already set up, and we were quickly settled in a home theater with a big, real canvas screen against one wall. In a corner, an old time movie popcorn machine kept churning away across from a bona fide jukebox. At the bar, in front of a whiskey collection that would have made E.A. salivate, they had root beer on tap.

Like Mom had said, who were these people?

I'd seen *Vampire Nurses* before; we all had. But as I watched the old familiar scenes, I couldn't believe it. It really was like I was watching Kathy on screen. I did double-takes a few times between the girl beside me and the actress on screen.

After the flick, Kathy's mom came down and told us some hilarious Hollywood stories involving some big-time stars and signed a few shirts. I looked at the walls of the home theater in the light; for a woman who hadn't made it big, she sure knew a lot of stars. There she was with John Wayne on a horse, Jimmy Stewart at a bank counter, Lucille Ball on a couch, and yes, the Stooges with the Empire State Building in the background.

After the movie, Kathy got out a roll of quarters for the jukebox and the records started as we cleared the folding chairs. Some of the records couldn't have been more than a couple weeks old; these were brand new songs. And then, like magic, the Everly Brothers' "Cathy's Clown" came up. I felt myself blushing as Roxanne came up alongside.

"Where did Kathy go?" I asked Roxanne, as Don and Phil Everly started to croon, "Here he comes . . . "

"Oh, she's upstairs. It's almost midnight, you know, she has to get party hats and horns."

"Midnight?" I asked. The last four hours had felt like minutes. Roxanne's date came along and pulled her to the dance floor, but she held back long enough to say, "You two are way overdue for your first dance. When I put on a Lettermen song on the jukebox, you bring her out on the floor. Don't worry, I won't play 'Cathy's Clown' again." She winked.

I expected to be nervous, but I wasn't. I thought: "Yes, we are overdue," and I intended to fix just that. But first, I needed some air.

I opened the patio door and walked out onto the boat bow–shaped deck that overhung Alum Creek. I watched the water, which somehow looked coal-black but glistened in the dim light as it churned slowly along, remembering how my life here had started eight months ago with the boat adventure on this very same stream, just upriver.

I heard the patio door open and turned—it was Kathy. I could hear the beginning of the Lettermen's "The Way You Look Tonight" and I thought, this is my cue. I felt a nervous lump form in my throat and I swallowed it, figuring she'd go back inside. But instead, she closed the door behind her.

"Would you like to go back in and dance?" I asked.

She just shook her head and came over and put her arms underneath mine and held me. We both shivered in the cold breeze.

As I looked at her, she shyly looked down and then back up. Gently, I leaned down and kissed her very softly. I pulled away, held her for a moment and then she put her hand behind my head and pulled me closer and we kissed again.

After almost a year we had finally overcome all the barriers. A thousand thoughts were going through my mind. I had completely forgotten everyone else until the door opened and Mrs. Martin yelled.

"Hey, you two, it's almost midnight. Get in here. You have other guests, dear!" I wondered if she had been there watching, but I admit I didn't care.

As the clock counted down we all began to count with it; when it chimed midnight, the song "Auld Lang Syne" was playing upstairs and I heard the adults clinking glasses. I had never been to a party like this, let alone felt like I was part of it. Yet here I was.

One a.m. hit pretty soon after that. Her parents' party was still going strong, so I knew I was walking home, but I didn't mind, I felt real warm. Kathy saw me getting my coat and went upstairs to get hers, too, saying, "Let's go out the garage door . . . don't walk through the party upstairs." I waited for her, and then we took the basement door into the garage.

"Are you glad you came?" she asked.

I could think of nothing to say except to pull her close and kiss her again. All I could hear was our breath and the snowfall.

She looked at me and grinned. "So you know . . . out on the deck . . . that was my very first kiss." Then she put her head up against my chest and asked. "Was it better than hers?"

I knew she was asking about Lynn.

I didn't want to tell her I had never kissed Lynn, or bring Lynn up at all. Mercifully, I was rescued by another couple who were looking for a quiet place, too.

"Uh, oh, this spot is taken," I heard the guy say. That was enough to break the mood. Kathy laughed it off with her usual style. "Will you be okay walking home, Larry?"

"Oh, I'll be fine. Good . . . good night."

"Good night. Happy new year."

Once I came to the bridge, a son-talker who was on his way home pulled up alongside me.

"Son, are you for wanting a ride?" I was wise to their game.

"Yeah, son, but be for turning the car off first."

He laughed. "Get in. You'll be for freezing out there, big shot."

It felt like 1964 was going to be a great year.

CHAPTER
FIFTEEN

My snow removal business was booming during winter break, but it didn't keep me from asking Mom to take me to the license bureau to get my temporary license on the sixth of January, my birthday. I had been driving Gramps's pickup and tractor on the farm since I was 12, even though Ohio technically didn't let you behind the wheel until your 16th birthday. I just needed road experience to complete the school's driver education. So when I got my temps, of course, I started to bug Mom and E.A. on the hour to take me driving. If all that stood between me and freedom was 12 hours in the car with E.A., so be it.

I also began laying the groundwork for freedom by asking Mom If she would sell me the '56 Chevy, as they now had gotten a newer '61 turquoise Chevy Bel Air on a holiday sale. The answer was no.

"E.A. still needs a car when he's home," Mom explained, "and so do I. I'm not sure if he is going to continue to drive trucks, though, so that's good news for you. If he gets another job with a company car, then maybe you'll get your own. But get your license first, and I can promise you a share of the driving time."

The first day back at school was a full day for Kathy, so we spent lunch period together for the first time since New Year's Eve—I have to admit, I'd missed her. We got caught up, and as we walked back to our next class she reminded me about the drama club's long-delayed play that Saturday night. I had tried to impress her about my soon-to-be-acquired driver's license as well as the prospect of having a car, but she mentioned her folks planned on getting her one once she turned sixteen and was more interested in the play.

"So as Mrs. Gibbs, I actually die in the play! Mom's been coaching me, I think I'm pretty good at it now." She laughed.

"I know you'll be great, Kathy. Just don't die for real."

"Promise. Oh . . . do you have a suit, Larry? It's not super formal, but . . . "

Well, I didn't, but Kathy didn't seem to care. She said to wear my best shirt and that'd be fine. It was too late to go suit shopping, anyway. So Saturday afternoon, I shined my old loafers and put on a clean blue shirt, gray slacks, and a tie E.A. loaned me that smelled a bit like a cheap hotel room. He tied it for me, I slipped it on, and then he near-strangled me in the car as he adjusted it before dropping me off. "Chuh, bud, the ladies love a good tight tie knot."

"They like a living guy, too!" I retorted as I loosened it.

Mr. Sullivan was the first to see me, and I must have looked uncomfortable as heck in comparison to my usual poise on the field. "Well, well, is this what a well-dressed center-fielder is wearing these days? Someone tell Mickey Mantle." He was a great principal and had seemed to work hard on at least recognizing all the students milling into the first non-athletic event since the assassination.

The audience was taking their seats when the Martins came in fashionably late and headed right up front to the parent seating. They had some older people who I assumed were grandparents with them and another well-dressed couple, and for all of them they had reserved almost the entire section, which I guess was an option. I was not one to try and draw attention to myself, but when her mom walked by and saw me a few rows back, she stopped.

"Hello Larry! How are you?" Then she leaned close and whispered, "You and Jack are the same size. I should have brought you one of his old sportcoats for the evening, poor thing." She gave me a quick but kind of cold hug and returned up front.

I let it roll off my back but looked at the worn spots on my loafers until the curtain raised and we were all enthralled by the play, me most of all. It went well, and I found myself appreciating the subtle touches after my time backstage with Henry. This time, though, everyone remembered their lines.

After the play I went to the cafeteria and waited for the cast. Ahead of me, the couple with the Martins had their son with them, and he was wearing a Columbus School for Boys jacket and tie and seemed to be looking all us Mifflin-goers over. That school was the premier male prep school in central Ohio; going there was a ritzy-class only sort of thing.

He seemed older than me, and this was confirmed by the pin he was wearing, which had "64" in big, gold script, meaning he was a senior at the School for Boys. I assumed he had known Kathy since the parents were friends. He beat me to meeting her when the cast came out.

"Kathy, you were outstanding!" he exclaimed. "I haven't seen you for at least two years. But when mother said you were the homecoming queen, I just had to come." He continued laying it on so thick I felt like I had to roll my pants up and put on some rubber boots. "Like mother, like daughter. You're so pretty." As he hugged Kathy's mom, I realized that maybe this was the new competition.

Kathy blushed and told him she was a sophomore attendant, not queen, but it was all downhill from there for me. I tried to sneak in a few asides about her delivery, but with her grandparents, the family friends, and Jay Gatsby making a fuss over her, I was about as popular as another litter of kittens.

It wasn't Kathy's fault. For one of the few times in her life she was in her own spotlight, not Aubrey's or her mom's. I didn't blame her or feel sorry for myself, at least too much. But like Gramps used to say when we were fishing and they weren't biting, "Son, let's cut bait and leave."

So I did.

The next Monday, I decided to play it cool and not rush over to Kathy first thing. After feeling over the moon about her two weeks earlier, I felt a little gypped, but I chalked it up to me being immune to puppy love this second time around. As a result, it was two days before we talked. To my surprise, it was Kathy who came over to my locker.

"I'm sorry, Larry. I think I know why you're giving me the cold shoulder. I wasn't expecting everyone. It was unfair to you, and I should have introduced you."

"I understand," I said casually. I'd made up my mind to go on the offensive as we started talking, and capture some of that New Year's Eve energy. "Hey, how about going on a double date with the couple we went to Brendan's Big Slice with last month? We could go over to the new Northland mall . . . " I realized I was rambling, but like a car without brakes I couldn't stop. "We could see the new James Bond flick, *From Russia with Love*. Mack took Trish, and he said it was great. You haven't met Mack. . . . " Kathy hit me with a bomb.

"Um, I'm actually going to the Democratic fundraising dinner downtown at the Neil House this weekend. Mom and Dad got us a table. With Brian. Remember? You met him at the play?"

Well, I hadn't met him, but I remembered him all right. The school hallway seemed to reel.

"Oh, okay, well . . . see ya round." I was deflated but I wasn't going to let her see it. Why were they going to a political dinner anyway? They couldn't even vote. I walked off with my head up, whistling one of my favorite tunes in an effort to disguise my hurt until I realized it was "Cathy's Clown." Then I just felt embarrassed.

As January dragged on, I found myself feeling out of the romantic loop again. Two more times I asked Kathy out, but apparently Brian had the inside track. Somehow I had gone from the New Year's Eve All-Star to warming the bench while he was hitting line drives.

When I got low enough to ask Aubrey about him, she read his resume from memory. Apparently he was Yale-bound that fall. I felt I had overcome my backwards habits enough to not have to compete with someone who was born wearing a Columbus prep school blazer, but apparently not.

"That's enough, Aubrey. I don't have any law firm partnerships I'm trying to hire for." To my surprise she turned genuinely sympathetic.

"Sorry, Larry. I really am. But you know, you should have made your move last spring. You two played hide and seek for six months or more with each other, and believe me when I tell you she was insanely jealous about your Linden girlfriend last summer. The whole Cubby thing was just to get your attention. Brian's only been in the picture since recently."

I was beginning to think Kathy was more interested in me when I had another girlfriend than when I was available. I felt like yesterday's news as Aubrey reached in my lunch sack but I swatted her hand. She stuck out her tongue but laughed.

"So it's back to the bench for me, then?"

"Look, you and I are friends. I don't always understand you and your crazy gang, but I think you're so darned honest, and I know this life here is different from where you grew up, so I'm gonna cut you slack. What's more, we all know you didn't ask to be here. So I'll tell you what's really up, no sugar coating." That was a new tone for Aubrey, so I paid attention.

"It's her mother, Larry. Bev is nice, real nice, although she's kind of a heel sometimes. What you see is what you get. She's a Barbie that never made it big back in California. So now, she is going to live her life through her daughter here in good ol' Ohio. You . . . probably get in the way of that."

"She just sees me as distraction, then?" I asked with an edge in my voice.

Aubrey sighed, shook her head and told me something I wish I hadn't heard, even though I knew it. "Well look, you're just a kid from a broken home, living in a rented American Veteran house on the edge of Shanty Town. At best, you're a toy, at worst . . . Larry, you ain't going to Yale, and you're probably draft bait in two years. She sees Brian as a potential son-in-law, real U.S. Senator material. Where are you headed if you don't get drafted? Maybe a year or two in the minor leagues at best? Come on."

"I couldn't have fixed that just by dating Kathy last summer. If what you say is true, her mom would have blocked it last year too."

Aubrey got up. "Cripes, I didn't want you two to get married. I just wanted you both to have a fun summer. You've got so much to learn." She leaned down, hugged me, and gave me a peck on the cheek. She started to walk away, then turned back around with that old Aubrey smirk on her face.

"Now, if you're looking to get hitched . . . there is always Lesser Brenda."

I had noticed at the pool last summer that Brenda could fill out a bathing suit real well. We all did. So I had to ask.

"Aubrey, why do you all call her Lesser Brenda?"

"Oh, thought you knew. Her stepsister is named Brenda too, she's a real knock -out. She goes to school down at Columbus Central High 'cause that's the area where her dad was living. Whew! Almost as good looking as me."

I just shook my head.

Thankfully, I was able to throw myself into preconditioning for baseball. I was determined to be in the best shape of my life, Kathy or no Kathy. For two weeks, I stayed after school each night running sprints around the field and doing agility and strength exercises I'd picked up in magazines. My best friend on the team, our backup shortstop, even started joining me, and out there in the cold I forgot about everything. We were determined to be starters this year and would find time to exercise even when we were supposed to be in home room.

But one day while I was down on the gym floor doing push-ups, I noticed a pair of brown, suede girl shoes in front of me. I looked up, and it was Kathy.

"Got a minute?" she asked.

"Sure, for you I do." We walked off aways from my friend.

"Larry, do you know that this Saturday is the Mifflin Winter festival?"

Well, I hadn't been here the year before, so I was unaware of what it was other than seeing the posters in the hall. "Yeah, I saw the ads."

"Well, I was nominated for the winter festival court . . . " I already knew that; I voted for her. But I let her go on.

"If I win, will you be my escort out on the floor for the coronation?"

I asked her point blank. "What about Mr. Columbus? Brian?" Kathy looked flustered but amused.

"Oh, Larry, I only went out with him because his dad is a judge and my dad is thinking about running for state legislature. The last couple of weeks we all have been doing the one big happy family routine around Columbus and making the rounds for Dad. Photo op, everyone smile!" she said cheesily, imitating holding a camera up to herself. That got me grinning. "Look, Brian has a steady girl at Saint Mary's School for Girls. I gave him a peck on the cheek for a photo, same as I saw Aubrey give you not one week ago. That doesn't make you guys a couple, does it?"

I admit, she was disarming and charming and beautiful as always. But I felt up to the task and kept the conversation smart. "How come you don't go to St. Mary's, anyway? You're Catholic, aren't you?"

"Because Dad graduated from Mifflin in '41. It's one argument Dad won with Mom a long time ago. I think she got a convertible for it."

Well, that conversation put a spring back in my step. I said yes, and of course, when the voting was done, Kathy was one of five girls selected for the court. Of those five, one would be selected as Winter Queen.

Now I had to buy a suit. There were no excuses, and I wasn't about to be outclassed by Brian next time he showed his face at Mifflin, St. Mary's girl or no St. Mary's girl. E.A. took me over to Penney's and we looked through the clearance rack, Mom's discount included. I found a sharp gray suit that needed some easy alterations and picked out a shirt, and E.A. found a great tie. Luckily, I could get the suit altered right there under Mom's discount and have it back a day before the festival. I plopped down some hard-earned snow-removal money and we headed home. Things were looking up.

As we drove by the Linden Air, E.A. announced: "Bub, I quit my trucker's job. Too much time away from you and the missus. Starting next week, I'm going to work for the Chevy dealer who helped us out last summer." I appreciated E.A.'s attempt at a compliment, but I knew E.A. loved trucking because of the greasy food at the stops. He had gained 35 pounds since last fall, and his doctor told him to get off the road, quit eating grease, get another job, and get over to the YMCA or Mom would be a widow. So he was going back to sales again. Hopefully that meant a company car for him and the family car for me.

On Wednesday, Kathy slid in beside me at lunch and I proudly told her I had gotten a nice suit. "I'll be sharp for our date on Friday," I said.

"I withdrew from the court, Larry," she said, sadly.

"What? Why? You were a shoo-in for the Queen!"

"Well . . . this year the school didn't have quite enough money for the whole thing. Who else but the Gents offered to pay the difference . . . but because the festival is sponsored by the Gents' fraternity, they got the planning committee to agree to them providing all the escorts. And if you're royalty, you're expected to go to the festival on Saturday with your escort."

"No way, Kathy!" She shrugged her shoulders.

"That's what I said. I won't go unless you are my escort and date."

At that moment, I had to step back and take another look at Kathy Martin. Maybe we did have a future. I gave her a quick hug, trying to be discreet but was too happy to care if anyone saw.

"I'll make it up to you, I promise," was all I said. Kathy smiled and looked proud of herself.

But as I was sitting in Algebra the next morning, I looked out the window and I saw the Martins' big black Lincoln roaring into the parking lot out front. Bev parked the car in the space reserved for the school superintendent, who was late, and got out in a huff. She was dressed to the nines and made her way into the school like a battalion leader. I was no Brian, but I could figure out what was happening.

We were dismissed soon after for lunch, and I passed the principal's office just as Beverly was thanking Mr. Sullivan at his door.

"Thank you so much. She isn't quite 16. I don't think she understands what an honor this is . . . thank you for reinstating her." As she came out, she passed by and looked at me like she was trying to remember where she knew me from. Then she connected the dots.

To my credit, I confidently said, "Hello, Mrs. Martin."

"Oh, Larry! What a nice surprise, dear. Did you hear Kathy has been nominated again for another court?"

Stupidly, I mumbled, "Ah, yes. I voted for her, a couple of times."

She gave a hearty fake laugh. "Oh, that's good of you. Listen, don't be a stranger, you're always welcome at the Martin Residence. Kathy considers you such a good friend. Buh-bye now!" She went off in search of Kathy at her honors English course.

With about 15 minutes left in lunch period, Kathy found me in the gym sitting with Roxanne, who was trying her best to get a story out of me for Overheard. Roxanne had long ago chosen to be a student office worker for the increased access to dirt, so she had seen and heard Beverly in the office, all of it. But she got her final scoop in a way she hadn't expected.

"Come on. I need to talk to you," Kathy said, looking at Roxanne glaringly. She stuck out her hand and I took it as she led me away. She started crying once we found a deserted classroom.

"Larry, Mom is going to make me go to the festival with a Gent and I just hate her for it. I explained you were my date. But she said 'Kathy, Larry seems to be a nice boy but I am just not sure he is the right one for you. I mean look how he monopolized you on New Year's Eve!'" She blew her nose on a handkerchief. "'Don't tie yourself down with one young man, especially one who. . .'" But I waved her off. Honestly, I didn't want to hear Bev's real thoughts.

Then a science teacher came in and politely said, "No fraternizing in the classrooms. Please now, both of you go on to your next class." Outside the bell rang, ending lunch. Kathy looked at me and just walked away, clutching her books.

The following evening at the basketball game during halftime, with my new $25-dollar suit hanging in the closet at home collecting dust, I watched Kathy go out on the stage, all smiles. She was chosen first runner-up for queen. As she accepted her bouquet, her mom was causing a small electrical storm with all her flash bulbs going off, taking photos of her and one of the newer Gents, who looked like a guy who'd just discovered a gold nugget in his ear.

As I looked at Kathy up on stage, I felt like I was seeing a rewind of my year here at Mifflin. First, finding out she had a crush on me, then the disastrous spring dance with Possum. Then summer at the pool and my goofy dive. Then Lynn. Then the ride on the Alpine lift at the fair. It was all in fast motion, but it ended with the kiss on New Year's Eve in the snowfall.

I wasn't one to give up. It wasn't my nature. Most of my life advice had come from Gramps, who I don't think ever quit anything and never let me either. But as I sat there, adding my half-hearted applause for the court, I came to the conclusion that what I was thinking about wasn't quitting, it was growing up. I couldn't come between Kathy and her mom, of course. Why go on making a fool out of myself? Okay, so I had struck out with two very beautiful girls. But some of the best plays in the history of baseball happened with two outs and two strikes. And I'd get another swing with someone.

I left the game early in the fourth quarter and walked home with a cold wind blowing out of the north like it'd come all the way from Lake Erie just to give me chills. On Saturday night I didn't go to the festival. Mom and E.A. were out, so Butch and Mack came over instead and I made Dagwood sandwiches out of everything in the fridge and even cooked some cheap, frozen grocery-store french fries as we watched *Sink The Bismarck* on our new 24-inch color TV. Even though the movie was in black and white, it seemed like we were in a movie theater.

I told my pals about my latest failure, and neither of them seemed all that sad. After they went home, I put the homecoming picture of Kathy that was in last fall's football program in my drawer by the feather clip.

CHAPTER
SIXTEEN

As February began, my sense of being romantically shipwrecked was eclipsed by a feeling that something big was happening at school. Homemade posters had appeared overnight in the hallways proclaiming stuff like "They're Coming," "Long Live King John," and all that. One had a stencil of Elvis, crossed out, with just "The King is Dead" beneath it.

I knew it was about the four long-haired guys who were going to be on the Ed Sullivan Show that coming Sunday night. I wasn't interested in them, but Mom and E.A. always watched him, so I guessed I'd end up seeing what all the racket was about. I didn't really care, and I wasn't an Elvis fan, so his being replaced didn't bother me either. Nope, for me, the Four Seasons forever; and if there was a king's crown, it was shared by two hillbilly brothers named Don and Phil Everly. Besides, a couple of bands from England could never replace all the American rock-n'-rollers.

Even if I had been interested in the new band, I was too busy with more important things to pay too much attention to all the talk. With Coach Barnhart having taken baseball over, preseason was actually exciting for us underclassmen, and he had us actively preparing like he had every intention of playing us all the way to a championship. Of course, the seniors laughed. One said he'd wait until the season started to really get in shape when he caught me doing a set of 20 sit-ups after we'd finished catch-and-throw exercises.

"You guys wait and see," he called to us underclassmen as his friends drove out from the parking lot. "Seniors always rule. It's a tradition for Mifflin Baseball. You guys'll be picking splinters out of your butts from the bench the entire season."

I was thinking of something to say back when Mack came over. His still being at school was unusual since his last class had been an hour earlier.

"Hey Mickey Mantle, wanna walk with me to Schottenstein's tonight?" he asked, talking about the main J.C. Penney competitor in the Northern Lights Shopping Center.

"Why don't you drive, Mack? And why aren't you gone, anyway?"

"Can't, I got a busted fan belt. Gonna have to leave her here until tomorrow when I can come back with one. Anyway, that's why I gotta go tonight."

"Sure thing. We're just finishing up here."

"Well, hurry, and don't waste time signing any autographs," he snickered.

I wondered what the rush was—it was Friday, and the store was open till 9:00. I hustled to get my stuff inside my locker, and we headed out at a decent clip. Mack seemed in a particular hurry.

It wasn't long before an old local mutt named Skip fell in with us. He didn't really belong to anyone—he just went wherever he could find food, which was often with Mack. I liked him because, like Gramp's dog Gypsy, he was a border collie, although the similarities ended there. Skip was pretty hefty. Over the summer I'd fed him quite a bit through the backdoor, mostly table scraps and old bologna, and would even leave out bowls of water for him during the hotter days. It was a relief to see him, as he'd not been around for a while and I imagined he had met his fate with the dog catcher like the big black dog Mack had thought was a bear.

"What's the rush, Mack?" I asked. We were running nearly faster than Skip could manage on the trail high above Sewer Creek.

"Do you know Bruce Mackley?" he asked from up ahead.

"Yeah, he's in junior high. His house is over on Lindale Drive."

"Well, he bought a shirt at Schottenstein's that only had one sleeve when he unwrapped it. I want one, too."

"All this for a shirt you could make yourself with a pair of scissors?"

"No, you idiot, there wasn't even an arm opening. It looked like he had one arm!"

I wasn't going to ask why this was a selling point, but Mack continued.

"Trish's dad played a joke on me when I was over there last night. He's a prankster, and I want to get him back by giving this shirt to him. He'll love it when he tries to put it on."

I raised my eyebrow. Mack had gotten back in pretty thick with Trish, and it was still funny to think of him drawing a ring around his nose the summer before. But all was forgiven, apparently.

"What did he do?" I asked.

"He and Trish were wearing bald wigs when I knocked on the door. I nearly turned around 'cause I thought I had the wrong house."

"Wait, wait, our Trish, I mean, your Trish? The Trish at school?"

"Yeah, she has a great sense of humor when she's around her dad."

I thought back to the fair and still wondered if we were talking about the same girl.

"So uh, you need a fan belt too?" I said, not really able to imagine Trish in a bald wig or Mack finding it cute.

"Yeah, that too, I guess." Mack slowed up. "I mean, really, I guess I just wanted to walk so we could talk. We haven't been to the woods much at all lately."

"That's true."

"You know that British group is going to be on Sullivan on Sunday, right?"

"Yeah, the Beatles or something. So what?"

"I'll be going over to Trish's for supper, and she said to ask you if you would want to come too and watch, it's their first show in America."

"You could have asked me that today when we were eating lunch with Butch. Do I really have to go all the way to Schottenstein's?"

"Well, no," he said. "But Butch is tired of girl talk, and this way I can ask you other stuff, like . . . well, are you going to go over and watch it at Kathy's house?"

"No, I don't think so, Mack. She hasn't even called, anyway. After the winter festival, I am beginning to see a pattern with her. Aubrey says it's her mom pulling all the strings. Maybe. Kathy's nice, really nice." I thought back to New Year's Eve. "But I don't want to be one of four or five guys she dates."

"Told ya!" he said. "I told ya a long time ago don't play with the Rat Pack." He had a smug look on his face.

By now we were a cherry bomb's throw from the highway—not that we would—so I told Skip to lay down and stay in the brush along the road. Shottenstein's looked more lit up than the sun after all that time in the dark woods. Mack immediately knew where to go for the fan belt, so the search was soon on for the shirt with one sleeve. We started looking at all the hanging shirts, then the ones in packages on the discount table, figuring maybe the store's staff had already done our work for us.

Apparently we were digging too deeply, as soon a prim-looking sales lady and a beefy security guard came over behind us.

"Hey guys," the store guard boomed from ten feet off. "I am going to ask you to step away from the table and turn towards me."

I was pretty slender so he just said to open my coat, but for Mack he made him take his coat off. The saleslady asked what we were doing. Mack, to his credit, told the truth.

"Bruce Mackley bought a shirt with one sleeve here, and I want one, too."

"Young man, we would not sell trash like that. Pay for your car part and leave."

The guard escorted us to the cashier and watched us pay before opening the doors. "If what you said is true, guys . . . why not just go home and cut the sleeve off an old shirt?"

"I told him to do that sir," I said. Mack huffed.

"Well, I don't want to see the two of you in here together again." The door slammed shut, the glass pane vibrating. Mack shrugged and we set off back into the woods. Skip was gone.

"Come on, Larry, it's getting dark, and he's got plenty of holes to sleep in. We can go faster crossing the creek without him, anyway. It's frozen."

It really was no big deal to cross the creek in the winter; we had done this before and knew the way well enough, avoiding half-sunk trees that would weaken the ice around them. As we stepped onto the ice to listen out for thin spots cracking, Skip galloped out from the brush ahead of us.

"Come on, Skip, lead the way," I said. He led on ahead as we got to where the stream got wider, about 10 feet across where the ice would be thick and allow for a safe walk. Mack and I both knew it to be pretty deep from seeing it in the summer, with no sunken logs or rocks to weaken the ice. Mack stepped gingerly out in front of me, but Skip bounded ahead.

Unfortunately for us, the up-and-down Ohio temperature had made the ice unpredictable. In less than three feet, Skip fell through with a crash and ke-dunk on a thin spot hiding beneath a dusting of snow. In the dim light of the city reflecting against the clouds, I could see Skip through the ice, like a dog in an aquarium.

All I could think of that moment was Gypsy and how frigid she'd be in that dark creek water. Thinking enough to get on my belly, I crawled over on the ice and tried to reach Skip's paws through the hole he'd made. Unfortunately, the entire pool gave way and down I went into six or more feet of water, face first... dirty Sewer Creek water.

To my credit, I kept my head and let myself sink feet first so I could kick hard against the bottom to go up. Sewer Creek didn't really have a big flow. This was just a pool gouged out long ago. There had to be a bottom.

 The water was so cold it was like ten thousand needles. I had read stories of those who survived the Titanic and said your fingertips were the first to go. I knew this wasn't that dangerous, but I needed to get out of there. The fact I had a heavy jacket on didn't help. It was like the opposite of a life preserver, an anchor. I managed to stand up, sort of, in the water and found my feet on the bottom, my hair barely out of the water.

Mack also kept his head and had immediately gone back to shore for a long tree limb, which he held out from the ground. Skip didn't need my help and paddled to the bank like an icebreaker, pulled himself up, shook off, and continued on without a care in the world. I hope he knew a good warm garage to camp out in.

As I struggled to the bank, spitting scummy, foul-tasting creek water out of my mouth, Mack looked pretty concerned until he saw I was okay. Once it was clear I was just wet and not injured, he pulled the limb away.

"Okay, are you coming Sunday or not? If not I'm just heading home and letting Skip bring back the fire department."

"Yeah. Yes! Now give me the stupid limb." I wondered why it was so important but realized I needed to hop in the shower sooner than later to keep from catching pneumonia.

Thirty degrees felt kind of warm as I stood on shore, but then the cold hit me like putting your head in the freezer in the hottest part of July to cool down. I needed to get home fast.

"Come on, Larry, your clothes will freeze before we get home if we don't hurry," Mack said, racing ahead. We got up on the trail and hit a brisk run, my limbs seeming to be on fire from adrenaline.

"Good thing we're tough, Larry or you'd be food for Possum's crawdads now," Mack said, laughing and huffing.

We got to the park and climbed up over E.A.'s dike, then ran as hard as we could, the wind feeling like a sheet of nails. Soon we arrived in my driveway, where Mom's car was parked. "Let me handle this." Mack said. He burst in the front door without knocking.

"Mrs. Darnell, your son was a hero today! He saved a poor dog from drowning, but you've gotta get him something warm, now!" As Mom came and looked at my frozen clothes, Mack continued. "I wish I was half as brave as he was to get that poor dog."

"Take your clothes off and pile them near the utility room," Mom said, seeing nothing was seriously wrong. "I'll wash them when they dry out. Was it the Sewer Creek you guys always talk about? You smell like a dead fish!"

Mack repeated the whole story with additional exaggerations. You would have thought I saved someone on the beach of Normandy and had received the Medal of Honor. Fortunately, Mom had a pot of chicken noodle soup boiling for supper, and the kitchen smelled heavenly.

"Well, you stay, Mack," she said. "I'm sure you had something to do with this, anyway." We ate after I had a hot shower and a change of clothes. Sewer Creek stank, but I realized we'd been lucky. It would have been different in the Alum, where there were vicious undertow currents in the deep part, especially with that ice forcing the water through like a narrow pipe.

I spent Saturday recovering and swinging a bat in the garage. E.A. had started working at the Chevy dealer and actually sold a car his first week there, so as a reward he got to bring one of the showroom's 1964 station wagons home. We went over to the school so I could drive around the parking lot some more and then, to my surprise, he told me to drive it back. I did ok, except I accelerated going into a turn and scared the daylights out of both of us. After he'd said a lot of words in a few new combinations, he concluded that we had some work to do before I went back on the road. But I was headed for my driver's license, sure enough!

I was still recouping Sunday afternoon when the phone rang and Mom said it was for me.

I heard Aubrey's familiar voice on the other end. "Laaarryy, Melanie and I are over here at Kathy's. We're going to watch the Beatles. Why don't you come over too?" Before I could answer, she said, "Oh, wait, here she is."

Off to the end, I heard a mutter, "Talk to him."

"Hello! Want to come over and watch the Beatles?" Kathy asked, very pleasantly.

"Well . . . "

"New color TV, Larry! And Dad is having seafood night tonight: lobster, shrimp, and king crab. If you don't like seafood, he's got some great ribeye steak. Wait 'till you taste his sauces!"

I knew Mack would kill me but I toyed around with the idea, and ribeye sounded delicious. Thanks to gramps's freezer back in Sunbury, we used to have them almost once a month.

"Who all is coming?"

"Just you. And me, and a couple of guys that Melanie and Aubrey know. You make six!" She told me who the guys were and I even knew them, so it seemed like a good fit. I thought about being on the deck with her on New Year's Eve and the fact that Mr. Yale or Cubby or the Gents were not in attendance, and it seemed like an easy home game. I knew I had to make a decision right then and there.

"What's your, uh, what does your mom say?

"Oh, don't worry. She's out in California for a reunion with some old movie gal pals."

So it's okay if I'm there because she isn't, I thought. If that's how it was going to be . . .

"Oh, gee Kathy . . . I am going to go over to Trish's with Mack to watch them."

"Trish? School Trish?" Suddenly Kathy's tone got a little defensive. "Are you going there with someone? I mean, if you're going to Trish's house, I just can't imagine who else will be there. . . . "

I thought that was a strange question, since I always seemed to be in competition with somebody for her affections. But I just responded pleasantly.

"No, just us three. No new color set, though. Besides, isn't Ed Sullivan in black and white?"

"Well . . . fine. If you change your mind, be here by 7:30 to eat. Dad starts boiling lobsters at 7:00. Hope to see you. Bye!" Click!

Later, I put on an old baseball shirt and some jeans, combed my beach-boy hair, and headed for Trish's. I had never had lobster before, but I imagined Trish's dad had whipped up something good, being a head chef and all.

Trish's mom answered the door. "Oh good, you came! Go on in. They're all here making a mess and pizza, I think." Then she patted me on the shoulder and whispered, "Thanks for coming. Go on in!" I had noticed she was trying to suppress a grin. I could see through the passage in the kitchen wall that Mack had a chef hat on and Trish was adjusting it.

But as I walked around the dividing wall and into the kitchen, I got tossed a curveball. There at the table was Lynn, rolling dough. Her long, dark hair was almost to her waist now; she had on a dark red Linden sweatshirt with flour all over it. The last time I had seen her was in the school foyer, while I was waiting for Kathy.

"Hi!" I said, not knowing what else to say or do.

I could tell we both had been set up. She clearly didn't know I was coming either and grew bright red. Mack and Trish were grinning like Cheshire Cats.

"Welcome to Chef Boy-ar-Mack's kitchen," Mack announced. "Hey, don't take your coat off. I need cheddar cheese and you got six minutes 'til Doris's Deli closes. Go get some. Chop, chop!"

"Is she open on Sunday?" I asked

"Yeah, she said she was going to be because of what's happening tonight on Sullivan. She thinks this will be a busier night for her than the NFL championship game was."

I felt glad for the excuse and turned to get out of there, wondering if it was too early to walk over to Kathy's once I dropped off the cheese. But Lynn dusted her hands and shirt off, let her hair out of the ponytail and grabbed her jacket.

"I'll go too," she said without even looking at me. And just like that, we were alone, together, walking down Woodland Avenue.

Neither of us said a thing for a few moments, then she started.

"Why are you here? They didn't tell me you were coming."

"I didn't know you were going to be here either, Lynn. Look, sorry if this is awkward for you. I'll leave when we get back."

Instead of answering, she just said, "I'm surprised you're not at Miss Perfect's house with all the high-society people and your beloved Rat Packers." She was playing offense already!

"I am not seeing her." I thought that might put out the fire, but I was wrong. I knew there was no point in repeating the discussion we had last November, especially while she was curling her hands into balls and blowing on them to warm them up. I tried to change the subject.

"How is your mom, Lynn? Bet—"

All I got was an ice-cold "FINE!"

"Ok—"

"You hurt me so much last December at that game Larry. I took a night off work to come and see you. I was going to tell you I understood your side of things and I even imagined us making up and sitting at the game together, but no. There you were with the living Barbie doll while she cuddled you during the national anthem. Jeez! I rode over with Jennifer in her car and I cried all the way home after I said hi to you."

By now we were at the deli. When we went in, Doris was wrapping up lunchmeats for the night. She shredded a quick half-pound of cheddar for us and sent us on our way, Lynn acting like I wasn't there the whole time.

After we crossed Agler road and got back to Woodland, I decided to try and stamp out the flames.

"Lynn, you're obviously mad. I'll just leave after I give Mack the cheese. Then everyone can be happy."

"Oh, I'm not mad at you, Larry. Mad isn't the word."

"Oh?"

"I hate you, I hate you, I HATE YOU!"

This, from the girl I had been so in love with last summer! She was staring dead ahead, but she wasn't through, not by a long shot.

"Don't worry. I got even with you. On New Year's Eve, I worked at the Neil House Hotel for Trish's dad. A guy from school I know from the concert band was there busing, too. We went to the after-work party for the staff together, and there was food and music. We danced a lot and he asked me out again, and I said yes! I've gone out with him seven times to games and school stuff."

Internally, my brain was screaming at me for not going to Kathy's and having to put up with this instead. Why didn't I go?

We were at Trish's now. I just handed Lynn the cheese and turned to go.

"Hey, I'm happy that things are better for you and your family. And I, uh . . . bye." Then I just turned and started to go, but I felt her hand grab mine. There were two tiny tears on her cheeks.

"I don't hate you. I'm sorry for saying that. But you hurt me so bad. The one guy I really believed in was gone."

"Well, it sounds like you've found someone. I hope it works out. Seven times, huh?"

"Oh, yeah, whoop-de-do. I went to the movies with him yesterday. He's a junior, and even though the prom is three months away, he asked me to go already."

"I don't need this. I'm going now." But she held on to me.

"Larry, I told him after he asked that, that I thought he was a nice guy but I just wanted to be friends. I'm not going to date him again.

He has a reputation around school as being a mama's boy, and who wants that?"

Why was she telling me this? Five minutes ago she said she hated me!

"Look. It's okay if you stay with us. We'll watch the Beatles, and you're wrong. They'll be the biggest thing ever to hit rock and roll."

I thought to myself that if I really hustled I could get to Kathy's by 7:30 at the latest and find out what lobster tastes like. But then she gave me that little pout she did all the time last summer. I knew she didn't do it on purpose; she just did it. I looked down at my worn clothing and knew this was just the impression Kathy's dad would want to get from that poor boy Kathy liked. And of course, the wind blew, and I could smell Lynn's hair, and she had a feather clip on, and well . . . I decided to stay.

When we got back, the smell of pizza in the oven filled the house. Mack had taken some sauce and added onions, peppers, salami, more pepperoni, and just about everything he could find in Trish's home cupboard and fridge. I noticed the pizzas had an inch of shredded cheese on them.

"Oh, ya know what?" Mack said, fake-thoughtfully. "We had cheese. I just didn't look hard enough." He started to smile but saw the quiet look on our faces and reeled it in.

When Ed Sullivan got started we went to their family room. Lynn was sitting in the love seat, something every house seemed to be getting, but it was awfully small. Mack and Trish and her mother were on the couch. I looked at my options and started to sit by Lynn.

"Can I sit here?" She just nodded. The love seat was small but we seemed a long distance from each other.

When the Beatles came on, the girls were on the edge of their seats going ballistic while Mack and I felt like we were pieces of old wood. They jumped up and were yelling and dancing in front of the TV with every camera pan to the boys' faces. I didn't mind too much. I hadn't ever realized how well Lynn could dance. The girls went through a pattern for the next nine minutes, proclaiming their undying love for whichever Beatle was on the screen.

"Paul! Ohhhhhh, it's JOOOHHNNN. Oh, please, George, are you married? How are you not?" But when they showed the drummer looking stupidly over his cymbals, they melted on the floor. Trish was trying hard to keep up with Lynn's moves, but Lynn could tear a hole in the carpet, she was so good.

"Slow down and show me that step, Lynn," she'd say every five seconds, only to get interrupted by a camera pan to Ringo shaking his hair out of his eyes.

As their first set ended, the poor people who came on afterwards as the interim act could not even hear each other perform, the crowd was so hysterical. Ed Sullivan looked like he had discovered atomic energy. Meanwhile, Lynn actually came over on the love seat and brushed my hair into a Beatles style. Trish rubbed Mack's burr cut sadly.

"Start growing hair, Mack!"

When the second set started the girls stayed in their seats because they wanted to actually hear them sing, but they couldn't help the occasional squeal.

"What do you think, Mack?" I asked during the second song, some ballad about holding hands.

"Eh, not as good as Possum and the Northglenners."

That got him slugged in the gut by Trish. Mercifully, the show ended after six minutes of singing, with Ed Sullivan thanking them and noting they'd be back in one week. Trish's mom got up and turned the tube off, with Trish and Mack going into the kitchen to help her clean up.

"Well, I guess I'll go, Lynn," I said, not expecting much of a response. Even though there'd been a caption on-screen saying John was married, Ringo, George, and Paul were still all fair game. "I don't think any guy is going to have a chance until at least Paul's off the market." I had a lot of strange feelings going on inside me and wanted to digest them all by myself on a walk home.

Lynn walked me to the door, and I decided to stick out a white flag.

"Well, till I see you again . . . bye. Maybe we'll see each other at the pool next summer." I respected her space and was content to leave it at that. I thought about the feather clip back in my drawer and how so long ago she had given it to me right here as I walked down the drive. Then behind me, I heard:

"Wait, wait!"

Lynn followed me out on the snow and gravel in her socks. "Ouch, oh, ahh, oo, ouch," she was saying over again. She caught up to me and brushed her long hair out of her eyes.

If this was a Cary Grant movie, like Mom liked to watch, we would have embraced and said how much we missed each other . . . but we didn't. We kinda stood there hoping the other one would do it first.

She reached into her jacket's big pocket and dug out a brown paper package, then looked at me with her big brown eyes that seemed so sad.

"Look, I didn't think you were coming, but I was going to give this to Mack to give to you. So here. DON'T open this till you're home!" Then she oh-ah-ouched back inside.

When I got home and was in my bedroom, I turned on my desk light and opened the package.

It was a porcelain white knight from a chess set. She had taped a faded note to it that said, "Sometimes, a girl needs a white knight." Then, in a different, fresher ink—maybe from after the basketball game—there was a PS.

"But if you're going to be my knight, I AM YOUR ONLY DAMSEL IN DISTRESS."

As I laid in bed thinking over the evening, I realized it had been six months since Lynn and I had actually been a couple. I was not sure if the note I had just read was a peace offering and an attempt to try again or just a way to finally admit she was maybe, just a little, in the wrong, too.

When I finally fell asleep, I had a dream that I was at a wedding. My wedding. Ten years had passed. It was 1974 and no one knew about the Beatles. I was at the altar waiting for my beautiful bride. On my right was Mack, then Butch. In the front row were Marcie and Trish, each of them were trying to keep several youngsters under control.

Mack nudged me and said, "Finally, after all you've been through, it's your day!" I heard the wedding song start as the bridesmaids started down the aisle. My heart was pounding.

Finally the organist began the part where the bride comes. Through the doors she floated, her white vail accenting her long dark hair, and it was obvious it wasn't Kathy. It was . . . But as I looked at the bride, I realized she was wearing a swimming suit. It was Lesser Brenda! She yelled from halfway down the aisle, "I won. I finally got you!"

Mack turned to me and said, "She always could fill out a bathing suit!"

CHAPTER
SEVENTEEN

One week later, when the Beatles did their second performance, Lynn did not come to Trish's and I stayed home. After a week of waiting to see her again and see what exactly being a damsel in distress meant to her, I found myself once again unsure where we stood or if we would ever get back together. Maybe she'd heard something else about Kathy and me. At any rate, there was no invitation to Kathy's for the second performance, either. I read Lynn's little note at least 20 times, trying to convince myself she had left the door open. But with her no-show, and no way to talk to her, I was in a kind of limbo. It drove me nuts that technically, I could call Kathy at any point but could probably guess how that would go since I stood her up on the first Beatle night. She had avoided me in school like the plague.

E.A. was ready for the Beatles this time. Before the show and after a half dozen Weidemans, he got the broom out of the closet, combed his dark wavy hair over his eyes with a bit of water, and played along with them when they came on. After a few songs I encouraged him to get his tuba out . . . so he did. To his credit, he made an all-brass "I Saw Her Standing There" sound pretty good.

At school in the halls, the Beatles remained kings. Even us guys got over our jealousy and were whistling or singing Beatle tunes in the locker room as baseball preseason started with conditioning and evaluation in the gym. Previously swept-back hairdos started to get noticeably longer on all of us.

On the rare warmer days we were outside throwing and trying to get in some batting practice. But as always, Ohio weather was unpredictable. The first weekend of March was forecast to be the arrival of spring-type weather but ended up being a rain-out. With nothing else planned, Mom suggested it was the perfect day to get my driver's license and I jumped on the chance.

I'd gotten through driver's education the previous fall with only a few scrapes, and of course E.A. had been letting me drive a little even after the tight-turn incident. His last challenge was parallel parking between garbage cans in our street while it felt like the whole world watched, but I got through it just as I did the final exam, with pure determination. The DMV was pretty empty thanks to the rain, and I soon held pure freedom in my wallet. Mack was the first person I called.

"Hey Mack, I got it! I can drive now! Wanna go somewhere? Get some burgers?" But he seemed distracted.

"Larry, if you're not doing anything this afternoon, uh . . . yeah, that one . . . " he said to someone who was there with him. "Come on over and listen to me and Possum's radio station. We started two weeks ago after the Beatle show and have time slots to fill. Possum, put that down."

For a brief moment, I envisioned them in a sound booth playing records and reading the news at one of WCOL's offices downtown. But that was obviously not the case.

"What time, Mack?"

"Be here at my place at two sharp. We start making calls first, then we play records. Last but not least," he imitated a drum roll on the receiver, "the big ... call ... of the day ... ay ... ay ... ay ... ay."

"Nice echo machine, Mack. Your house? Radio station?"

"My house, 2:00 p.m."

So I put on my Mifflin baseball windbreaker and walked through a slushy combination of rain, sleet, and snow. I had looked at Mom with the keys in hand but she shook her head. "It takes years to know how to drive on ice," she said. So much for my license and total freedom.

When I got to Mack's, I just went in the unlocked door. Neither of his parents' cars were home as usual, and I was soaked through and through, almost as bad as the Sewer Creek ice bath, though not as smelly.

I expected to find Mack and Possum in the kitchen, where the Halls' telephone was, but all I could see of the phone was a black extension cord stretched to the max around the doorframe and down the hall to Mack's bedroom out front. Mack was lying on the bed, watching Possum sing the song "Telstar" by the Tornados into the phone, which was held from flinging back into the kitchen by a stack of newspapers. It was a hard song to sing because, well, it was an instrumental. But Possum was doing a good job, alternating between humming through his nose and singing lyrics he was making up on the spot about the original Telstar communications satellite that had been launched in the summer of 1962. When he was done, he thanked their opening listener who they had called and promised to send him a free clavioline, which I guess was what the Tornados used for the sci-fi-sounding melody instead of their noses.

"This isn't a radio show ... " I ventured, thinking how embarrassed I would be if Butch dropped in just then. Mack made a silence sign by slicing his hand down through the air.

"It's how we open our program, Larry. We're in the space age now!" Possum explained. "LIVE, from W-M-A-C-C-C-C! Okay, Mack, you ready for our man-about-town segment? You're on!" With that, he got the phone book, opened it at random, and picked a name.

"Mr. Harold Connors is our lucky pick!"

"Dial him up, Possum." Mack gingerly lifted the phone from underneath the newspapers and stretched even further to his bed. On the sixth ring, a grouchy-sounding man answered.

"Connors Residence. You're interrupting my afternoon nap. This better be important."

Mack thought a bit and went into a sultry Lauren Bacall voice.

"Harold, I am here at the airport. Come get me! I need a ride. I need to see you."

"I don't know who you are," Mr. Connors said in a hushed tone. "What do you want?"

Mack was in his stride now. "Please Harold, don't do this, is your wife there? Harold, we must talk, I need money. I am desperate, Harold, please."

At that point we heard a woman, I assumed Mrs.Connors, in the background.

"HAROLD! Is that one of those hussies you work with? Give me that phone."

Mack wanted to continue but it was clear it was heating up at the Connors household. Possum interjected.

"Mr. Connors, please bear with us. This is Possum and Mack from WMAC radio, you're our man about town today!"

"Harold, give me that phone, now!" Mrs. Connors was yelling in the background.

"Honey, Janet, it's a radio joke, it's, uh, Possum and Mack from a radio station. It's a joke. Please, honey, put the lamp down!"

Mack saved the day. "Harold and Janet, for being such good sports today, we are going to give you a free, large garbage-all-the-way-pizza from Brendan's Big Slice." Mack jerked his hand toward the phone, and Possum joined him at the receiver. In unison, they said, "Just go in and sing 'Lunch is on Possum annnd Maaack!" Mack pushed Possum away. "You and your lovely wife enjoy a night out on romantic 17th Avenue at Brendan's Big Slice, near the trailer park, okay?"

"Boy, oh boy, you guys had me going. I fell like a marble off the table. Honey, put that suitcase away. It's a joke! We're going out for dinner!"

"Have fun, Mr. and Mrs. Connors," Possum yelled. Mack hung up.

I wasn't sure what to think about the whole set-up. It was hilarious, but I wondered about this new alliance between these two.

"Possum, get that record player out from underneath my bed. It's right by the firecrackers," Mack instructed. On top of the turntable was a pack of dusty Oreos.

I guess even after a year of adventure and even romancing some girls, I knew deep down that Mack still was just a big kid who loved to prank, and he felt he could do that with Possum. He sure wouldn't have done this with Butch, and I tended to be just about as serious. It was the only explanation for this strange afternoon.

"Okay next up, put on the Robin Hood record, Possum," Mack said between dusty Oreo bites. "And find me a contestant for name that song!"

Possum closed his eyes and opened the phone book to Mr. Byron Granger, Karl Rd., in Columbus. On the third ring, a very nice older woman answered.

"Grangers, hello? Who is this?"

"HELLO! This is Possum and Mack on W! M! A! C, C, C! You have been chosen from over one hundred thousand names. What do you think about that?"

"Uh, oh my, I've never won anything in my life. What should I do?"

Possum explained that the station would play a song and if she guessed the title, she would win a free meal from the Big Bev Restaurant, a steakhouse in nearby Whitehall. He then asked if she was ready. I saw him switch the record speed to seventy-eight before playing about ten high-speed seconds.

"Well, Mrs. Granger, what's your guess?"

"I . . . I'm not sure. They sing so fast. It's, uh, the Chipmunks singing their Christmas song."

"OHHHHH no, Mrs. Granger," said Mack. "So close, so very close, but no. We'll play it again on regular speed for you."

Possum put the record on forty-five. This time you could hear the theme to one of the Robin Hood shows that had been popular a few years back.

Robin Hood
Robin Hood
Coming around the bend
Robin Hood
Robin Hood
With his group of men
Robin's as sly as a fox
Little John's as strong as an ox . . .

At that point Possum scraped the needle off the record. Mack quietly mouthed "be careful" but turned his attention back to the phone.

"Well, Mrs. Granger, what do you think?

"Uh, well, all they say is Robin Hood, so that's my guess."

"Aw, no! Mrs. Granger you're so close, so close, but no! I'll tell you what. I will let the studio audience vote."

I held my thumb up, Possum's went down. Mack told Mrs. Granger it was a tie but that he held the deciding vote and he was going to give her the free meal at Big Bev's.

"Oh, thank you Mr. Mack Possum, thank you. I'm shocked."

Possum leaned in. "Remember, Mrs. Granger, just walk into the Big Bev and sing this song for your free meal: 'Lunch is on Possum and Mack!' So long!"

Mrs. Granger wasn't done yet. "But! Uh, Mr. Mack Possum, I know it's a bother, but may I sing on the radio, please? I can't wait to tell the girls at our Thursday lunch at the Food Corral about this."

Mack looked at Possum, Possum looked at me and I just shrugged.

"Go ahead, Mrs. G!" Mack said.

She began to belt out the first few words of "Danny Boy." At first she was on key, but then she began to shriek and hold the notes forever. Once Mack and Possum were done rolling on the floor, Possum blew a cavalry charge with his bugle into the phone and they hung up on her.

"Well, that was awful," I said, putting my coat on to go.

"Wait, wait, Larry, you don't want to miss the big call of the day!" said Possum.

"Can it get any bigger?" I asked.

"Yes, sir! I'm going to call Melanie and ask her for a date."

"Melanie? Melanie Ryder from the Rat Pack? No way, Possum."

"Oh, yeah way," Possum said. "She is in my study hall and she loves me. You won't be the only one with a Rat Pack girlfriend, Larry." Mack raised his eyebrow and glanced at me, but Possum was already dialing. I sat back down again. This had potential for disaster, and I wanted to see it happen. On the sixth ring, Melanie answered.

"Ryders, you got Melanie here."

"Hi, Melanie, this is Possum. You know, Carl Carlson from school in your study hall, third period."

"Yes, Possum, I know you. What do you want?" Melanie sounded bored.

"Remember you said you'd go out with me?"

"No, I said if you were the only person on earth, I'd think about it. But only if I wasn't busy."

At that point I heard another girl in the background ask who was on the phone. I knew that voice. It was Kathy.

"It's, uh, Possum, Carl Possum something."

"Who all is there? What is this?" I heard Kathy ask.

"Well, actually, you're on WMAC, we're broadcasting from Mack's bedroom. Melanie is the big call of the day."

"So, who all is there?" Kathy asked again. "Wait, you know me, Possum. Larry kinda introduced us at the pizza place."

"Ahhh, yes!" said Possum, like he'd been recognized in the street by an old friend. "So me and Mack and Lar-" At that point I threw a pillow at Possum and shook my head. But now Kathy was getting pushy.

"Is Larry there? Tell me the truth!"

"Nope, he's not here!" Mack yelled. She then asked to speak to Mack, but Possum held on to the phone.

"I'm Larry's best friend, no worries. Talk to me."

"When you see him, tell him to stop giving me the cold shoulder and talk to me! It was bad enough he stood me up the night of the Beatle Show! Larry is who I want to date. I REPEAT, I want to date Larry! Mack, can you hear me? Is he seeing the Indian again?" Mack yanked the phone away from Possum.

"Well, time is up for today's program, folks! Live from WMAC, don't step in the cow patties, all you Mifflinites!"

He hung up and glared at Possum. I put on my jacket again and Possum pulled his paper bag from underneath Mack's bed.

"Wait, who's doing your paper route today, Possum?"

"Uh, Teddy is my new sub. I'm so busy with the band and the radio station that I hired him to do it for half what I make. It's a great deal for him."

I wondered if Teddy would get paid as I picked up yesterday's paper from the side of Possum's bag and started to look at the sports section. Then an article in the metro section caught my eye:

Local Restaurants Sour On Bogus Prizes

A number of restaurants in the Northglenn and Whitehall areas have called police hotlines about customers arriving and demanding free meals given to them by a supposed radio program. Police are making an attempt to trace the origin of the calls but have had little luck in resolving what they believe to be just a prank. Police remind residents that there is no radio station in the Central Ohio area with the broadcast sign WMack and request that residents report further . . .

I showed the article to Mack. He had already read it and said today's show would be the last now that I'd gotten to experience it.

"You're fired, Possum. The station is closing."

This didn't seem to alarm Possum, who tossed his harmonica, bugle, and records into his newspaper bag.

"As long as I can add it to my resume," he replied. "Say, Larry, when I date Melanie, maybe we would let you and Kathy double date with us, since you can drive now. That would be great wouldn't it? And you can pick us up. I don't think Melanie has a car."

"Possum," Mack said as he pushed him out the door. "She is not going to go out with you. Ever."

We could hear Possum playing taps as he walked away. After Possum was out of hearing range, we broke out a couple of root beers and Mack fried some Spam with cheese and melted butter. Mack called them his heart-attack specials.

"So, what are you going to do?"

"About what Mack?"

"Come on, about Kathy or Lynn. They're both gorgeous, they both seem to like you. What's keeping you from making a decision, anyway?"

"We're back to serious Mack now, I see."

"Not serious, just real. I can goof off and still care about my best friend, right?"

"Lynn and I fought bad before we watched the Beatles show, you could tell. Later she gave me a note saying she wanted to be my damsel in distress, but who knows if there's hope or not when I can't even call her? Do I sit on my hands and wait for her?"

"Want my opinion, for what it's worth? I'll tell you who you belong with. If you don't like my answer, then give me back that sandwich cause I ain't feeding traitors!"

I gulped down half the sandwich.

"Too late, but let's hear it."

But then there was a knock at the door; looking outside I could see it was Trish.

"Hey guys, how'd the radio program go?" she asked. They both had smirks on their faces and I smelled another set-up. I went to the door to see if Lynn was there, but she wasn't.

Mack answered her.

"Not bad, Possum went out with a bang. Come on, Larry, we're going to take you out to supper."

"We just ate, Mack!"

Mack burped and said it was an appetizer.

"Please say 'excuse me,' Mack!" Trish said, laying down the law.

"Excuse you, Trish," Mack said, burping again. Trish gave Mack an if-looks-could-kill glare. I didn't want to be in the middle of that, so I called Mom and told her I'd be eating with Mack and Trish. When I got off the phone they were looking longingly into each other's eyes, so it seemed like last fall's tensions over manners had mostly evaporated. We got in his '57 Chevy, and he started it up with a roar.

"Gonna paint this baby candy-apple red this summer," he said as we raced down Perdue Avenue towards East Linden. I had to laugh at them as a couple: Mack had taught Trish to shift gears as he worked the clutch.

"Where are we going?" I asked as she slammed the Hurst Shifter into fourth gear and my forehead bounced off the back of the front seat.

"We're eating at Maddie's. I told Lynn we were bringing you over," Trish replied with a grin. Resigned to my fate as a captive prisoner, I watched the familiar houses whiz by. Amazing how fast you could get there in a car, considering I always walked this route.

As we stood waiting to be seated, I saw Lynn in full waitress mode. She smirked a little when she saw us and motioned to the hostess to seat us in her area. The new Maddie's was twice the size and twice as homey; the old gentleman who owned it had spared no expense, and the regulars were rewarding him with gangbuster business. We sat down in a corner booth.

"Well, isn't this a surprise," she said with a grin as she brought out the waters. I also saw her lean over to Trish and whisper "Thanks" and then, "Back with the menus in a second."

She smacked me playfully on the head and laughed. Mack nudged me and winked.

"I get it," I said with a playful groan.

Over behind the counter I saw who I remembered as Lynn's mom, watching me like a hawk. To complete the family, a younger girl, maybe 11 or 12, went by with the busing cart putting silverware and napkins on the clean tables. She was a little fairer than Lynn, but she had the same nose and smile. I guessed it was her little sister, Kristy. It seemed like a fifth of the workforce was related to Lynn.

"Hiya, Trish, is this the famous Mack?" Kristy said while staring at me.

"The only one there is, Kristy," Trish said while holding her fingers behind Mack's head like horns. Kristy continued to look at me but laughed.

We ordered, and Lynn was all business until the end, when she took her break and sat down beside me, pushing me further into the booth. But then she leaned over and whispered.

"Did you read the note I gave you? With the knight?" She was nervously biting her lip as she waited for me to respond.

"Yes," I said as quietly as I could.

At that point Trish and Mack got up and went over to the bakery part of the restaurant and were looking at the pastries. I heard Mack say, "Nothing for me, I'm watching my figure." It was obvious they were just giving us space.

"So does being here mean you are a one-damsel type of white knight from now on and forever?"

I looked into her eyes, and this time they weren't nervous but seemed bright with hope. My heart beat my brain to the draw.

"Yes, that's what it means, Lynn."

"Okay," was all she said, squeezing my hand under the table. She got up like nothing had happened, but entering the kitchen she turned and gave me the warmest smile I'd seen since last summer. I got out my wallet and figured I'd give the biggest tip I could, but Kristy playfully came over with the busing cart as she cleaned up a table across from us.

She started to sing in a little sister sing-song while looking away. "I know who you are . . . I know who you are . . . my sister loves you."

CHAPTER
EIGHTEEN

From that night at Maddie's on, I was constantly plotting when I could see Lynn again. I was even thinking about it outside the school during lunch the next Monday, sitting on the stone steps at the school's entrance when I heard soft footsteps behind me. I turned and saw it was Kathy, brushing off the low brick wall before sitting on it and swinging her legs.

"So, did your friends Mack and Possum tell you I spoke to them Saturday?"

I decided to be coy. "No, when did you see them?"

"I didn't. They called Melanie's house acting like they were on a radio station or something. That Possum guy wanted a date with Melanie and I asked to speak to you. It sounded like you were there. You were there, weren't you?"

"I try not to get mixed up in those hijinks." I looked off in the distance and tried to be cool like Steve McQueen, but I could feel Kathy drilling holes into my head with her eyes.

"I wanted to tell you that I am not interested in anyone else, so if you weren't there, I'm saying it again."

"Gee, Kathy, I want to believe it, I really do. But three times this school year, I wanted to be your guy and got sidelined. First it was Joe the Fullback, then Brian the future senator, then the Gent who looked like he had rubbed a bottle and got you as his first wish. I don't really want there to be a fourth time, you know?"

"Oh, come on, my mom just made me . . ."

"Is your mom ashamed of me or what? Am I not good enough for her? 'Cause that's the way it seemed."

"Larry, in a couple years we will be in college, right? And then who cares what she thinks. In the meantime, they've got their appearances to keep up and I've got mine."

My folks had never talked about college because I knew they didn't have the money. But that was beside the point.

"Doesn't it bother you to be moved around like a chess piece?" I asked quietly. I tried to see life from Kathy's perspective and understand how she felt about having her mom trying to constantly relive her life through her daughter. My mom never quite got over not being a 20-something anymore, I don't think, but at least she didn't try to relieve it through me. It couldn't be fun . . . but then there was that New Year's Eve memory. Even though I was back with Lynn and wanted to be a hundred percent, having that moment with Kathy was a hard thing to just forget about. My thoughts gave her some time to think about a response.

"No! Well, yes. Look, Larry, right now Mom wants me to date around and be involved in everything, pad my resume for college applications. She wants me to be the first two-time homecoming Queen." At that, Kathy actually laughed and put a plastic smile on her face and waved like a puppet. I couldn't help but chuckle.

"Do you think you really could achieve that with me as a boyfriend?"

She hesitated long enough that I knew that she knew the real answer. But now she was looking at me like she had on the deck. I avoided her glance and gazed over at the baseball field, where the janitors were putting lime on the foul lines for our first scrimmage game tonight. I figured I should tell her about Lynn at some point during the conversation but wasn't sure how.

"I am a one-girl guy, Kathy, I told you at the beginning. I don't two-time, I don't like being two-timed."

"And you love Pocahontas, don't you?"

She immediately regretted that, I think. Not so much that she said it, but she said it to me. She looked like she'd accidentally cussed in church.

"Oh gosh, look, I'm sorry. I didn't mean that how it sounded. Maybe I've been around Aubrey too much. A lot of the girls called her that last summer. I didn't ever, honestly. I mean, she's beautiful. If she came from a wealthy family, she'd have it all, I'd be jealous of her."

I felt the sting of that last sentence all the way to the soles of my feet. I must have thought too long because Kathy simply nodded her head and sighed.

"Look, when Mom caught us kissing, she told me the next day to not get so involved with just one guy because you ruin your chances to be popular. Especially if . . . Well, look, I want it to be us. Mom doesn't have to know!"

"That's good, because she'd try to give me one of your dad's old suits if she did."

"I get a big allowance. We could go over to Penney's today, there is a nice lady there in clothing, she'd know what you'd look good in."

I wondered if she meant my mom.

"No, Kathy I won't do that. You gotta realize . . ."

"But I could help you become more . . . more—"

"More like Brian or one of the Gents? Nah, I'd rather not. Look Kathy, you're wonderful, truly beautiful. You know that Johnny Tillotson song, 'Poetry in Motion'? That's you." She blushed a bit. "But I think we hafta just realize we come from opposite sides of town and we can't get over that. Your mom can't, anyway." I got up to leave.

"What does Lynn have that I don't have? Tell me . . . tell me!"

I was stunned she actually called her by her name. I simply reached over and hugged her gently as she sat on the stone guardrail.

"You've got everything, Kathy. You don't need me."

Later that night we played Whetstone, a major City League school, in a scrimmage game. I started the game in center field and played the first five innings, and then the coach put in the seniors. We had a three run lead when they took over, but by the bottom of the seventh we were behind by two. They were obviously not in shape, except for our ace pitcher, who wasn't part of their clique. He kept his head and didn't give up, but we lost anyway. Still, us underclassmen held our own against the powerful Whetstone Jaguars and the scoreboard proved it.

At the team meeting after the game, one of the seniors, who also had Gent connections, stood up and interrupted the Coach. "Mr. Barnhart, maybe you're not aware of the senior rule. You started mostly underclassmen, and we lost the game."

Coach stood there and said, with zero emotion, "I went with my starters and was doing fine. You seniors lost the game. Four errors, five strikeouts. All by seniors."

"Seniors don't sit on the bench," he protested.

"It's my team now. I make the decisions."

Right then, six of the seniors went into a huddle about 10 feet off. Coach Barnhart waited for them silently. I felt like I saw a little smile in the corner of his mouth. The guys came back looking full of themselves.

"Mr. Barnhart, we quit."

Coach was chewing gum, and he rolled it to the side of his mouth. Without skipping a beat he responded, "Don't forget to turn in your equipment!

Only our two senior pitchers stayed, including our ace, but the other one had been on the reserve team for the two years prior. It was one hundred percent Coach's team now. He looked at Mr. Arwell, who was the assistant coach when it wasn't wrestling or dance-chaperoning season. "Jim, let's bring up Kinset and Norman from the reserves." Then he turned to us.

"You're the varsity team. Anyone else want to quit?"

"NO!"

Then he put a hand on our senior pitcher's shoulder. "Billy, you're the captain. This is your team as much as it is mine, now." He turned to the freshman catcher, who was a big, stout kid for his age. "You're my catcher. Can you handle it full time, all nine innings?" He looked around at the team and just nodded. As a group, we stood in a circle and put our hands on the coach's hand.

Our new captain yelled, "On three: One, two, three . . . TEAM!"

From then on, things were different in baseball. There was no room for loafing; Coach Barnhardt kept a tally and made us run sprints, sometimes even backwards, for mistakes we could have avoided. We were able to get in a few more scrimmages before the weather turned ugly again, and while our inexperience showed, we were a tougher opponent and managed to beat Columbus West, who had a long history of winning seasons. Most of all, Coach knew how to teach baseball. And we ate it up.

All that stopped on the last Thursday of March, when it went from seventy degrees in the morning to a full-on blizzard at 5:00 in the afternoon. The snow lasted two days and put a halt to spring ball. On Friday, school was canceled—and when the buses couldn't make it through town with their chained-up tires, you knew it was bad. I slept in until 9:00 and shoveled snow all the rest of the day, wishing I was patrolling center field somewhere.

When I got home at 5:00, I immediately sat down to count my riches only to get an unexpected call from Butch. Usually he didn't call. You just kinda knew when he wanted you by instinct, like when you sensed a storm was coming. I picked up the phone and didn't even have a chance to say hello.

"Hey, Larry, the gang is sledding tomorrow. Be at the park at noon, no later. Oh, bring some firewood if you still got some." Something about the way he spoke made it seem like this was the last sledding day ever, but maybe that was just Butch and his decisiveness.

"Sure, Butch, what's the occasion?"

"It snowed, ya dolt, that's what."

So next morning, I got up, ate, and took heavy twine from the kitchen utility drawer to tie the last of my firewood in a bundle. The snow was compact enough that I could just drag the whole bundle behind me on its bark like a sled, which was handy as I didn't own one. I could have bought one like the old wood-and-steel one back at Gramps's, but I wanted my mom's old '56 Bel Air more and I knew it'd help if I kind of "bought it" from them. Besides, according to Mack, you usually used garbage can lids, big pieces of cardboard, or whatever you could find.

As I entered the park I heard a rumbling sound over on the hill, unlike any sled I'd ever heard before. Then I saw Butch and Marcie roaring down the hill on an old refrigerator door. They were flying like a bobsled in the Olympics, with the refrigerator door sounding like a cement mixer on high gear. I walked over to where they had crash-landed and helped Butch pull the door back up the hill, which was smooth as glass from all the times they'd gone down.

When we got to the top, Butch took my firewood and threw a good portion in the burn barrel he had going. It went off in a spout of sparks.

"Go on, Larry, try it. I gotta dry my mitts. Ya can't steer at all, so use your boots to stop or you'll go into Sewer Creek."

"Already done that once this winter."

I got positioned and stuck my feet in the shelves while Marcie came up from behind and gave me a running start. Just as I started to go, I saw Mack arrive with some big cardboard pieces and heard him challenge me to a race, but then he vanished in a blur.

Onboard it sounded like a snowplow breaking the sound barrier. The snow was so slick I felt like I was pulling Gs like you read about Air Force test pilots doing. I stuck my two feet out and managed to dig into the snow without breaking any bones, stopping six inches short of the old snow fence by the creek. It was rotten old splinters bound up with rusty fencing; the fridge door could have flattened it easily if I'd not started braking halfway down the hill.

"Wow, what a doozy!" I said to Mack, who arrived a few seconds after. We lugged it back up the hill together, only to find Trish and Lynn by the burn barrel. Lynn was wearing a big parka with fur around her face like she was about to climb Mt. Everest.

"Hey, Lynn, I didn't know you were coming today. Are you cold?"

She smiled. "Heard you guys were sledding. And for goodness sake, it's like minus 20." It was only 30, but Lynn was more of a summer girl. Butch was tossing more of the firewood into the barrel and seemed to smile to himself.

"Take her for a ride on the door, Larry," he said. "Mack, help me get this fire going. Once you guys walk back up you'll get good and warm."

So I got on, and she clambered on behind me.

"Wait, what do I hold on to?" she yelled as Marcie gave us a good push, and down we went.

"Me!" I shouted back as she wrapped her arms around my shoulders. When we stopped, she was laughing hysterically.

"Oh, that was fun! Man, you guys do all kinds of great stuff." She lay down beneath the quickly darkening clouds that now looked like rain and made a snow angel. I let her finish before pulling her back to her feet. As we walked back up the hill I pulled on the rope with one hand, and I felt her take a hold of my other mitten.

"Pull me up the hill, too. Whew!" she said, dragging her feet. "And what are you grinning about? You look like the cat that ate the canary."

Well, I felt like a million bucks. She seemed like the old Lynn again. I turned and put a gloveless hand on her cheek.

"Just happy you're here, Lynn. I never knew I could miss someone so much."

When we got to the top, the crowd was getting bigger, including adults. Marcie got on top of Butch's shoulders and made an announcement that everyone was invited back to the Blains' farm for cider and hot dogs and marshmallows cooked over their produce barn's wood stove once we'd had our fill of sledding. We went up and down for another half-hour before hot cider started sounding good, although from tugging the fridge door and Lynn up the hill I was getting pretty hot inside my flannel jacket.

Possum arrived just as we started to go. Butch told him he would get one year taken off his probation if he took the fridge door back to Butch's house before meeting up with the gang at Marcie's, and Possum bowed and raced off, the fridge bouncing behind him. Free of the door, we all took Lucky Duck Trail down through the woods; the creek wasn't frozen because of the recent warm weather, but the snow covered everything up to the water's edge. We must have looked like the front of a Christmas card as the six of us walked along the trail.

When we came to Troll's cave, Trish and Lynn made Mack stop and explain what it was.

"Trolls live in there in the summer, of course," Mack volunteered. "Sometimes Possums, too."

"The trolls go to Florida for the winter, though," Marcie added.

"I wanna look in there," Lynn said kind of cautiously.

Mack and I went in first, just to make sure there wasn't anything too bad. All we could see was an old blanket, some newspapers that dated back a few years, plus the remains of some campfires and a very large snake skin that had been shed.

Lynn peeked in behind us. "Any trolls?"

"Nope, gone till spring," I joked. Of course, at that point she had to come in and she jumped back when she saw the snakeskin.

"Yuck! What on earth is that?" Lynn was a city girl at the end of the day; she was all sorts of brave, but she probably had never seen a dried snake skin.

"Snakes have lotsa suits of clothing," Mack said. "He probably left it here by mistake."

"No, Mack. What is it?"

Mack insisted the snake would come back for it when it needed it.

"Unh-uh, quit it. You're both making fun of me."

Lynn and Trish quickly had enough of the cave. We left and were soon inside the Blain barn over the hill. I never quite realized how close it was; in fact, Marcie mentioned it was technically on their property.

Marcie's dad had a big pot-bellied stove roaring, and it was almost too warm for coats inside the shack. Once we arrived, Marcie's mom and Dad went back to the house and came back with cider and food. We all crowded around the potbelly stove to start roasting dogs.

"You guys have so much fun," Lynn said, holding her hands close to the almost-glowing cast iron of the stove. Then she stood in front of me and was dancing to the tunes on the radio that was playing in the barn. "I wish I could go to Mifflin and do this every time it snowed."

"Me too, Lynn," I laughed. "But it's not every weekend we do stuff like this."

Marcie's dad asked us to follow him to the lean-to against the barn. We found Marcie there with a little lamb in her arms. Behind her, I saw about 20 ewes inside in the main barn. Off to the side, in smaller separate pens, were several ewes that had new lambs.

"What are they, Marcie?" I asked. I knew most sheep breeds, but these I didn't recognize. They were white with black spots and had horns; a few of them had four. I had never seen them at a fair.

"Jacob's sheep. They're a Scottish breed, I guess," said Marcie. "Some people say they're descendants of the sheep Jacob chose from his father-in-law in the Bible, but we just have them to eat the grass in the orchard and grapevine areas." She nudged Butch. "Would you choose 'em?"

Butch didn't get the hint, or at least didn't let on that he did.

Lynn asked to hold a lamb, so she and Marcie and Trish got in with one of the older ewes. The girls were of course in love with the lamb and never wanted to leave. "This mama is Baa Baa," Marcie explained, patting a fluffy, gentle ewe with big eyes. "She's calm. She won't mind if we hold her little girl."

Lynn cuddled the lamb and cooed to it. As I looked at her from the other side of the pen, I tried to imagine Kathy doing this. It was a strange thought but I couldn't shake it out. Lynn was so sincere and wholesome. It made me want to kick myself for the way I had reacted to all that had happened to us, and wonder what I ever saw in Kathy and her suits and allowances and fancy foods.

We left after about an hour, Butch staying behind. True to tradition, Possum arrived just as we were heading out.

"Hey gang, I'm here. Where is everyone going?"

"Back home, but there's food in the barn," I told him, knowing he'd be third-wheel for either Mack or me if he didn't get distracted. That was all he needed to hear, and he was in the barn in a flash. The four of us walked out to Agler Road and headed for Northglenn, with me falling back with Lynn while Mack and Trish walked ahead.

"Uh, are you staying the night?" I asked.

She shook her head. "No, I was here last night. I gotta work tomorrow. I came over because Kristy's grandparents came down from Akron to see her today . . . so I usually leave when they come. Mom and her meet them downtown."

I wondered what it'd be like to have to have to leave when your sister's grandparents who were not yours came to visit . . . because you weren't welcome. But Lynn never complained. She just kept that pretty chin up all the time.

"So you'll just have Trish and Mack take you back, I guess?"

"Unless I find someone to walk me home."

I suppressed a grin. "I volunteer. You have a suitcase at Trish's?"

"No, just a grocery bag with my stuff." She stooped to get a handful of snow. Mack and Trish were a few feet ahead of us so I yelled up to them.

"Mack, we're stopping at my house and then we'll get Lynn's stuff and I'll walk her home."

"Good, I don't want to waste gasoline driving anyone home in this slush," he said, acting gruff. But he laughed as Trish tugged on his ear. Behind me I heard the swing of an arm and felt the thud of a snowball on my back.

When we stopped at my house, no one was home. I tore out of my heavy winter gear in my room as fast as I could and put my baseball windbreaker on in case it rained, because outside a warm wind was blowing all of a sudden. March could and did do everything, sometimes in the same day.

I looked at the feather clip, which I had rehung on the bedpost, and thought how strange it was that Lynn was right here in the house. What a feeling! I shook my head and ran downstairs, and we headed over to Mecca Drive for Lynn's paper-bag suitcase.

Finally, it was just us and the old familiar road from last summer. I started to talk, but Lynn interrupted.

"Have I ever told you my Cherokee name?"

"No. I guess I never thought you had another name."

"When my father was here three years ago, he told me what name he had given me after he found out I was born."

"It's not Lynn?"

"It's 'Ahyoka.' In Cherokee it means, 'she brought happiness.'"

"That's beautiful, Lynn." I felt like I didn't have the right to repeat it.

"I'm gonna have it added to my legal name when I get old enough. Until then, I'm Lynn Bennet, no middle name. What's yours?"

"Thomas. It means . . . uh, 'sometimes, he is stupid.'"

Lynn laughed and we walked another block.

"How many days till your birthday, Lynn?" I knew it was in mid-April, but it was another thing she had been vague about. This time she didn't hesitate.

"Ten days from now, next Thursday."

"Do you think you can go out on car dates then?"

"Maybe if I find a guy with a car." Then she got serious. "Okay, Larry Sometimes-Stupid. Let's clear the air. What's in the past is in the past. Right?"

I feel like I had as much to gain from that as she did.

"Y—"

"And we learned and we're stronger for it, right?"

"Ye—"

"And you're my guy, right?"

I wondered if I was going to get a word in edgewise.

"Objection, Miss Bennett. My client hasn't actually answered, but he says, 'yes.'"

She smiled but wasn't through as we got to the old apartment building that was my stopping point.

"Good. Then I am going to tell you something about me you don't know. Even Trish doesn't know. But you need to know it." I gulped. What could this even be?

"Mom says she likes what she hears about you, but she wants me to show you something, and she says it'll make a difference. Time to prove one of us wrong."

Now my mind was racing.

"Come on," she said, as she took my hand and started down Denune Street past the rundown apartment where we always stopped.

We walked a quarter of a mile until we came to Cleveland Avenue and Tubby's Tavern. Tubby's was nothing more than an old three-story house with the bar on the bottom floor, probably some old house built before the Depression. I was going to joke that we should look for E.A.'s car when she stood before it and crossed her arms.

"Okay. This is where I live."

"At Tubby's?" I said dumbly.

"No, idiot, up on the third floor. Come on, Mom isn't home, but you can come up." We walked up a shoddy stairway to the third level, past a kitchen ventilator belching out fried air. Lynn unlocked the door and we went in.

I could tell this apartment had been the attic years ago when this was just another house on Cleveland Ave. There were just splintery wood floors and two windows, front and back. The one in the now-living room had a pane boarded over. There were two other rooms, plus a bath, all tidy but small.

Lynn matter-of-factly got us a drink by turning the cold water spigot on the kitchen sink. The handle was replaced by a rusty old pair of vise grips, but I recognized the glasses as the heavy red glass ones from Maddies.

"We get the chipped ones for free," she chuckled, handing it to me. "Home, sweet home."

I looked down the way into the one bedroom. It looked like she shared it with her sister. There was an old surplus army bunk bed, plus a dresser with a photo I recognized.

"I still have the picture your dad took of us at the airport last year in my room," she said, grinning. "Just put it back out recently. Well, what do you think?"

"At least I know where to pick you up, now?" I smiled. I could tell a load had been taken off Lynn's shoulders.

"Remember last summer when I had to actually tell you it was ok to hug me? Because you're so dimwitted sometimes." I nodded. "Well, I am reinstating that privilege now. You don't have to ask or wait for me to start it."

So I hugged her for a good minute or two and then she said that I'd better go. "Mom will be home soon. She said I should tell you, but she didn't actually say I should bring you in the apartment, and she can be weird about these sorts of things."

As we went back down the stairs, it was raining softly but it seemed more intense with the snow that was rapidly becoming an iced-over glacier. As I turned to walk home a '57 two-tone green Dodge Coronet pulled in the back lot. I could see Lynn's mom and sister in the car. Happily, they didn't see me. Lynn kept my windbreaker but I didn't even notice the rain, I was feeling so good.

Late Sunday evening I was upstairs trying to do my homework but thinking about the night before. The rain had continued, and a weird sort of fog had descended on Mifflin as the snow slowly melted. Then Mom came up and had a concerned look on her face.

"Larry, are you in some kind of trouble?"

"No . . ."

"Because there is a mean-looking guy at the door who wants to see you."

"What's he look like, Mom?"

"Well, he looks like James Dean, down to the old leather jacket." I laughed. Mom had never met Butch. I went down, let him in, and introduced him to Mom. Butch was strangely polite, winning Mom over in a heartbeat.

"My goodness, you really do resemble James Dean. Back in the '50s, he was my favorite, before he . . ." With that her voice trailed off.

Butch showed a completely different side of himself and just smiled. "It is really nice of you to compare me to him, Mrs. Darnell."

Mom said she had some cookies that would be up in 15 minutes, so we climbed the stairs to my room.

As usual, Butch sat right on the floor and stared at me. I think he did that to make you nervous, but this wasn't the first time he had tried that on me and so I went first.

"So, what's up, Butch?" I asked. "Been seeing a lot of you, lately."

"Ok, here's why I'm here. First, Marcie's parents sold the farm and are moving their operation to Plain City, about an hour from here. A housing developer bought the land and will start tearing down the buildings and bulldozing it up for lots."

I opened my mouth to say I was shocked, but he waved me off.

"I've known about it since late January. Last night was kinda the end. It's never good to know something's the last time, because everyone acts weird. So I'm just telling you now."

"So what happens to you two guys? You're gonna drive all the way out there every weekend?"

"I'm getting there. Don't rush me. You know I turned 18 last November. I know that seems way off in the distance for you, but it ain't. So about the time those creeps from England started ruining the radio, I enlisted in the Navy for six years. Wasn't going to wait for them to come get me."

"Wow!" was all I could say.

"Got my first choice of assignments 'cause of the long contract. Gonna do PT boats like JFK."

"When do you go, Butch?" He shrugged and dropped the bomb.

"In two weeks. I'm quitting school soon. I'm only a junior, and I ain't staying in school 'till I am almost 20. Nothing I'm gonna learn there I can't learn while gettin' paid in the Navy."

"So what does Marcie think about all this?" I asked with some concern.

"She hates it, whaddya think she thinks? But what are we going to do? She's got two years of school left, by then I'll probably be in some crap swamp in Asia." Then he smiled. "Navy PT crews go everywhere, pretty far inland sometimes. I told 'em I got some experience with boats."

I laughed. "Yeah, ya do."

"Well, Marcie's gorgeous, and she's gonna find someone else. Not gonna let it be while I'm writing' her sad letters and staying away from the local girls, ya know? So we're over." Butch acted tough, but I knew why he turned around suddenly. He looked at the picture of me and Lynn sitting in the C-121 Cockpit. It was the same one Lynn had. I'd taken it out the night before when I got back.

"You made the right choice, friend. I know it was a hard time." Then he stood up, stretched, and cracked his knuckles. "Buuuuuuutttt . . . I like Lynn even more because she kept me from havin' to kill you if you went with the queen of River View."

Mom brought up some cookies. He wrapped half-a-dozen in a napkin, ate one thoughtfully, and headed out. "See ya!" was all he said as I watched him walk alone into the fog.

CHAPTER
NINETEEN

With Lynn's birthday in early April, I'd wanted to do something special for her for weeks. She had teased me about going to a fancy restaurant, The Top of the Town, in Columbus, and I had enough cash in hand to pull it off. But Mom told me I wasn't ready for big city driving, so that was out. Instead, the gang just had a party for her at Trish's, cake and ice cream. After visions of us sitting in the Top's big leather booths eating prime rib, it felt a little childish, but she seemed to enjoy it.

Afterwards, I humbly drove us up to the A&W Root Beer stand. She said she loved the frosty mugs and was a good sport, even putting a straw in her root beer and blowing bubbles.

"See Larry, I couldn't have done that at the Top. Kids do it all the time at Maddie's, and it's pretty fun." Somehow, Lynn had a way of making any place seem like it was exactly where you wanted to be, and I cheered up. After that, we headed out to go clothes shopping—all and all, not bad for our first car date.

We made a big effort those last few weeks of April to see each other as much as we could, now that we were "official." It was hard with our schedules—and yes, the different-school problem was more inconvenient than I anticipated, even with wheels. But summer was just around the corner, and I knew I had made the right decision. Still, both of us talked about how we were going to make this work next year during school—Lynn seemed to bring it up way more often than I did. Despite that, we really didn't come up with any concrete ideas. But if it meant me going to Linden's football games to watch her march in the band and her coming over to watch my games, I was okay with that.

Out on the baseball diamond, things were good, too. By the first week of May, we were solidly in third place in the regional league and pushing our way up towards second place. Only longtime rivals Gahanna and Hilliard stood in our way. In hushed tones, guys on the team were starting to believe we could win the league, especially since we'd beat Hilliard's summer team last Fourth of July. Of course, you didn't want to jinx it by actually saying so too loud. But the team was really jiving as a unit, and I wasn't too surprised when our shortstop asked me to wait up for him as we left the school after trouncing Grove City.

"Hey, are you gonna be home tomorrow afternoon, Larry?"

"Sure, Curt, what's up?"

"A little surprise, buddy. You'd be doing me a huge favor if you helped me out with a . . . project."

"Ok, as long as it's before 2:00. Lynn and I have a date to go on a picnic after her work shift ends at 4:00. I'm going to ask her to the spring dance next weekend." Roxanne was in charge of the rescheduled dance this year and had hired the Midnight Ghost from 1230 AM, the new WCOL radio, to MC. This dance was open to the entire school and would be my and Lynn's first appearance at my school, really. Curt just gave a thumbs-up and got in the car of another friend, who was taking him home.

I found time to wax the '56 Bel Air the next day while waiting for whatever Curt had planned. It had set out for most of its life, and the red was more pink than Campbell's-soup-red, now, and the white was a dirty cream color. Mack told me not to worry because as soon as it was mine he was going to paint it metallic black. Then I'd get chrome rims and accessories and be able to show up in style. Inside, E.A. was having his own celebration of good news after having been chosen salesman of the month. The only guest at his little party was Mr. Wiedemann's. Mom was out back suntanning; it was all the rage in women's magazines. By the time I was wiping off the last of the wax, E.A. had turned professional crooner, serenading the roast that was thawing on the counter and cha-cha-ing with the broom. I knew he was really lit when he got down on his shoulder on the tile floor, like Curley did, and went around in circles saying "wooooooooo-woooooooo-woooooooooo."

"The inmates are running the asylum," I thought out loud. Just then, Curt pulled into the driveway in a new Thunderbird convertible, and I couldn't believe who was with him.

Yes, just as E.A. was putting on a Las Vegas show in our front windows, we were visited by the Rat Pack. Aubrey, Melanie, Lesser Brenda, and in the front seat, beside Aubrey, Kathy—all of them grinning like vampire nurses. Quickly, I checked E.A.'s condition. He appeared to be dizzy from his Curley imitation and was standing at the counter getting his breath. I ducked back outside just as Aubrey leaned over and laid on the horn, yelling "Hi Larrrrrrry!"

Curt pushed her back over and got out as the girls started to pile out, too. Right then, E.A. stuck his head out the window—there was still no screen after the infamous Old Crow evening—and yelled.

"Hey, Bub, what's with the horn? Can't a guy have some peace in his home?" Then he saw the girls and did an overeager doubletake. "Well, who are these little chickadees?" I knew he would come out and pulled Curt aside.

"What on earth's going on? Since when do you have a Thunderbird?"

"It's Kathy's. She let me drive 'cause we're going to teach them how to play baseball today. Aren't you glad to see us?"

"We? Heck no, I'm not. Lynn would kill me if she knew they were here. I might kill you for bringing them here!"

"Aw, come on, the Mifflin girls are playing the Gahanna girls next Saturday before the dance for a charity softball game. Lynn who?"

"Lynn, my real and actual girlfriend. And what do we care? We'll be on our road trip to London and we'll barely be back in time to make it to the dance!"

I looked over his shoulder at the Rat Packers. London, Ohio, was a small farming community to the south of Columbus, and it was our farthest trip of the year—not quite England, but it sure felt like it. Right then, I'd have settled for being magically transported to either of them.

Instead, I was still in Mifflin when E.A. came out in a holey sweatshirt, striped Bermuda shorts, and black knee socks pulled as high as they'd go. Lesser Brenda started laughing uncontrollably. He immediately started telling the girls why the Space Program would fail under Lyndon Johnson. Aubrey and Melanie tried to act interested. Kathy had her arms folded and probably had an opinion, but was just staring at the ground with an occasional stolen glance at me. I knew bad things happened in threes, so I kept on looking out for Possum coming down the road, or worse, a surprise visit from Lynn. But Mom saved the day when she put on a long shirt over her bathing suit, came to the fence, and said she wanted E.A. to come inside.

He held his nose like something stank. "Hey, I am talking here!"

Mom held her ground and got louder. "Now, E.A."

He came to attention and saluted the Rat Pack. "I shall return."

"Get them outta here, Curt, before he comes back," I hissed.

"Aw, Larry, come down to the park with us," Aubrey pleaded.

"Come on buddy, you owe me. I can't do this alone. Unlike you, I actually would be happy to date any of them!" Curt insisted.

"What? What on earth do I owe you for?"

"Taking you and" —then he pointed at Kathy— "her to Brendan's Big Slice Pizza last winter. Come on, man. I can't help it didn't work out."

"Oh, that's low Curt," I winced. But I guessed he was right. "Fine. Go now, I'll come for 20 minutes only, and I'll drive down by myself."

When I got to the park, Curt was pitching underhand and Kathy was batting. I went out to left-center field before he could ask me to switch and stayed as far away from the others as possible. The others were scattered around waiting to bat, chasing the occasional grounder that Kathy managed to hit. But Melanie made a beeline for me as the ball went in the opposite direction.

"She's still got a thing for you, ya know," she said this as she nodded at Kathy.

"I'll tell you what I told her and everyone else who asks, Melanie. It's over. I am back with Lynn, hopefully forever. Matter of fact, we have a date in an hour and 15 minutes. So I'll be going soon."

Melanie just shrugged and went in to bat as Kathy put on Curt's spare glove and started for the outfield. I wasn't sure if she was coming out where I was but I wasn't taking any chances. I pointed to my wrist like I had a watch and yelled at Curt that I had to go. I could feel him drilling holes in the back of my head, but for the first time in my baseball career it felt good to get off the field.

The arrangement was that Lynn would bring the sandwiches from work, and she asked me to pick up some other things at the deli, so I went home, changed, and left as quietly as I could so as not to disturb a dozing E.A. on the couch. But what should I find parked outside Doris's but the T-bird. Curt and Aubrey were at the counter ordering.

"Hey, I thought you were going on a date," Aubrey said. "This it?"

"Still am, and no."

"Who is it, Larry, someone new or the Indian Princess again?"

I ignored her and Curt asked me to help him carry their food and drinks. I figured I owed him that much after bailing so I placed my order with Doris and helped him carry out trays of sandwiches and slaw.

"I got a sure thing here," he said under his breath.

I ignored him too.

As I opened the door to go out, Kathy and Melanie were sitting with their backs turned to me. Lesser Brenda was facing me. They were all smoking Kools, E.A.'s favorite brand, and they seemed pretty good at it. Melanie had her transistor radio on so they did not hear me, but I heard Kathy loud and clear, in between puffs.

"I bet he's going out with that little squaw again . . . she belongs back on the reservation, making those feather things she wears in her hair. Nothing but trash. Aubrey found out where she lives. Did you know it's over a ba—"

At that point Brenda was motioning toward me mouthing "right behind you."

Kathy turned and stared at me. You could have cut the tension with Possum's rusty old Swiss army knife. Finally, she exhaled a "Yeah, I said it," and blew smoke at me. "You two deserve each other."

Whatever fascination, or idea of Kathy being an unobtainable girl, or whatever I thought she was before kind of wilted up and died right then and there. I set their food down, clapped Curt on the shoulder, and left.

I passed Aubrey on the way out and decided I'd have the last word this time. "You guys are pathetic. Except for Melanie." Then I left to go pick up Lynn. I told her about the whole event and when she laughed, it seemed like the era of the Rat Pack was over for good.

The following week, the second-last at school, was good and quiet. I believed the Rats had finally got the message, and Aubrey even seemed to avoid me in the halls. The only real setback that week was that on Thursday London High School's athletic director called Coach Barnhart and asked if we would like to play a night time double-header instead of in the afternoon. They were one of the few schools with baseball lights, and he said that because of the time change to an evening game, we could expect a crowd in the hundreds. That was good for us—most games were played in front of a few dads who got off work and maybe a few girlfriends—but it meant the dance with Lynn was nixed.

Coach told us at our meeting on Thursday. "Guys, you're going to have to miss this year's spring dance. We have a chance to play under the lights in front of a crowd. I know a lot of you had girls you were going to take to the dance, but this is huge for our team and really adds value to all the hard work we've done."

"Well that stinks, Larry," Lynn said when I told her on our now-nightly call after her shift at Maddie's. She sounded disappointed. "I was finally going to make you get out there on the floor."

"There'll be more dances," I said.

"Yeah, true. Hey, I did have some good news."

"What's that, Lynn?"

"So we found out tonight that Mom is going to take over the restaurant in a few weeks. Dominic bought an old nightclub with some of his buddies and wants to put Mom in charge here so he can focus on being the hottest spot in town, velvet ropes and everything. Real swanky."

"Do we get VIP membership?" I joked.

"Not for two more years!" Lynn laughed. "But it's a great thing for Mom. She has worked here for eight years, ever since she divorced Kristy's dad. Now she'll be making a hundred dollars a week! Can you believe that?"

"Holy smokes!"

"Hey, they're here to pick me up. Gotta go, bye!" I swear she said "—love you!" before she hung up, but maybe I was just imagining things.

Coach gave us Friday night off to rest and relax for our road trip the next day, so I headed home from school and collapsed on E.A.'s throne in the living room, contemplating going over to Maddie's. Mom called with her perfect timing just then and said that E.A. had a fleet deal going with the city of Delaware, so they might be late. That meant I was on my own. Pretty soon, I heard the familiar whistle call of Butch coming down the street. I got up and went out to find him and Mack.

"Wanna go to the bait store at Agler and Sunbury? They're selling candy bars five for a dime," Mack said.

"Sure, why not? But why aren't you driving, Mack?" I asked as we started walking, with Butch up ahead.

"I primed the car again, it's over at the garage I work at. This time next week it'll be candy-apple red with flames on the side. But I gotta let that primer set for a few days."

Up ahead, Butch laughed.

"You're gonna be police bait for every cop who hasn't met his ticket quotas."

"That's if they can catch me," Mack said. "Hey, can we swing by Henry's? He owes me money for some M-80s." Usually Butch didn't like add-ons to adventures once they got started, but this time he said sure. Word was out that Timid Teddy had finally stood up to Henry, who was sporting a fat lip. That was worth the extra five minutes' walk.

When we got there, Possum was sitting on the ground with Henry standing before him up on a box like Caesar about to give a speech. Henry saw us and shouted through an obviously swollen lip. "Hey guys, you're just in time. Wanna hear the funniest joke in the world?"

Teddy was off to the side in a lounge chair reading a Catholic Digest. "Not if it's off-color. I mean it. I don't want to hear trash." he said, not even looking up. Henry ignored him as we leaned against their chain link fence.

"Okay. What are the three fastest forms of communications on earth?" He paused for effect as I noticed his dad looking out the window. "Give up?"

We nodded.

"Okay, television . . . no, wait, um."

"Telephone!" Henry's dad whispered from the window.

"Oh yeah, yeah, Telephone . . . telegraph . . . " At this point, Henry and his dad both began to laugh. "And . . . he-heh, tell-a-woman!" Possum immediately started rolling on the ground in laughter, holding his stomach like he'd been shot by a cannonball. Henry's dad was wiping legitimate tears from his eyes as if Henry had just won an academy award for best joke.

"Teddy, get your brother a Coke. He deserves one!"

Teddy got up grumpily and said okay. When he brought it out, Henry popped the top with his all-purpose knife.

"Dare me to chug?" Possum egged him on and he started. One gulp, then two, then three. On the fourth, Possum raised his hand and asked if he could have some. At that point, Coke started to gush over Henry's swollen lower lip, then it started to come out of his nose. He turned and spit Coke all over the side of the garage.

"Darn, Henry," his dad said sadly. "You would have made it if you hadn't been distracted." Mack started to ask for his money but Butch said to forget it. "That was worth the price of admission right there, Mack." Possum asked for a sip of what was left, but Henry wiped his lip tenderly and finished it.

"Hey, wanna hear it again?"

At that point we left and continued on to the bait store. Butch said we were stopping to pick Marcie up, so we swung up the lane that went back to their farm only to find her, her father, and a man in a 1964 El Camino that had some company's logo on the driver's door. The guy was putting a signpost in the ground by the road. Marcie looked relieved to see us and immediately cut out from her dad and the builder.

"Tell them, Marcie!" Was all Butch said.

"Uh, okay, guys, we sold the farm to a developer. It all kind of happened so fast. They're going to put in apartments and single homes on our land, just like where you guys live."

"Where are you going to live, Marcie?" Mack asked.

"Dad bought a farm that has a large orchard on it near Plain City about 40 miles away. We already have a contract with the local grocery stores for sweet corn and other produce. With the money we're getting for this land, we can buy five times as big a farm and still have some left over."

"Who'd want to live here?" laughed Mack.

"I did," was all Marcie said.

"They say Columbus is going to get big soon and developments are going to be popping up all over," I said, trying to help Marcie out since I already knew about it.

She just nodded and continued. "Anyway, Dad already planted the corn and some of the vegetables over there. We're moving the rest of the farm over after school's finished."

"So all apartments and homes?" I asked, continuing to play along. I wasn't sure if Marcie knew that I knew, but didn't want to betray Butch if she didn't.

"Right up to Sewer Creek. Even Troll's Cave is going to get leveled, I think."

"Better make sure Possum's not there," Mack said, although I could tell this was a shock for him. Butch resolutely said nothing. Even if Butch wasn't heading into the navy, I knew this'd be curtains for them as a couple. Butch wasn't the type to drive 40 miles to see a girl. Not that he didn't care, but it just wasn't Butch.

But tonight, they were still together, and Marcie even held Butch's hand for a second before he stuck it in his leather jacket. As we walked across the bridge to the creek we stopped and did what we usually did, which was spit into the water below. Marcie saw a log floating under us, hawked up a big loogie and really let it fly.

"BULLSEYE!" she yelled.

"Don't do that Marcie," Butch said kind of cranky like.

"Eh, who cares?" she retorted.

There was a rather large woman at the bait store with a bandanna wrapped around her head reading a glamour magazine about how anyone could look like Raquel Welch in ten days or less. Mack immediately got down to business and asked where the discount candy was.

She ignored him. "Honey, I was a-hearin' you're a-movin'," she said when she saw Marcie.

"That's right, Tami," Marcie said. For the first time, I saw tears in Marcie's eyes. The woman didn't notice and pointed Mack to a boxful of all types of candy bars.

"There's them candy bars you was askin' fer. Don't go pickin' through them, just take the first ones off the top there, Chubby." When she returned to Raquel Welch, Mack dug in and found all the ones with peanuts, then laid out about a dollar in dimes.

"Count that for me, Marcie honey," she said, still reading.

Something was odd; there were dusty candy bars on the dirty old shelves, too, but they looked different from the ones in Mack's hands. Then it hit me: the wrappers were the old ones. Baby Ruths hadn't been in wrappers like that for years. I tried to get Mack's attention, but Mack had already finished one so I figured the harm was done.

Butch laid 40 cents on the counter, and we all got ourselves a pop from the cooler. Then we went out back and watched a doe with a young fawn prance about in a flat, sandy area where the Alum would wash up in rainy seasons. Now it was green as an emerald with new grass and trees, even kinda picturesque. Butch laughed and told everyone not to chug like Henry had.

In a minute, a grungy old man came out on the rear porch of the bait store and started to use the outdoor facilities off the porch, into the valley. The doe and her fawn bounded off, and as he watched them go he saw us.

"Get outta my backyard now, ya hear?" That was as good a time as any to leave. When we took our bottles back to collect the glass fee, the big woman was making some sorry-looking baloney sandwiches with even droopier tomatoes and lettuce for some fishermen who had stopped in for bait. She wrapped the sandwiches up in the parts of the magazine she'd finished and I saw a blob of tomato slide over Raquel Welch's face. I lost whatever appetite I had for dinner at home, at least for right now. We left and crossed back over the bridge.

Where the log had been was now a huge snapping turtle, milling about above the deep waters. Marcie couldn't resist and fired another salvo onto its shell.

"Bullseye again!" She yelled. Butch was obviously irritated.

"Marcie, stop it now. It ain't ladylike."

"Make me!"

When we got to Marcie's lane, she turned in right away. "Wait up, I'll walk with ya," Butch said.

"Don't bother." She said as she walked off by herself.

I looked at the sign the employee had brought. "Coming soon!" it read. "New homes under $10,000 on quarter-acre lots."

"I guess the trolls have to move," Mack said.

"Maybe they'll go to Shanty Town." The joke fell flat. Butch was obviously mad as we walked away. For some stupid reason, I made a risky remark.

"Butch, you shouldn't have yelled at her. That's just Marcie, it's the way she's always been, it's the way she'll always be. She's just upset about all this." Butch stopped and looked me right in the eye. "Wouldn't you be, too?" I said, lower.

He pointed his finger at me like a challenge.

"Ohhh crap!" I heard Mack say.

"You son of . . . " I got ready to defend myself like he had taught me. But then he smiled.

"You've come a long way, friend, since you came here. There was a time you never would have said that." Mack laughed up ahead and resumed his candy bar: crisis averted. Butch came a bit closer and lowered his voice.

"You were always my right hand man, I could always count on you." He spoke a little louder so Mack could hear. "Guys, I quit school today."

"You can do that?" Mack asked. I saw him getting ideas. Butch nodded solemnly.

"Yep. I joined the Navy. I leave next week for the Great Lakes training center." Then it all hit me, even though I was pretending not to know. Life suddenly felt like a pinball machine. First Blains' farm, now this. What next?

"Nothing left for me here, guys," Butch continued, jerking a thumb back at Marcie's farm. I was glad Butch had told us both, but now I felt like I had got a second punch in the gut. Somehow, the fact it was no longer a secret made it real.

When I got home, I sat on E.A.'s big easy chair like I'd started the evening and reviewed the events of the last few hours as the last of the spring sunlight fell on the tree outside and into the living room.

First, Henry spit Coke all over his garage, and it looked like Timid Teddy wasn't so timid anymore. I'd heard of boxing priests in Ireland. Maybe he was going to become one.

Second, Mack ate some five-year-old candy and seemed like he'd live.

Third, Marcie and Butch were through, and we were losing both of them. I knew she'd be welcome in the group for however longer she was here, but who was I kidding? Without Butch there was no group. Those were big, military surplus boots to fill.

Like clockwork, there was a knock at the door. I looked over to see what looked like a familiar flat top in the dim light.

"Yes, Possum?" I said wearily.

"I ain't Possum, ya dolt."

"Door's open, Butch," I laughed.

I made each of us a big corned beef and Swiss cheese sandwich that easily weighed three times as much as the bait shop's baloney sandwiches, and we sat out on the front steps. Uncharacteristically, Butch lowered his voice like someone was listening, even though it was just us in the dying light.

"Listen, will you take me to Fort Hayes downtown next Tuesday morning at 700 . . . uh, 7:00 a.m.? You'll only miss one class and you should be back by 8:30."

"Sure, I'll get a teacher's pass from the coach. He's a Korean War veteran. He'll be cool with that."

"Thanks. Mom's berzerk over this, and our car isn't running." We ate our sandwiches in silence, and he got up to leave.

"Got any more cookies?" He grinned.

"Sure!" I wrapped a few in baking paper. "Hey, Butch. Make Possum a full member before you go, huh?"

"Never!"

But Sunday night, when we all met at the park to say farewell, Butch's mood seemed to have changed. It was just us guys: Butch, me, Mack, Possum, and even Henry, who seemed to have found another crowd lately. After some hot dogs, chips, and candy bars from Mack, we sat around a glowing fire, waiting for the goodbye to happen. Then Butch got up, pulled his switchblade out and snapped it open.

"Possum, get over here." Possum looked at me kinda scared, but I just nodded. He got up in front of Butch.

"Possum Carlson, I hereby grant you full membership in the gang." He then put the blade on each of Possum's shoulders. "With all its rights and privileges and, uh, responsibilities." Then he put his switchblade away. Possum was at a loss for words for the first time ever. Finally, after a few tears trickled down his cheek he turned to me and said, "Larry, I'm a full member, a full member!" I just looked at Butch and smiled.

Tuesday morning, with my signed pass in hand and permission from Mom, I left at about 6:15 to go over to Butch's. To my surprise, he was standing on the corner of Northglenn and Woodland with a small satchel. I knew better than to ask him why, but he told me anyway.

"Mom threw me out and told me never to come back. I spent the night at Mack's. He would have taken me this morning, but I wanted it to be you."

We rode straight down Cleveland Avenue in the cool, dewy spring morning until I turned into the fort's gate. There was an MP in a chrome helmet who saluted us and asked our reason for entry. Butch said just said "Induction" and the MP motioned to a few parking spaces outside a big, brick building.

"Butch—"

"Don't get all mushy and talky. Let's just say goodbye and be done with it. You know this is you in two years, right?"

"Maybe I'll see ya then."

"Maybe."

"Goodbye, Butch."

"Goodbye, friend. I mean that." Then he got out and came around to the driver's side. "Hey, you weren't going to back down on the bridge last week, were you?"

"No. After all we've been through? That would have been an insult to you. I was ready to lose a few teeth."

He laughed and punched my arm about as hard as he had hit the guy at the drive-in last fall.

"Ow! What's that for?"

"'Cause you're still a punk."

He smiled the biggest smile I'd ever seen from him as he went through the door to the induction center. That was the last time I ever saw Butch.

CHAPTER
TWENTY

O ur team was still in the hunt for a championship as May started to wind down, and school with it. The second-to-last Saturday in May, the Gahanna Lions came to try us out in a double header in Mifflin and lost each game. I had pushed my average up towards .300 and I had an even better day against the Lions than our team did, going three hits for seven at-bats for the day.

It probably helped that my dad came to watch and Lynn sat with him. In the second game, I hit a line shot into left center that probably didn't stop until it landed in Montana, and Lynn did her shrill whistle accompanied by my dad hitting even higher notes. I had my own cheering section to beat out the rest of the bleachers. After the game the coach said he'd bring ear plugs the next time my dad and girlfriend came, and then he reminded us we had the Hilliard Hawks the following week.

"If we win, guys, we're the champs! That's huge for me," he admitted with a grin. "But even bigger for you. You earned it."

I walked Lynn home after Dad dropped us off at the Darnell mansion. With the endless summer ahead, we had stopped worrying about the problem of different schools, at least for now. These days, things seemed to be looking up for the Bennets: her mom was making more money, which meant Lynn finally getting to keep some of her own tip money. If Lynn could get a car, well, we'd see. I didn't mention the hope to her, as she seemed happy she was just finally able to get herself and Kristy ice cream on a whim instead of saving for it.

That Tuesday, we played our last non-conference game of the year. I still didn't have everyday driving privileges, so I hoofed it across the bridge toward home after the game. It gave me a chance to walk by the Blains' old place, where I saw Marcie's jeep by the house and Marcie herself at the end of the lane, digging up the old mailbox.

"Hi Larry," she kind of said into the wind.

"Hey Marcie. Whatcha up to?"

"I told Dad I wanted this, so I guess he told the construction workers to leave it alone. I've been walking down here to get the mail for as long as I could walk." She gestured up the road.

Two weeks might as well have been two centuries. The fields of crops had already been bulldozed and graded out level as a pancake; the orchard was gone, all of its old, carefully tended trees piled up in a big heap ready to be burned or mulched. The barn was gone, too, probably taken for scrap by the Amish in the surrounding area. The house looked haunted. All the windows, the doors, and anything else worth a couple bucks for resale was gone. I guess the Mifflin Township Fire brigade was going to burn it down for practice sometime the next week.

"Come with me Larry. You'd wanna see this," Marcie said, walking ahead of me in the damp dirt and clay, already starting to dry out and get dusty in the sun. We walked down to Sewer Creek, but I didn't recognize the area one bit. "Don't you know what we're standing on top of?" asked Marcie, pointing down.

"Not at all."

"This is where Trolls Cave used to be. You can tell by how it aligns with that tree line." But it was hard to recognize even the untouched trees in the distance. The turn in the creek had been straightened out, and a large portion was now in a huge culvert, stinking and reeking. I wondered how long it would be before the new residents called the zoning board about Shanty Town.

When we got back to the house, Marcie wiped a few tears out of her eyes and got two root beers out of a styrofoam ice chest in the back of her jeep.

"Hey, how about a toast to the old Blain Farm? Just us two lost farmers?" I chuckled and banged the cap off both our bottles—not that Marcie couldn't, she just seemed real broken up and trying to hide it. We clicked our bottles in the hot summer sun.

"You're the only one of my friends who understands how hard this is. Everyone else lived in the sort of place they're building here. They'd say it's an improvement."

At that moment I envisioned Gramp's farm looking like this and winced. "Yeah, Marcie, I get it, I do." We didn't say anything for a bit and then I changed the topic. "Hey, have you heard from Butch at all? Any letters?" I knew in basic you got to write letters and figured Butch would start to miss Marcie in all the stress of getting yelled at, day in and day out. It had been almost three weeks since I had dropped him off and I tried to imagine him with a buzz cut.

"Nope. We're through. It was fun while it lasted. I really cared for him, I know he cared for me, too, but it's over. You gotta grow up and not get your hopes up about those things. Come on, I'll walk you out the lane. About time I get going, anyway." We headed out and for the first time I was awkwardly quiet around Marcie. She broke the silence at the road. "Hey, you take care of Lynn. Don't lose her this time, dumbo. She's special."

"Thanks. But look, this is all kind of sad. When I see you in school tomorrow, lemme buy you lunch as a sendoff."

She shook her head. "No, Larry, this is it. Today they let me take my finals so I can get over and help Dad organize the farm. It's just me and the mailbox, headed back to Plain City tonight."

I looked at the slender girl who was almost as tall as me and could only think to quietly say, "Well, bye pal."

She sniffled and took a breath. "Larry, I just have to ask. . . . Have you ever thought . . . if there were no Butch and no Lynn, maybe you and me could have, uh . . . "

With that, she coughed out a sob, leaned in, and gave me a sudden hug, then turned and ran down the lane, back towards the jeep and what was left of her home.

I walked home feeling a little strange, but I realized Marcie knew me as the only other person she knew that loved farm life. And she was hurting. In that moment, she would have said she had a crush on Possum if it meant holding onto that little farm.

School was winding down to the last few days, and excitement for summer was at an all-time high. Morningside pool was going to open with a bang the first Wednesday of summer break, with Jerry Shaver bringing his dance party to the park. The big news was that it was Donatella's last show and a new Miss Teen Beat would be chosen. We all knew that the rumors circulating around school were bound to be true: Aubrey had auditioned and would be a shoo-in for the job. She was so sure that she had told Mrs. Barnhart that she probably couldn't be a cheerleader this year and she wanted Kathy to take her place, or at least that was what Coach had said when he heard us talking about it during warm-ups.

Of course, Lynn and I were going to go, and I had the car lined up for the evening. The only thing left in the school year was our showdown with the Hawks from Hilliard, and I could see myself strutting into the pool as a member of the winning team that the year before couldn't have shined Hilliard's shoes. It'd been worth having to miss the spring dance to beat London and claim the spot as the Hawk's year-end opponent.

Everyone was feeling good about the game, and on the way over there as the bus rattled along the road, the coach stood up and gave his last pep talk of the year. "Guys, whatever happens I am proud of you, but I think we've got a real chance to repeat last Fourth of July. Billy, you're pitching the first game. Paul, you're up on the second game. Let's show those Hawks what Mifflin can do!" We left the bus with our heads high.

I don't think any of us were ready for what happened that afternoon. We lost the first game, twenty-seven to three. It was like batting practice for Hilliard. Twice they batted around in an inning, and I swear their star hitter yawned before smacking one of Billy's curveballs. The second game was a little better, I guess: 11-2. I tried my best, lining a shot off the pitcher's shoulder and scoring on Curt's double. But the bus ride home was solem.

Coach was trying to contain his anger—not at us, but maybe at himself. Finally, he just said: "We're obviously not their caliber yet," and that was all. The sting went away a little two days later when we found out our ace pitcher and our third baseman made first team all-league, with Curt and me making honorable mention all-league.

Not bad for sophomores with a strong team to play for in their junior year. We had some ace incoming sophomores.

The last morning of school, I went to my locker to clean it out. Roxanne had the locker next to me, and I found her doing the same into a big garbage bag.

"You better be sure to go to the pool dance tomorrow at Morningside. Trust me, I've heard a few things. Something big is going to happen."

"Will do, Roxanne."

Oh, and please introduce me to your girl from Linden! I bet we'll be friends."

"Okay, Roxanne. But please leave the reporter's notebook at home."

"Never!" But I knew Roxanne was a good person to have on your side. It's just that I was hoping to have Lynn mostly to myself.

Between baseball and finals, I'd not seen or talked to her in almost five days, which felt like five weeks. I guess it was a preview of what it would be like sometimes next year, being at different schools.

When I opened my locker, a bunch of empty Land-O-Lake butter carton stubs fell out on the floor. On the back was a girl's scrawl:

"Don't bring girls from other schools to our events next year. Especially ones with feathers in their hair!"

I looked down the hall to see three Gents in their yellow blazers, laughing.

"Funny, huh?" I yelled. "Let's settle this right here and now."

"Are ya sure, without Butch here to protect you?" one of them chuckled.

"You're first," I said to the one talking. But at that point they looked behind me, laughed, and went down the stairs. Standing behind me was not Roxanne but Possum, with his fists up and the meanest look he could muster.

"We would have got 'em Larry," he said.

"We would have, pal," I said. "Thanks for having my back."

"That's because I'm in the gang now."

The night before the pool party, Lynn called from Maddie's. I was so glad to hear her voice, I felt like I was hearing her for the first time in years. She'd worked all that weekend so she could take the night of the dance off.

"Larry, we are so busy with school graduation dinners, you wouldn't believe it. I barely have time to even call you, but I miss you and—"

"You are going to be there at the pool tomorrow night, aren't you, Lynn?"

"Yes, but you go on over when it starts. Mom's covering for me and I will leave as soon as I can get off. I'll just walk over."

"Sure?"

"Yes, no worries. I don't know when Mom's getting back. She hasn't told us where she was going."

So on June third, I cleaned the car out, washed it for the third time that week, and put on my best jeans and a brand new Yankees t-shirt with Mickey Mantle's lucky number seven on it. Then I put on just a dab of some expensive cologne that Dad had got at some swanky Hong Kong emporium and felt like a million dollars; he had given it to me because it made Betsy sneeze. When I turned on the car radio, they were playing a real oldie by Duane Eddy, "Rebel Rouser." I turned it up all the way and felt cool as anything. This was Butch's favorite song, and I admitted to myself for the first time of many that summer that I missed my friend.

Mack and Trish weren't going to the dance, so it really would be just Lynn and me. In a turn of events that would have made no-ring-in-my-nose Mack from last year happy, they were headed for Columbus Motor Speedway. Trish was really getting into car racing, and in return Mack had picked up some etiquette.They were working out well together. I rolled into the pool just as the sax in the song was fading.

Of course, the first thing I did was look for Lynn, but she wasn't there yet even though the dance had already started. As expected, the Rat Pack was taking up the first five picnic tables with a sprinkling of Gents scattered among them, all ready for Aubrey's big night. I intended to keep my distance and have no trouble from either group, so I headed straight for the concession stand and got a couple of bratwursts and a Dad's Root Beer to sip while I waited for Lynn and watched the couples dance.

In a moment, Jerry Shaver came out in a gray three-piece suit with his hair slicked back and mingled with the kids who weren't dancing, jokingly pulling wallflowers onto the dancefloor. He wasn't able to keep Aubrey off his shoulder as she laid it on thick to cheers from the Rats.

"Come on, Jerry, tell us who won Miss Teen Beat!"

"Yeah, spill the beans!"

Ever the pro, he just shrugged his shoulders. "Hey, I'm just the disk jockey, they don't tell me nothing," and went back to resume

MC-ing while Donatella Montabella worked the folks at the table. She was a few octaves lower than usual tonight; it seemed like she'd really grown up since the last dance. You could tell she was ready for college.

As I started in on the second brat, I saw Lynn come in. I almost dropped the brat—boy, she looked stunning, dressed up like never before. She was in a new outfit she had got at Penney's on her birthday, a dark blue blouse with white pedal pushers like Mom said were the latest style. She also was wearing a brand new feather clip, too, vivid and turquoise against her long black hair, with matching wrist bracelets and neck choker. I waved but she didn't see me . . . and sat down with two guys from Linden.

I knew I was on display to half a dozen pairs of Rat Pack eyes and felt my stomach creeping into my feet. But then one of the Linden guys pointed over to me, and she started around the pool.

When she arrived, she hugged me for what seemed like minutes and finally burst open with a smile. "I have so much to tell you, but first, I'm starving. Get me a burger with a pickle, no mustard or ketchup. I don't want any stains on my new outfit, okay?"

"Yes ma'am, and for your drink?" I said, playing waiter to the waitress.

She held up my Dad's Root Beer. "Got it right here, server boy, but you can get yourself another one. Then meet me over at that bench, I've got some news that I don't want anyone else to hear just yet."

I came back with her burger and sat down expecting anything and everything. She looked like a kid waiting to open Christmas presents.

"Love your new jewelry," I blurted.

She nodded giddily. "Yes, isn't it great? Dad sent it to me. It's from New Mexico. He bought it there from a real craftsman, all handmade, too."

"That's gre—"

But she couldn't hold her excitement any longer and burst out with a long, carefree laugh.

"Larry, we're getting a house. Mom told us just today. It was a big surprise. She signed a two-year lease to rent a home yesterday. It has a yard, big trees, a garage, three bedrooms, two baths, a furnace—not little kerosene heaters. And a brand new General Electric oven! And—" She was talking so fast that I couldn't keep up with her.

"That's grea—"

"But . . . I have to change schools."

Oh boy, I thought, feeling the other shoe drop. At least now she lived close enough to see in person. This was probably in Plain City. Just when we had worked this out. . . .

"Where, uh, is your new home, Lynn?"

"Well, on Lindale Drive."

I nodded dumbly. "What town?"

But Lynn started to grin.

"I mean, what school will you . . . wait, Lindale? Like, the next street over from where me and Mack and Trish live?"

She grabbed my hands and nodded fast.

"You'll be going to Mifflin?"

"Mhm!"

I could have almost kissed her, but I settled for a big hug.

"Lynn, that's wonderful. That's the best news I've heard all spring!"

"That's why I was late, we weren't at work after all. We went over to see it and get the keys. We're moving in this weekend! Speaking of which, are you free on Saturday to lift some boxes?"

I would have cleared my schedule even if I'd planned on trying out for the Yankees that Saturday. Right then, Jerry announced the next to last dance, but we just stayed there and talked. We were both so excited that we were totally oblivious to everything else going on, making plans about how it would be living just five minutes from each other and riding to school together, having dinner at each other's houses. We were like kids in a candy store that had just opened up. When we finally came down off cloud nine, the dance was over and Jerry was calling all the couples up.

"Okay, you guys and gals, one last song, one last dance, and then we have to say goodbye to Donatella and find out: Who! The! Next! Miss! Teen! Beat! Is!"

"All right! Go Aubrey!" the Rats and Gents cheered. I could see Lynn roll her eyes, but then she took my hand unexpectedly and pulled me straight to the dance floor.

"Come on, you're not getting out of it this time." I looked down at my feet, and I swear I had two left shoes on.

Jerry put on "Let It Be Me" by the Everly Brothers, and as its chords echoed off the concrete, Lynn began to sing along softly, the two of us holding each other tight like something brand new was beginning, even if we had been dating for a while. The only problem was, she was swaying gently to the music and I looked like one of the statues down by the Statehouse.

"Come on, Larry, dance. After all those shindigs at Mifflin, you gotta be good!"

I gulped. "I never learned to dance."

But that didn't stop her. I just followed her lead till I picked up on her steps. We did fine.

When it was over, Jerry said. "Okay, sit down, everyone. The time has come to say goodbye to a dear friend. Come on over here, Donnatella. Ladies and Gentlemen, a big hand for Donatella Montabella. The only person who has ever been Miss Teen Beat for two years!"

We gave her a big round of applause. She was trying not to cry as she began to speak. She must have sucked down some helium, because her high-pitched voice was back.

"WOW! Just wow! Gang, what a ride. How many dances have we done, Jerry? Over a hundred?"

Jerry nodded. "Plus, two years' worth of the Saturday Dance Beat show on channel nine."

She was crying now, so Jerry took over. "Everyone, Donatella starts her freshman year at Ohio State University this fall. She is going to be a swell teacher when she graduates, and who knows, you might bump into her your freshman year if any of you go!"

This gave Donatella time to recover, and she kind of sobbed through her next few words as she read them from what looked like pink diary paper.

"Ok, gang, time to introduce the new Miss Teen Beat. It was a real hard choice for the production team at the station. We liked them all. Over 50 great candidates to choose from, and even Jerry didn't get to know who we picked."

By now she was standing directly in front of Aubrey. Kathy was hugging her and I heard her say "It's you, I know it is!"

"So without any further delay, let's do this Jerry!" Jerry stretched out his hand towards Aubrey, who started to stand up, but then Donatella walked over to the small maintenance shed. Jerry looked confused. As Donatella swung open the door, the DJ put on . . . the "Bristol Stomp."

Possum came bounding out and proceeded to dance around the entire floor doing what was now known as the Possum Stomp. At first, I thought it was another of his shenanigans, but on his second pass around the floor Donatella joined him and did the stomp with him. The whole audience—the part that weren't Rat Pack or Gent members—burst out in applause.

Jerry was speechless. I guess he really didn't know who had won. He tucked his mic under his arm and asked an assistant if this was for real. When the technician nodded, he sighed and said, loud enough for me to hear: "This is going to be a long year. That's the kid who made a shambles of the dance at Mifflin two springs ago. I know the execs are trying to get rid of me . . . "

But unlike at the infamous dance, Donatella seemed to have changed her mind about Possum now. When the song ended, she danced up to the stage for a final bow, and Jerry, fully recovered, went back to his professional voice and congratulated Possum.

"Ladies and gentlemen, our new, miss . . . ah, excuse me, mis-ter, Teen Beat!" Donatella grabbed the mic.

"Gang, your new Mr. Teen Beat, Carl 'Possum' Carlson, is from right here at Mifflin High School. He's going to make you all so proud!" The assistant gave Possum some roses, and Donatella put her crown on his huge, six-inch-tall flattop. Somehow, he saw me in the crowd and gave me a big thumbs-up. I returned it.

Lynn turned to me dumbstruck. "Is this for real? Did he really win? This is crazy. I knew two girls from school who tried out for this, and they're gorgeous. Possum's, well . . . "

"A full-on gang member," I said with a smile. At that point, Roxanne sat down by us and winked.

"Told ya something big was going to happen. Hey, this is Lynn Bennet, right?"

"That's right. Lynn, Roxanne, school reporter. Roxanne, Lynn, my girlfriend. I actually just found out she will be coming to Mifflin next fall!" Roxanne grinned and was going to say something but was drowned out by Aubrey two tables over.

"I can't BELIEVE I lost to that moron! He is a moron and an idiot, and this was rigged. I want a recount, right now!"

Roxanne's boyfriend came to the rescue and told us the gang was going over to Brendan's Big Slice and invited us to ride with them.

"No thanks, I'm going to drive Lynn home. But count us in, next time, okay? She lives here now!"

"You drove tonight?" Lynn asked. "I forgot to ask, I figured I'd have you walk me to the corner one last time."

"Sure did, and no more corners for me. I'll take you home. And by the way, it's a yes to Saturday. I'll bring the Chevy—it's got a big trunk."

"Before that, Larry, come over to Maddie's tomorrow so I can introduce you officially to Mom and Kristy. You should meet them if you're going to be coming over." She was beaming. As we got ready to leave, I looked over and saw at least 15 girls around Possum asking for autographs. He looked like he was in heaven.

When we got out to the car, I opened the door for Lynn and she hopped in. But when I got in on my side, she was already sitting in the middle. I slid in beside her and turned on the car. I'd left the radio on, and the Midnight Ghost was just announcing the start of his 10–2 show.

"Hey, all you young lovers out there in radioland. The Midnight Ghost is declaring this the first day of summer vacation. School's over, and so are all the graduations. So open those windows and get ready for the best summer of your lives, 'til the next one. If you're out cruising or maybe up at the dam watching those submarine races, this song is for you. Turn to that gal or guy you're with and give 'em a big kiss, and tell 'em you love 'em." Then, you could hear him lean into the mic and whisper: "'Cause the Ghost said to!"

With that, he put on Percy Faith's "Theme from a Summer Place." We both listened for a while, hand in hand, until Lynn looked at me and innocently asked, "What are the submarine races?"

I just laughed. "Well, uh . . . " She had her hands folded in front of her. She appeared to be deep in thought as Percy Faith's orchestra really got going.

"I know this is a special night for us," she whispered. "I, uh, never actually kissed a guy, let alone told someone I loved them." She quickly added. "Except when I said, 'love you,' to you a week ago on the phone, accidentally. I mean, not accidentally, but . . . "

She paused as the song reached the end. Slowly, she turned and looked at me. It seemed her brown eyes were full of hope, love, and maybe a little nervousness. Without really realizing it, I put my hand out to gently touch her cheek, got very close, and kissed her. My heart told my brain to get out of the way and to get these next six words exactly right.

"I love you, Lynn . . . Ahyoka Lynn Bennet."

She put her head on my shoulder and said, "No one has ever really called me that." Then she put her arms around my neck and kissed me back. In my limited kissing experience, it was by far the best ever.

Suddenly, I was aware we were the last car in the lot except for the Channel Nine crew, who were loading up their station wagon.

"I'd better get you home, Lynn," I said.

"Larry, wait one more minute," she said, putting her hand on mine as I got ready to shift. "After the night I met you over at McDonald's, the next day when I got home from Trish's, I wrote in my diary, 'Last night, I met the boy I am going to marry.'" She shyly looked down, then straight at me and put her cheek against mine and whispered so tenderly. "I love you," and kissed me again.

In a moment, I turned the car lights on and pulled out onto Hudson Street and headed for Tubby's Tavern. It was only her home for a few more days.